Praise

New York Times

D0091463

THE

"Filled with believable characters and hard, realistic dialogue, [this] perfectly paced novel offers a suspenseful story laced with more than a few shockingly unexpected plot twists."

—*Publishers Weekly Signature Review*

"A violent, tension-packed, well-written thriller spiced with Box's vivid portrayal of the Western landscape that he loves." —Associated Press

"A nonstop, action-filled race against time. Rolling down the superhighway of suspense, this thriller will leave readers breathless."

—*Library Journal* (starred review)

"Be warned: this is one scary novel."

—*Toronto Globe and Mail*

"*The Highway* is the summer's most terrifying novel . . . Prepare to be scared." —*Orlando Sun Sentinel*

"A fast-moving, edge-of-your-seat page-turner. I really couldn't put it down." —Criminal Element

"Get off the genre interstate and take *The Highway*."

—*Billings Gazette*

BACK OF BEYOND

"May be his best yet . . . a roller-coaster ride of unexpected twists and turns . . . one of the most suspenseful wilderness thrillers since *Deliverance*." —Associated Press

"Once again, Box provides the complete suspense package." —*Kirkus Reviews* (starred review)

"A great creation." —*Houston Chronicle*

"Grade A . . . page-flying suspense with superior character portrayal . . . a great adventure." —*Cleveland Plain Dealer*

"Terrifically entertaining stuff that comes together with a bang in the end." —*Booklist*

"A perfect introduction to the novels of C. J. Box." —*Petrona* (UK)

"Tough, gripping . . . [with] atmospheric volatility." —*The Australian*

"Sprawling, ambitious . . . palpably compelling." —*Publishers Weekly*

"Timeless . . . gripping . . . resemble(s) an Agatha Christie closed-community whodunit but with horses, bears, wolves, and hunting rifles." —*Sunday Times* (UK)

"Box . . . knows life and death in the backcountry like few other writers today." *—Library Journal*

"The type of entertainment and escapism that drives us towards crime fiction in the first place."
—Bookgeeks.co.uk

"A taut tale . . . that hooks you." *—USA Today*

"If Box isn't already on your list, put him there."
—Toronto Globe and Mail

"The best of Box's novels that I have read."
—Powerline

"A brand-new, stand-alone thriller which may just clinch it for [Box]." *—Daily Mail* (UK)

"A riveting, unforgettable work . . . beautifully written and wonderfully told." —Bookreporter.com

"Rewarding . . . we dare you to try to figure out the mystery before the end . . . Grab this book." *—City AM* (UK)

"Perceptive . . . well-rounded . . . smooth, muscular writing keeps the tension rising." *—Financial Times*

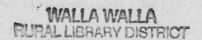

ALSO BY C. J. BOX

THE HIGHWAY

M
BOX
2013

C.J. BOX

St. Martin's Paperbacks

This is a work of fiction. All of the characters, organizations, and events portrayed in this novel are either products of the author's imagination or are used fictitiously.

THE HIGHWAY

Copyright © 2013 by C. J. Box.

All rights reserved.

For information address St. Martin's Press, 175 Fifth Avenue, New York, NY 10010.

Library of Congress Catalog Card Number: 2013009869

ISBN: 978-0-312-54689-2

Printed in the United States of America

St. Martin's Press hardcover edition / July 2013
St. Martin's Paperbacks edition / July 2014

St. Martin's Paperbacks are published by St. Martin's Press, 175 Fifth Avenue, New York, NY 10010.

10 9 8 7 6 5 4 3

*For my daughters, Molly, Becky, and Roxanne
. . . and Laurie, always*

Be self-controlled, be vigilant; because your adversary the devil, as a roaring lion, walketh about, seeking whom he may devour.
—I Peter 5:8

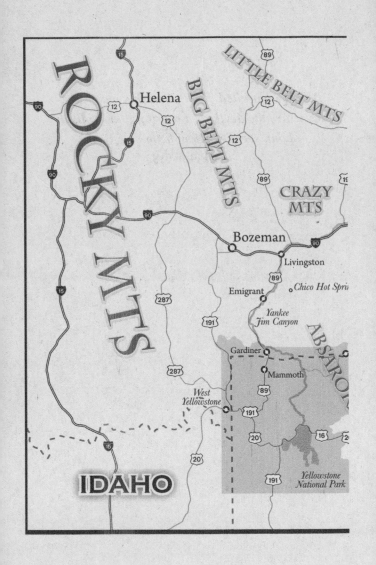

Map by Molly Donnell

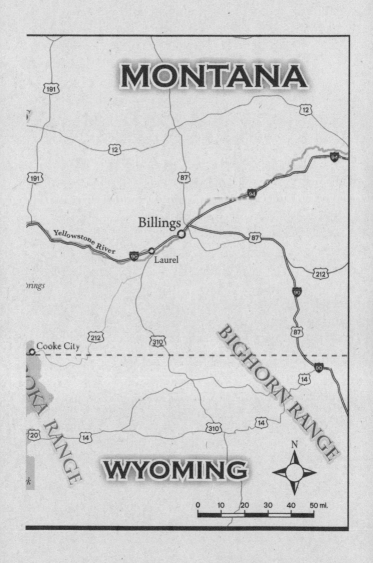

The Night Before

10:13 P.M., MONDAY, NOVEMBER 19

I.

Lewis and Clark County Montana Sheriff's Department Investigator Cassandra Dewell winced when a pair of headlights broke over a rise onto a long treeless bench in the foothills of the Big Belt Mountains north of Helena. She was on the worst assignment of her nascent career, and she hoped it would be a failure. If she was successful, her partner—a dark legend, her mentor, named Cody Hoyt—would likely lose his job and go to prison.

When the headlights appeared she was eating from a small box of chocolate-covered cake donuts, playing that stupid game she played with herself. One every hour, just to "keep her energy up." It had been three hours and the box of twelve was gone.

She was parked high on a windswept ridge. Her position gave her a sweeping view of the valley below, and a wide angle on the only two-track that led from

the county road to the murder house. On the car seat
next to the empty donut box was a departmental camera equipped with a telephoto night vision lens.

Cassie's eyes burned with fatigue. She'd not seen her
son in twelve hours and her mother was angry with her.
But when she recognized the dark outline of the vehicle
below as it switched off its lights and continued slowly
down the road toward the house, she said, "Goddamn
you, Cody."

II.

He drove slowly in the dark, squinting over the wheel
of his departmental Ford Expedition, trying to see the
two-track road, but he mostly drove by feel. When
the front tires began to drift out of the ruts he nudged
the wheel and put them back. Although it was cold outside, in the low thirties, he kept his driver's side window down. He could smell pine and sage and dust from
his wheels. The sky was clear, filled with stars, and there
was enough of a moon that the twin tracks of the road
appeared pale and chalky.

On the seat next to him was a wrinkled paper sack
filled with items that warmed his heart.

He was working late to plant evidence that, he hoped,
would lead to the arrest and conviction of a reprobate
named Brantley "B. G." Myers. Planting evidence re-
quired stealth, skill, and planning. Cody was up for the
job. In fact, it was one of his specialties.

The road was in the open on the bench. To his right,
the terrain rose up and out of view. To his left it main-

tained a plateau for a mile or so and then sloped off into a massive swale. There was a small lake reflecting the starlight and moonlight in the basin of the swale. A rim of ice framed the open water along the banks of the lake. Ducks and geese covered the lake like errant punctuation. To the right of a road leading down to the lake was the dark low-slung rectangle of a rambling log home—the crime scene he was about to disturb.

He crept along, hoping he wouldn't hit a cow or an elk on the road, hoping he wouldn't drive right off it and have to use his headlights to get back on.

Nestled in the trees on the top of the hill to his right, three-quarters of a mile away, were three cabins. Each was at least five hundred yards away from the other. The lights were on at all of them, yellow squares in the dark trees, and the occupants, if they were watching, could clearly see down the slope to the road he was on. He didn't want them to know he was there. He didn't want *anyone* to know he was there. Especially the sapphire miner named B. G. who owned the cabin on the far right and who had a telescope set up on a tripod at his picture window so he could spy on his neighbors below and keep track of vehicles on the remote county road.

B. G. had always rubbed Cody the wrong way. But more than that, B. G. was a killer. Cody glanced up in the general direction of B. G.'s cabin and sapphire mine, and whispered, "Fuck you, B. G."

He slowed and hung his head out the driver's-side window so he wouldn't miss the turnoff to the log home down by the lake. He saw it a hundred feet ahead and made the turn without tapping his brakes and therefore flashing his brake lights. The SUV was in low gear and he kept it there, letting the torque of the engine propel him slowly down the slope. Sure, he'd leave tire tracks, but it didn't concern him. After all, he'd been in and out of the place three times that day. When the home loomed in front of him he swung around it and parked in back out of view of the three mountain cabins.

Cody had taken his usual precautions to go off the grid. As he'd cleared town, he'd reached down under the dashboard and snapped a switch that killed the GPS locator unit the department used to keep track of their detectives, and the digital odometer. He'd installed the kill switch himself, breaking department regulations. And he'd not told Edna, the dispatcher, that he'd taken his vehicle out from his home, which was another breach. As far as she knew, he was relaxing in front of his big-screen or reading one of his books. He had maintained radio silence since he left town.

Cody had uncombed sandy hair streaked with silver-gray, a square jaw, high cheekbones, a broken nose, brown eyes flecked with gold, and a mouth that wouldn't smile so much as twist into a smirk. He looked at himself in the rearview mirror. His eyes were clear now and had been for two damned years since he'd stopped drinking. They looked somewhat blank, even to him. Cody wasn't completely sold on sobriety but he confessed that to no one. He wore jeans, cowboy boots, a loose long-sleeved fishing shirt, and a flocked Carhartt thermal vest. Under his untucked shirt was his .40 Sig Sauer, a set of handcuffs, and the seven-point gold sheriff's department badge.

As he got out and dropped down to the frozen ground, he glanced up the slope to see if he could be seen from B. G.'s place. He couldn't.

He reached inside the cab for the paper sack and clamped it under his arm.

B. G. wouldn't do well at the state penitentiary in Deer Lodge, Cody thought. Once word got out among the population what kind of reprobate he was. Which made Cody smile.

III.

Everything about Cody Hoyt was exasperating, Cassie thought as she peered through the binoculars. When he was at a crime scene he was methodical, detail-oriented, curious, and thorough. It was like he emerged from a cynical and disheveled shell with strangely clear eyes. But the rest of the time . . .

Cassie Dewell was thirty-four years old with short brown hair and large brown eyes. She was twenty pounds overweight and self-conscious about it. She was the kind of woman constantly described as "having a pretty face," which left the rest to be surmised. She'd been paired with Cody two weeks before after Sheriff "Tub" Tubman fast-tracked her promotion as a response to a series of articles in the Helena *Independent Record* about the lack of diversity in the department. Cassie was well aware of the circumstances and she would have resented it if she didn't need the job and increase in salary to support her son, her mother, and herself. That Tubman held the promotion over her was something she'd need to deal with when this assignment was over.

Cassie was a local Helena girl born and bred. Her late father was a long-haul truck driver and her mother— who described herself as a "free spirit"—was living with Cassie and her son. When Cassie had taken the promotion, Tubman had assured her she'd have plenty of time to be with her family. He'd lied.

That morning, inside the cabin below, they'd found the body of Roger Tokely, fifty-eight, slouched forward in a straight-back chair, head bent, as if examining something on the floor between his feet. His beer belly prevented the body from falling forward to the floor. He faced a big-screen television mounted on the eastern wall in front of him. His arms hung on either side of his body, palms out. He wore baggy gray sweatpants and a yellow T-shirt. His feet were bare and swelled grotesquely, the thick toes looking like stubby purple Vienna sausages.

There was a large pool of blood on the floor beneath Tokely's chair. Cody guessed it was thirty inches across. The outside four inches of the pool was clear and the inside was dark and oval-shaped.

Next to the pool on the right side of the body was a stainless-steel revolver.

Cassie thought suicide. Cody thought homicide. Not only that, he said he was pretty sure who'd done it. Someone named B. G.

He said, "B. G. is a six-foot-five reprobate who lives right up there on the ridge."

There was no evidence she could see pointing to anyone.

"Don't worry," Cody had said with an evil grin that chilled her and confirmed her worst fears about her partner, "we'll prove it."

IV.

Cody didn't turn on the lights and moved by feel and memory into Roger Tokely's kitchen. The lounge chair where Tokely's body had been found was still there in a muted pool of moonlight. The bloodstain had not yet been cleaned up but the murder weapon had been taken for evidence.

On the side of the kitchen counter was a garbage container. With gloved hands, he opened the lid. The smell of rotted food wafted out. Then he opened the small paper sack he'd brought with him and glanced inside. The contents had been taken from B. G.'s Dumpster. Inside were crumpled fast-food wrappers and a half-eaten McDonald's cheeseburger that might yield DNA. The scraps would tie B. G. to the scene of the murder.

He'd try to act surprised when the evidence tech announced the discovery.

* * *

As Cody climbed into his Ford he thought he heard the distant sound of a car starting up. He stepped back into the grass and peered toward the bench on top, then scanned the dark treeline. He didn't see a vehicle, or headlights. Still, it unsettled him.

Tuesday, November 20

There's a killer on the road
His brain is squirming like a toad
—**Jim Morrison, "The Hitchhiker"**

1.

He called himself the Lizard King. The prostitutes
known as lot lizards feared him. More precisely, they
feared his legend, the *idea of him*. None of them who'd
ever seen his face up close lived to describe it.

He was parked in the back row of trucks with his
diesel engine idling, his running lights muted, his hair
slicked back, and a bundle of tools on the floorboard
on the right side of his seat within easy reach. He was
hunting but there was no need to go after his prey. The
lot lizards would come to him.

The truck stop was four miles west of Billings, Montana, off I-90. A cold mist hung in the air and moisture
beaded on the windows and the paint jobs of more
than seventy big trucks. The black asphalt lot shined as
if freshly varnished between the rows of semis, reflecting the lighted highway signs and hundreds of streams
of horizontal running lights from the parked trucks

themselves. The air outside hummed with rumbling engines. Tendrils of steam rose from beneath the engines and combined with the undulating waves of heated exhaust that rose from beneath the big rigs.

From his high perch in the dry and warm cab, his sight lines were clear. The truck plaza itself was filled with activity and he noted it carefully. Vehicles entered and exited the long banks of fuel pumps in front of the garish low-slung building a hundred yards away. Professional truckers filled 150-gallon aluminum tanks with diesel fuel on one side of the lot, passenger cars and vans filled up with gasoline on the other.

Inside the truck stop restaurant, waitresses served the $10.95 T-bone special advertised on the marquee near the exit. Drivers lounged in the "trucker's only" section checking e-mail, comparing road conditions, or drinking coffee. Truck stop employees cooked up fried chicken and potato wedges for the lighted bins at the front counter and manned the cash registers selling salted snacks, energy boosters, beef jerky, and drinks.

This was the way it was on the open road; islands of lighted activity in a sea of prairie darkness. Cars and families on one side, truckers on the other, but sharing the same facility. Two vastly different worlds that met only at places like this. Inside, truck drivers and citizens barely acknowledged each other and the modern truck stop was designed so there would be little interaction. Sure, the drivers would get on their radios and laugh at the rubes they'd run into inside and mock their looks or stupid conversations, but inside they were segregated between the amateurs and the professionals,

the clueless consumers—the civilians, the amateurs—
and the cloistered universe of the providers.

He was on the road so much his outlook on it had
changed completely over the years. It no longer seemed
like he was moving, for one thing. Now he felt as if he
were stationary while the road rolled under him and
the scenery flowed by. The world came to *him*.

Like the captain of a large ocean vessel, a large swath
of the landscape was off-limits to him, as he was con-
fined by the shipping lanes that were interstate highways. When he parked his truck at a rest area or truck
stop for the night he couldn't venture into town because
he had no way to get there unless he walked. It was like
a captain who had to anchor his boat and take a dinghy
to shore.

Oh, how he resented the smug people in those towns.
They thought their food, clothing, furniture, appliances,
and electronics simply appeared at stores or on their
front doorsteps. They didn't stop to think that every
item they ate or wore or used was likely transported
across the nation in the trailer of his truck or those like
him, or that the hardworking blue-collar rednecks they
avoided in real life and despised on the road were the
conduits of their comfort and the pipeline of their
wealth.

It was the Tuesday before Thanksgiving, so there was
more traffic on the highways than usual. It would be
much worse the next day as families moved across
the country with a lull on Thanksgiving and another
spike on Sunday as people returned home. He was used

to it. The rhythms of the road were like rivers that flooded and receded in perpetuity.

The Beartooth Mountains to the south were light blue with new snow and the lack of stars indicated heavy cloud cover. It was still warm enough on the valley floor that the moisture hadn't turned to snowflakes, but there was a snap in the air outside and he watched as travelers left their cars and zipped up coats on their way into the truck stop. He snorted at an overweight family of fools wearing T-shirts and shorts who practically ran from their passenger van to the door that led to the restrooms. *Fucking idiots.* What if they broke down wearing clothes like that? Who would they look for to rescue them? *Me,* he thought. The invisible, faceless trucker.

In the darkened cab of his eighteen-speed Model 379 Peterbilt, the Lizard King was alone, quiet and still, the cab perched over 550 horses of steel muscle under the iconic squared-off snout. The truck was flat black, stripped of chrome, and as subtle as a fist. It was a trucker's truck the way a Harley-Davidson was a biker's bike. He'd even painted the twin stacks with black chimney paint to eliminate any hint of flash.

Without looking down, he let his right hand slip down on the side of the seat until he could find the string that held his bundle together. He pulled the cord and the bundle unrolled. His fingertips traced each item. Everything had been wiped clean and sterilized since its last use: the tire thumper, which was a short lead-filled wooden baton used to check the pressure of his eighteen wheels, the pliers and wire cutters, two pairs of handcuffs, four knives—the heavy hunting Buck, the short folding Spyderco, the long thin filet knife, and the stainless-steel hatchet. His lightweight Taurus 738 TCP semiauto in .380 ACP. In an oblong, hard, and hinged box once used for sunglasses was a syringe filled with Rohypnol. And his vintage fourteen-inch long Knapp butcher saw with the aluminum T-grip and both bone and wood teeth on opposite sides of the blade. It was designed for the rapid field butchering of big game. He ran his thumb gently along the bone teeth.

Satisfied that everything was in order, he removed the tire thumper and placed it on the dashboard next to his roll of one hundred-mile-an-hour brown Gorilla tape. Both were standard items used by every trucker and they wouldn't draw a second glance. He bundled the rest of the tools and reached under his seat for the satchel, which contained heavy plastic bags, the wire ties, his folding shovel, the 300,000 volt Stun Master stun gun, and the three-inch-wide roll of duct tape. He put the bundle of tools back into the satchel and zipped it closed.

If things went well, he wouldn't even need to reach for the satchel. *If things went well . . .*

The Lizard King glanced around the cab to make sure he'd completed all the items on his mental checklist. The carpeted floormats had been pulled and stashed, leaving a bare metal floor. Both seats were fitted with clear plastic covers. All logbooks, maps, and other paperwork—anything that could absorb fluid—had been stashed away. He turned in his seat. The cloth drapes separating the cab from the sleeping cabin had long ago been replaced by clear shower curtains that allowed him to see clearly into the back. On his bunk was a specially adapted cover made from blue tarpaulin, and plastic sheeting lined the walls. The single small window of the sleeper was blacked out.

He'd forgotten nothing. There was no cloth or porous surface for blood, hair, or fiber to cling to inside, and the cab and cabin could be hosed clean in a few minutes by a power washer.

He was ready.

He waited for the segregation between the professionals and the amateurs to breach. It did when a rusted-out van cruised the trucking lanes and parked in shadow on the side of the truck stop. North Dakota plates.

Two lot lizards got out and the van drove away. That meant they had thumbed a ride or made arrangements for a pickup later. Meaning there would be no telltale vehicle left at the truck stop to raise any alarm. That was good.

What wasn't so good was that there were two of them. It wasn't unusual; they tended to partner up to some extent. Which meant if one of them vanished the other would know.

One lot lizard, who was short and heavy and dark— maybe an Indian from the res to the south—started off for the far corner of the lot. She'd work that side first, he guessed. He breathed a sigh of relief.

The other one put her hands on her hips and looked in his direction.

She looked thin and gaunt and had long stringy blondish hair haloed by the blue overhead lamps and the mist. He couldn't see her face yet because of the darkness. A long sweater or shawl-like cape hid her figure, which was one of the tricks of the trade. She teetered on high heels and held her hands out to her sides as if for balance and she baby-stepped toward the parked lines of trucks.

Perfect.

He stubbed his cigarette out and squinted through the curl of smoke and the rain-smeared windshield. He could feel his insides start to knot.

Since that morning outside of Chicago the Lizard King had been planning the hunt. He'd awakened in his bunk thinking about it, and at breakfast he'd gone through his mental checklist. It had been several weeks, and he was due.

He pulled a fifty-three-foot trailer known as a "reefer," meaning the inside of the box was controlled by a separate diesel refrigeration-slash-heating unit mounted on the front. Depending on the contents of his load, he could keep the box cool to freezing, and his loads were primarily pallets of fresh or frozen food. He ran coast-to-coast, picking up apples in Yakima, Washington, and delivering them to Boston, and completing the circuit with yogurt from Connecticut or potatoes from New Jersey to be delivered in the west. The loads and destinations varied from circuit to circuit, and sometimes he forgot what he was hauling. It took him four and a half days to run from one coast to the other, and he generally completed two full laps of the nation before returning home. His life was a rhythm of three weeks on the road, a week at home to recuperate and get repairs, then three more weeks of running. He was on his way home after nineteen straight days on the road; meaning no more than eleven hours of driving in any fourteen-hour period, and ten hours of rest in order to legally drive another eleven.

The Lizard King knew mileposts on every highway in America and knew which truck stops to fuel up and which ones to avoid. He timed his routes to avoid as many weigh scales—called "chicken coops"—as possible and he'd rather use his piss-jug than be forced to stop at highway rest areas frequented by homosexuals known as "pickle parks." Like all truckers, he did his best to avoid states with overbearing troopers and stupid regulations like Minnesota, Ohio, California, Oregon, and Washington, and he gave a wide berth to other trucks from companies known for poorly trained drivers.

It had taken just one glimpse of a young woman the night before, red-haired and college-age, her car filled with boxes and clothes she was taking home for Thanksgiving break, who passed him on an incline and swung back into his lane so recklessly that he had to tap his brakes and lean on his horn. When he was able to catch back up with her in the passing lane she looked up and their eyes met for a brief second. Then she flipped him off with dismissive contempt. That's all it took. Rage blasted through him and orange spangles erupted in front of his eyes.

Before he could swing his rig over into her lane and force her off the highway she stomped on her accelerator and shot ahead. Their bumpers almost kissed but she gained distance. He cursed the half-load in his trailer that held him back. It was like dragging an anchor behind him. He cursed that red-haired girl until her taillights faded away in the dark.

He'd kept an eye out for her all the way to Janesville, Wisconsin. But by the time he got to Chippewa Falls he'd lost her somewhere. She'd either continued to speed home straight ahead or she'd taken an exit off the interstate.

She had no idea, he thought, how lucky she was. Outside West Fargo, he'd barely slept and he thought of what she'd look like bound in cuffs and tape with a whole new attitude toward him.

So after breakfast, in light rain outside of Mandan, he parked at a rest area and pulled on his raincoat. The first thing to do was to make his loaded eighty-thousand-pound truck invisible. He did it by covering the transmittal dome of his Qualcomm unit with a shower cap lined with aluminum foil and sealing the bottom with tape. This way, neither his employers nor curious troopers could track his movements or his speed.

His anticipation built throughout the day as he rolled west. He paid special attention to the radio and slowed in advance of the speed traps or scales outside Wibaux and Bad Route, Montana, and he didn't stop for lunch or mandatory rest periods although he lied in his logs to say he did. He shot across I-94 in Montana maintaining the perfect speed of sixty-three miles per hour for maximum fuel efficiency for his Caterpillar C15 motor to get as far ahead of schedule as possible. They shouldn't expect him before 10:00 P.M. If the dispatcher, that bitch, said she had trouble tracking him via his Qual-comm, he'd curse and say it must have malfunctioned again like the last time.

He gained four hours, he figured, by the time he hit Miles City, Montana. Four hours of free time, where no one would be watching. He'd carry that four free hours with him as he pounded west, and not withdraw a minute of it until he got to the truck stop outside Billings.

Four hours was more than enough time to do what he needed to do. He'd done it in two, so he was sure of it.

He'd arrived early to the truck stop, an hour before dark. At that time there was plenty of room in the back row of the trucker's lot when he arrived, and he took a middle space without neighbors on either side.

Choosing the back row meant something to other truckers. Either the driver wanted to get some real sleep in his cabin behind the seat, or he wanted privacy to rest or do paperwork, or, in this case, he was sending a signal that he was available to the truck stop prostitutes who worked the facility. The lot lizards.

He carried a duffel bag across the lot in the dusk and

went straight to the trucker's entrance of the building. Inside, he paid eleven dollars for a shower. He shaved and changed into a disposable one-piece Tyvek jumpsuit with elastic bands on the sleeves and cuffs. The jumpsuit got no strange looks in the trucker's lounge because truckers wore all kinds of strange clothing. A driver with a full beard, a multicolored serape, and flip-flops sat at a table reviewing his logbook. The man didn't even look up. One driver he knew drove in his underwear with the heat on high.

Still, though, when he became the Lizard King he knew his presence made a statement. People shied away from him when they saw him coming. Conversations stopped as he passed by, like there was some kind of malevolent black cloud hanging over his head. And when he stared at others they tended to quickly look away. It used to bother him, but now he took a kind of perverse pride in it. He didn't want to make new friends, anyway. What was the point?

The Lizard King had never felt brotherhood toward other drivers. In fact, he found many of them as disgusting as the amateurs on the road. He noted how many piss-jars and urine bombs had been tossed on the side of the road, how many Walmart bags of feces. He'd seen the cutaways in the floorboards of some trucks, and he cringed when he witnessed fat truckers parking as close as possible to the truck stop restaurant so they wouldn't have to waddle far to eat. And then there were the Bible-thumpers . . .

He avoided the public retail section of the truck stop, and took a long route back to his Peterbilt through dozens of idling trucks so no one would track where he went. As he passed between two semis in the first row he was dismayed to find a small knot of five drivers shooting the breeze back and forth. Three men leaned against the fuel tank of a blue Mack on the left and two others mirrored their posture against a red Kenworth on the right. He had no choice but to walk right through them and to betray no surprise or caution. To his chagrin, they were arguing about a Bible passage.

"That ain't what it means," one of them said. The man was tall and well built and clean-shaven. He wore a yellow chamois shirt and a ball cap that read TRUCKING FOR JESUS. His Mack truck had the same logo painted on its door behind him. He said, "Listen: 'The discretion of a man defers his anger, and it is his glory to overlook a transgression.' That's in Proverbs. It means look the other way."

The driver he was arguing with leaning against the Kenworth had bushy muttonchop sideburns and wore a cowboy hat. He shook his head and said, "No, you listen. Romans 12:20 says, 'If your enemy hungers, feed him; if he thirsts, give him drink; for in doing so you shall heap coals of fire on his head.' That says to me God will get your revenge for you so you don't need to do any thumpin'. That says God don't look the other way but you should."

"God doesn't do revenge," the man in the chamois shirt said, rolling his eyes. "He does love and forgiveness. Maybe you ought to do the same."

"And I will if I know God will do the thumpin'. But

if he's just going to let the bad man get away with it—naw, that don't seem right."

"You're readin' it wrong, friend," Chamois said. "Remember that later in Proverbs . . ."

"Excuse me," the Lizard King said, "just passing through." He wanted to get by them as quickly as possible. He hoped they were so deep into their discussion they wouldn't even recall him later if asked. The front row truckers weren't all Christians, but many of them were. They'd park next to each other in their sanctimony and self-righteousness and spout verses and lessons to each other while looking down on people like him. He avoided them whenever possible.

The Bible-thumpers sometimes hung bras out their drivers' side windows at night as a way of warding off the prostitutes since it suggested a husband and wife driving team inside. It was a message known well among truckers, but not all the whores knew what it meant, which caused great consternation among the faithful.

"Hey, you look familiar," the muttonchop driver said to the Lizard King.

Since he couldn't just charge through now without making more of an impression than he wanted to, he glanced up at Muttonchops and said, "Sorry, I don't recall."

But he did. The truck stop out of Amarillo. Muttonchops had been down there, parked in his Kenworth in the row in front of the Lizard King, when that fat lot lizard in the Ugg boots and micromini waddled her way to his Peterbilt. The Lizard King was ready—*oh, he was ready*—but as he reached down to let her in he looked up to see Muttonchops watching him through his side sleeper window.

It ruined the moment, and destroyed his plans. If Muttonchops was later questioned and could say he saw the fat lizard get into the Peterbilt . . .

So instead of inviting her in and starting the process, he'd opened the door and as she reached up for his hand to climb inside greeted her face with a kick from his size twelve hunting boot. She fell in a heap on the pavement, blood streaming out of her nose. She was angry but not nearly as angry as he was as he slammed the door shut. He hoped like hell Muttonchops didn't get a clear look at his face that night when he opened his door.

"McAllen, Texas, then?" Muttonchops said, not sure. "The Flying J down there?"

The Lizard King shrugged. "Nope," he lied. "I ain't been down there in years."

The McAllen truck stop was one of the better locations for lot lizards in the country. It ranked right up there with the Vince Lombardi Service Area on the New Jersey Turnpike or any truck stop in Gary, Indiana. Other infamous lot lizard high spots included El Paso, Detroit, and the Port of Albany in New York. Although truckers rarely used CB radios anymore, they still had them. Lot lizards knew it, and he'd hear his radio crackle with, "Anybody need company tonight? If you do, take it to 21. This is Barbie Doll . . ."

Once the lot lizard and the trucker switched to the other channel—along with everyone else parked at the stop who wanted to listen in—there would be a discussion of services, prices, and the location of the man who wanted company. The Lizard King didn't ever respond. He waited for them to come to his door.

"Feel free to join us, brother," Chamois said. "You're more'n welcome. You don't have to know nothing about the Bible. My friend here doesn't, either."

Muttonchops said, "Hey," as if offended and a couple of the others laughed.

"Thanks," the Lizard King said, waving over his shoulder but not looking back.

"You a Christian, son?" Chamois asked.

"Sure," he said without conviction.

"God bless you, buddy," Chamois said. "Whatever you are. Whatever the deal is with you."

And one of the others said, "He needs it."

The Lizard King didn't stop or turn around to see who said it. Was it Muttonchops? Did Muttonchops just remember where they'd met and what nearly happened?

As he reached the back bumper of the trucks and turned left, he shot a quick look over his shoulder at the Bible-thumpers. They were still looking in his direction, and Muttonchops was in the middle of them, talking low.

"He needs it" stuck in his craw as he watched the skinny blond lot lizard climb up into a cab ten trucks away. Who were they to judge him, those bastards? he thought. Weren't they supposed to show some tolerance? Wasn't their whole act about forgiveness?

She was making her way toward him, truck by truck. Most calls were refusals, but four trucks away he saw a hairy arm reach down from a cab and a big hand grasp hers and pull her up. The lights in the cab went out and he saw cheap curtains pulled sharply across the sleeper cab window. He'd gotten a glimpse of her thin and haggard face from the interior dome light of the cab before it went out, and it wasn't a face to write home about. But it would do, he thought. He slid the elastic cuff up over his wristwatch and checked the time. In about five minutes she'd be done. It rarely took longer than that. Truckers wanted blow jobs and not much conversation. Rarely did they want anything else that would take more time. Five minutes tops, and the lot lizards backed out, usually grasping stained and crumpled tissue.

He hoped she had all her teeth but if she didn't, he hoped she had none. He remembered that one in Utah after he'd knocked all her teeth out . . .

There were more and more semis entering the truck stop by the minute, and more cars. They were pouring in. He couldn't account for the sudden traffic, but the more chaos and confusion on the lot, the better for hunting.

He sat back, trying to stay calm until she reached him.

He visualized the dispatcher, that dried-up old crow, trying to track him by his Qualcomm and flipping out because she couldn't locate him or his truck.

His ears hummed with tension and he was so preoccupied he almost didn't hear the rapping on his driver's door. The sound jerked him out of his internal debate, and suddenly all was quiet and he was focused.

He wondered how the hell she'd gotten there so fast. Had everyone else rejected her? Or was there a new one, a new lot lizard he hadn't seen?

He reached over and grasped the door handle and opened it a few inches. It was that damned Chamois and Muttonchops.

He didn't open his door more than two inches, so they couldn't see inside.

"Hey, buddy," Chamois said, "We just heard I-90 West will likely be closed all night."

"Why?"

"Big propane truck jackknifed a few miles past Laurel. The Montana State Patrol shut down both lanes."

That explained the sudden arrival of traffic, he thought.

"No shit?" he said, angry they were there but assuming they'd interpret his curse being about the highway.

"Yeah," Chamois said, "We're likely to be here all night. The Montana state boys are taking every precaution that jackknifed truck don't blow up."

He looked down through the gap between the door and the frame. Muttonchops stood shoulder to shoulder with Chamois but he couldn't see his face. The Lizard King wanted them to leave. Their presence might spook the lot lizard working her way to him. Or they might turn on her, the Bible-thumping bastards.

"Well," the Lizard King said, "thanks for letting me know. I may give it a try later, though. I'm not that far from home base and there are a few other routes I can take."

"Where's home?" Chamois asked. "Livingston, Montana?"

He was taken aback that they knew, but then realized they'd read it on his door.

"Yeah."

"That ain't that far."

"That's what I'm sayin'."

"Well," Chamois said, as if killing time for a reason the Lizard King couldn't discern, "you'll have to decide for yourself which road you take."

He said it in a way that caused the Lizard King to think it had nothing to do with the highway.

"That I'll do," he answered, trying to keep his rage from overtaking him. These bastards were *mocking him.* "In fact, I'll do whatever the hell I want and I don't need any help or advice from you," he said, slamming the door shut.

As he watched them walk away toward their trucks in the front row, he saw Muttonchops playfully punch Chamois in the shoulder as if they were sharing a joke. He thought of shoving his gearshift into second and mowing them down.

Then he saw her, the blond one. She was descending from the cab four trucks away. The lights inside came back on. And she was teetering toward him on her high heels.

Everything was set up perfectly, but too many factors nagged at him. The closed road, for one. And all the attention the Bible-thumpers had paid him. One of the beauties of the road was its anonymity. The Bible-thumpers would likely be five states away by morning. Still, though, they'd seen his face. They knew his rig. If they were somehow found and questioned later . . .

A voice in the back of his head squawked: *Abort-abort-abort.*

But the closer she got, the more his entire body coursed with electricity and it seemed like his nerve endings were firing, shooting sparks. It had been so long, and he was ready to explode. He thought of that red-haired girl calling him a loser. Those Bible thumpers mocking him. His perfect, perfect plan and preparation.

He almost felt sorry for the lot lizard because she had no idea what kind of hell she was getting herself into.

2.

Eighteen-year-old Danielle and sixteen-year-old Gracie Sullivan were traveling north on I-25 in Danielle's red 2006 Ford Focus with the green Colorado PLNTDNL license plates and music blaring, the wipers smearing spots on rain and snow across the windshield, and the check engine light on. PLNTDNL stood for "Planet Danielle" and it was her car.

Gracie was simply along for the long ride to Omaha to be with their dad for Thanksgiving. Their parents had divorced years before and the girls rotated holidays between Denver, where they lived with their mother, and Omaha, where their father had most recently moved with his software engineering firm.

He even sent them a GPS and a road atlas for their Thanksgiving trip to Omaha. The atlas was in the backseat, where Danielle had tossed it after determining their route. The GPS was still in its box in the trunk unopened, because Danielle didn't want to take the time and trouble to figure out how it worked. Their bags were stuffed in the trunk and the backseat floor was littered with fast-food bags and wrappers and empty plastic water bottles.

Danielle was at the wheel. She drove like she lived—with wild impulsive fits and starts. Gracie would watch the speedometer slow to fifty while Danielle searched for a song she liked on the sound system or texted on her phone, then gritted her teeth when her sister sped up to eighty with the rhythm of the music. It drove Gracie crazy.

"At least go the friggin' *speed limit*," Gracie said, wide-eyed and pleading. "Don't you have cruise control? Why don't you set it so you don't kill us before we get there?"

"We'll be fine," Danielle said. "Stop freaking out."

"You drive like a crazy person."

Danielle let up on the accelerator pedal and reset the cruise control at exactly seventy-five. "There. Are you happy now?"

"Yes!"

"This is boring."

"That's okay!"

They'd left that morning at nine. It was eight hours to Omaha; north on I-25 to Cheyenne, then east on I-80. Gracie wished she was old enough to have a driver's license so *she* could drive. Danielle was dangerous. Lanes meant nothing to her.

Danielle was dark-haired, big-eyed, with a full figure and a wide mouth. She was everything Gracie wasn't.

Gracie was pencil-thin with reddish blond hair, freckles across her nose, and of course she wore glasses
because contacts irritated her eyes.

"And you need to stop texting," Gracie said.

"You are such an old lady," Danielle replied. "You
should have blue hair and a walker. And orthaconic
shoes."

"*Orthopedic.*"

"Whatever."

"Look," Gracie said, "I was up until two this morning
getting all my homework done. I'm tired."—Danielle
rolled her eyes. She *never* did homework.—"and I want
to get some sleep. But I can't sleep with you speeding
up and slowing down and weaving all over the road."

Danielle didn't respond and didn't indicate she even
heard her. She was looking at her phone.

"He won't answer," she said.

"Who, Justin?"

"Of course Justin. Who else?"

"Oh, stop it," Gracie moaned.

"He always asks about you. He thinks of you as the
dorky little sister he never had."

"*God!*"

"I tell him how smart you are, how you got all of the
brains while I got all of the rest. How all the teachers
can't believe we're even related and blah-blah-blah."
She wriggled her fingers in the air while she talked
because she knew how much the gesture annoyed
Gracie and always had. "And he asks, 'Is she still a flat
little plain Jane?' "

"He did not!" Gracie whined. The fact was, Danielle

was more than a little correct. Justin was a genuinely great guy, smart and athletic, always positive. He was a reader, too, and Gracie and Justin had discussed books while Danielle stood aside rolling her big blue eyes. Gracie and Justin probably had more in common than Danielle and Justin, Gracie thought. They had both read the entire Harry Potter series, for one thing. But Justin had moved with his mother to Helena, Montana, in the spring. Danielle hadn't seen him since, although they were in constant contact via cell phone, Facebook, and Twitter.

"Well, no, maybe he didn't exactly say it," Danielle said, enjoying the torture of her sister, "but he was thinking it. I know this because the two of us, Justin and me, are like one. I'll bet you never in a million years would have guessed we'd still be together two years later."

"You're right," Gracie said. "How long before he figures out you're dumber than a box of rocks?"

Danielle ignored that. She said, "We are, you know, like *one being*. Like we had a mind-meld. We can finish each other's sentences. I bet you didn't know that about us."

Gracie said, "Anybody can finish your sentences. All they have to say is, 'That's, like, friggin' awesome.' See how easy it is?"

"You can be such a little bitch," Danielle said, stung. "I'm tired!"

"Then go to sleep," Danielle said. "Leave me alone."

Gracie sighed and sat back. She tried not to think about Danielle, or the fact that the moment she closed her eyes her sister stomped on the gas pedal and started texting on her phone.

Gracie slept hard, and when she awoke she sat up and rubbed her eyes. She was surprised to see that it was late afternoon and the sun was slanting shadows across the empty landscape.

"You snore," Danielle said.

There were distant mountains to the west and it took her a moment to say, "Where are we? This doesn't look like Nebraska."

"Really?" Danielle smirked. "It doesn't?"

"Danielle," she said, alarmed, "where are we?"

Her sister flipped her hair back and said, "Somewhere between Casper and Sheridan, Wyoming."

Gracie was suddenly wide-awake. "You missed the turnoff. We're in Wyoming instead of Nebraska. We're north instead of east. Turn around!"

"Calm down," Danielle said. "I know what I'm doing."

"What?"

"I'm going to Helena to see Justin. He won't answer my texts and he won't take my calls. There's something wrong and I have to see him."

It took a few seconds for Gracie to comprehend what she'd been told. When she did, she said, "Have you lost your friggin' mind?"

"No, I've found it," Danielle said theatrically. "Someone has gotten to Justin and I won't let it happen."

Gracie shook her head in disbelief. "Turn around or I'm calling Mom."

Danielle snorted.

Gracie realized why when she reached into her bag on the floor of the car and her phone wasn't there.

"Give it back," Gracie said.

"I will when you calm down," Danielle said. She refused to meet her sister's eyes, and for once concentrated on the road ahead of her. Gracie had rarely seen Danielle so determined . . . or so irrational.

"I'll clear it with Dad," Danielle said. "If he's okay with it, you should be okay with it. He's the one making the call here. Mom will have Thanksgiving with Aunt Susan and it won't matter where we are if Dad says it's okay."

"But he *won't*," Gracie pleaded. "He'll tell us to turn around and now we won't get there until the middle of the night."

Danielle said, "So you'll agree that if he says it's okay, you'll calm the fuck down?"

Gracie balled up her hands and pounded them once, hard, on her knees. "This is so stupid I can't believe it."

"Hush," Danielle said, "I'm calling."

As soon as Gracie heard Danielle say, in her most girlish and syrupy voice, "Hi, Daddy, it's Danny," she knew how the conversation would turn out. And she hated her father for it.

Danielle activated the speaker on her cell phone and Gracie could hear both sides of the conversation.

Their dad was a pushover, especially for Danielle's pleading, and especially since he still felt guilty about the disaster of their back-country trip to Yellowstone Park two years before. He was still trying to make up for it and the only way he knew how was to give in to anything Danielle asked of him and to try to get himself back into her good graces.

"Does your mom know?" Ted Sullivan asked. Gracie could hear the fear in his voice.

"Not yet," Danielle said. "But don't worry. I'll tell her."

Silence.

Finally, Ted said, "But if I know what you're doing and I don't tell her . . ."

"I'll handle Mom," Danielle said with confidence.

Ted obviously wasn't convinced, though. He said, "She asked me to call her when you girls arrived. I can't call her and lie. I just can't."

Danielle frowned for a moment, then grinned. "I've got it," she said. "Just don't call at all. Tell her tomorrow you forgot. That sounds like something you'd do. By then everything will be fine."

"Boy, I don't know," Ted said with doubt in his voice.

"Daddy, we all know how scatterbrained you can be. This won't be the first time you forgot something."

"That's true," he said.

"Dad!" Gracie shouted. She couldn't remain silent another second. "Did you *forget* you have *two* daughters?"

"Hi, Gracie," he said sheepishly.

"Maybe I don't want to go, did you think about that?" Gracie said. "Did you think maybe I don't want to spend Thanksgiving with Danielle's boyfriend?"

Before Ted could respond, Danielle switched off her speaker and pulled the phone up to her ear. "Daddy, you really like Justin, don't you? Remember when you told me that?"

Gracie was so angry she could barely hear the rest of the conversation. It went on for another five minutes before Danielle said, "Goodbye. I love you, Daddy," and dropped the phone into her lap.

"He says he might fly to Helena for Thanksgiving to be with us," Danielle said. "So will that make you happy?"

"Not really," Gracie said. "He's such a wimp at times."

Danielle told Gracie Dad seemed to enjoy being in on the deception because it was something he could share with his girls.

"He can be such a limp weenie." Danielle laughed.

Gracie didn't like to think of their dad like that. She wanted him to be brave, tough, admirable, and stoic. But Danielle was right.

After an hour of angry silence, Gracie pointed at the red CHECK ENGINE light.

"Hey, what's with this little engine thing that's lit up?"

"Don't worry about it," Danielle said.

"Shouldn't we get it checked?"

"By who? We're in the middle of friggin' nowhere if you haven't noticed," Danielle said, gesturing outside toward the darkening mountains in the distance. They'd just entered Montana. The last sign they'd passed said they were entering the Crow Indian Reservation. "Just don't worry about it. It's been on for hours."

"Danielle!"

"We'll ask Justin to check it out when we get there. He knows something about cars, I think. Just quit worrying about everything all the time." Her sister noted the time on her phone and changed the subject. "It's four. Time to text Mom and tell her we can see Omaha from here. There's no reason to make her worry."

Gracie winced. "You mean, other than you're lying to her."

"Better that than spending her whole holiday worrying. And I promise to call her when we get to Helena. I'll take all the blame, don't worry."

Danielle sent the text and threw back her head and laughed. "I can talk anybody into anything," she said, looking over and batting her eyes, letting her voice take on the syrupy tone she'd used on their dad. "It's just this thing I have. This gift. This wonderful skill."

Gracie clamped her jaws tight and fumed. But it was true, and it was unfair. Her beautiful and oh-so-popular older sister had the ability to manipulate people in amazing ways and she had no qualms about doing so.

"I can't believe you're doing this," Gracie said, shaking her head. "I can't believe I'm letting you."

"It's because you love me," Danielle said. "And who can blame you?"

"*God!*"

"Justin loves me, too," Danielle sang. "He said I'm the best thing that has ever happened to him. And you know what? I am. He might have forgotten it a little or gotten, you know, distracted. But once he sees me again, and remembers what it's like to be on Planet Danielle . . ." she saw no need to finish her thought.

"You can be such a—"

"Wonderful sister," Danielle interjected. "That was the word you were looking for. We're here because of love. You love me and you want to support me in my relationship with Justin, even though you are a little jealous because he's so hot and sweet and sexy."

"I'm worried about this engine light," Gracie said.

"Forget about it."

"I can't forget about it. What if the car breaks down? Then what do we do?"

"It won't break down," Danielle said, petting the dash with both hands. "It loves me, too. My car would never let me down."

Danielle interrupted her monologue long enough to hand Gracie's phone back to her and open her own. Gracie watched her sister speed dial a number.

"He won't pick up," Danielle said to her in a stage whisper. Then, on Justin's voice mail, she said, "Guess who is driving right now to Helena to spend Thanksgiving with her boyfriend? Call me."

Danielle closed her phone and beamed.

3.

Cassie Dewell sat in a hard chair across the desk from Sheriff Tubman in the Law Enforcement Center and became proportionately more alarmed as his mounting glee became apparent. She found herself squirming in the chair, trying to find a comfortable position. She wasn't even aware at first that her hands ached because she was squeezing them together between her thighs.

Tubman slowly studied each of the printed photographs she'd brought him, his eyes dancing across every inch of every one, the set of his mouth pulling back into a smile of satisfaction. After he studied a photo, he placed it faceup and side by side on his desk in chronological order as they'd been taken. Soon, the photos stretched across the desk from corner to corner in three neat rows.

She had no desire to look again at the photos. After all, she'd taken them the night before. She was sick about what she'd set in motion. What Tubman had forced her to do.

The large envelope containing the prints had been locked inside her briefcase under her desk the entire day. They were there when she and Cody met to start assembling the murder book on Roger Tokely. Cody was patient with her and walked her through the process of methodically assembling the crime scene reports and photographs, the preliminary coroner's report, the case file time line, the written recap of their initial investigation.

They were there when the crime scene techs, twenty-year veteran Tex McIntire and Alexa Manning, his new twenty-seven-year-old lesbian assistant (further proof of Tubman's diversity program at work), burst into the investigator's office to announce their find in Tokely's garbage can. Not only did they locate a credit card receipt signed by Brantley Meyers, aka "B. G.", but they'd also bagged fragments of food that might determine B. G.'s presence, via DNA, inside the Tokely residence on the night of the murder.

She'd watched Cody closely when they heard the news. He seemed genuinely pleased.

Cassie knew what she had. And she dreaded showing the photos to the sheriff. He'd been out all day on a campaign swing to Lincoln and other small communities in northern Lewis and Clark County. With each hour, her tension increased. She'd passed on lunch when Cody asked, and said she was trying to diet. He nodded

back knowingly, practically telegraphing his approval
to try and lose a few pounds, but reminded her of the
maxim he'd always lived by: "Take every possible opportunity you can to eat and take a shit, because this
county is 3,500 square miles, a third of it roadless."

As soon as he was gone she drove to Taco Bell and
ate herself through half the menu, it seemed. Stress
did that to her. So did boredom. So did *everything*, she
thought ruefully.

Sheriff Tubman had returned to the Law Enforcement Center at four thirty and looked in on Cody and
Cassie. When she looked up and met Tubman's eyes he
knew immediately.

"Got a minute?" the sheriff asked her.

"Yes."

"My office, please," he said, and shut the door behind
him.

Cody had asked her what the meeting was about.

"How should I know?" she lied.

"Tell him he's a prick," Cody had said. "Tell him
I've seen better leaders on the end of my fly line."

"I'm sure I'll do that," she responded, and grabbed
the handle of her briefcase on the way out.

It was more than two weeks since daylight savings time
had ended and she hated how early it got dark. As she
sat across from the sheriff she looked over his shoulder
through the window. White-blue lights were strobing
to life in the parking lot. She could see clerical staff
trundling out to their cars in heavy coats, condensation
puffs revealing their conversation. After five, the LEC

cleared out. She wished she was one of them. And given what was about to happen, she wondered for the first time since accepting the job if she was really cut out for it.

"Here you can clearly see he's turned his headlights out," Tubman said, looking at the first two photographs. She'd used the night-vision setup on her digital Canon Rebel. Cody had taught her how to use it, she thought with a stab of guilt. The full moon had really helped as well.

Tubman said, "The only possible reason he'd do that would be so the citizens up on the bench wouldn't notice a vehicle. That's the only real explanation, since we all know the Tokely residence was empty."

She nodded once but said nothing.

"What's this in his hand and under his arm?" Tubman asked, looking at the next few photos. "It looks like a bag of something. A paper bag.

"And here he is standing on the front porch looking back. Trying to see if anyone is watching him. Is it possible he could see you?"

"No, sir."

"That's obvious," Tubman said, practically rubbing his hands together with joy. "Because in the next shot he's bending down picking the lock. That's breaking and entering right there, as well as proof that he's trying to do something worse. Because if he had a legitimate reason to go back into that house, all he had to do was file a request for the keys from the evidence room."

She tried to swallow but her mouth was dry.

"So we jump ahead," Tubman said. "The next few shots show nothing, just his vehicle and the dark house. But that tells us something right there, because he made a decision *not* to turn on any lights. Why would an investigator do such a thing? Why would a red-blooded, honest cop sneak into a crime scene and bump around in the dark? Gee, that's a tough one," Tubman said with heavy sarcasm.

"And here he comes out of the house. How long was he in there, Investigator Dewell?"

She cleared her throat but had trouble speaking.

"How long? I didn't get that."

"Seven minutes, sir."

"Seven minutes. That's a very short period of time to do a thorough investigation or follow up on a lead, don't you think?"

"Please, sir," she said.

"Okay, be that way," he said dismissively. He turned his attention to the last few prints.

"He comes out after seven minutes and what do you know? He no longer has the paper bag! He must have thrown it away inside because he's such a stickler for littering, don't you think?"

She said nothing.

"And here he is looking around again. Trying to see if anyone saw him. Do you think at that point he was suspicious of you?"

"He might have heard my car, sir. I started it up because I was freezing and I wanted to turn the heater on."

"But he didn't see you."

"No."

"And he hasn't asked you what you were doing last night?"

"No."

Tubman sat back in his chair with a grin and looked at her. He said, "Good work, Investigator Dewell. Damned good work. I've finally gotten that son of a bitch, thanks to you."

She looked away.

"I know you didn't feel comfortable following him when I asked you," Tubman said. "But you did your duty. You should be proud. No one wants a crooked cop in their department, much less a crooked partner. Why do you look like I shot your dog?"

"I just don't feel good about this," she said. "He's such a great cop in so many ways."

"Bullshit," Tubman said sharply, sitting forward and glaring at her over the prints. "He's been a pain in my ass since we hired him. There's a good reason why he got kicked off the Denver Metro police force—because he's a renegade. He might have solved some cases but who is to say he didn't plant evidence then?"

She said, "He had the highest arrest rate in Denver. I looked it up. And he's got the highest rate here. He's your best cop when it comes to solving felonies. You *know* that."

"What I know," Tubman said, "is that the happiest day of my career is when I see his ass going out my door."

Before she could respond, Tubman reached for his phone and punched the intercom button.

"Hoyt," Tubman said, "I need to see you in my office."

He grinned as he lowered the handset onto the cradle.

Cassie felt like she'd been punched in the stomach. She said, "You're going to do this while I'm in the room? You're actually going to do this now? So he knows who brought him down?"

Tubman waggled his eyebrows like Groucho Marx. He said, "I need a witness to the execution."

"I'd rather it not be me, sir."

"You're looking at this all wrong, Dewell," Tubman said. "You brought down a crooked cop. The *Independent Record* will love it. The Billings *Gazette* will love it. And the voters will love it."

She took in a ragged breath of air and exhaled it through her nose. "I'm not running for anything," she said.

"Keep up this good work," he said, "and someday you might be. I mean, plenty of years from now." He meant it as a good-natured joke but she didn't smile.

There was a knock on the door.

"Come in, Investigator Hoyt," Tubman said.

Cody took in the scene quickly. She watched as he squinted at the prints, at Tubman's triumphant grin, and turned to her without saying a word.

His face didn't twitch but the light went out of his eyes as he looked at her. They were the eyes of a man who had lost it all.

4.

The Lizard King watched as the lot lizard approached the Mack parked next to his. She tottered on her high heels and held her arms out for balance as if navigating a high wire. She'd be at his truck in five minutes, tops. Less if the driver refused. Because she was on the other side of the Mack at the driver's door, he couldn't see her.

He was barely breathing, and he felt himself becoming aroused. Not by her, but by what he was going to do to her.

The dome light went on in the cab of the Mack as the driver opened his door to answer the knock. The Lizard King could see the back of the Mack driver's bald head and a dark crown of fuzz that wrapped from ear to ear in the back. The bald head nodded up and down. He was talking to her.

"Come on, buddy," he whispered. "Do it or don't.

Quit fucking negotiating. Get out your forty bucks and stop trying to *make a deal*."

The last three words came out in a shout.

The Mack cab light doused. He couldn't see inside but he hadn't seen her enter. The driver pulled the wrap-around cab curtain closed.

There were four kinds of sleeper cabs on the road, from the "coffin" type with a tiny twenty-four-inch bed accessible through a porthole-like hatch to the lavish studio sleepers that were practically camper trailers with wide beds, showers, sinks, and entertainment centers. Between the extremes were "condos" where the bed lifted to the ceiling to allow some headroom and "midroof" models where the bunk was on the bottom with storage compartments on top. The Lizard King preferred the midroof, but all of the designs were big enough to allow two people to cavort inside. Lot lizards didn't need much space.

Then there she was, coming around the front of the Mack, her hand out on the grille of the truck for balance. The driver in the Mack had sent her away. She was shaking her head as if she couldn't believe it. It was obviously a refusal from the driver. Maybe he'd said something, or gotten a quick free grope, he thought. She paused and quickly composed herself; smoothing her hair down on the sides and tugging at the hem of her skirt. Then she put on her game face and looked up and started toward his door as if nothing had happened.

The ten seconds it took for her to rap on his door

seemed like an eternity. Then he heard it: three blows. These girls weren't subtle, he thought.

He reached for the door handle with his left hand and cracked his door a few inches. With his right he reached down and touched the plastic grip on the stun gun with the tips of his fingers.

"Yes?" he asked.

"Are you looking for a little company tonight?" she asked. He could see one eye through the crack. Too much dark eyeliner, as usual. The collar of her coat was faux fur and it sparkled with flakes of snow.

"I am," he said.

"Are you alone or do you have a partner, too?"

"Just me."

"Then," she said, drawing out the word, "why don't you open your door and let me inside so we can party?" She gestured toward the slightly open door: "I'm skinny but I ain't *this* skinny, dude." Her laugh was rough—a cackle.

He shot a quick look through the windshield. No one appeared to be watching, but with those Bible-thumpers one never knew. He looked across. The driver in the Mack had apparently settled into his sleeper for the night. The Lizard King could see bands of light blue from a television under drawn curtains.

He opened the door and could see her in full. She was older than he'd hoped. Her eyes peered from dark hollows, like a raccoon. Her face was angular, emaciated, with a gash of bright red lipstick. She didn't part her lips when she smiled up at him. Probably ashamed of her teeth, he thought. As he reached down for her hand she hesitated for a moment, looking up at him. She seemed taken aback by the white Tyvek jumpsuit, and when she saw his face she recoiled.

"Are you coming in or not?" he asked, annoyed.

Although she seemed to be reconsidering, she extended her hand. He grasped it and pulled her up into the cab. As she wriggled over and sat on his lap he shut the door and the dome light went out. He could feel her bony hips through his suit. There wasn't much meat on her. And she could no doubt feel how hard he was beneath her.

"You're ready for me, ain't you, cowboy?" she said.

He grunted. Her coat and hair smelled of damp and stale cigarette smoke.

"So how do you like it, sugar?"

He said, "Rough."

She froze, but before she could reply he reached up and plunged the twin prods of the stun gun into her bare neck beneath her jawbone. There was the angry snapping sound of electricity and she arched her back with more strength than he thought possible for a meth head.

He took the stun gun away and could smell burned flesh and hair in the cab as her body went limp. He roughly pushed her off him and she fell away and thumped on the bare metal floor at his feet.

Then, as he reached down to pull her back into the sleeper cab, she started to convulse. Her arms and legs jerked spasmodically and her head turned to show a gaping mouth. Teeth missing, he thought. He was right about her. He shrunk back, alarmed and angry. *What was happening*? One of her feet twitched so rapidly her shoe came off and bounced off the door. She'd struck back wildly with her fist and hit his ankle.

She made an "uunnh" sound and stopped moving. Her head was still twisted to the side and a long thin breath clattered out of her. He knew she was dead.

He cursed aloud and kicked the body hard. Nothing. This had never happened before. Was she so strung out the voltage triggered cardiac arrest? He didn't know and didn't care.

He just knew he was angry and not at all satisfied. He hated that bitch for dying on him so soon.

He bellowed, *"Goddamn it!"* and thumped the steering wheel hard with the heel of his hand.

And he heard the laughter and looked up. Chamois, Muttonchops, and the other Bible-thumpers had once again assembled between two trucks in the front row. They weren't looking at him, but they were laughing and gesticulating over some private joke. It was like they were mocking him.

The Lizard King rolled her body over. There was blood everywhere, rivulets coursing through steel channels on the floorboard and pooling in dents where the metal was screwed to the frame. Then he saw the curved bone handle of the knife sticking out from her breast. Right into her heart. Her ratty purse fell away as he rolled her to her back.

So she'd packed a knife of her own, he thought. A

cheap hunting knife hidden in her soft cloth purse. Without a sheath. And when she fell to the floor the blade pierced through the purse and her own weight sunk the blade into her chest.

Stupid, *stupid* bitch, he thought.

5.

In Helena, Montana, eighteen-year-old Justin Hoyt scooted his chair back from the table and the laptop and listened again to the voice mail. He held up his hand to his friend Christian to shush him while he called. Christian hovered behind the sofa in the family room off the kitchen, watching ESPN Sportscenter with the sound off and making comments along with the two other guys and two girls crammed onto the couch. The coffee table in front of them was littered with empty beer bottles, an open laptop showing YouTube videos, and an iPad.

Christian, who was a tall and wide-shouldered linebacker for the Helena high school football team and who'd volunteered his home for the party because his parents were in Great Falls, rolled his eyes and lowered the volume on his iHome with a remote. He was pale-featured and wore his hair in a semi-buzz cut that looked like a beige carpet sample. A couple of other boys, who were pounding beer after beer in the kitchen and were also on the football team, howled in protest that they *liked* that song.

"Just a minute," Christian said to them with mock seriousness, "Justin is listening to something *really important.*"

"I hope it's not his dad coming over," one of the girls said. "That dude scares me."

"Thanks," Justin said. Like his friends, he wore a gray BENGALS FOOTBALL hoodie, jeans, and a baseball cap. He had borrowed Christian's laptop to try and track Danielle and Gracie and it sat open in front of him. Justin hadn't drunk any beer and had made a promise to himself to hold off until his guests arrived. And then maybe just one. He had no natural attraction to alcohol, maybe because his life had been shaped by it—courtesy of his father.

"Guess who is driving right now to Helena to spend Thanksgiving with her boyfriend? Call me."

He felt his insides contract and he looked up.

"What is it, man?" Christian asked.

"Remember Danielle?"

Christian rolled his eyes. "The crazy bitch?"

"I never said that," Justin said quickly.

"But you thought it, man. What about her?"

Justin gestured toward his phone. "She left me a message saying she's coming to see me. Tonight."

Christian's eyes got big and he looked around before he burst out laughing.

"For Thanksgiving," Justin said. "She's coming *here.*"

Christian leaned in close to Justin. "Didn't you say you dumped her finally?"

Justin felt his face blanch.

Christian leaned back and grinned. "You didn't pull the trigger on it, did you? You wussed out."

How could he explain? Justin thought. Danielle was relentless. She didn't take hints. And she blew right past any mention he made about his new life in Montana, the new friends he'd met, the football team, *the new friends he'd met* . . .

He didn't hate her, he thought. He just didn't like her anymore. She was too much—dominating every conversation, telling him what he should think, what bands he should like, how he should apply to Colorado State University because that's where she would likely go.

They'd been through such a trauma together two years ago in Yellowstone they'd emerged extremely close. They'd been through a trauma that would have ended badly if Justin's dad Cody hadn't intervened and saved them. But afterward, after Justin moved to Montana with his mom and Danielle returned to Colorado, the separation made him realize *she drove him crazy.* He'd asked himself if he would even want to be around her at all if she didn't look like that. And his answer was no.

Christian said, "Didn't you say that if you could take her sister's personality and put it into Danielle's body, that—"

"Shut *up,*" Justin said, giving Christian the evil eye and checking around to see if anybody had overheard.

"I was goofing around. And that was just between us, dude."

Christian replied with a broad conspiratorial wink and drained the last of the beer bottle he held in a meaty hand. "Hey, I get it," Christian said. "I've seen her profile on Facebook. She's *smoking* hot, man."

"What are you guys talking about over there?" one of the girls from the family room called out. "Christian, you went to get me a beer, remember?"

"Coming up!" Christian called back, walking into the kitchen to pull another beer bottle from the cooler of ice.

The girl, named Kelsie, got up from the sofa and smiled at Justin and shook her head to indicate Christian was an idiot. Kelsie had short red hair, sparkling green eyes, a little too much makeup, and breasts that strained at the buttons of her blouse.

She said, "I heard. So is this the girl that kept you unavailable to the fine girls of Montana?"

He didn't respond.

"Justin, are you there?" she asked, annoyed. Justin heard Christian curse in the other room and looked up.

"Sorry," he said. "I'm not sure what I should do."

"Tell her to turn around," Kelsie said. "Yes!" Christian agreed as he walked back. "But tell her to sext you some photos first."

"Shut up, Christian," Kelsie said coldly. Christian shut up.

Then to Justin: "Tell her to *go home*."

"You don't know her," Justin said, sighing. "Plus, she

has her sister with her. They're on the highway hours from Denver."

"She's manipulating you," Kelsie said. "Can't you see that?"

He slumped back and looked at the ceiling for any answer other than *yes*.

6.

In the shadows of the rear row at the truck stop, The Lizard King dragged the body into his sleeper cab and wrapped it in plastic sheeting and secured the bundle with hundred-mile tape before sopping the floor clean of her blood so his boot soles wouldn't stick to it. Then he stripped off his bloody one-piece, tossed it into the corner of the sleeper, and pulled on another. The inside of the truck would have to be thoroughly washed out and disinfected as soon as he could do it. But not here. Not with a body in the sleeper. He couldn't risk the chance of letting anyone look inside until he figured out how to dispose of the body and the bloody rags. Luckily, there were plenty of empty miles between the truck stop and home.

He sat back heavily in the driver's seat after he'd stashed all his tools and weapons. The Bible-thumpers were still out there.

His blood was up and he suddenly wanted to kill them all. But there were five of them and one of him, and they stood in between the shelter of the truck trailers so he couldn't run them down.

Furious, he released the parking brake and slammed his gearshift into low and the Eaton-Fuller transmission bit in. The laughing Bible-thumpers were bathed in his headlights as he revved the motor and lurched forward toward them. They scattered except for Chamois, who held his hand up as if that could stop tons of steel and rubber.

But the Lizard King didn't drive over him. Instead, he cranked the wheel sharply and roared out of his space and down the driveway, nearly clipping the bumper of the truck next to him with the end of his trailer.

He wanted to get out of the lot as quickly as he could, to leave this place of wicked humiliation. The faces and trucks of Chamois, Muttonchops, and the others would forever be burned into his memory. He'd never forget them, and he'd get his revenge one by one. He didn't care if it took years to get them all.

In the meantime, he'd have to take it out on somebody, some bitch.

He roared out the exit to the highway going way too fast. In his rage he didn't check his mirrors before sliding onto the interstate.

7.

Danielle had her phone on her lap, texting furiously and giggling. Justin had replied.

"Justin is sooo excited for us to get there," she said to Gracie.

"He is?"

"Don't sound so . . . pissy," Danielle said.

"What did he say exactly?" Gracie asked. She couldn't imagine Justin texting that he was "sooo excited." Gracie was constantly taken aback by her sister's blissful ignorance on so many serious subjects. But she couldn't fault Danielle's ability to get what she wanted when she wanted it and to drag others along into her orbit. Like *her*.

"So what did he say?" Gracie asked.

Danielle shot her an annoyed look. "He said, 'Okay.'"

"That's it?"

"He's a man of few words," Danielle said with her patented lah-de-dah intonation, although the set to her face belied her tone.

The thing was, Gracie thought, Justin wasn't necessarily a man of few words at all, although he probably didn't get many in when Danielle was talking. The simple "okay" in response wasn't encouraging. And of course Danielle knew it.

Despite the situation Danielle had put them in, Gracie felt an unexpected wave of sympathy for her sister. Danielle, despite her bluster and lah-de-dah, was fragile and needy. Their parents' divorce, when Danielle was thirteen, had crushed her and she'd yet to recover. Danielle was too emotional, too desperate for male attention. She'd surrounded herself with boys as if trying to fill the void left by Ted. Before Justin, Danielle was a little slut. Gracie had been embarrassed by her sister, and was too often chosen as a sounding board by the boys Danielle had thrown aside. But after Justin, Danielle straightened up. In a way, Justin had taken Danielle off the market and allowed her to grow. Even a distant Justin gave Danielle an excuse to take herself out of the game. He was good for her in ways he didn't understand, and in ways that were unfair to him, Gracie thought. She didn't blame him for perhaps wanting to be cut loose. But at the same time, she didn't want her sister to spin out of control.

"I'm in prison on the Planet Danielle," Gracie moaned.

"What brought *that* on?" her sister chirped. "Besides, you could be worse places."

Gracie glanced over at the display panel and changed the subject.

"That light is still on," Gracie said.

"Oh, that again." Danielle sighed.

"When is the last time you got the oil changed in this car? Do you even know?"

"Barely . . . out . . . of . . . Billings," Danielle said while she punched in the letters of the text to Justin. Then: "Mom sent me a text back. She said to say hi to dad. Woo-hoo! We're still in the clear."

"I see some lights up ahead," Gracie said, gesturing with her chin. "There's a truck stop or something. I wonder if they'd have a mechanic working or we could find someone to take a look at this?"

Danielle looked up, angry. "We're not stopping to waste time. Justin or his dad can look it over when we get there. They'll fix it."

"What if we don't make it?"

"What if monkeys fly out of your butt?"

"Really, Danielle—"

"We're gonna keep driving!"

Gracie took a big gulp of breath and held it in.

The lights of the truck stop drew closer. There looked to be a lot of activity on the lots; plenty of cars and big trucks. Someone, possibly, who could help them.

Gracie said, "If you don't stop to check on the car, I'm calling Mom."

Silence.

"I'm not kidding," Gracie said, holding up her phone to show her sister she was serious. "We can't take the chance this car will blow up. Then what would we do?"

"You can't keep threatening me with that every time you want your way. It's childish."

"*I'm* being childish?

"Yes. Stop it with the 'I'm calling Mom' crap."

"Then take the exit so we can get your car looked at."

"Who is going to pay for a mechanic? Did you think of that?"

"You have a credit card," Gracie said.

"Why should I use *my* money?"

"*Because it's* your *car!*"

Danielle rolled her eyes theatrically once again, but flinched when Gracie touched the button on her phone that lit it up in anticipation of placing a call.

"Don't," Danielle said.

Gracie pressed the speed dial for home. The rapid sound of the connection being made could be heard through the speaker.

"Okay!" Danielle yelled, "I'm turning in."

Gracie killed the call before it could be answered.

Danielle shook her head and tapped the brakes. "You're such a baby. See, I'm turning in."

Danielle eased to the right and slowed to turn on to the exit to the truck stop. Gracie lowered her phone to her lap and breathed a sigh of relief. Then, out of nowhere, a massive toothy semi-truck grille and front bumper filled her window just a few feet away. Gracie screamed.

The powerful bass roar of the diesel engine from the truck right next to them vibrated through the floor-boards of the little car.

The truck tire was so close she could see beads of water on the chrome of the fender. Danielle jerked the wheel to the left and for an instant the inside of the car exploded in light from a single full-sized truck head-light. Somehow, they avoided getting hit. Although the near miss hadn't been Danielle's fault, the truck driver hit his horn and the sound was earsplitting.

"Jesus Christ!" Danielle gasped. "What happened?"

Gracie was practically on top of the center console, and would have scrambled even further if the seat belts hadn't restrained her. Her heart whumped in her chest.

"That big truck," Gracie said, barely able to speak, "He came out of there and didn't even slow down. He nearly ran us over."

Now the big black truck was in the right-hand lane pulling away from them, a line of amber running lights strobing through the interior inside their car.

Gracie was shaken, and eased back into her seat. The truck pulled away.

"He nearly killed us!" Gracie said. "And we missed the exit because he was in the way."

"*Asshole!*" Danielle screamed at the taillights of the big rig. "You're an asshole!"

Gracie regained her ability to breathe in and out. She looked into the side mirror to make sure there wasn't another oncoming truck bearing down on them but the highway behind them was clear.

Danielle suddenly accelerated.

"What are you doing?" Gracie said.

"I'm going to *pass* that asshole," Danielle said through gritted teeth.

8.

The Lizard King saw a flash of red just outside the driver's side window and glanced over to see the little Ford Focus careen into the passing lane where he'd accidentally forced it. The car had been in the turning lane but he'd been so consumed with his situation he hadn't seen it coming. And because of the darkness and his high vantage point, he couldn't see the driver.

"Watch where you're going," he said aloud. To himself as well as to the driver of the Ford.

He dismissed the other car while he took out part of his frustration on his empty passenger seat, hitting it over and over with his fist as he drove, stopping only to shift into higher gear as his rig picked up speed.

He pushed his truck hard. It felt good to drive fast; eighty thousand pounds hurtling down the highway like a bullet shot from a gun. The lights of the truck stop receded in his mirrors.

Still, though, his nerve endings were sparking like live wires. The humiliation back at the truck stop hadn't stopped his needs, but prolonged them. The pressure built inside him. He had a vision while he drove of his skull exploding like a melon on his shoulders, spattering the inside of the cab with brain matter.

The next several miles of the highway was a long straight 5 percent grade. He'd driven the stretch a hundred times. The grade slowed his truck down to the speed limit and he grabbed a lower gear. The long hill was known to truckers as a "dragon fly"—dragging up one side and flying down the other.

Then, in the driver's side mirror, he saw the headlights. He recognized the little red Ford coming up behind him as the one he nearly hit, but he didn't even look back except to note in his rearview mirror that there were two people in car. They weren't big people. Probably still pissed about being cut off. He didn't care. He wanted to leave them behind. He wanted to leave *everything* that happened at the truck stop behind.

Because the Peterbilt was slowing down climbing the mountain pass, the little red car was catching up. In fact, it was right behind him, so close he could see two faces painted red by the glow of his taillights. Young people; girls. Two young girls.

Two young girls on a desolate stretch of interstate highway in the dark.

He shook his head and bared his teeth as the Ford eased into the passing lane. It was a stupid move to try and go around him, he thought. He glanced over as he drove, wondering if he'd see them closer at all or simply the top of their car as it passed him. Over the years, he'd seen all kinds of scenes in cars when he looked down through the windows; kids driving with their legs folded Indian-style while yapping on their cell phones, couples humping in the backseat, reprobates smoking crack, men masturbating with their pants gathered around their thighs, women performing blow jobs on the driver.

Now, he wondered, were there other passengers in the backseat? Men, husbands or boyfriends? Maybe children?

For the Lizard King, passenger cars and trucks on the highway and the people who drove them existed in a kind of low-level subspecies; an annoyance and a hazard. They existed in a world far below him both literally and figuratively; amateurs in the world of professional drivers. They existed because *he let them exist,* because he could so easily crush them, drive them off the road, or run them down. The drivers of these little cars didn't realize they were on borrowed time and that in any conflict with an eighteen-wheeler, they'd lose.

The angle was just right and he could see both the driver and the passenger through their windshield in his side mirror. Two unaccompanied girls. No one in the backseat. Colorado plates that read PLNTDNL, whatever the hell that meant. So they were hundreds of miles from home with the entire huge state of Wyoming between their home and him. The driver was older than the passenger. She was a looker. Oval face, big pouty mouth.

The passenger was younger and his amber running lights reflected in her glasses. She didn't look old enough to have a driver's license.

The girls had no idea how far they were over their heads, he thought. How typical . . .

They were of that "self-esteem" generation he despised. Unlike him, they'd grown up stupid with every adult they knew praising them, telling them how wonderful and special they were, making sure they never lost a contest or a competition, teaching them nothing but contempt for men who kept the nation running by working long hours with their hands and dripping sweat . . . like him. And he'd known someone like that, in fact a few of them. They belonged to a generation of know-nothings with heightened self-esteem and no respect for working men like him who'd done it the hard way, and were still doing it the hard way. . . .

When the little car was about ten feet from catching his rear bumper, he grinned and jerked the wheel hard to the left, cutting it off.

The headlights vanished from both of his mirrors.

He had the same thought he had earlier when the lot lizard approached his truck: they had no idea what kind of hell they were getting themselves into.

9.

The double rear wheels of the trailer sprayed a mist on the windshield that blinded Gracie, and Danielle gasped as the huge truck suddenly swerved into their lane. The truck was so close Gracie could see its underbelly; long metal shafts, glistening hoses, swinging suspended tire chains, elbows of steel.

Gracie felt the Ford slowing down. She couldn't see anything ahead now except glowing red taillights undulating through the moisture on the windshield. For all she knew, Danielle was in the process of driving under the rear end of the truck trailer.

"Turn on the windshield wipers!" she screamed at her sister.

"I am!"

"Slow down!"

"What do you think we're doing?"

And Gracie realized it was true: the taillights filling the windshield were pulling away. Danielle had the wipers on high now, and the glass cleared. The big truck was a quarter mile in front of them, far enough now that the double sets of tires didn't spray them.

"He did that on purpose!" Danielle seethed.

"I think he did," Gracie agreed, completely unnerved by the thought.

Just before the huge truck had swung over to cut them off she'd caught a glimpse of the driver's face in his mirror. He was fat and doughy with a square head and light-colored wavy hair and eyes set too close together. But she hadn't seen him well enough to identify him if asked.

"He did that on purpose," Danielle said again, this time in awe. "He could have killed us."

"*Again,*" Gracie said.

"What an asshole."

Gracie nodded.

"Is it possible he didn't know we were back there? Maybe he was texting or talking on his phone or something?"

"I don't know."

"What an *asshole.*"

The grade of the road got steeper as they sped back up to the speed limit.

As it did, the big truck slowed. It was still in the passing lane.

"I'm going to try it again," Danielle said, stomping on the gas.

"Danielle, don't!"

"What," her sister said, "you want to follow this jerk all the way to Helena? I want to get rid of him once and for all, the asshole."

And with that they once again closed the gap between the Ford and the truck.

Gracie sat back deep in her seat and tried to say a prayer for them. She was unpracticed and couldn't concentrate. They'd caught up with the rear wheels of the tractor itself and were nearly parallel to the door of the cab. The Ford wouldn't go any faster up the grade, but neither could the truck. Gracie knew that if the truck driver swerved again into their lane he'd force the Ford off the road. She could only hope—and pray—that Danielle would shoot around him before he could change lanes again.

She looked over and watched the progress. Danielle stared straight ahead, leaning over the wheel, a look of crazy determination on her face. Through her window she watched their progress. One set of wheels by, then another. Amber running lights coursing through Danielle's window as if being pulled through. Then the tires of the cab of the truck and the door. There was frontier-type lettering on the door but it was too high for Gracie to read in full. A name in script she couldn't make out and the words, *Livingston, Montana*. She turned to look ahead and focused on the road, on the white stripe on the left side of the left lane, keeping a steady eye on it so the mist being thrown from underneath the tires of the truck wouldn't further blind her. She didn't know how well Danielle could see the road. They were nearly past.

Gracie jumped when cold wet wind howled through the inside of the little car.

"What are you doing?" she yelled at her sister.

In Gracie's peripheral vision she could see Danielle leaning out her window with her left arm extended. The door of the truck just hung there, not receding, not pulling ahead.

"Loser!" Danielle screamed through the open window, raising her middle finger outside, "Fucking loser asshole!"

"Stop it!" Gracie yelled. "Get back in the car and go!"

"Loser! Asshole!"

"Danielle!"

With a satisfied smirk, her sister brought her arm back into the car and floored it. The massive headlights receded in the rearview mirror as they approached the summit of the long climb. Danielle reached over and hit the button and the driver's window whirred back up.

"Ha!" Danielle said. "I told him."

"Could he see you?"

"I think so," she said. "I saw him lean over and look at me. I could just see the top of his forehead. He had the forehead of a loser."

"You're crazy," Gracie said, meaning it. "Why did you have to yell at him? Why didn't you just pass him and leave things alone?"

"And let him get away with it?" Danielle said. "No fucking way. He's lucky we didn't call 911 on his ass."

Gracie sat still until she could breathe again. "Please stop talking like a truck driver," she said.

10.

The Lizard King had been preoccupied by the body in the back. When he'd swerved earlier that damned body had been thrown out of the bunk in his sleeper. It had landed with a thump behind him, and he was looking at it on the floor—he could make out its blank dark eyes through several layers of plastic—when the Ford made its move. By the time he looked up, the car was parallel to the cab. And when he stretched and looked over . . .

They were right *there*, the two young snotty girls in the little red Ford. Right below his passenger window. They were too far along now to easily force them off the road because he could no longer use the trailer as a bludgeon. When the car didn't advance, he was curious and strained up in his seat to get a look at them.

That's when he saw the contorted face of the looker thrust out of her open window. She was screaming at him but he could make out the words: *Fucking loser asshole*.

Loser.

It was like a hard slap in the face.

And because of the steep grade and his load holding him back, the Ford pulled away. He couldn't push his rig any harder to catch up on the hill.

He bellowed in rage as the car passed him and gained distance before it summited the long haul and vanished down the other side.

As he topped the hill, he looked out ahead of him. He could see for miles. In the distance, maybe a mile away, were the two tiny red taillights of the Ford. There were no other cars on the interstate in either direction for as far as he could see.

Less than ten miles ahead was the roadblock set up by the Montana Highway Patrol. He'd no doubt catch up with them there. He envisioned a scenario where he pulled them out of their car and tore them apart with his hands.

Then a cold and razor-edged calm took him over. He'd felt it before, many times. It was the feeling he got when he was stalking prey.

The Lizard King reached into his jumpsuit and pulled out his cell phone and speed dialed his partner.

"I'll be there tonight," he said.

"You got a load?"

"Negatory."

Silence. Pained, angry silence.

Then he said, "Remember that situation you said

you wanted a while back? You know what I'm talking about."

After a beat, his partner said, "No shit? Is this gonna happen?"

"Maybe, maybe not."

"But it could is what you're saying."

"There might be an opportunity," he said. "I won't know until it happens." Thinking, they could pull over to switch drivers. They could take an exit for a rest area. They might even stop to stretch, or walk around to keep awake, or to look at something. He'd have a chance as long as it wasn't public, like a service station or a convenience store . . .

"What kind of opportunity?" his partner asked. His tone was anticipatory.

"Maybe a double load."

Then, his partner's tone rose. "You're kidding?"

"Nope. Get receiving ready."

"I'm tied up right now, damn it."

"It's a fresh load if it happens," the Lizard King said. "Real fresh. A *double* load. We don't want it to spoil."

His partner moaned. It was a sound that slightly unnerved even the Lizard King. Then, "It may be a couple of hours."

"That ought to work."

"I wish you woulda told me earlier. I've got a situation."

"Three hours, possible double load," the Lizard King said. "Freshest meat you've ever seen."

"Holy hell."

"You said it."

"Don't screw it up. Please don't screw it up."

"Fuck you," the Lizard King said and snapped his phone shut, thinking maybe he shouldn't have told him until he had the double load secure.

Because if it didn't pan out, he'd never hear the end of it.

11.

Cassie had been home just long enough to feed her dog, look in on her mother and Ben, her five-year-old son, and change out of her uniform. While she pulled on jeans and took an inordinate amount of time in her closet before deciding on a long-sleeved Henley and a suede leather vest, she tried Cody's cell phone. No answer. She debated whether to call his house and decided against it. Jenny, his ex-wife, had recently moved back in with him. If she picked up the phone and hadn't yet heard what happened that day, Cassie didn't want to be the one to deliver the news. And if Jenny *had* heard, Cassie didn't want to hear what Jenny thought about it. She'd met Jenny once and recalled an intelligent, attractive, very strong-willed woman. She'd thought better of Cody after meeting Jenny.

But Cassie couldn't discern what Jenny had thought about *her*—a younger single mother who was Cody's

new partner. And now the one, Cassie thought, who set
up her husband to be fired.

So she pulled on her parka, told her mother and son
she'd be back soon, and went out to find Cody. She
needed to explain herself, justify her actions, and make
him understand what she'd done wasn't personal. Cassie
was scared, though. Cody could be intimidating and
he had an explosive temper. He might rip into her, even
though she thought she might deserve it.

She drove her Honda past Cody's house. His old
pickup wasn't there.

Cassie located Cody's pickup where she hoped it
wouldn't be: the Jester's Bar downtown on North Rod-
ney. She parked her Honda Civic a block away, got
out, and took a deep breath of cold thin air. She jammed
her hands into the pockets of her parka, pulled them
out again, and nervously smoothed down the front of
her coat. A streetlight hummed above her through the
leafless trees and threw cold blue light on the broken
sidewalk.

Jester's was a serious old-school bar located in the
corner of a shambling historic stone building across
the street from the brick building housing the Lewis
and Clark County coroner's office. She'd never been inside the bar—she wasn't much of a drinker and her son
prevented nights out on the town—but she'd heard the
stories. Local cops were sent there frequently at closing
time. The bar offered no food or big-screen TVs and
catered to hard customers. From the outside it looked
as inviting as a prison cell except with neon beer

signs—Ranier, Pabst—filling the square windows. Three Harleys sat out front pointed out toward the street, front wheels cocked to the side.

Cassie paused at the door. She could smell cigarette smoke and hear the click of pool balls. She almost turned around and walked back to her Honda. Instead, she steeled herself and pulled the door open, to be greeted by a sensory rush of smoke, stale beer, and Lynyrd Skynyrd from the jukebox.

It was dark inside and unevenly lighted. The mood was as intimate as a small beat-up warehouse. There were photos tacked to the walls and names carved into the pine paneling. The floor was gritty with dirt.

Every head in the place swung toward her; the three bikers at the table near the bar, two tattooed pool players leaning across green felt, an emaciated cowboy emerging from the men's zipping up his Wranglers, the pockmarked and pony-tailed bartender stubbing out a smoke, and the skanky old crow with dyed red hair and a tight black T-shirt seated on her stool.

And, in the corner in the back, illuminated harshly in yellow from a hanging lamp over a pool table, was Cody Hoyt. He was on a stool with his back against the wall at a high round table. Both his hands were on the table, framing a smoldering ashtray. A single tall glass half full with clear liquid sat near his elbow. His hooded eyes bored holes into her.

She nodded at him and took three steps in his direction and hesitated. He gave no indication he wanted her to join him. She flushed and looked around, embarrassed by the situation. One of the bikers winked at her.

The old crow at the bar made a cackle that ended with a sharp punctuation of phlegm.

Then she turned back around and approached her former partner but didn't take a seat. In her peripheral vision, the pool players quickly racked their cues and headed for the back door, their game unfinished.

"Mind if I join you?" she asked. She hoped her intonation wasn't as limp as it sounded to her.

Cody didn't say yes, didn't say no. He simply glared at her.

"I'd like to talk with you, if you don't mind," she said softly. "About what happened."

He blew out a sharp puff of smoke from his nostrils but he didn't reply.

"Cody," she said, trying to hold his eyes and not look away, which was difficult, "I didn't mean to set you up. That was never my intention. I feel terrible about what happened. Sheriff Tubman . . ."

A terrifying grin cracked Cody's face at the mention of the sheriff's name and it froze her for a moment. She'd forgotten how mean he could look.

" 'Can I get you?" she heard just over her shoulder.

Relieved, she turned. The pony-tailed bartender stood a few feet behind her. He was short and wiry and wore a long, sheathed bowie knife the length of his thigh.

"What?" she asked.

"I said, 'What can I get you?' " he said.

She hesitated. "Maybe a glass of wine?" she said.

The bartender smiled coldly. "Red or kind of red?"

She didn't ask. She said, "Red."

He nodded, and turned his attention to Cody. "You gonna drink it this time?"

At first she didn't understand. Then she had a vision of Cody ordering alcohol, staring at it, and sending it back untouched. She wondered how many times it had happened before she arrived. The thought stabbed her in the heart.

Cody nodded slightly. But the bartender didn't move. Finally, the man said, "Do you two plan to be here very long?"

Cassie squinted at him, not understanding.

The bartender chinned to where the pool players had been before they left so quickly. "Look," he said, lowering his voice so only they could hear. "We've got regular customers coming in until we close. They like to be able to relax, you know? Kick back? It ain't usual for a couple of county cops to be sitting in here, you know?"

"We're off duty," she said.

"Still, you stink of it," the bartender said. "No offense."

She could feel her face flushing again. Cody cleared his throat and readjusted himself on his stool so his jacket opened and his .40 Sig Sauer could be clearly seen in its holster. He said to the bartender, "Get us our drinks, you mouth-breathing little ferret. And keep them coming if we want them. Because only one of us is off duty. The other is just an angry man with a gun who could blow chunks of your heart out your back before you cleared that knife. And believe me, I'm in the fucking mood to pop somebody. Do we have an understanding?"

The bartender's eyes got huge and his mouth just hung there. After a few beats, he nodded and turned meekly toward the bar.

"I could *never* do that," Cassie said, climbing on a stool and leaning across the tabletop toward Cody. She said sadly, "Please tell me you're not drinking?"

"Not yet. Maybe I'm building up to it, though. This is club soda," he said, pinging a fingernail on the rim of the glass. "It tastes like . . . the end of the world as I know it."

Then he growled, "This is where it helps you to be a chick. Because if you weren't, I would have kicked your ass the second you walked in that door."

She'd heard stories about the infamous Cody Hoyt even before she graduated from the academy. He was a polarizing presence within law enforcement and throughout the state. Some LEOs (law enforcement officers) hated his guts, others winked when his name was mentioned. No one, it seemed, was neutral.

Cody had grown up in East Helena, from a long line of Hoyts, who were known as white-trash outlaws. The Hoyts were poachers, cattle rustlers, small-time crooks, and grifters. Somehow, Cody had chosen law enforcement and had worked himself up through police and sheriff's departments in Montana, Wyoming, and eventually became the lead homicide investigator for the Denver Metropolitan Police Department. His record of convictions was remarkable, but as his reputation grew so did the whispers. He not only cut corners, department gossips (and defense attorneys) alleged, he invented new corners to cut. Although his work resulted in a firefight that brought a serial pedophile down, his methods—including the appearance of his uncle Jeter brandishing a ten-gauge shotgun—got him thrown off the force.

Given his reputation, most Montana LEOs were surprised when he landed a job as investigator at the Lewis and Clark County Sheriff's Department. Stories of his carousing rivaled stories of witness intimidation, brutality, and tampering with crime scenes. But again, his results were inspiring. Two years before—after being suspended for shooting the county coroner in what was later deemed an accident—Cody came to the conclusion that a serial murderer responsible for the death of his AA sponsor was on a multiday wilderness horseback trip in Yellowstone Park. So was his estranged son, Justin.

Without authorization or backup, Cody had recruited an old-time wilderness guide and ridden into Yellowstone in a fury. When it was all over, bodies littered the trees and two large-scale conspiracies were brought to light, including one that involved the department. Cody had reconciled with his son and convinced his ex-wife to move back to Montana. Rather than prosecute his subordinate, Tubman—under pressure—had supported Cody. But he'd bided his time until he could pull the trigger.

Cassie realized now she'd ended up as the one holding the gun.

* * *

After the bartender delivered the drinks—a plastic cup of cheap Merlot for Cassie and an amber shot and a pint of beer for Cody—Cassie handed the man her credit card.

"Cash only," he said, but without the attitude from before. She dug into her purse and handed over her only twenty and he went to make change.

"Run a tab," Cody called after him. The bartender nodded.

"Can we talk about this," she asked Cody insistently, "or should I just go home? This isn't much fun for me, you know. I know about you," she said, gesturing toward the drinks on the table. "I know you've been clean and sober for three years. I know that's why your wife and son moved back. Everybody in the department warned me about you when I got hired. How you'd show up drunk in the morning, how you'd insult anybody who crossed your path. How you bent the rules when you wanted to. But I also heard you were the best investigator around and you'd cleaned up your act. I wanted to learn from you. I wanted to work with the best."

"If you wanted to work with the best," he said, "why'd you sneak around behind my back and fuck up my career? Hmmm?"

She wasn't sure how to answer, except to say Tubman had ordered her to follow him. It wasn't like she could refuse . . .

"Bullshit," Cody said, cutting her off. "You could have handled it a dozen ways if you had any . . . *balls*. I understand you're bright-eyed and bushy-tailed and you're eager to please. But you haven't been around much. You don't know how things work."

She sipped her wine. It was awful. She took a gulp. "What could I have done?" she said. "He gave me an order."

Cody rolled his eyes with disgust.

"What?"

He fixed his horrible smirk on her and held out a hand and started counting the fingers on it with the other. "One, you could have said you lost me when I drove out of town. Two, you could have accidentally deleted the shots after you took them. Three," he said, making sure she noted he was extending his middle finger toward her, "you could have told Tubman to fuck himself and send somebody else, because partners don't rat on partners. Four, you could have begged off at the last minute. Said your son was sick or your mom fell down and broke her hip. Some kind of bullshit that would stick. And five, we could have worked it together so we still got the bad guy which, last I looked, was what I thought we were supposed to do out here."

She held her tongue because she could tell he wasn't done.

"How many murder cases have you worked?" he asked.

"You know," she said.

"That's right: none. How many major felony cases? Oh, same number: none. But you went to the academy and you got hired right away and promoted right over the heads of people who've been in that department for years. So I guess you know it all."

"I don't know it all," she said with anger, "and I never act like I do. And I could have partnered up with Markey or Stegner or Curley. But I fought to be able to work with you. And you know why? Because I'd heard you were the best. That you were a bulldog and that you'd cleaned up your act."

His face reddened and his eyes bulged. He looked like he was ready to explode. She looked away because the intensity of his glare was almost violent in itself. Then he surprised her by snorting again and he laughed softly, shaking his head. He seemed suddenly more interested in the untouched shot and beer than he was in her confession.

After a long pause, he said, "I know it was Tubman and you're too green to go up against him, plus you owe your job to him. He used you, and you let yourself get used."

"I know. I'm ashamed of myself."

"Are you?"

"That's why I'm here."

His eyes bored into hers. She was surprised when they softened.

He said, "You'll find, Cassie, that it's us against the world. We do our damnedest to put away degenerates and douche bags so innocent people won't be hurt by them, but all the forces out there are set up to make us fail. We've got county attorneys that won't take on a case unless it's airtight, judges who want to invent the law instead of enforce what's there, defense attorneys who want to show publicly how fucking incompetent we are, and juries who want to stick it to the man. So when we've figured out that someone is guilty as sin, sometimes we need to stack the deck a little. You know what I'm saying?"

She shook her head, but was both scared and a little thrilled to hear what he'd say.

"Somebody's got to defend innocent people," he said. "They need a dark angel. The deck is stacked against them, too. All those good citizens out there just want to raise their families, go to work, go to church, and keep their heads down. They don't give a shit about county politics or political correctness or who's running for sheriff or the sheriff's fucking diversity program. They just want to live their lives. Somebody's got to step up and protect them, you know? And who is tougher on bad guys than me?

"Look," Cody said, "B. G. did it. The two of them are big-time growers fighting for market share. I know these people because I grew up with them. I went to school with B. G., and he's been a dirtbag in training from the minute he was born. B. G. went to Tokely's house on some pretext and shot Tokely with Tokely's gun, then made it look like a suicide. He murdered a man. We're supposed to be against that. And I don't give a shit about Roger Tokely, either. He was a reprobate just like B. G. But if we leave B. G. out on the street, look what we've done. We've allowed him to continue to beat the shit out of his wife and kids for years and they'll never turn against him because he's got them under his thumb. Worst of all we've showed him he can beat us. So the next time he gets high, maybe it's one of those innocents out there who gets it. Maybe it's your mom, or your kid, or my son. B. G.'s a typical douche bag. He's been getting away with crap for years. He's human shit and I just want to flush him away."

She flinched when he suddenly reached back, but instead of the weapon he slapped his wallet on the table and opened it.

"This is Justin," he said, jabbing his finger on a photo of a strapping, smiling teenager in a football uniform. "He's just a great kid. He's smart, he's kind. He's empathetic in a way I just look at and wonder where the hell it came from. I still can't believe he's my son, because all that bad Hoyt blood must have ended with me somehow. But I look at this kid, Cassie, and I say to myself I will never let him get hurt by some dirtbag like B. G. So B. G. has to go, simple as that."

She looked up and was surprised to see the softness in his eyes.

"All I was doing in that cabin," Cody said, "was spreading some bread crumbs around that would lead to other evidence. Now the techs are motivated, they'll find more and more to place B. G. in that house. By the time they've got enough to arrest B. G. we might not even need to use the trash I put in his garbage can. The stuff I did wasn't enough to railroad B. G.—but it was enough to get everyone looking in his direction. That's all I wanted, was to put the spotlight on him. And that's sometimes how you have to work it so the right scumbags go to prison."

"But it isn't ethical," she said.

He laughed. "No, it isn't. Which is why I did it myself and didn't try to involve you. You've still got ethics, or so you think."

"I didn't want to believe you'd do something like that," she said. "I felt if I followed you I'd be able to prove to Tubman you were clean."

"You felt wrong," Cody said. "You," he said, jabbing his finger toward her, "let yourself get used. He used you to get me. And you just happily went along with it until you realized what you'd done. Now you come in here for what? Forgiveness? You want me to pat you on the head and tell you what a good girl you are? You want me to tell you thanks for saving me from myself? Is that what you want?"

She shook her head.

"The problem with people your age," he said, "is you never understood the difference between thinking and feeling, and to you feeling is more important, which is bullshit. You *felt* like you were doing the right thing, so you did it. You *felt* that it was probably okay to screw your partner because your boss told you to do it. You *felt* like all you needed to do was come in here tonight and I'd see how genuine your all-important feelings truly are and I'd say, 'It's okay, Cassie. You meant well. All is forgiven, Cassie.'"

She felt like he'd slapped her repeatedly. She tried to blink away tears that were ready to burst behind her nose and inside her eyes.

"Well," Cody said, reaching out for the shot glass and then recoiling as if the glass of bourbon stung him, "you're not forgiven. And I *feel* like I'm going to get hammered tonight. Care to join me?"

"No," she said.

"Then goodbye, and don't let the door hit you on the ass on your way out."

"Please, Cody," she said, "Don't do this. Don't hurt yourself. Think of Jenny and Justin and all you've built up."

"This is it for me," he said. "I had a nice run but this is the end of the trail. When I got kicked out of Denver I thought I'd never get another gig in law enforcement. The only reason I wound up back here where I grew up was because Tubman thought I had the goods on him. Now he's got worse on me. And he'll make damned sure I never get another law enforcement job in Montana or anywhere else."

With that, he suddenly tossed back the shot and chased it with half the pint of beer. She watched with fascination and horror as his eyes glistened and he smiled manically.

"Damn," he said, "that was good. I miss this. And I want another one."

"Cody . . ." she said.

He dismissed her and signaled for another round. Then he arched his eyebrows and said, "Leave or stay, I don't care. But if you stay, things might get ugly."

She watched as he downed the rest of the beer in time for the bartender to deliver another round. A second glass of wine appeared as well. Cody took the shot glass from the bartender's hand before he could set it on the table—and downed it.

"Keep 'em coming," Cody ordered.

Then to her: "Don't get me wrong. I admire your guts coming here tonight. That shows me something. But I've got a question for you."

"What?"

"Who is going to protect these people now?" he asked. "You?" He said it with incredulity.

She felt her face flush hot again, and she sipped the glass of wine for something to do.

"Cody," she said, reaching out and putting her hand on his arm. He looked down at it suspiciously. "What do you have on Tubman?"

Cody froze for a moment. Then, that evil grin she both loved and hated stretched slowly across his face.

12.

It was only minutes but it felt much longer as the head-lights of the black truck retreated behind them. As they reached the top of the hill, Danielle kept the pedal floored, prepared to shoot down the other side. They'd played enough mountain yo-yo with big trucks on the drive north that day Gracie didn't mind that her sister wouldn't slow down and let the momentum of the black truck catch up with them.

Gracie's stomach hurt. Seeing that truck grille so close to the car had unhinged her. Passing the truck with her sister screaming insults had unhinged her in a way she couldn't explain.

She hated her sister for putting them in this situation and hated herself even more for going along with it. Cars, trucks, big lonely highways at night were *serious*. Steel and speed and pavement and weather didn't give a couple of teenagers a pass. This was the real world and Gracie wasn't sure she liked it. Danielle didn't seem to notice because she lived, as she claimed, on "Planet Danielle." But Gracie couldn't live there, even though it was probably more fun.

Danielle was texting furiously on her phone. "I told Justin what happened," she said. "He said to me, 'Good driving back there.'"

"Great," Gracie said sullenly.

"Yeah," Danielle said. "I let that guy have it. I guess you should thank me for saving our lives, I guess."

"Gee, you think?"

Danielle shrugged and flipped her hair back. The close call and hearing back from Justin seemed to have filled her sister with confidence and arrogance, which was her normal state.

Gracie said, "Did you text him about the engine light?"

"No way. I don't want to worry him."

Gracie covered her face in her hands.

After a few moments, Danielle's phone chirped. She looked at the display. "Oh, no," she said. "Shit!"

"What?" Gracie was suddenly buoyed: *It was their mom. She talked to their dad. They were busted. They would have to turn back or drive to Omaha.*

"Justin says he looked on the Internet and there's a big wreck or something on the highway. It's closed up ahead of us. Shit!"

Gracie didn't have the same reaction. She thought, *We can turn around and forget this whole thing. We*

can drive straight through the night to Omaha to Dad.
We can get ourselves out of this! Relief flooded through
her.

Danielle said, "He says not to worry. There's another
way to Helena but we'll need to get off I-90."

Gracie didn't want to reveal her true thoughts, and
said, "We shouldn't leave the interstate. I don't want to
go out there"—she gestured with her chin toward the
black mountains to the south—"we don't want to be on
crappy little country roads."

"Don't be such a baby," Danielle said, dismissing
her. "He says it's not a bad drive but we'll need to go
back through a corner of Yellowstone Park. He's going
to e-mail me a map."

"No way," Gracie said.

"That's what we'll do," Danielle said flatly. "It's
time we got over that Yellowstone trip. This is our opportunity to put it behind us."

"No way," Gracie said.

"We're looking for the exit to Laurel," Danielle said,
"Highway 212."

As she said it the headlights lit up a green highway
sign that read: LAUREL 4 MILES.

"We're in luck!" Danielle sang.

"Let me talk to him myself," Gracie said. "Call him
and hand over your phone or I swear to God I'll make
you turn around at the next exit and drive to Nebraska."

Danielle huffed and rolled her eyes. She said, "Don't
you trust me?"

"Ha!"

Danielle punched the speed dial, held the phone up

to her ear, and said to Justin, "J-Man, Gracie needs to hear from you directly. She's getting cold feet and she's making squeaky noises about not coming. So just give her the directions and she can navigate us there."

Gracie couldn't hear what Justin replied because her sister kept the phone close to her face, but whatever it was made her smile. But she held out the phone.

"Justin," Gracie said. "I'm nervous about going off the interstate. Are you sure we should do this?"

His voice was deep and calm but resigned. He said, "Hey, Gracie. It sounds like you guys are coming to visit. I wish I would have known about it."

"Me, too."

"I can't believe your mom let you."

"She didn't." Gracie turned away from her sister, who was glaring. "So Danielle didn't tell you?"

"Tell me what?" There was panic in his voice.

"She thinks we're driving to Omaha to be with our dad right now."

"Shit, Gracie," Danielle said. "You're such a narc."

Gracie ignored her. "She did talk our dad into it, but you know how he is. But Mom doesn't know."

Justin sighed. "There's probably no talking Danielle out of it, is there?"

The question confirmed Gracie's suspicions. She shot a quick glance at her sister, who looked back anxiously. Gracie felt a sudden and unexpected pang of sympathy for her sister. Justin wasn't enthusiastic about seeing her after all. He might have given her signals— the texts and calls that weren't returned certainly should have conveyed something—but Danielle had blissfully

chosen not to notice. Danielle was rarely denied anything by anybody.

"Maybe *you* could do it," Gracie said. She held the
phone tight to her face so Danielle couldn't overhear
Justin's side of the conversation and realize what they
were talking about.

"Do what?" Danielle asked.

Gracie ignored her.

Justin said, "I can't just tell her not to come now.
You guys are close and it's dark. It might be dangerous
to drive back all that way tonight."

"That would be okay with me," Gracie said.

"But would she do it?"

Gracie looked over at her sister, at the determination
in her face. At the way she gripped the wheel.

"Probably not," she said.

"Maybe you guys can stay here tonight and I can
talk with her and you can go see your dad in the morning. I can talk to my mom about making up the spare
bedroom. But telling her . . . man, that won't be fun.
You know how she gets when she's mad . . ."

"You're telling *me*?" Gracie said.

Justin laughed.

"What are you two talking about?" Danielle spat.
"Are you talking about me?"

"Okay, so what we'll do is make sure you get here in
one piece." Justin sighed, "Then we'll worry about the
rest later."

"Okay," Gracie said. She anticipated Danielle trying
to wrest the phone from her and dodged her sister's
outstretched and grasping hand.

"Let me look at the computer," Justin said, and she could hear keystrokes. While he found the site he wanted, he said, "So you bumped heads with a trucker, huh? Some of those truckers think they own the road, don't they?"

"This one did." She glanced up and there were no headlights in her rearview mirror. "He's way behind us now."

"Cool," Justin said. She could hear voices of other boys in the background. Someone whooped, and Justin shushed him. "Okay, I'm sitting at my friend Eric's computer and I've got Google Maps up. Where are you exactly?"

"Just a few miles from Laurel," Gracie said. "Maybe three."

"Great. I see where you're at. The Montana Department of Transportation site says the road is closed between Park City and Columbus. But you'll hit Laurel before you get there and that's the place where you can get off the interstate and go around. It says they might keep the road closed all night so this is the smart thing to do. Now let me talk you through this. I've gone on this road before with my dad, and it's a really cool drive. It goes right on top of the mountains and drops down and cuts the corner of Yellowstone Park and comes back up into Montana."

"Yellowstone," she repeated. "That place doesn't have a lot of good memories."

Danielle had stopped grabbing at the phone now that she was assured they were talking about the route to Helena.

"Believe me, I know," he said. "But you won't even be close to where we were on that pack trip. Not even close. And you won't need to get off the paved road. You'll barely be in the park and if you keep going you'll come up through Mammoth Hot Springs and be back on track."

He outlined the route on 212 from Laurel south through Rockvale to Red Lodge, and from there to Cooke City and Silver Gate via the Beartooth Highway and into the northeast corner of the park. Then they should exit the park at Gardiner, Montana, and drive north on Highway 89 to Livingston through the Yellowstone River canyon back up to I-90 and on to Helena via Bozeman.

"It sounds complicated," she said.

"Yeah, but it isn't," he said. "There are only a few roads and I'd guess there won't be much traffic at all except for other people who know how to go around the closed road. I'm looking and it doesn't seem to be snowing on top of the mountains. That could be a big problem. But right now it looks like a clear drive and I'll be right here the whole time tracking you on the screen. If you get confused, just call and talk to me."

She took a deep breath but said nothing.

He said, "It's too bad you guys don't have a GPS."

"Oh, but we do have a GPS," Gracie said, shooting a look toward Danielle who looked back as if wounded. "It's in the trunk of the car."

"The trunk?"

"She's *your* girlfriend."

Justin laughed wearily, and said under his breath, "Not for long."

"Hey," Danielle protested. "Quit talking about me, you two. I'm right here. And if you want to pull over somewhere, I'll get the GPS out and try to figure out how it works. Geez . . ."

"You heard?" Gracie asked Justin.

"Tell her it's a good idea. That way we'll both know exactly where you are."

"One more thing," Gracie said, "The check engine light is on. I don't know what that means and neither does Danielle."

Justin sighed and asked how long.

"Forever," Gracie said.

"Is the car getting hot or doing anything strange?"

"Not yet."

There was a long pause and she could hear him asking one of his friends about it.

"Eric says it could be a short or it could be serious."

"Great."

"He can look at it tomorrow morning," Justin said. "I mean, if you get here."

Gracie sighed.

"But, Gracie," he said, "keep in touch with me. There are some cell phone dead spots, but if I know where you're at and something happens I can call my dad. He'll know what to do."

Gracie recalled meeting Justin's dad Cody. He scared her at first, but she ended up liking him. And he seemed to like her.

"I don't know where he is right now," Justin said. "He didn't make it home for dinner. But he's got a cell phone and I'll give him a call if we need to."

She found herself smiling and felt her shoulders relax. Justin's voice was soothing, and he was saying all the right things. Danielle, she thought, never did deserve him.

Gracie felt a pang and lowered the phone to her lap and covered the receiver with her hand.

"Danielle," she said, "maybe this is a really bad idea. It's not too late to turn around and go back."

"What? Are you out of your mind? We're practically there."

"But—"

"But nothing," her sister said, tears glinting in her eyes. "We've come all this way to see Justin, and I'm going to see Justin."

And Gracie realized Danielle wasn't oblivious after all. She *knew.* She just couldn't accept it and probably thought she could talk him out of it. And maybe, Gracie conceded, that would happen. Danielle could be very persuasive, especially with boys.

Gracie raised the phone. "Okay," she said, "what do we do when we get to Laurel?"

Danielle let go of the wheel, pumped her fist in the air, and shouted, *"Yes!"*

13.

The Lizard King looked ahead and to the left on the highway and saw the familiar halo of the inferno lighting up the misty sky—the refinery on the outskirts of Laurel. Rolls of steam lit by flames from the flare stacks hung low to the ground in the low pressure and mist, making the facility look otherworldly.

It fit his mood. He was locked in, engaged. His rage had receded into a dark steel box in the back of his mind to be unleashed later.

Since the red Ford had passed him a few miles before, he'd pushed his Peterbilt hard on the flat, keeping his eyes out for the two little taillights. He'd passed several other cars and trucks, and he was surprised he hadn't yet caught up with the Colorado girls. He kept thinking of the dark-haired one and the way she'd sneered at him. Thinking of that full red mouth and that glimpse of white teeth.

How the boys must like her, he thought. She was one of *those* . . . filled with attitude and always flipping her hair around. It was always gratifying, he thought, how quickly their attitudes changed in the right circumstances.

Part of his ritual with the lot lizards, usually toward the end, was to ask them, "Tell me what you were like in high school?" He made them re-create those years, even to the point of describing what they wore and who they hung with. Most of them had never graduated, but a few had. And most of them had been druggies and losers. A number of whores couldn't even recall the details.

But there were a few—he thought specifically of that redhead from Amarillo with the butterfly tats— who could recall high school with clarity and fondness. She told him how she bounced between the cheerleading crowd and the heavy metal drug crowd. How she'd gone to three of four proms but skipped the last one because by then she was into meth and goth. How she'd barely graduated and gotten hooked up with older men who didn't look out for her best interests. But he didn't care about what she'd become—it was obvious. He pressed her for details of her first three years. As long as she was talking, he kept her around. She admitted, finally, she'd probably been too cruel to some of the boys who weren't good-looking or athletes. When he asked her if she regretted the way she'd been, she didn't comprehend the question.

Then he ended it.

She had been his favorite so far.

Two things would ruin his night, he thought. The Colorado girls could just keep going past Laurel until they were slowed down by troopers enforcing the roadblock. There they'd sit with dozens of other vehicles with more stacking up behind them. It could be hours, and there would be too many eyes.

They could also turn off the highway before they got to where the crash was located. Maybe to get gas, maybe to get some food or directions. Either way, he'd probably lose them.

Or . . .

Far up ahead, in the fused ambient light of the mist from the Laurel refinery, he saw the red Ford. The girls were easing over to the right with the turn signal blinking.

He felt a charge of electricity shoot through him. *The Colorado girls knew the way around the roadblock*. There was still a chance their destination was this way, maybe Red Lodge, but he'd bet dollars to donuts they'd be taking the same route he intended to take—over the Beartooth Highway, into Yellowstone, out Mammoth, and toward Livingston to get back on the interstate.

The Lizard King eased off the pedal and downshifted to slow down the truck. He didn't want to get close enough that they'd know he was still with them. He pulled over onto the shoulder and doused his headlights after he braked the truck to a stop. Good thing, too, because the Colorado girls had stopped as well.

He didn't hit his emergency flashers because he didn't want them to see him. The big rig sat still in the dark on the side of the highway, lights out, steaming and rumbling in the cold night.

The body of the lot lizard was surprisingly light. He hefted it back onto the bunk and secured it with long strips of tape. Just to make sure, he pressed his palm against the plastic sheeting where her mouth was. No warmth. No reaction. The body was already stiffening up. He wondered if bodies stiffened quicker when there was no meat on them.

He found his binoculars in a side pocket on his door and sat back in the driver's seat and brought them up as the dome light of the Ford went on and the dark-haired passenger got out. He focused on her as she opened the trunk and was rewarded with a fine view of her heart-shaped ass that sent a tingle down his inner thighs. She found whatever she was looking for, slammed the trunk lid, and climbed back into the car. He waited until the Ford's brake lights flashed and it started up the off-ramp to Laurel before lowering the glasses and reaching for the gearshift. He held in place until they were moving again.

As he climbed through the gears and rolled past the refinery he placed two calls from his cell phone. The first was to his dispatcher. He held the phone away from his ear until her railing subsided and then raised it back up.

"I told you," he said, "Your Qualcomm unit is acting

up, just like before. It ain't my fault you installed a defective unit."

"I still can't find you," she said. Her name was Yvonne and she was a bleached-blond fatty with moles on the folds of her neck. Like all dispatchers, she thought she was God.

"I told you," he said, "I'm sitting in traffic outside of Park City. The state patrol has the roads shut down and I don't know how long I'll be sitting here before they let us go."

Yvonne started screeching about his failure to call her sooner or she could have *told* him about the accident. That it could be hours before they'd open the interstate again.

"What do you care?" he said. "I'm half empty and every delivery was on schedule. I'm on my own time now."

"You know you need to come into the office," she said contemptuously, and he hoped no other truckers were listening in. "You've got a month's worth of logs and receipts to turn in. DOT wants an audit on all our drivers like I told you weeks ago."

"Screw 'em," he said. Nearly adding, *Screw you, too.*

The Lizard King was an independent contractor, although it didn't ever seem like it. The trucking company he was signed on with took 15 percent of every payday in exchange for brokering trips and administration. Between his company, the state regulations and rules, and the ever-growing federal regulations and mandates, it seemed like there was a conspiracy to throw every long-haul trucker off the road. There was the

Federal Motor Carrier Safety Administration, the Safety Measurement System (CSA scores), random drug testing, rising fuel costs . . .

He pressed the phone against his groin so she could talk to his genitals.

Finally, he said, "I'll call tomorrow after I get some sleep."

"You need to get that Qualcomm looked at—"

He punched off.

Then he made another call as he exited the ramp. The Ford was a long way ahead but he could see the lights. It didn't turn at Laurel, which meant they were headed for the Beartooth Pass. As it rang, he could imagine her cursing, pushing away her lap blanket, and struggling to get up to answer the phone. He could see her two large hands folding over the grips on the walker like reptilian claws and the lenses of her steel-framed glasses winking in the reflected light from the television screen. Her massive thighs rubbing together as she moved, those fat white cylinder-like ankles pinched into dirty shoes . . .

Just picturing her as she grunted and shuffled in that close house with dark paneling that smelled of stale cabbage and bacon and rotten garbage made the bile rise in his throat.

14.

Danielle and Gracie were in Yellowstone and it was spooky. The roads were fine—no snow—but it was oppressively dark and it seemed like someone had flipped a switch and turned out all the lights. The sky was clear and it had stopped raining but the only illumination came from a thin sliver of moon and the gauzy, ghostly wash of a million stars that seemed close, as if tamped down by an unseen hand from above. The road was banked with walls of thick black pines that occasionally opened up to reveal grassy meadows. Although the tires hummed on the pavement, Gracie got a sense of immense quiet all around them. They'd encountered no oncoming cars since they'd entered the park out of Silver Gate, a tiny and sleepy town where the only human activity existed around a couple of bars.

"We're back," she whispered to Danielle.

"So let's get the hell out of here as fast as we can."

"The speed limit is forty-five," Gracie said.

"Screw that."

But her sister's emphasis wasn't on the circumstance that they were back in Yellowstone, Gracie thought, but because she wanted to see Justin and talk to him. Talk him back onto Planet Danielle.

Simply being in the park wasn't as horrifying to Gracie as she'd anticipated it would be. The things that had happened to them there were the result of evil people, not the place itself. She still had nightmares, but they weren't about Yellowstone. Her nightmares came from what she saw and experienced when the door had opened to reveal evil and violence that until that trip had been closed to her. Now she knew what some people—despite their manner and packaging—were capable of. It still shook her to her core.

And there was a bizarre kind of symmetry going on, she thought. They'd met Justin and his father Cody in Yellowstone and the bonds they'd forged were so strong that here they were, some time later, going to see them in Montana.

Gracie didn't know how she felt about leaving the interstate highway. Despite their size and dominance and the close encounter they'd had with one, the stream of big trucks was also reassuring because it meant there were people on the road if something went wrong. Now it felt like they would be alone out there.

They rounded a corner to a constellation of piercing green dots ahead in the road. Danielle braked and waited for the small herd of buffalo, whose eyes reflected back green in her headlights, to amble across the cracked blacktop.

"That's why you shouldn't go so fast," Gracie said. "Can you imagine hitting one?"

"My poor car," Danielle said, petting the dashboard.

Danielle had attached the GPS unit to the windshield by its suction cup assembly and after fumbling around for twenty minutes finally figured out how to plug it into the AC outlet. Its glow and brightly delineated roads and lines was a comfort to Gracie and made it seem less like they were in the middle of Siberia. The feature she prized the most was the readout that claimed they were three hours and thirty-eight minutes from Helena.

"Oh my God," Danielle gasped.

Her tone frightened Gracie, who peered ahead on the two-lane to see what had alarmed her sister.

"No signal," Danielle said, staring at her phone. "I forgot there's no cell service in this stupid place."

Gracie said, "I can't believe you forgot that. Don't you remember getting hysterical about it when we were here? I do."

Gracie sniffed the air and asked, "What's that smell?"

"What smell?"

"Like something burning. Don't you smell it?"

Danielle rolled her eyes. "It's nothing to worry about."

"How do you know? It seems like it's coming from the motor."

"Because I know my own car," Danielle said with

anger. "She's been running for hours and she's probably getting tired. Just don't worry."

"You mean you've smelled this before?"

"Of course," Danielle said. "Besides, we're in Yellowstone with all the geysers and such. They all smell a little like toilets."

But Gracie wasn't sure she believed her.

There was a long straight run and Danielle obviously felt comfortable speeding up. To the south was a wide-open vista that stretched out for several miles until it butted against dark tree-covered foothills. A wide black river serpentined through the meadow, the surface of the inky water reflecting the sliver of moon and the stars. Elk and bison grazed near the banks framed by wisps of thermal steam. Huge white trumpeter swans nested in the tall grass near the river. Danielle seemed transfixed by the screen of her cell phone and the NO SIGNAL message where bars should have been.

"It's really kind of pretty," Gracie said.

"What is?"

"Look out there. You can see wildlife in the starlight."

"I thought they were cows."

"This is Yellowstone Park, Danielle," Gracie said. "They don't graze cows in a national park."

Danielle seemed to be thinking it over. Then she said, "I heard cow farts are one of the leading causes of global warming. That's why we shouldn't eat so much red meat."

Gracie sighed.

But as they started a slow turn away from the Lamar River valley, she noticed a tiny wink of light through the back window in her rearview mirror a long distance behind.

"At least we aren't the only people on the road," she said.

"What?"

As they crossed over a long expansion bridge with a thin angry river far below them, Gracie could see a smudge of light ahead coming from beyond a shoulder of mountain. Then a small wooden sign reading: MAMMOTH HOT SPRINGS, 2 MILES. She glanced at the GPS. Three more hours.

"We're just about out of the park," she said.

"And I have a signal!" Danielle shrieked. As she said it her text box lit up.

"Two texts from Justin," Danielle said. "That's so sweet. He was worried about me." To the phone, she said, "Don't worry about me, J-Man. I'm coming to save you." She began to text.

Fifteen minutes LATER, Danielle's phone chirped. "He wants to know where we are."

A beat passed, and Gracie said, "So tell him."

"Where are we?"

Gracie sighed, looked at the GPS display, and said, "Tell him we're in Montana again. We just drove through Mammoth Hot Springs and Gardiner and we're going north on Highway 89."

"Slow down," Danielle said, tapping the keys.

"You could look at the screen, you know. It says we're close to Yankee Jim Canyon."

"Yeah, yeah," her sister muttered.

The highway paralleled a river and there were high canyon walls on both sides. The night sky was a belt of stars straight above them, its expanse narrowed to a trough by the walls. Gracie thought the sky looked like a mirror of the river they were driving by.

Suddenly, the car lurched.

Gracie looked up, "What was that?"

"I don't know," Danielle said. But when Gracie leaned over and checked the temperature gauge she saw the needle had not only entered the red but was pressed tight to the far corner of it. The engine lurched again and went silent. It was as if the soul of the little car had left it, leaving the slowly rolling husk.

"Oh, no," Gracie said.

"What is it?" Danielle asked, frantic. The Ford slowed.

"Something happened to the motor. The steering wheel is all stiff."

It was a struggle for Danielle to crank the wheel even a quarter of the way but she was able to slightly turn the front wheels. When she pressed on the brake it barely responded, as if the life had gone out of it.

"Oh, no," Gracie said again as the little Ford coasted to a stop a few feet before the front bumper tapped a crooked delineator post. The headlights still shined and the GPS screen glowed, but the car was dead.

Danielle tried several times to start the motor but it

simply produced a grinding sound. She pumped the gas furiously and tried again. Nothing.

"We're going to be here *all night,*" Gracie cried.

"Shut up and don't think the worst. Here, you try it," Danielle said to her sister.

"What can *I* do?"

"I don't know," Danielle said, quickly getting out and walking over to Gracie's side. She opened the door. "Scoot over and give it a try," she said.

For the next few minutes, Gracie twisted the key in the ignition but the engine didn't start. Instead, there was the angry grinding sound.

"I'm just draining the battery doing this," she said.

"Did we run out of gas?" Danielle asked angrily.

"No, we have half a tank. It must have something to do with that engine light. The fricking light."

"Are you sure you can't get it started?"

"Do you want to try again?" Gracie asked, a crack in her voice.

"This is terrible."

"No kidding."

They sat in silence and darkness. The display on the GPS began to fade. Gracie could feel cold seeping into the car from the floorboards.

"I can't call him," Danielle said softly, sniffing back a tear. "I've lost the signal again in this fucking canyon."

Gracie said, "We could walk back to Gardiner. It's only a few miles back there, I think."

"Or we should stay with the car," Danielle said. "And wait for somebody to stop and help us."

That's when the headlights appeared on the road behind them.

Gracie cracked her door so the dome light would come on, but didn't open it any further. She turned in her seat.

One set of headlights, coming fast. And a long string of amber running lights flowing behind, like the tail of a comet.

"It's slowing down," Gracie said.

"That's friggin' awesome." Danielle grinned.

"Danielle . . . it's that truck."

Bright headlights lit up the inside of Danielle's Ford and Gracie turned to Danielle. The grille of the black truck filled the back window and she heard the hissing of air brakes. The harsh white light made her sister's face look cartoonish. But there was no doubt Danielle was terrified.

"Lock the doors!" Gracie yelled.

And the lights behind them went out, leaving utter darkness. Gracie heard the *thunk* of the electric locks and thanked God the battery had enough power to perform the function.

The truck was so close behind them the Ford vibrated from the heavy engine.

Gracie craned in her seat, looking back. Her eyes couldn't adjust to the darkness due to the blinding light a moment before. Green diamonds and orbs strobed in her eyes from the aftereffect. But she thought she heard a door slam.

"Maybe he'll help us," Danielle said, barely above a whisper. "I wish I wouldn't have . . ."

There was a beat of silence and the passenger window exploded inward. Danielle screamed. Gracie tried to scream but nothing came out but a wheezy croak. She turned to see Danielle put her arms up to block the huge hands of the driver who was reaching inside.

What happened next came in rapid flashes.

The driver appeared to be reaching for Danielle's throat as if to strangle her but there was something dark and squared-off in one of his hands. Gracie heard the angry crackle of electricity and Danielle's sudden "*Ungh!*" followed by the sight of her sister stiffening like a corpse, raising herself out of her seat, her eyes rolling white back into her head, her mouth slack . . .

Gracie turned away. Tried to locate the toggle to unlock her driver's side door so she could get out and run. Tried to remember whether the toggle was on top of the armrest or in its side or on the dashboard . . .

The hot smell of urine filled the car.

And in her peripheral vision, a big white form moved hurriedly from right to left in front of the car. It was the truck driver, wearing all white, something plastic, a glimpse of his big blocklike head . . .

She found the button and jammed it forward and all four door locks popped open.

Gracie pulled back on the door latch and it started to swing open when the driver wedged himself into the opening and reached toward her. She heard a thump on the top of the door frame as he hit his head trying to bend inside, the blow significant enough to rock the car.

It staggered him a moment and he paused, and she threw herself away, started crawling over the top of Danielle's convulsing body toward the passenger door. But the driver recovered and she felt his fingers grasp the top of her waistband and jerk her back into the driver's seat.

"Hold still, you little bitch," he croaked and she saw him for the first time—huge, rough, flushed, fleshy— lips curled back to reveal crooked yellow doglike teeth, fresh blood from his forehead or scalp coursing down— and got a glimpse of the electrical device he had poised over her face and plunged into her neck.

The sensation was sudden and massive and debilitating. She no longer had control of her body, which stiffened, and she had an image of lightninglike electricity firing out from the tips of her fingers and toes. Every muscle and sinew seemed fused together with steel and she felt welded into a single mass of flesh.

But she was still conscious. She had no concept of time or motion, but she could hear the sound of his boots scraping gravel outside the car.

And she could feel the sharp prick of a needle through the fabric of her jeans into her inner thigh.

15.

The Lizard King reached up and grasped the stitched nylon strap through the loop and leaned back on his boot heels and pulled it down hard. The trailer door slid down on its dual tracks with the sound of rolling thunder, but in the instant before it sealed he got a last look at the three still bundles of limbs and clothing inside, looking like oversized dolls tossed aside. There was a glimpse of thick dark hair from the older one and the soles of splayed running shoes from the other. They weren't secured to the bare metal floor or the walls of the container and they'd no doubt flop around when he made turns or sudden stops. Unlike the third bundle that wasn't going anywhere.

But they were both breathing when he lifted them inside, and they'd likely be alive—if bruised—when he got them to his destination. When the bottom of the door fitted into the channel he reached across his body and yanked the handle of the locking mechanism over so the upturned steel arm slipped snugly under the outside bolt of the bed. He threaded the hasp of a combination lock through the eyebolts of the mechanism and snapped it shut. The trailer was now locked securely from the outside. There was no way to open it from the inside. The trailer had vents in it so they wouldn't suffocate, and he adjusted the reefer unit to sixty-eight degrees so they wouldn't freeze to death.

His heart was beating madly and pulses of blood whumped in his ears but he was methodical in his movements and actions. All his work had taken place in the open on the side of the highway. His headlights were still off so they wouldn't light up the little Ford he'd parked behind, but anybody driving by might recall seeing the huge Peterbilt pulled up tight to the car on the shoulder. It would look, he hoped, like he'd stopped to help out the occupants of the car. Since the smashed passenger's window could be seen from the road, he carefully pushed all of the remaining broken glass inside so it wouldn't draw attention. He realized while he was working how visible his white Tyvek overalls were. The material seemed to absorb what little light there was and it could draw attention he didn't welcome.

It was a miracle, he thought, that no one had driven by on either side of the highway since he'd stopped. In the back of his head a clock ticked, and he knew his odds worsened by the second. He'd accomplished his task within five minutes of stopping and the hard part was already done, but everything could be ruined if someone passed by and saw him. Or stopped to see what was going on. In that case, he'd have a decision to make. Involuntarily, he reached down and touched the heft of his .380 in his overalls pocket.

He lumbered out onto the asphalt of the highway to assess his situation. The Yellowstone River roared on the other side of the road. He could see white water lace streak the black surface of the water below. There were no houses or lights on either side of the canyon yet. The canyon walls were dark and high on both sides and the stars were oppressive in their silent intensity. The air smelled of juniper from the brush leading down to the river and diesel fumes from his idling truck. He looked both ways on the highway, knowing he would see headlights long before he heard a vehicle approaching. The road was empty.

The Ford couldn't have broken down at a more perfect location, and he reveled in his luck. Gardiner was miles behind and out of view. Ahead on the highway, two miles north after the walls narrowed precipitously for a while, the canyon opened up on the opposite side across the river into a wide bench. That's where the religious compound was located, where there were people and a smattering of lights and a clear view of the highway. Those members always seemed acutely aware of vehicles and traffic, and if the Ford had broken down there he would have kept on driving. But it didn't.

He took a deep breath and walked back to the Ford. He noted an odor he hadn't noticed before: the acrid smell of hot burnt oil that wafted up from beneath the hood. He wondered how it was the girls couldn't have recognized the odor while they were driving. Maybe, he thought, they smelled it and had no idea what it was. That didn't surprise him. Teenagers weren't like they used to be when it came to cars or car care. They just got in them and drove off; he'd seen it. As long as the stereo system worked—that was all that concerned them. As a young driver so many years ago, the Lizard King treasured and babied his first used car, a 1978 Chevy half-ton pickup. He knew everything about it and he spent nights and weekends tuning the engine and keeping it in prime running condition. It disgusted him how little kids cared anymore, as if their cars were an entitlement and driving their right.

Unlike him. He'd parlayed his love and competence for wrenching and driving to truck driving school, where he'd paid $3,000 to earn his first commercial driver's license (CDL), then hired on with Swift Trucking on their "Train, Lease, Drive" program that eventually paid for his first rig. That was four trucks and three million miles ago.

He threw open the driver's side door of the Ford. The dome light came on but it was muted and weak—the sign of a dying battery. He rooted through his cargo pockets past the stun gun and the pistol and withdrew a mini-Maglite flashlight and twisted it on. With the flashlight clamped between his teeth, he leaned into the car. It was a mess, which confirmed his disgust. The floors and dash were littered with junk but he found what he was looking for: their two cell phones. He knew from experience that there was no service inside the canyon where they were located but that there would be a signal within two miles when the canyon walls receded and the Paradise Valley opened up to reveal the compound. He was blessed with luck! It was meant to be!

The phones, he knew, might contain GPS capability. But no matter. He grasped a phone in each hand as he backed out of the car and turned and fast-stepped across the road.

The phone in his right hand came to life and he nearly dropped it out of surprise. He lifted it and saw the call was coming from someone named Justin. Surprisingly, there seemed to be sections of the canyon where there *was* spotty cell service, and this appeared to be one of them. He refused the call and quickly powered the phone off and threw it toward the river.

As he reared back to throw the second phone there was a pinprick of light in his right eye. Someone was coming from the north. He threw the phone anyway, heard a second distant splash far below, and jogged back toward his truck trying to assess how much time he'd have before the vehicle arrived. The road to the north paralleled the serpentine river, so the oncoming car was temporarily tucked out of view. He figured he had two minutes until it arrived.

Opening the door, he emptied his pockets on the floor of his cab, his .380, the stun gun, the case with the syringe (now empty), the flashlight, and the handcuffs. Running his hands down his jumpsuit as if frisking himself, he was satisfied he'd left nothing behind. He quickly shed the Tyvek overalls and kicked the bundle off his boots. He stuffed the white mass into a dark plastic trash bag and shoved it under his driver's seat to be disposed of later.

And suddenly the oncoming car was upon him, much sooner than he'd anticipated. A yellow wash of head-lights lit him up as he stood but he fought the urge to look over his shoulder and show his face.

The car passed by but he could hear the motor de-compressing as it did so, and he shot a glimpse under his right armpit to confirm that yes, red brake lights flashed. The car was slowing down.

Why? He wanted to shout. What had they seen?

He watched as the car pulled over to the opposite shoulder five hundred feet away and began a U-turn.

The Lizard King felt his face and scalp pull tight with rage. Everything had gone so well, and now this! He considered clambering inside the cab and roaring away before the car could reach him. But to do so would definitely create suspicion when the driver arrived to find the empty Ford. So he stayed where he was, fro-zen in time and space, but let his right hand creep back up into the cab until his fingers grasped the grip of the .380.

The car that had passed him stayed in the highway lane instead of pulling over. It slid up beside him and he squinted against the beam of the headlights, trying to figure out how many heads were inside; deciding that if there were more than two he wouldn't fire be-cause it would get too complicated . . .

The car was a late-model four-door sedan and as it

arrived the passenger window rolled down. Inside was the grinning face of his partner.

"Scared you, didn't I?"

"I should fucking shoot you anyway," the Lizard King said, pulling the gun down in full view of the driver.

"Good thing you didn't."

"Yeah—good thing."

"Jesus Christ, what happened to your face?"

The Lizard King absently reached up and dragged his fingertips through blood. He'd completely forgotten about his wound. The blood was hot and sticky.

"Guess I banged my head in all the excitement."

"You better clean that up. You look like hell itself."

He nodded.

His partner gestured toward the dark Ford. "Is this the double load you mentioned?"

"It is."

"Young ones?"

"Like I said."

"Anyone come by and see anything?"

"Only you."

"*Fantastic.*"

"Everything ready at the place?"

His partner nodded. The grin seemed plastered to his face and in the green light from his dash he looked malevolent, like a gargoyle.

"You had better get in your rig and get going," his partner said. "I didn't see anyone behind me but that doesn't mean someone might not show up."

The Lizard King nodded. Now that the situation had

defused itself he felt equal measures thrilled and exhausted. *This was going to work.* He said, "You going to follow me in?"

His partner said, "In a minute. Once you're clear I'm going to push that car farther off the shoulder into the brush. I don't want anybody seeing it or noticing the license plate until we get back here to drive it away."

The Lizard King shook his head, "That car won't run. I think the engine is seized up. You can smell it. We'll need the tow truck to get it out of here."

"Shit."

"It is what it is. But believe me, this will be worth it."

"That good, eh?"

"One of 'em, at least. I didn't get that great of a look at the other. But this is exactly what we talked about that time, remember? And they're not meth heads."

"Kind of like Christmas, eh?"

"Yeah," the Lizard King said. "Oh, there's a dead one in there, too. It was an accident."

"You've been a busy man."

"I'm motivated."

His partner nodded, then conspicuously peered out through his windshield ahead and checked his rearview mirror. "Still clear," he said, "You better go. It's going to be a busy night."

"See you soon," the Lizard King said, turning to pull himself back into his cab. "I'll drop off the precious cargo before I unload."

16.

Danielle's cell phone rang once and stopped. Justin held his phone away from his face and stared at it, unbelieving. He made sure he hadn't misdialed and confirmed that he hadn't.

Christian said, "What's up, man? Didn't she want to talk to you?"

"She hung up," Justin said, surprised. "One ring. Maybe she was in the middle of something and she'll call me right back."

"*Right,*" Christian chided. He had a baby face despite his size, and it took only two beers for a blush of pink to bloom across his cheeks. He'd had at least two, Justin guessed.

"I don't know," Justin said. "Maybe they're still going in and out of cell phone range. Last I heard they were going into the Yellowstone River canyon out of Gardiner, so that might be it."

"Yankee Jim Canyon!" one of the boys on the sofa cried out. "I went on a white-water raft trip there last summer and froze my balls off."

"Sweet," one of the girls said, and the other laughed.

"Try again," Christian said to Justin.

He punched the button. This time the call went straight to voice mail: *You've reached the voice mail of the awesome Danielle Sullivan. Please leave a message and I'll call you right back unless I don't. Ciao!*

"That's weird," Justin said. "She doesn't take my call and then it goes straight to her mailbox."

"Try it again."

This time, Justin heard a recorded message from Verizon saying the number he was calling was not available.

"It's like she turned her phone off. That's just weird. Danielle *never* turns her phone off. I doubt she even knows how to do it."

Christian shrugged. "Maybe her phone ran out of battery and she doesn't know it. Or she forgot to bring a car charger. Didn't you say she was kind of an airhead sometimes?"

Justin didn't remember saying it but thought he probably had because she was.

"In fact, I'm going to try Gracie's phone next."

Justin scrolled down his contacts list for Gracie's number and tuned Christian out. He wasn't in the mood for Christian, and especially Christian with a few beers inside him. The party had already lost some people, who had moved on to other parties. Christian had called Justin a "buzzkill" because, he said, "nobody likes seeing a dude sitting at a table working phones and a computer when they want to kick back and relax."

Gracie's number repeated the same message from the carrier. He closed the phone, frowned, and looked up. Christian stood there, hovering. Justin responded with a shrug. "*Both* of their phones are off. That just doesn't make sense."

"Screw her," Christian said. "You've got better things to do. I know *I* do.

"Who knows, man," Christian said. "Maybe they stopped for gas and she met some studly biker. You know, chicks just say they want nice boys. Really, they want the bad ones."

From the couch, Kelsie said, "Christian, you don't know what you're talking about as always."

"It's true," Christian said to her, walking into the kitchen to pull another beer bottle from the cooler of ice.

In his absence, Kelsie got up and joined Justin at the table. She sat close and said, "If those girls don't show up, Justin, you know who to call, don't you?"

He looked up to confirm he'd heard her correctly and she smiled. She was sweet, cute, and available, he thought. Danielle would make mincemeat out of her if they were ever in the same room.

He waited ten minutes, then called both numbers again. Same result. He was getting worried. If they'd had car trouble, or had been in an accident , . .

Justin stood, closed his laptop, and shoved his phone into the pocket of his hoodie.

"I'm out of here," he said to Christian.

Kelsie sat back, hurt.

"I'm sorry," he said. "But if they show up at my house and I'm not there . . ."

She crossed her arms over her breasts and glared at him.

He went out into the night with his laptop under his arm and his cell phone in his hand. He climbed into the older model Toyota Camry his father had somehow obtained the year before from the county impound lot, and sighed deeply as it warmed up.

He wondered if Danielle was gaming him, making him worry so he'd be more grateful to see her. She was capable of it, he knew. But if Gracie was along, Danielle couldn't get away with that, he thought.

It didn't feel right to have a girl, even one as smoking hot as Danielle, so determined to be with him that she'd drive hundreds of miles herself. It should be the other way around, he thought. Maybe the whole thing was a ruse? Maybe Danielle had been in Denver or Omaha the entire time and the long drive was something she made up to shame him, to make him remember how close they'd been and how much he'd miss her if she was gone?

Involving Gracie was the kicker, though, and pushed him back over the line. He'd seen how tough and resourceful her sister could be. Gracie wouldn't get involved in a deception.

Justin thought about the sequence of calls and texts

earlier. She's been in constant contact with him, seemed thrilled to hear back from him, and then . . . nothing. He could think of no reason she'd simply turn off her phone. And if her phone had run out of battery power, she would use Gracie's or call from a pay phone to check in. Danielle hated a vacuum and felt obligated to fill it.

He thought he knew what to do next, but he hesitated. He kept looking at his phone, willing it to ring and for Danielle to be on the other end. He sent three texts, one after the other, asking if she was okay, asking her to call. He copied Gracie in each time. When neither responded, he once again tried to call and once again got the message.

The last thing in the world he wanted to do that night was to tell his mom what was going on. She didn't like Danielle and didn't approve of him pledging himself to a girl in another state throughout high school. Danielle had been clingy and proprietary. His mom would go ballistic if Danielle simply showed up for Thanksgiving. And she might not believe that Justin wasn't in on it.

Should he call Danielle's mother? He barely knew her.

He did know Ted Sullivan quite well. But what he knew of him didn't fill Justin with any confidence. Ted would likely get hysterical and create problems that didn't yet exist.

Then there was his dad. He wouldn't be as emotional or judgmental about the situation. After all, he'd saved all their lives. But his dad was at best unpredictable. When Cody Hoyt had his fuse lit, anything could happen. Justin wasn't sure he wanted to be the one holding the match.

17.

At the table in the back corner of Jester's Bar, Cody leaned toward Cassie, bared his teeth, and said, "That's right. Tubman owns sapphire mines. Three of 'em. He leases them out with a contingency agreement. Tubman gets forty percent of the proceeds if the miners hit it big."

Cody's face was close enough to Cassie that she could smell the alcohol on his breath. Two shots of Jim Beam, two bottles of Coors Light. Certain words—*sapphire, contingency*—were strung out and loopy when he used them. His once clear eyes were now slits. A veiny bloom of tiny red blood vessels had appeared on his nose and cheeks.

Since they'd been there, Cassie had counted thirteen people who'd entered the bar, seen them in the corner, and left without buying a drink. Thirteen people who had either had encounters with Cody Hoyt or knew of him by reputation and didn't want to be in the same room with him. The bartender glared at them every time the door shut. Cody was either oblivious to what was happening, or didn't care.

"I don't get it," she said, barely sipping on her third glass of wine. She was feeling it. But she wanted the dirt on the sheriff and in order to keep Cody talking, she needed to play along—even if there was no way she could keep up. She said, "So what if he has some mineral leases? There's no rule against it that I know of."

"There isn't," Cody said. "And from what I understand, he married into it. His wife Dixie's family has lived in the county for years. The mines are in her name, but you know how that goes."

Cassie shook her head, not understanding.

Cody rolled his eyes, apparently annoyed that she couldn't connect the dots.

"There are a few legit miners," Cody said. "Some of them are as honest and hardworking as the day is long. But think about some of 'em we've dealt with like Tokely and that fucking B. G. We know they use the mines as cover for dealing, right?"

"We suspect it," Cassie corrected.

"We *know* it," Cody said. "And guess what?"

"What?"

"Two of the mines Tubman owns are worked by Tokely and B. G."

"Oh," she said.

"That's right. So haven't you ever wondered why—as a department policy—we take it easy on those people up there? Haven't you ever wondered why we don't do any surveillance in the Big Belts? Haven't you ever wondered why Mr. Law-and-Order Tubman hasn't done a high-profile raid up there and hauled their asses in?"

"I hadn't thought about it," she said. "I haven't been here that long."

"Don't get me wrong," he said. "I don't give a shit about them either. Live and let live, I say. I don't care if they're high on weed all the time or even if they shoot each other, as long as they keep it to themselves and don't involve any civilians. But you'd think our sheriff might care, wouldn't you?"

"I'm not sure where this is going," she said.

"Where it's going," Cody said, "goes back to that contingency agreement I mentioned. Tubman gets forty percent of the gem revenue. But it seems to be an all-cash business, just like dope. So how do we know that forty percent comes from the sale of sapphires?"

She sat back. "You're saying Tubman is involved in drug dealing?"

"Nope," Cody said. "I'm saying he gets payments from those people. I doubt he asks for copies of receipts from gem sales, is what I'm saying. Guys like B. G.—do you think he keeps good records? Do you think B. G. keeps one set of books for gem sales and one set for drug sales? Hell no, he doesn't. He commingles all his cash and he pays Tubman a percentage overall. Tubman probably never asks where the money came from, and B. G. probably couldn't tell him anyway. But I've done some snooping. Tubman has a nice house worth three-quarters of a million, plus a property up on Flathead Lake. That's a highbrow place. He's got snow machines and four-wheelers and who knows what else. You think he was able to afford all those things on his sheriff's salary?"

She nodded her head. "So how do you know you're right about this? If the mines are in his wife's name, how can you really say the sheriff is doing something crooked? It could be her money."

Cody simply grinned at her. "Think what the newspaper would do with that info come election time?" he said. "All they have to do is report the facts. Voters might not look too kindly on a sheriff who appears to be getting rich doing his job. And you can bet anyone running against him would bring it up. If Tubman spends all his time defending himself, he looks tainted. And in local politics, perception is reality."

He signaled for another round.

"Please, not another one," Cassie said. "We've got to get you out of here before—"

"Before what?" Cody asked. "I've got nowhere to go, thanks to you."

The bartender arrived with his head down. He looked whipped.

"I see what's been happening, partner," Cody said to him. "You've been losing a lot of business tonight."

The bartender nodded.

Cody shifted in his stool and reached back and opened his wallet again. This time, he handed the bartender a Visa card.

"Buy everyone left in the place a couple of rounds," Cody said to him. "And one for yourself because you look like you need it. And another wine for the pretty lady here."

"I'm fine," Cassie said quickly.

"I'll be the judge of that," Cody said. To the bartender: "Keep it flowing until I tell you to stop. For everybody in the place. They'll call their friends back and we'll all have a good old time."

The bartender left with the card, and announced to his remaining customers that the party had started. The bikers lifted their beer bottles in Cody's direction. Cody took it all in, acknowledging the accolades.

To Cassie, he said, "This is how drunks make friends."

She shook her head, "I've never seen you like this."

"This is the real me," he said. "I used to be a fun guy before I turned into a sober curmudgeon."

And your son and your wife came back, she thought but didn't say.

As the bartender delivered drinks to everyone, Cassie said, "I was asking you how you knew all this about the sheriff."

"You were?"

"Yes."

He held her eyes with his, and he smirked. "Have you ever met Dixie Tubman?" he asked.

"The sheriff's wife?"

He tilted his head and grinned. It was an unfamiliar man-to-man gesture that unnerved her.

"Before Jenny came back I catted around a little," he said, still smirking. "Dixie gets kind of lonely in that big house all by herself when Tubman is away giving speeches or politicking."

"*You slept with the sheriff's wife?*" she said, raising her voice. Someone had fed the jukebox and the guitar intro to Lynyrd Skynyrd's "Gimme Three Steps" was playing.

"I fulfilled a need." Cody winked. "Didn't do much actual sleeping. Damn, I always liked that song."

She rubbed her eyes. "I'm trying to wrap my head around this," she said. "So how did you find out about the mines and the contingency agreements?"

"Pillow talk." He laughed. "When she wasn't biting the pillow, I mean."

"Don't be an asshole."

"I used to be an asshole when I drank," he said frankly. "Everybody told me that. So many people told me I began to believe it might be true."

"Does Tubman know?"

"Know what? That I was an asshole?"

"That you slept with his wife!"

"Keep it down, girlie," he said, "All I know is *I* didn't tell him." He reached out and put his hand on hers. She pulled her hand away.

He was obviously drunk, she thought. The evening had taken a turn she had dreaded but anticipated. Men like Cody—in fact, most men she'd been around—would eventually make a play. It wasn't that they pined for her, or wanted her, or even thought much about her during their day. It wasn't even *personal,* which kind of hurt. It's just what they did, what they were hardwired to want to do. She'd once mistakenly believed a situation like this might turn out to mean more. Hence, her son.

"So no more about the pillows, is what you're saying." He chuckled.

She turned and slid off her stool. The wine fogged her brain and she reached out to steady herself.

"I'm not going to stay," she said to him. "I'll drive you home."

"Home?"

"You're right," she said. "I don't think you want Jenny to see you like this. So I'll drive you to a motel for the night."

"What about your place?" he leered.

"My mother and son wouldn't like it," she said. "And I wouldn't, either."

Then he looked up over her shoulder and his face changed. The leer was gone. Suddenly, he looked stricken.

She turned and recognized Justin from the football photo Cody had showed her.

18.

Justin drove Cody home in his car. Cassie Dewell followed them in Cody's pickup after Justin agreed to return her to her Honda later. His son drove with barely controlled fury, but laid out the circumstances of the night; how Danielle and Gracie Sullivan had suddenly stopped communicating with him.

Cody sat in embarrassed silence although his heart was racing and the comforting buzz of alcohol coursed through his blood stream. Home was a beige two-story ranch with a double garage, on a block lined with beige two-story homes in a new development on the north side of Helena. So new that he could still see the seams of grass sod on the front lawns and all the cue-stick-sized tree trunks were secured with wires to T-posts so the wind wouldn't blow them away. Justin swung into his driveway and nearly kissed bumpers with Jenny's car, missing it by inches.

Cody said, "I can't ask you to lie to your mom. But you could just not say anything."

Justin refused to look over at him. He said, "Just help me find those two girls. Then you can go out and destroy yourself again."

It was like a knife to the heart, and Cody moaned. He rubbed his face with both hands and tried to will himself sober. He hated the role reversal; his son as the parent, himself as the miscreant. He was embarrassed for Justin and angry with himself.

Justin got out and Cody followed. Cody's boot caught a crack in the driveway concrete and he tripped and righted himself by grabbing the hood of the car. Justin simply looked at him, shook his head, and went inside the house.

Cody stood there for a moment breathing in cold air, feeling the frigid sheet metal of the roof numb his bare hands. He watched Cassie park his truck in front of the house and was still there when she walked up.

"You look like you're waiting for someone to pat you down," she said.

"Feel free," he said sullenly.

She shook her head. "Just remind Justin I need a ride back for my car."

"Come inside out of the cold," he said, standing up. He was grateful he didn't swoon. "No reason for you to stand around out here."

She started to object but he said, "Please."

She sighed and nodded.

"Jenny might start swinging," he said. "You might have to protect me."

"I'll probably help her," Cassie said, deadpan.

He paused inside the front door and kicked off his muddy boots. One thing he liked about the place was that it still smelled new—new paint, raw lumber, fresh carpet. It was the first new house he'd ever owned and he wondered how long it would take him to damage it. Every hovel he'd ever lived in he'd left with fist-sized holes in the walls, carpets stained from whiskey spills, and bullet holes in the molding. But that was before he stopped drinking and raging and before Jenny decided to give him one more chance.

She was standing at the top of the landing with her arms crossed, looking down at them. Justin stood behind her. Jenny had long dark curly hair, blue eyes, a pug nose, and was fit and trim due to her daily runs. She wore a loose-fitting sweatshirt and tight jeans.

As he evaded her eyes she said, "Are you going to introduce me?"

"Oh," he said, "This is Cassie Dewell. She's my . . . *used to be . . .* my partner."

"What happened?"

Cody paused, hoping Cassie would say the right thing. But she remained quiet other than to say, "Nice to meet you" to Jenny.

"I got suspended again," he said. "Well, *fired* actually."

He would have preferred it if Jenny cursed or threw something at him. Instead, she closed her eyes and slowly shook her head. Her disappointment cut deeper than cursing or anger.

"I'm sorry," he said, looking down.

"Justin," Cassie said from behind him, "About that ride . . ."

Cody didn't want Justin or Cassie to go. He didn't want to be alone with Jenny.

"What did you do?" Jenny asked coldly. "I mean, before you went out and got shitfaced?"

He didn't respond.

She said, "When you didn't come home for dinner all kinds of things ran through my mind. You were on a case, or you were lying somewhere bleeding to death— all the things all cop's wives think. But then when Justin told me what was going on and said he needed your help, I thought of all those times *I* couldn't find you. But I talked myself out of it. I actually began to trust you again. Now you show me I was wrong."

He closed his eyes. He had nothing to say.

Finally, after a moment, Justin said, "Mom? Can we please do this later?"

Cody thought that if Justin were close enough he'd kiss him. Jenny was protective of Justin—Cody thought unnecessarily so—and on the very rare instances where their son was upset Jenny got the long knives out to protect her child. Even from Cody. And from her own justified anger.

Justin said, "Those two girls are out there somewhere."

Cody sheepishly looked up at his ex-wife. Jenny seemed to be conflicted what her course of action should be.

Cassie surprised him by saying, "Mrs. Hoyt, for what it's worth, the second Justin showed up Cody stopped drinking. I know because I was there."

"How sweet of you," Jenny said acidly.

"It's my fault all of this happened," Cassie said. "I really feel responsible."

Jenny said, "It must have been hard pouring drinks down his throat."

"Mom, *please*," Justin said.

Cody took a deep breath and said to Jenny, "Let me see if I can figure out where these girls are. You could help me out by making some coffee."

Jenny finally nodded, and turned on her heel for the kitchen. Then she stopped short, and said to Cody, "Justin said it's been hours since those Sullivan girls texted or called. You know how it is with these kids, Cody. They're never *not* texting each other. I'm afraid something has happened to them."

I'm afraid something has happened to them. The words hung there. They weren't unfamiliar to Cody. He'd heard them countless times from the other side of his desk at the sheriff's department from husbands and wives, boyfriends and girlfriends. People always assumed the worst when a loved one was missing. Sometimes, they were right.

Cody nodded and mounted the stairs to the living room. He was drunk but the immediacy of the situation seemed to have sobered him some. His head hurt—one of the signs that either the hangover would start to kick in or he'd need another drink to stave it off. There was no alcohol in the house. Jenny made sure of it. And he knew he'd cleaned out all of his hiding places two years before.

He grabbed a hardwood chair from the table in the kitchen, carried it over to where Justin was on the couch, and swung it around and sat down so he could face his son. He motioned for Cassie to come and sit next to Justin.

"Before we panic," Cody said, "let's review the situation and get all the facts in order so we can do the right thing and not waste anyone's time. Justin, when was the last text from Danielle?"

"A few hours ago."

"When exactly?"

Justin looked up blankly.

"Look at your phone," Cody said, trying to remain patient. "Check the log."

His son started scrolling. Finally, he said, "The last text from her was at eight twenty-seven. She said they were in Yellowstone Park."

"Where exactly? It's a big place."

"She didn't say."

Cody squinted and sat back. "Why in the hell were they in Yellowstone?"

"There was a roadblock or something on I-90," Justin said. "I looked at the map and figured out how they could go around it and get back on the interstate past the roadblock."

"Yellowstone?" Cody asked again. "You had them go *back* there?"

"Dad," Justin said, "I didn't *make* them do anything. They wanted to get here as fast as they could and it looked like the best alternative route. That's all."

"I wonder if it creeped them out," Cody speculated. "Maybe they got into the park and everything they went through before came rushing back so they freaked out and turned around and went home."

"No," Justin said, shaking his head. "They were fine with it. They're not like that. You should know them better than that."

"Well, I don't," Cody said. "I met them that one time and we didn't exactly have a get-to-know-you chat. Gracie was all right, but her sister—"

"Her sister *what*?" Justin asked, his voice cracking.

"She just seemed kind of, well, unserious." Cody said.

"She's my girlfriend, Dad," Justin said. "But I wanted to break up with her. She seemed to know that and wanted to come up here and talk me out of it, I'm sure. There is no way she'd just turn around and go home without telling me."

"Let's start over," Cody said, shooting his sleeve and looking at his wristwatch. "Okay, so you last heard from her at 8:27. It's 10:15 right now. That means she's been in radio-free Montana for one hour, forty-five minutes or so. Son, I know that seems like forever to you but it's really not very long. You know the cell service in the park is awful and it cuts in and out all the way up to Gardiner, if that's the way she was coming."

"That's the route we talked about," Justin said. "But she should have been well past that by now. She should be back on the interstate less than an hour from here. I did the math."

Cody paused for a moment to do it himself. "Okay, you're right if she didn't get held up somehow," he said. "And that's a big if.

"Think about it," Cody said, "They could have made a wrong turn."

"Maybe," Justin said. "But they said they had a GPS."

"Okay, but who knows—maybe there was road construction in the park. There is always road construction going on in there and they never seem to get it done. Maybe—"

"I checked the Yellowstone Web site," Justin said, shaking his head. "They have all the road alerts posted. There's some construction way south of Mammoth down by Old Faithful, but that's only in the summer."

"Maybe they ran out of gas."

"Then by now they should have found some and been back on the road," Justin said, his jaw set.

"There are so many possible reasons why they haven't called," Cody said. "Their phones may have run out of juice and they forgot to bring a charger—like you do all the time. A cell tower could have gone down, or there might be a service interruption. Maybe they hit an animal. Or, God forbid, got in an accident. That's certainly possible."

Justin shook his head. "But it doesn't make sense, Dad. I called both their numbers and they *refused* the calls. They didn't go to voice mail. It was like they saw my name and refused the call."

"That is strange," Cassie said. Cody had practically forgotten about her.

He said, "But who knows? It could have been a problem with the cell service. They're probably just broken down or something."

Justin closed his eyes. "In that case, someone should know about it. Wouldn't a wreck have been reported by now?"

"Maybe," Cody said. "But those roads are remote and the place is under the jurisdiction of the National Park Service. The feds do things their own way. Not a lot of people travel through Yellowstone this late in the fall. It would be possible to have an accident and not get help for a couple of hours."

"Which means," Jenny cut in as she returned from the kitchen, "those girls might be hurt. And if that's the case, we need to find out where they are and let their parents know what's going on."

Cody asked, "Do you know if they were in touch with their mom in Colorado?"

And, if possible, Justin's face turned even whiter than it had before.

"What the hell do you mean she doesn't know?" Cody shouted.

"It was Danielle's decision not to tell her," Justin said, staring at his shoes. "She lied and said they were driving to Nebraska to be with their dad for Thanksgiving."

"Ted?" Cody said, "Ted is in on this?" He recalled Ted Sullivan with distaste. But as soon as he said it he wasn't surprised. He said to Cassie, "Ted Sullivan is a pain in the ass. He thinks the way to be a father is to be best buddies with his kids and let them do whatever the hell they want so they'll like him, even though that almost got them killed before."

"Justin," Jenny said, "I can't believe you went along with this. How are we supposed to call Danielle's mother and tell her we don't know where her daughters are?"

"I know," Justin whispered.

"But we've got to call her," Cody said. "And maybe, just maybe, she's heard from them. And what about Ted? Do you think he's been in contact with them?"

Justin shrugged.

"What a mess," Cody said, sitting back in the chair. His headache was getting worse.

"Cody," Jenny said, "What are we going to do?"

He rubbed his eyes. "First, I need a couple of ibuprofen. Then I'll call the highway patrol," Cody said. "I'll find out from the dispatcher if anybody has reported an accident or a breakdown between Gardiner and Bozeman. If not, I'll try to raise somebody in law enforcement in the park to see if they know anything."

"And if they didn't?" Jenny asked.

"I'll put the word out to start looking for them. Justin, what kind of car is she driving?"

Justin said, "It's a little red Ford Focus. I don't know the year but it's used."

"Do you know the license plate number by any chance?"

"P-L-N-T-D-N-L."

Cody wrote it down on the palm of his hand. "What does that mean?" he asked.

Justin smiled a little when he said, "Planet Danielle."

"Planet Danielle," Cody repeated, shaking his aching head.

While Cody downed five ibuprofen tablets in the kitchen he felt a presence behind him. Expecting Jenny, he turned so she could let him have it. He was surprised to find Cassie.

"Let me help you with this," she said.

He waved her away. "What is it you propose to do?"

She shook her head. "I don't know. But it's the least I can do."

"That's true. But I'm not even sure what you could do at this point."

"Then let me know when you figure something out," she said.

"Run out and get me a bottle of Wild Turkey," he said.

"Except that."

19.

Gracie rolled over and felt like throwing up but she couldn't open her mouth because it was taped shut. She knew if she got sick she could choke to death. In a primal reaction, her eyes bulged wide as she tried to control the rising waves of nausea. Her belly heaved but she fought against it, willing herself to stay calm, willing her body to try not to expel what was inside her stomach. Although she was conscious she couldn't see a thing. Was she blindfolded as well? If so, she couldn't feel the blindfold.

Although she couldn't see, she had the impression she was in a long dark metal cylinder of some kind. It was dark and cold and the ground was pitching and she thought, *I'm in a spaceship.* The steel floor trembled and shook, it smelled of sawdust and varnish. She tried to reach out to push herself to her hands and knees but her limbs wouldn't respond. Her stomach ached and splashes of color and sound swirled behind her eyes until she closed them again. She managed to roll to the side until her progress was stopped by something long, still, and stiff. It gave a little under the pressure from her body and she thought she felt the knob of a knee or an elbow in her ribs.

She scooted back, then rolled again toward the object so she was on her side facing it. She used the crown of her head to poke at the object to try and determine what it was. The middle was stiff but elastic. Further up was a soft rise—breasts—and she could make out the jut of a chin and then a brow. But the object didn't move or breathe and the crackling and rustling sound she heard meant it was covered in some kind of plastic. The realization overcame her: *Her sister was dead and cloaked in plastic sheeting.*

Instinctively, Gracie scrambled away, inadvertently kicking the body. She was horrified and couldn't process what she'd found.

Her progress was stopped by another object. It took her a moment to realize that the body now pressing against her back was heavy, warm, and still.

Danielle. She recognized her sister by her scent. But unlike the other body, Danielle was surely alive if still under. Gracie snuggled against her sister, spooning with her in reverse, feeling the warmth against her back and hearing slow, labored breathing.

She tried not to think of the other body but she wondered who it had been and why it was there.

* * *

Gracie tried to remember what had happened but it came in erratic bolts of mental videotape: the blinding headlights of the big truck pulling in behind them, the flash of pure white clothing as the driver, who appeared as a silhouette framed by the high headlights, had swarmed her, locking her head in the crook of his arm, and the sharp bite of a needle in her thigh. Locking up, feeling her consciousness fade away, impulses in her brain misfiring . . .

Then nothing, and even now she wasn't sure if she was awake or dreaming or in some kind of state in between.

Gracie tried to say, "Danielle?" to the body beside her but her voice was muffled. She realized her hands were bound behind her back and her ankles were tied or taped together as well.

She bent her head back and thrust out her chin, still fighting the nausea, and felt an edge of the tape near her jawbone come loose. Pinpricks of sweat broke across her scalp and forehead as she tried to hold it in. Then, by dropping her chin to her chest and catching the loose adhesive of the free corner of the tape to her collar, she was able to wrench her head to the left and tear more of the tape from her mouth. Her lips felt suddenly cool from being exposed to air, and she retched, emptying the contents of her stomach on the steel floor until there was nothing left.

Then she wiped her mouth the best she could by rubbing it against the clothing on her shoulder, and leaned in closer to her sister and said, "Danielle?"

Her sister didn't respond. She breathed in the smell of Danielle's hair, and closed her eyes and burrowed through the thick dark hair until her chin was against her sister's throat. She could feel a slow pulse beneath Danielle's skin and the swell of her sister's breasts as she breathed.

"Thank God," she whispered. Then, to Danielle: "Wake up, Danny. Please wake up."

But despite her pleading, Danielle didn't stir or open her eyes.

That's when she heard a squeal beneath the floor of the room—the squeal of brakes.

They were in the trailer of the truck, and it was moving. She had no idea how long they'd been there or when the ride would be over.

The smell of her own vomit joined with the sawdust and varnish and cold stagnant air inside the container. Whatever was in the syringe was taking hold of her again, pulling her down, and she felt herself swoon. There was some comfort when she closed her eyes again, and she knew she wouldn't last very long before she passed out again.

20.

Cody's cell phone lit up and he snatched it up from his home office desk and looked at the display: dispatch calling back.

"Edna," he said, "Tell me something good."

"Everybody always asks me that," she said, "and I always let them down."

He frowned. His head was pounding. The ibuprofen had done no good. Every cell in his body screamed, *More alcohol!* at him—a familiar feeling. He idly wondered what proof was listed on the bottle of Listerine in the bathroom.

Cassie was in the kitchen with Jenny. He had no doubt they were talking about *him*, since he was probably the only thing they had in common.

Edna was the senior dispatcher at the L&C Sheriff's Department and she'd only recently given up trying to marry Cody off to someone—anyone—to complete one of her life goals. She hated the idea of single cops in the department, and she claimed she'd played matchmaker to eighteen relationships over the years. Of those, half were still married. Cody was grateful Jenny had come home for many reasons, but getting Edna off his back was an unexpected bonus.

"I checked with state dispatch as well as the NPS emergency center in the park," she said. "There are no reports of accidents involving a car of that description either on state highways or in Yellowstone. I asked the troopers at the I-90 roadblock to look for a car of that description and we're waiting for a callback."

"Crap," Cody said.

Edna said, "Of course, that doesn't mean they're not out there somewhere, but no one has called it in."

Cody said, "That includes the Beartooth Highway, the road in Yellowstone from Cooke City to Mammoth, and Mammoth to Livingston?"

"You don't have to repeat it," she said. "I got it the first time. No one has called anything in on a red Ford Focus with Colorado plates."

"Damn," he said, leaning back in his chair. He'd been checking on his computer to monitor the roadblock on I-90—the Montana Department of Transportation site still said the road was closed. That was good because it isolated hundreds of westbound vehicles in one place and if the girls were stopped in traffic they'd be located. But the odds weren't good, since Justin said they'd taken the alternative route.

"We need to put out an alert on that vehicle," Cody

said. "Let everybody know to keep a lookout and call you if they find it. Let the Wyoming folks and the Idaho folks know about it, too, just in case those girls really screwed up and went out another park entrance. Can you do that, Edna?"

"Already done," she said. "This isn't my first rodeo, Cody."

"Here are the descriptions of the occupants of the car," Cody said, giving Edna the details from memory.

"One of them is your son's girlfriend?" Edna asked.

"Yes." Then: "Sort of. Used to be."

He thought of something. "Edna, have there been any reports of cell phone outages? That could explain the lack of communication."

She said there had been no reports. Then she asked him to hold on for a moment, and he could hear the beeping of numbers being punched on a keypad, then Edna saying, "Just checking" to someone. She came back on the line and said, "I just called my sister Sally's cell phone in Gardiner from my cell phone. It went right through."

"Another theory knocked down," he grumbled.

"I'll let you know the second I hear something," she said. "But you know how kids are. They could just be lost, or whatever."

"Well, we need to find them," he said.

"Have the parents been notified?"

"No. I'll do it but I want to make sure I can tell them something one way or the other. In fact, can you look up a number for me in Omaha? Ted Sullivan. He's the father."

What wasn't said between them was that the most horrific duty of anyone in law enforcement was to be the one to notify parents of missing or hurt children. Cody had done it too many times, and it tore his heart out. And he rarely even knew the victims.

"I'll do that and get back to you," she said.

"Send the number in an e-mail," Cody said.

"Ten-four," she said. Then: "I called a state trooper I know who is stationed between Livingston and Gardiner. He used to be married to Sally. His name is Rick Legerski and I left a message on his voice mail about what was going on. I hope you don't mind that I left him your number."

Cody sat back. "*Thank you*, Edna. That was good thinking." He jotted the name down on his pad.

There was a long moment of silence before Edna said, "Cody, I heard you were suspended today."

"Just a flesh wound," Cody said. "Doesn't mean anything."

"Will I get in trouble with the sheriff for helping you out?"

"Maybe," Cody said. "If you want to tell him."

"I won't."

"Besides, would you really not want to find those stupid girls?"

"Of course not."

"Well, then," he said.

"Dispatch clear," Edna said.

He mumbled a thank you and closed his phone.

* * *

"No luck?" Cassie asked from the door. He realized she'd been there since the phone rang and had been listening in.

"Not yet," he said.

She looked over her shoulder in the direction of the living room, obviously checking to see where Jenny and Justin were, then stepped in and closed the door behind her.

"Cody," she said, "what do you really think?"

"I honestly don't know," he said. "But I do know it's not going to help anybody to panic. We're pulling the trigger on this thing pretty fast. If someone called in the situation to me at my desk, given the short time period that's lapsed between the last text message and now, I'd counsel them to calm down and wait for at least a couple more hours."

She nodded. "This Danielle," she said. "Is she trouble?"

Cody said, "Oh, she is. But she's that kind of trouble boys find irresistible. You should see her picture."

Cassie said, "Justin showed me a shot of her on Facebook. She looks like the kind of girl who used to take me aside and tell me I could be pretty if I just *tried*."

Cody smiled.

"So," she said, turning serious, "what do we do?"

He nodded at his phone. "We wait. Somebody out there will locate them." He didn't say how. Or what they'd find.

She came over and leaned against the edge of the

desk, facing him. She said, "What does your gut tell you? Just between us?"

He looked away for a moment, then back at her. "We give it a couple of hours. The word is out to the highway patrol, local law enforcement, game wardens, and park rangers. There may not be a lot of 'em out there this time of night, but if they're out on patrol there aren't *that* many roads to check."

She took in a deep breath and crossed her arms. "And if after a couple of hours we don't hear anything?"

"Then we start to get worried," he said. "This is the kind of situation where time is everything. If they are in trouble, well, we can't act fast enough.

"In fact," he said, squinting up at her, "if we don't hear anything soon I'm going to head down there and start rousting people."

"You're in no condition to drive," she said.

"I'll be fine," he said. "In fact, I've probably logged in more road miles drunk than most people have sober. But I can't just sit around. I've got to get into the middle of things and start knocking some heads. Many times, a case doesn't get solved until all the players involved—local sheriffs, cops, state guys—are properly motivated. And if there are suspects, I want to be the one asking questions. We can't wait until morning."

"I'll go with you," she said. It was a statement, not a question.

"Nope," he said. "You won't."

"Really," she said. "I can take a sick day."

"Forget it," he said. "You don't want to be around

me if I have to use some unorthodox methods to get answers, if you know what I mean."

She said, "I read the report about what happened in Yellowstone. I know there were some allegations of brutality. One witness said you shot him in the knees and hung him from a tree."

Cody shrugged. "Otherwise, the bears would have eaten him. I saved his miserable life. But you don't want any part of that. You want to be as far from that kind of thing as possible at this stage of your career. Besides," he said, "How do I know you wouldn't just report me again?"

"You're a son of a bitch," she said angrily.

"Yes, I am."

"Look," he said, "if you want to help you can help me more by staying here. If I get onto something down there I'll need someone to work the phones and access all the databases. I can't rely on anyone else in the department, considering my situation. So if you keep yourself available, you could be a hell of a lot more help than if you tagged along."

She started to argue, but thought better of it. "Makes sense," she said.

"So if this thing goes to hell, keep an eye on e-mail and keep your cell phone on."

She nodded.

The door opened and Jenny came in. Justin hovered just behind her.

"Anything?" she asked.

"Not yet," Cody said. Justin's shoulders slumped in despair.

Over his shoulder, a chime on his computer sounded. He glanced over and saw it had come from Edna.

"Everybody out," Cody said, "I need to collect my thoughts before I call that idiot Ted Sullivan and tell him his daughters are missing."

21.

A single dark cloud scudded across the slice of moon, halving it, while the Lizard King adjusted the control for the RPMs on the ancient Case backhoe. The powerful old engine revved roughly, rattling the metal floor of the cab, but settled into a banging muscular rhythm that could be heard for miles if there had been anybody out there to hear it.

Mountains rose on all four sides of the deep little valley and they were blacker than the sky. The night was still and cold. And beyond the growl and glow of the backhoe in the mountain meadow there was utter darkness.

The four lights mounted on the roof of his open cab threw harsh white light on the matted grass in front of the machine. He dropped the outriggers on both sides of the backhoe and triggered the stabilizers. They bit into the soil with a hydraulic hiss and he could feel the backhoe sit back on its haunches and settle in. He placed his gloved hands on the two tall lollypop sticks between his knees. The left stick maneuvered the hinged hydraulic arm and the right stick controlled the bucket curl. The scarred steel teeth of the bucket plunged into the soft soil and the motor strained as he lifted the first big mouthful and dumped it to the left of the backhoe. The ground was dark and moist with a few large rocks, and he should be able to dig a square pit that was fifteen feet long, twelve feet wide, and six feet deep within a couple of hours.

He knew this because it wasn't the first excavation he'd performed in the narrow valley. In fact, if one looked closely, the valley floor was riddled with them.

The Lizard King was both incredibly excited and exhausted. He'd not slept for twenty hours and the night had been a roller coaster of anger, lust, fear, and triumph. He hadn't been home yet and his cell phone was filled with messages. Since he knew what was on them and who had left them there was no reason to listen. No reason at all.

To the right of the hole he was digging was the little red Ford they'd towed in. In the glow from the light bar above his head he could see the reflection of his white Tyvek jumpsuit crumpled on the front seat of the car. On the passenger seat was a bundle of clothes and shoes that had been removed from the comatose girls. Everything would soon be buried under tons of dirt. Including that green Colorado license plate.

By morning light there would be no visible trace of the red Ford or the items inside it and the backhoe would be garaged in the county machine shed.

He thought of those two thin, flawless, half-naked bodies they'd unloaded. They were so unlike the lot lizards he'd brought back the last few months. Sure, there had been treasures from time to time when he got lucky and the circumstances were right. But for too many months, they'd had to make-do on a steady diet of lot lizards.

Then he pushed the thought aside as far as it would go so he could concentrate on his work.

22.

As Cody reached for the landline phone to call Ted Sullivan's Omaha phone number, his cell phone lit up. The display showed a 406 area code—Montana—but he didn't recognize the number. In his move for the phone he'd knocked over half a cup of coffee Jenny had brought in for him—his third so far. Hot coffee flooded across the surface of his desk and a rivulet poured into his crotch where he sat. Cody kicked his chair back, daubed the spilled coffee with the sleeve of his shirt, and opened his phone with his free hand.

His voice croaked, "Cody Hoyt." His throat was raw from cigarettes. The caffeine hadn't sobered him up much but had simply made his nascent hangover more wide-awake.

"This is Trooper Rick Legerski of the Montana Highway Patrol. I got your number from Edna Mulcahy in Helena." His voice was deep, gravelly, gruff, and no-

nonsense. Cody could hear a radio or television in the background and assumed the man was calling from his home.

Cody introduced himself while sopping up more coffee with a series of Kleenex tissues from a box he kept on his bookshelf.

"Edna tells me you used to be married to her sister," Cody said. This is how it went in Montana. Longtime residents sniffed around each other until they found someone they both knew. Usually, it didn't take long.

There was a moment of silence.

"Sally, yeah," the man said with a sigh. "Do you have any ex-wives?"

"One," Cody said.

"I've got two. Love is grand, but divorce is a hundred grand. But enough about that.

"Yeah, Hoyt," Legerski said, changing the subject, "I've heard of you before." His voice was cautious and a little weary. Cody recognized the intonation and had heard it many times from older law enforcement types.

He smiled. "You've heard all good things, I imagine."

"I knew your uncle Jeter," Legerski said. "In fact, I busted his head open once when I spotted him weaving across the center line outside of Ekalaka with a dead bull elk in the back. He refused to take a Breathalyzer and got belligerent so I . . . subdued him."

"So that was you," Cody said. "I remember hearing that story."

"His head was as hard as a rock," Legerski said. "It bent my baton and I had to get a new one."

Cody chuckled.

"And your name has come up a time or two around here," Legerski said.

"I suppose it has."

"You're looking for a couple of missing teenagers in a vehicle," the trooper said, done with small talk.

"That's right," Cody said, and repeated the make and model of the Ford as well as the names and descriptions of Gracie and Danielle Sullivan.

"Colorado plates?"

Cody spelled the license plate and recapped the story.

Legerski said, "I haven't been down that road through Yankee Jim Canyon tonight but I haven't heard of anything unusual. I was dispatched up to a roadblock on I-90 most of the night and I just got home and clocked out. I was just about to eat a late supper when I saw Edna called."

"Sorry to bother you at home," Cody said, not sorry at all. But he needed whatever help he could get so he said it.

"Part of the deal," Legerski moaned. "A Montana state trooper is always on call."

Cody rolled his eyes and pressed a ball of tissues into his lap to soak up more liquid.

He'd always had a knack for visualizing the details of people on the other end of the phone by the way they spoke, their choice of words, and their intonation. His former partner Larry used to bet him whether his premonition would be correct when compared to the real person when they finally met them. Most times, Larry had to pay up.

Because of the anecdote about Uncle Jeter, who had died three years before, Cody guessed Legerski was in his late fifties or early sixties, probably close to retirement. He was likely a big guy, as most troopers were, and because of his drawl Cody painted a drooping thick gunfighter mustache on a hawk-beaked craggy cowboy face. Since he'd mentioned working out of Ekalaka in Eastern Montana, Cody assumed Legerski was a lifer and had moved around the state throughout a long career. Ekalaka was in the middle of nowhere. Livingston and Gardiner were in Park County, which was considered a high-profile and plum location because it bordered Yellowstone. So Legerski had moved up through the years. Which meant he got along within the state bureaucracy—the Montana Highway Patrol was a division of the state Justice Department—in ways Cody had never gotten along within his. Legerski's tactic of introducing himself with a story about splitting open Uncle Jeter Hoyt's head was right out of "Old Cop 101," and designed to put Cody on the defensive right away and establish that Trooper Rick Legerski was a tough old bastard who had seen a lot and wasn't impressed much by local sheriff's department investigators.

Cody usually got along with tough old bastards, he thought. Except when he shot them.

Cody outlined the possibilities—breakdown, accident, cell phone outage, wrong turn somewhere. He repeated the line about "not *that* many roads to check."

Legerski took umbrage to that. "There ain't that many *paved* roads down here," he said, "but that don't mean there aren't a lot of roads. We've got hundreds of

miles of dirt and gravel roads. Old logging roads, old
ranch access roads, fire roads, and two-tracks known
only to poachers and old-timers. If those girls took one
of those because their GPS steered them wrong or they
were just dumb, that opens up a shitload of more possibilities. If they left the pavement at some point they
could be high-centered in some wash or gulley out of
cell phone range and we might not be able to find 'em
for days."

Cody winced. He listened haphazardly to Legerski
outline two incidents he'd worked; one where a couple
of elk hunters had knocked the axle out of their Jeep
and didn't get back to the highway for three days, and
another where "some shithead Iraqi or Pakistani tourista"
drove a Prius up a logging road and was found half-
eaten by a grizzly bear ten days later. In both cases
they'd flown a helicopter over the heavily timbered
mountains but the vehicles hadn't been spotted. Park
County was still in litigation trying to get other govern-
mental entities and federal agencies to share in the cost
for the search.

Trooper Legerski, Cody thought, likes to talk.

"Okay, I got it," Cody said. "And it's possible they
took a wrong turn somewhere. But from what my son
tells me these girls were in a hurry to get to Helena.
One of them, at least, has a level head on her shoulders. I doubt they'd just drive off the highway into the
trees."

"I don't know why anyone would be in a hurry to get
to Helena," Legerski said, and laughed at his own joke.

"Yeah, yeah," Cody said, waving it aside. Montanans loved to disparage their state capital. "But let's assume for now they didn't leave the road. How likely is it they're broken down somewhere and no one has called it in?"

Cody heard a long wheezy intake of breath that he recognized as being from a fellow smoker. Then, "It's possible, I guess," Legerski said. "Not that many folks use that road this time of year. The touristas are all out of the park this late in the season because all the hotels and campgrounds are shut down. The road's used mainly by locals this time of year and they'd likely notice an unfamiliar car on the side of the road and call it in."

"So they might be down there along the road somewhere? Maybe in Yankee Jim Canyon where the cell service is bad?" Cody prompted.

"Anything's possible, I guess."

Cody wanted Legerski to offer to drive the road. The trooper was under no obligation since no one had called in a report of an accident or breakdown and he was off duty, but . . .

"I'd do it for you," Cody said finally. "If you ever need a favor in Lewis and Clark County, I'm the guy to call."

Legerski's laugh seemed mocking and inappropriate, Cody thought.

"You must think we're real rubes down here," the trooper said.

"What are you talking about?"

"You must think that we're so far off the beaten path that we don't know about the Internet or something."

Cody felt the hackles on his neck rise and vowed to himself to keep calm and not blow up.

"'Cause I got an e-mail sitting right here in front of me says you got suspended today. That as of right now you've been busted back to civilian."

Cody wondered who'd sent it. But it didn't matter.

"I'll be reinstated within a week," Cody lied. "In the meantime, there are two girls out there lost or hurt or worse on your roads."

"Well," Legerski said, "I suppose I can change back into my uniform and take the cruiser back out. But you'll owe me if I don't find anything."

"I owe you anyway," Cody said. Thinking, Now Justin owes *me*.

"Yeah, I wasn't doing nothing anyway," Legerski said sourly. "Just getting ready to grab some dinner and go to sleep for the night."

"A Montana state trooper is always on call," Cody said.

"You're kind of a smart-ass, aren't you? For a guy asking for a favor?"

"You're right," Cody said. "So thank you. And give me a call either way, okay? I'm sure I'll be up. And if by some chance we hear from those girls, I'll call you right away."

"Call me on my cell," Legerski said, giving Cody the number. "I can't do any more overtime and if HQ knows I'm going out on a private call they'll raise hell. So let's keep this between you and me—back channel."

"Fine," Cody said, well aware of how many times he'd gone off the radar screen himself.

As he began to close his phone, he heard Legerski say, "Hoyt? You still there?"

"Yeah."

"There's one thing and we can talk about it later, I suppose."

Cody frowned. "What's that?"

"This isn't the first," the trooper said.

Cody sat up. "What do you mean?"

"Nobody wants to entertain this theory very much, especially the suits in HQ," Legerski said. "But this isn't the first time a car with females in it just up and vanished down here."

Cody felt his scalp crawl. He said, "Come again?"

"Look, I better get going. But tell me your e-mail address before I go. I'll fire you an e-mail with some links in it you might want to check out."

"What do the links go to?" Cody asked.

"You'll see," Legerski said and hung up.

"Oh my God," Ted Sullivan said when Cody told him. "Oh my God!"

"Don't panic, Ted," Cody said. "We don't know enough yet for you to get hysterical."

Ted Sullivan had light auburn hair so thin his freckled scalp undergirded it and hazel eyes that darted from one thing to another and seemed to focus up and to the left of the person he was speaking to. The one word Cody had heard over and over from others talking about Sullivan when they'd first met in Yellowstone was "weak." Gracie hadn't said as much, but she did concede her father was "not strong." Cody had learned that Sullivan was a software engineer of some note within his own particular circles, something about cloud technology, and he'd been divorced for seven or eight years from Danielle and Gracie's mother. He'd moved around the country with different firms and was now in Omaha. Cody was aware Ted Sullivan probably made ten times as much money as he did, but that didn't impress him. Little about Ted Sullivan impressed him. But as a father himself, he almost felt for the guy. No one wanted to be on the other end of this particular phone call.

"Marcia is going to kill me," Ted said morosely.

"She should," Cody said. "You deserve it. Justin told me that Danielle called you and how you went along with it. We just found out about the scheme tonight."

"She'll take me back to court," Ted said. "She'll get my visitation rights taken away."

"Enough about *you*, ass-hat," Cody barked. "When was the last time you heard from *them*? Have you gotten a call or a text in the last four hours?"

"No."

"Did you try to call them?"

"Well . . ."

"So you didn't, okay. As I thought, you're no help right now, but you need to know the situation." Cody said. He noticed both Jenny and Justin were peeking in the room at him, probably because his voice had gotten so loud. He waved at them to go away. Neither moved. Jenny frowned back at him.

"That's just not true," Ted said. "I know for a fact

that both Gracie and Danielle have GPS-embedded phones because I bought them for them. All we have to do is trace their whereabouts through cell-mapping software. They also have a Garmin I sent them. We can contact the company and—"

"Ted," Cody said impatiently, "GPS doesn't work if they're out of cell range. This is Montana. And don't you think that if their phones were working we wouldn't be in the situation we are now?"

"Oh."

"Okay," Cody said to Ted while nodding at Jenny that he'd received the message from her to cool down, "You need to take off your geek hat and let their mother know. And when you do, find out if they've been in touch with her and when it was and exactly what they said. Give her my number if she wants to talk with me directly."

Sullivan moaned. "You have no idea how she can be."

"Yeah, Ted. You're the only man with an ex-wife, so I wouldn't know how that is," Cody said, glancing at Jenny who looked back steaming. "You need to call her, Ted. Tell her what's going on."

There was a beat of silence. "Can you . . ."

"No," Cody said. "I don't even know her name or number."

"I could give it to you."

"*Call your goddamned ex-wife, Ted!*" Cody shouted. "Man up and call her."

"Okay." His voice was a whisper. Then, "I'll be on the first plane to Helena in the morning."

"Don't come, Ted," Cody said. "I've seen you in

action. Stay the hell in Omaha by the phone. I'll keep you posted on anything we find out."

"But they're my daughters," Ted said. "They're all I've got."

Cody started to yell again but caught himself. He thought of what he'd do in similar circumstances, and he couldn't blame Sullivan for wanting to be there.

He said, "I can't stop you but if you come here you're on your own if you do. I don't want you around me trying to help. I've seen your version of help before. It results in a clusterfuck and dead bodies."

There was a long silence. Jenny had covered her face with her hands and was shaking her head from side to side. Cody thought maybe he'd overdone it.

Then Ted said, "Call me the second you find out something."

"I'll do that," Cody said, and closed his phone.

"Great bedside manner," Jenny said. "I can see why you used to be the star of the sheriff's department."

"Best they've got," Cody said. Thinking, *And the best they've ever seen.* At least that used to be the case when he had nothing to lose. He corrected himself: "Best they had."

At that moment his e-mail chimed again. Cody looked up to see that the message had been sent from TROOPER-RICK@gmail.com.

The subject line read: THE CHURCH OF GLORY AND TRANSCENDENCE.

He mouthed, "Oh, *shit.*"

Then, to Jenny and Cassie: "I'm going to gear up and

drive down there. I want to talk to this trooper before too much more time passes."

They argued about him driving, and Jenny agreed that Cassie should drive Cody's pickup. He nixed it.

"We've had this discussion," Cody said, forwarding the e-mail to Cassie's e-mail address. "She's going to man the command center here." To Cassie, he said, "I just forwarded you something. Read it over and give me a call on the road. Let me know what it says and what you think."

She nodded.

To Jenny, he said, "I'll see you tomorrow, I hope."

As he passed them in the doorway, he said to Justin, "Call me the second you hear from them if they text or call you. I wouldn't mind coming back and getting some sleep. I've got a hell of a headache."

Cody unlocked the door to the room in his basement where he stored his gear and flipped the light on. The heavy-duty steel shelving was packed with equipment. There were shotguns, hunting rifles, revolvers, semiautomatic pistols, a collection of brass knuckles, fixed-blade tactical knives, night vision goggles, sets of body armor—even a Kevlar helmet.

He selected an AR-15 rifle and a Benelli M1014 12-gauge combat shotgun and propped them in the corner to take along.

Cody packed a gear bag with two .45 ACP 1911 Colts with extra magazines, night vision goggles, body armor, .223 rounds for the AR-15 and 12-gauge buck for the shotgun, binoculars, rope, handcuffs and flex-ties, a pair of radios, and several cell phones. While he was bent over buckling a holster with a 9MM Model 26 "Baby" Glock to his ankle, the door was pushed open.

He looked up to find Jenny standing there with her arms crossed over her breasts. She didn't have a key to the room and simply referred to it as his "man cave." Her eyes swept the contents.

Most of the items still had evidence tags attached from the Law Enforcement Center to which, unbeknownst to the sheriff or the supervisor, he had a key.

"Cody . . ."

"I never take anything that might be used in court," he said. "Only stuff that's leftover before it gets sold or destroyed."

"That's not why I came down here."

"I know," he said. "You don't have to say it."

"I'll wait until you get back," she said. "Right now you need to help your son and find those girls."

"Thank you."

"But, Cody . . ."

He nodded, and said, "I thought you were going to wait."

Her eyes flashed with anger.

"Sorry," he said.

"Just promise me one thing and keep it this time."

"What?"

"Promise me you won't take another drink tonight. I know how you are. Once you get started, you don't stop. You *can't* stop. And you've got a head start."

"I stopped for two years," he said.

"Until tonight. You started drinking again when your son needed you."

"I didn't know it at the time," he said.

"Just promise me."

"I promise." Thinking, *She didn't say anything about a minute after midnight.*

Then, as he stood and gathered his weapons and gear, he thought, *No.* Not tonight. He had a job to do. This is what he'd explained to Cassie at Jester's. This, right here, was why he existed.

"I promise," he said again.

23.

Gracie awoke. She was in a different place.

The floor she lay on was hard slick cement instead of vibrating steel. But it was dark, like before, except for a slight airy hum somewhere in back of her. She was in a fetal position on her side, her knees tucked up almost beneath her chin. There was faint orange light in the room, emanating from behind her, but there was enough illumination for her to see that her knees were bare and white.

Painfully, she stretched out. Her arms raised up above her head—no bindings—and her legs straightened along the floor. The tape on her mouth had been removed but her lips and cheeks were still gummy with adhesive. She'd been stripped to her underwear and wore only her panties, bra, and socks. The thought of someone taking her clothes off while she slept disgusted and frightened her.

She reached down the length of her body and slipped

her hand between her legs. Although she'd never had sex and didn't know what it felt like afterward, she was sure she hadn't been raped.

She flopped over to her back and her naked shoulders made contact with the cool concrete floor. The ceiling was dark and without features. The air in the room was musty and there was a sharp unpleasant odor on the fringes, something old and permanent. Some kind of human odor.

She still had no strength and it was hard to connect with her own body. A headache pounded between her ears and it was so all-powerful that she thought a quick movement would again lead to nausea.

Gracie rolled her head to the right. A wall, also concrete, without a door or a window. Faint pale lines about an inch apart like tooth-tracks from a rake, swept across the surface in an arc. The wall she thought at first was pitted wasn't pitted at all, but flecked with dark stains and paintbrushlike smears of black.

Her heart raced, and with it her head pounded even harder.

It was silent inside the room except for that soft hum, but she had trouble hearing because of the liquid pulsing in her ears as she comprehended the nature of the place she was in.

She rolled her head to the left. Danielle was there, also undressed except for her underwear—a lacy black bra and ridiculous magenta-thong panties—her face hidden by a cascade of black hair. But there was rhythmic breathing, and Gracie heard Danielle issue a soft moan. She was still alive but unconscious.

"You want a blanket?"

The voice made her jump. It was low and raspy and it came from behind her out of view. Gracie rocked back on the crown of her head, chin up, to try and see who had spoken.

"Here," the voice said, and Gracie's head and torso were suddenly covered with a scratchy blanket that had been tossed on top of her with a soft *whump*.

Moving slowly to not trigger the nausea again, Gracie lifted her right arm to move a corner of the blanket off her face. The fabric smelled slightly of sweat, dust, and urine. Once her face was clear she shifted her hips so she could look up and see.

The figure—it took a moment to recognize it as a woman—sat with her back to the far wall, a bare knee propped up. Gracie couldn't see all of her because she was half in shadow, but what she saw was white and skeletal. A thin scabbed-over ankle, a bulbous knee like knotty pine, the sharp angle of a corpselike shoulder, and oily hanks of long blond hair. One eye looked out from a sunken dark socket and it was lit orange by the electric heater that hummed beside her. The heater was the source of the sound and the only bit of light in the room.

The woman shifted and lowered her knee and her leg stretched out along the floor. There was something wrong with the gesture, something incongruous about her. Gracie realized it was because the woman only had one full leg. Her other thigh, which lay flat on the concrete floor, stopped just above where her other knee should have been.

"Lost it when I was little," the woman said, and gestured toward the door. "They took my prosthesis and they won't give it back. Like I was ever gonna fuckin' run away," she said, hissing out the words.

When the woman opened her mouth again Gracie saw a dark maw with no teeth.

"Now that they got you little girls they won't have no use for me," she said, and a single tear snaked down her cheek.

24.

After dumping the body of the lot lizard in the trunk of a car next to the house, the Lizard King stood silently on the broken front porch of the house he'd grown up in, trying to calm his breath and slow his heartbeat. He'd dropped the two girls off, hidden the body in his sleeper while his truck was unloaded, then driven home. The events of the night had been fantastic but now he wanted to calm down. He welcomed the utter and pure exhaustion that came after the rush, because he knew the next few days would be incredible.

There was a light on inside.

He thought for a moment that he might just turn on his boot heels, get in his truck, and stay in his sleeper for the night. But being back in those familiar surroundings would bring it all rushing back again, the events of the day, and he'd never get to sleep. Plus, the cab reeked of disinfectant from being thoroughly scrubbed down. So he hoped she'd simply left a light on for him or forgotten to turn it off—it happened more and more often—and he reached down for the door handle.

The house itself was close, tiny, tired, and sad. It was obscured from the dirt road out front by sixty years of gnarled and tightly packed Russian olive bushes that rimmed all four sides like medieval walls. There was no garage—not even a carport. The paint peeled on the asbestos siding and most of the shingles on the roof were cracked. There was always a certain smell around the house, sickly sweet and ancient, from the coal that was once burned in the stove to warm it. That smell seemed to live in the walls itself. But compared to the odors inside . . .

He opened the door and stepped in quietly and eased it shut behind him. The light came from the kitchen and it was muted and lit floating dust motes kicked up by his entry. There was a tunnel of sorts through the living room to his bedroom. His shoulders brushed against a column of boxes and plastic tubs that rose from the floor to the ceiling. He had to turn slightly to make progress. The floor was gritty with dirt.

There was a side passage off his route to the kitchen and he took it so he could turn off the light. There was so much loose paper stacked throughout the kitchen and the rest of the house that leaving a light on was a fire hazard. He was always telling her that, always complaining about the stacks of newspapers and mail, about the columns of boxes, crates, and things she called her "collectibles" or her "memorabilia" that now

filled the entire house except for his bedroom, telling
her that the house was a fire hazard and a health hazard
because of the old groceries rotting in the refrigerator
and cupboards. . . .

Once, during a screaming argument, he'd told her he
would borrow the Case backhoe and knock the house
down and bury everything inside it. He'd told her the
county would likely give him a medal for good citizen-
ship for eliminating an eyesore. She'd screamed back at
him, asking, "*Where would I live? What would I do?*"
Breaking down into tears and sobs that disgusted him
but somehow touched him at the same time and made
him soften his demand. She'd promised to clean the
place out, to sell what she could and have the rest hauled
away. Except, of course, for her most valuable "collectibles," she'd said, already backing off before doing
anything. Adding that she'd also have to save her
"memorabilia," like the footlockers that once belonged
to his dead sister JoBeth and all the medals and trophies
she'd won in high school. Those she'd have to keep, of
course. But the rest: gone!

She knew she had a problem, she said. But he'd been
cruel and inhuman to point it out. After all she'd done
for him, she said.

That was seven years ago. Since then, the hoarding
had gotten worse. He'd not seen the top of the stove or
the surface of the kitchen counter in years. JoBeth's old
bedroom was packed with boxes, clothing, papers,
boxes filled with grocery bags and rubber bands—
packed so tight the door barely closed.

There were missing cats. He'd brought them in and

released them to silence the constant rustling he'd heard deep within the piles of "collectibles" and "memorabilia." But the cats had vanished. She claimed they must have run off. He suspected they were long dead, moldering, crushed under the debris.

The only room in the old house that was habitable was his own. Sure, it was dark and small. The things on the walls—his first set of mule deer antlers, his diploma from graduating from Livingston High, the curled and yellowing ripped-out photos of hot rods and pickups and Dallas Cowboy Cheerleaders—hadn't been updated in years. But the room itself gave him warm and familiar comfort. It was his place to gather his thoughts, to dream, to masturbate. In a brushed-steel lockbox under his bed were his keepsakes and souvenirs from his successful hunts. He knew he shouldn't keep them, and especially not in a place so close to him. But he couldn't help it. He'd tried to dispose of the box once—taking it out to the pasture to bury—but he couldn't do it. The contents were too important, and nothing he'd yet encountered would arouse the feelings he got when he rummaged inside.

He blamed the intense need he had for keeping the souvenirs on *her*. That evil wormlike trait had been passed on to him.

Before she got really bad, she used to enter his room while he was away. He knew it because the sheets on his bed were occasionally changed. And once when he returned the pinups of women he'd put up on the walls were simply gone. She denied she'd removed them but of course it was her.

Now he kept his door triple-locked and never left the keys. He never let her in there. *Ever.*

He'd often wondered how it was possible to so bitterly hate someone he loved. He chalked it up to blood ties and left it at that.

He slid through an opening in the stacks to enter the kitchen to turn off the light and there she was, glaring at him through her steel-framed glasses, a shapeless and massive woman in a flower-print housecoat the size of a mainsail. She was sitting at the table. Her elephantine ankles anchored her to the floor like tree stumps.

Her face was wide and fleshy, framed in a silver-white helmet of tight curls. Every week, no matter what, she made her appointment with her longtime hairdresser in Livingston. Her hair had never changed in style or length since he'd been alive. Why she cared about her hair and nothing else was another thing about her he couldn't understand.

"It's about time," she said fiercely, biting off her words.

She was at the ancient table shoved up against a wall. The table had a foot of open surface on it, where she sat behind a plate and a bowl with something brown in it. Her meaty hands were curled on either side of the place setting.

"I didn't know you'd be up," he said.

"Of course I'm up. I made you dinner hours ago and waited and I'm still sitting here waiting. Your stew is cold now. I suppose you can still eat it but it's cold. It's as cold as your heart."

"Stew?"

"Dinty Moore," she said, shifting slightly back in the chair and lifting her chin. "An entire can of Dinty Moore."

"How long has it been here?"

"I don't know," she said, blinking.

He paused. "I *hate* Dinty Moore stew."

"You didn't used to," she said sharply, defensively. "You used to love it."

"I never loved it. I never liked it. JoBeth loved the stuff—not me."

"Oh, how you lie. You even lie about JoBeth."

He shook his head. He thought again about getting the tractor and leveling the place. With her in it.

His cell phone vibrated in his pocket—a message. He ignored her and drew it out, read the screen, and dropped it back into his shirt.

"I have to go out again," he said.

"What about this stew?" Her tone was filled with outrage.

"I don't care," he said, backing out, "Eat it. Put it in the refrigerator if you can find room. Store it in Jo-Beth's room if you can even open the door."

"You're going to waste it?" she said, angry. "Where are you going, anyway?"

"To the shop."

"The shop is closed. It's nearly midnight." Then, "Are you up to something, Ronald?"

"Just work."

"Just work," she mocked. "You come home at midnight, you stay long enough to insult me and my cooking, then you walk back out the door."

"There are some loose ends," he said.

"We need to talk about Thanksgiving. It's coming up."

"Let's do what we always do," he said. "Talk about it and then do jack shit when Thursday comes."

"That's a cruel thing to say."

He shrugged.

"This stew," she cried from the kitchen as he pin-balled his way through the stacks of collectibles toward the front door, "You're just going to *waste* it?"

Wednesday,
November 21

Destiny picks flowers, know it's just like this:
Hardest part of dyin', is knowing what you missed
—Jalan Crossland, "Hard Ol' Biznis"

25.

2:30 A.M., WEDNESDAY, NOVEMBER 21

Cody swung his pickup into the near empty parking lot of the First National Bar of Montana in Emigrant. His tires popped through the gravel and he pulled up so close to the entrance the front grille of his pickup nearly kissed the gray and sagging hitching post. There were only two other vehicles in the lot—an ancient Willy's Jeep with a ragtop and a gleaming Montana State Patrol car. This was the place. Cody glanced at his wristwatch. He was on time.

When Trooper Rick Legerski had suggested the First National Bar as a place to meet and two thirty as the time, Cody had objected.

"Isn't there anywhere else?"

"You have a problem with it?"

"I don't drink," Cody said.

"That's not what I heard. Anyway, you don't have to. It's the only place open this time of night. Meeting there will give me time to patrol Yankee Jim Canyon into the park and back again and look for that missing car. If you keep your eye out on the way down to Emigrant, we'll pretty much have seen the entire route you described and the First National is right in the middle."

Cody grudgingly agreed.

He drove from Helena to Livingston via Highway 12 through Townsend, Three Forks, and Bozeman. The last time he'd taken the route was two years before on his way to Yellowstone to try and save Justin. He'd been held up in Townsend and nearly burned to death in Bozeman in the Gallatin Gateway Hotel, but he'd made it through. Mission accomplished.

This time, it was to try to find his son's ex-girlfriend. There was a huge difference in degree and motivation, but he welcomed the diversion the situation presented—and the timing. Otherwise, he'd have been back in Helena, probably drunk and shooting out streetlights or shouting and waving his pistol on Sheriff Tubman's front lawn. That's the way things progressed when he went on a bender, which was the path he'd been on before Justin showed up at the bar. In a strange way, Danielle and Gracie Sullivan had probably prevented him from completely going off the rails.

But despite the ability to focus on something besides his own predicament, he couldn't help but speculate about his future while he drove. What would he possibly do next? Where would he get a job that paid enough to maintain his house payments? Another job in law enforcement was probably out of the question because he had two strikes against him and a reputation the size of a truck. Private security jobs paid crap in and around Helena. As he passed through Townsend he recalled working on a ranch there as a teenager and knew he was too old and lazy and inept at physical labor to even consider it again.

Provided Jenny chose to stay with him, she might have to try and find something to help make ends meet. She worked part time at the hospital as an administrator, and her current salary allowed them a few extras. Now, though, she might have to look for a second or different job. That would be a fun conversation to have with her, he thought sourly.

He'd once kicked around the idea of becoming a private investigator after he'd been fired from the Denver Metro PD but he discarded it at the time. Now, though, he might actually have to look into it seriously, but he wondered if there was enough work out there to make it pay. The PIs he'd crossed paths with in Montana were all ex-LEOs, and lived hand-to-mouth because there wasn't enough work to go around in a rural mountain state. And he knew that even if he could figure out a way to make a living—doubtful—the work would be unsatisfying. Cody's primary motivation, the thing that made him stay sober up to now and get up in the morning, was to crush bad guys. It was the only reason he kept going. He had a special knack for it because he was bad himself and always had been, therefore he had special insight. He doubted he could transfer his blinding passion to photographing cheating spouses or tripping up insurance claimants. And deep within himself, he always knew that if he couldn't smash bad guys the only career he could imagine that could provide the same rush and intensity was to become one of them. Rob banks, maybe. Kill for hire. Those were things he could do. The possibility was inside him like a sleeping viper. Deep down, he always knew he could out-bad any bad guy. And outthink any run-of-the-mill cop.

Criminals he put away were incredibly stupid—like B. G. He wouldn't be like that. He knew not only how criminals thought, but how cops thought, too.

He took a deep breath and rubbed his eyes. Not now, he thought. He refused to take this train of thought any farther down the track. The viper would have to remain in its nest for now.

After cruising through Livingston on dark and silent streets, seeing no sign of a red Ford Focus downtown or in any of the motel lots, he took Highway 89 south toward Gardiner. He drove peering both ways for the Sullivan car. There were few houses or lights, and the moon was the only source of illumination.

He saw no cars on the side of the road matching the description, and none passed him coming from the south.

The highway was a lonely place after midnight in southern Montana.

Emigrant was one of those towns that was more a location on the map than a real town, since the only building was, in fact, the First National Bar, established in 1902, or so the hand-painted sign read outside. The bar sat just off Highway 89, thirty miles south to Gardiner and twenty-three miles from Livingston to the north. Across the highway, down a two-track asphalt road and out of sight from Emigrant, was Chico Hot Springs, an ancient sanitarium turned resort. It was a shambling, funky place with a big thermal hot pool, rooms, a restaurant, and a bar where Cody had once taken Jenny and gotten in a bar fight with two fake cowboys from Bozeman. He remembered it well. Jenny left him the first time after that.

It was known as Paradise Valley. The Gallatin Range was west, the Absarokas east. To the north behind him were the Crazy Mountains. And straight south on Highway 89 through Gardiner and the northern entrance to Yellowstone National Park. Hollywood stars and hedge fund managers played rancher on small spreads throughout the valley and the Yellowstone River flowed through it. This time of year, though, the hobby ranchers were usually decamped for the winter and the valley was dark, silent, and cold. Espresso stands were closed for the winter, and the upscale eateries stopped selling *The New York Times.* Meanwhile, herds of elk and buffalo drifted northward from Yellowstone Park to reclaim the grass, with wolves and grizzlies shadowing the flanks of the herds, looking for opportunities. Ranchers fed cattle hay from flatbed sleighs and snow machines replaced horses and four-wheelers. If one didn't know better, a visitor might think every human being in the area during the winter was named "Carhartt" because of the label on most of their clothing. During the winter, the Paradise Valley became western again.

Cody checked his phone before opening his door. On the three-hour drive south from Helena, he'd checked in frequently with Justin, Jenny, and Cassie. Justin hadn't heard a thing from the Sullivan girls, and he was starting to panic. Jenny had talked to Ted Sullivan and their mother, who was, as Jenny put it, "going back and forth from hysterical to murderous." She wanted to kill Ted first, and Danielle second. Jenny said she talked her down and promised to stay in touch with any news.

Cassie had opened the e-mail sent to Cody and had done some additional research on her own from her home computer. As she came across more information she'd e-mail the link to his phone with her own comments. Because he'd been driving, Cody hadn't had a chance to read anything yet. But she'd called with one particular item that piqued both their interest, and Cody planned to ask Legerski about it if the opportunity presented itself. But first he wanted to hear Legerski's thoughts. Local cops—especially longtime locals in small communities—were generally in touch with the mores and culture of their constituents. Too often, Cody thought, investigators from outside the community didn't pay enough attention to the theories of the locals. It was a lesson he'd like to pass along to Cassie Dewell.

Cody was impressed with Cassie since they had talked in the bar. Her guilt fueled her investigation, and he didn't want to let her off the hook until the Sullivan girls were found. The situation—him in the field, Cassie working the phones and databases at home—

reminded him of the successful arrangement he'd had with his former partner, Larry Olson. They'd been a great team. The two of them had the highest percentage of solved homicides in Montana.

When they were working, Larry punctured holes in Cody's enthusiasms and filled the vacuum with research and evidence. Cody kept Larry operating at a high level by challenging him and threatening to go off on his own tangents. Every case, it seemed, was a race between Larry's brains and desire to contain Cody and Cody's kick-the-door-in fieldwork. Maybe Cassie could be his new Larry, he thought. At least for tonight, as long as he needed her. After that, he thought, he'd cut her loose for what she'd done to him.

He got out and took a deep breath of the cold night air. The moon was bright and lit up the snowcapped, eleven-thousand-foot Emigrant Peak. The Absarokas dominated the eastern night horizon like a buzz saw that was switched off. At the foot of the mountains the river serpentined through the valley floor flanked by twin columns of massive skeletal river cottonwoods, their leaves gone. The river reflected the moon on treeless stretches. It was always ten degrees colder near Yellowstone than in Helena, and Cody noticed the difference.

He slipped his phone into the breast pocket of his jacket and one of the .45s into the back waistband of his jeans. He tugged the hem of his jacket down to hide it.

Then he pulled on a L&C Sheriff's Department baseball cap with an emblem on the front and turned

toward the ancient bat wing doors that lead to the alcove of the First National Bar of Montana.

Montana Highway Patrol Trooper Rick Legerski sat
alone drinking coffee at a small table in the middle of
the bar. There were no other patrons. Cody stifled a
smile when he saw him: Legerski looked *exactly* like
he'd thought he would, although thicker through the
chest and bigger through the belly. He looked up with
warm blue eyes.

"Cody Hoyt?"

"Yup."

"Welcome to Emigrant."

"Thank you."

The First National Bar was ancient and inviting,
with pine paneling, low lights except over the pool table,
and dozens of elk, moose, deer, and antelope trophy
heads mounted on the walls. Local cattle brands were
burned into the tabletops and plank wood floor. It
smelled of sawdust, cigarette smoke, spilled beer, ma-
nure, and greasy food. Cody kind of fell in love with it.

"Got some coffee brewed in the back," Legerski
said, nodding toward the bar. Cody followed his eyes.
A large-framed bald man wearing a Carhartt vest over
a red plaid hunting shirt nodded his head slightly. Cody
thought the man didn't really want to be there spinning
his wheels with two customers who drank coffee. He
got the impression Legerski and the bartender were old
friends by the way they communicated without words.

"Black," Cody said to the bartender.

Cody sat down opposite Legerski. The trooper raised his eyebrows.

"See anything on your way down?"

Cody shook his head. "You?"

"Sorry. Nothing."

"Shit."

"Word is out everywhere," Legerski said. "I heard the description of the vehicle and the girls over the radio. They're looking for them in four states, but nobody's found 'em yet. Edna really got the word out fast. She's a good one, that Edna. Tomorrow the word will get out around here by breakfast and who knows?"

Cody nodded.

"They just opened I-90 again," Legerski said. "I was up there helping out for a while. But before they opened it back up the patrol up there inventoried all the cars waiting in line. No red Ford Focus with Colorado plates."

The bartender brought Cody a heavy mug and set a thermal carafe on the table for the both of them, then hovered. Cody read in Legerski's expression he expected Cody to pay, which he did.

"Extra ten bucks in there," Cody said to the bartender, "For keeping the place open."

The bartender nodded in silence and clumped back over to the bar. By the way he started wiping down the counter and running water into a sink it was obvious he was closing down for the night. But his body language suggested he was listening in on them and trying not to be obvious about it.

Cody said, "I do appreciate you taking a run down to Gardiner and checking for that car. And getting out of bed to do it."

"No problem."

"Do you have any kids?" Cody asked.

Legerski shook his head. "Not technically," he said. "My second wife had a couple of future wards of the state, but we're divorced. But no, none of my own."

Cody sipped the coffee. It was strong and bitter and hot and it burned the tip of his tongue. "Jesus," he said.

"I should have warned you," Legerski said. "Jimmy's not known for his coffee."

Legerski produced a detailed Montana Department of Transportation map, unfolded it, and spread it across the table. For the next few minutes he pointed out all the side roads and wrong turns the girls could have taken between where they last communicated as they exited the park to Livingston. Cody listened patiently but found the speculation to be of no value. He'd already gone over it all in his mind. Sure, they could be anywhere within the park or in Wyoming, Idaho, or Montana. But that wasn't the point and it didn't help explain why they'd stopped communicating or why their distinctive car hadn't been located.

Cody put his cup in the saucer and lowered his voice. "When I talked to you earlier you said something about this not being the first time some girls came up missing around here. Care to expound on that topic a little?"

Legerski paused and looked into Cody with well-practiced, all-seeing cop eyes. Searching Cody for something. Cody just looked back, squinting through the smoke of his third cigarette since he'd walked in.

"First, some ground rules," Legerski said. "Because I live here and I know everybody. Sometimes it's a fine line between being in town and of town, if you know what I mean."

"I do," Cody said.

"I'm involved in civic organizations like Kiwanas and the Lions Club," Legerski said. "I referee high school football and basketball. I see these folks from the valley every day. So I can't let it get out there I've got a hate on for any of 'em."

"Believe me," Cody said, "I get it. Whatever you tell me stays with me. I'm good for my word."

"I've heard that," Legerski said. "But I've also heard some other things."

"Those being?"

"That you can get out of control. That you're a loose cannon at times. That you get drunk and shoot the county coroner at a crime scene."

"All true," Cody said, "but you knew that."

"I also heard," Legerski said, lowering his head while he lowered his voice, "you're in a lot more shit than you let on when you told me you'd be back on the job within a week. Despite that sheriff's department cap on your head. From what I heard, you're out of the department. You might even face charges."

Cody took a deep breath and sighed. "Yeah," he said.

"So right now," Legerski said, his eyes betraying embarrassment on Cody's behalf, "you have no authority or jurisdiction here. This is just a conversation between an off-duty trooper and a regular citizen. We're just two guys talking. Nothing more than that."

Cody let it sink in. He nodded.

"Does anyone know you're here?"

"Why do you ask?"

Legerski met his eyes straight on. "Just covering my ass. If you go off and do something stupid, I don't want it coming back on me. I have a couple of years left until I retire with full benefits."

"Spoken like a state employee."

"That's what I am." Then he set his jaw. "I have no obligation to be here right now talking to you. I'm off shift."

"I apologize," Cody said. "I appreciate your help. And to answer your question, my wife and son know I'm here. The sheriff doesn't know a thing." He decided not to mention Cassie.

"No one else?"

"The Sullivan parents—one in Colorado and one in Nebraska. They're worried. That's why I asked if you had kids of your own. Then you'd understand the urgency. I know I'm not likely to find these girls tonight and you know it. We've got experience in these kinds of situations. But they've got to have some hope. My son does, too. At least if I'm down here, I'm doing something besides sitting on my butt waiting for a phone call."

Legerski nodded and seemed to be thinking about it before proceeding. Then, with a what-the-hell grimace, he said, "How much do you know about the Church of Glory and Transcendence?"

Cody leaned in closer. "Some, I guess."

"What? Tell me so I don't have to cover familiar ground."

Cody had been recalling what he knew on the drive down after being prompted by Legerski's e-mail. He said, "The church was founded in the mid-1970s in California, I believe, by a woman named Stacy Smith. Smith claimed she'd been ordered to create the new movement from God himself. I don't know a lot about what they believe, but I've heard it's a mixture of New Age bullshit that includes Christianity, Buddhism, mysticism, and other stuff. Fairies, alchemy, all kinds of crap."

Legerski chuckled but didn't correct him.

Cody said, "Stacy Smith was a charismatic true believer, and her personal magnetism and fervor attracted hundreds of followers in a short time. Because one of the primary beliefs of the church was that the apocalypse was coming, she wanted to relocate the church and its crazy followers to someplace isolated and safe. Hence, Montana."

"Why do they always think that?" Legerski asked rhetorically, and they both laughed.

"Anyway," Cody said, "A big ranch resort was for sale just down the road on the other side of the Yellowstone River. It was perfect for the church so they bought it and moved everybody up here. When was that, 1980 or so?"

"Nineteen eighty-one," Legerski said. "Five thousand acres and twenty or so buildings. That was before they started big-time construction."

"Okay, I was close. So hundreds of the true believers moved there, probably thinking it was a great location because they hadn't lived through a winter yet. Lots of folks in the area were worried at first because a lot of people considered the church a cult. But the faithful turned out to be pretty nice neighbors overall, right?"

"Right, for the most part."

Cody didn't pursue the other part yet.

"They sold good pies and preserves," Cody said. "I remember stopping at their outlet once. So even though people were suspicious, Stacy Smith kind of won everybody over. This is live and let live country, and even though more and more people showed up to move across the river on the church compound they pretty much stayed to themselves and didn't bother anybody."

Legerski nodded.

"But then some followers quit the church in the early nineties and they didn't have much good to say about Stacy Smith and the practices of the church. Nothing horrible—no sex stuff or anything like that—but they did tell everyone that the church had been amassing quite a weapons cache in preparation for the apocalypse. That news got the feds worried, of course, and they raided the place. They found years' worth of food stockpiles in underground shelters that were supposed to keep the members alive through a nuclear war, or whatever. And they *did* find a lot of guns. A whole shitload of them."

"Right," Legerski said.

"So as a result, the word got out that these peace and love religious folks were armed to the teeth. Stacy

Smith started to be seen as a kook instead of a sweet inspirational leader. Then the feds started looking at their tax status and lowered the boom on 'em. Stacy Smith got old and sick and was forced to turn the reins over to other people in the church, and the new guys agreed to give up the weapons and sell some of the property to pay off tax bills. After that, I haven't heard much about them for years. I've heard they don't have many members anymore and that the place might come up for sale again."

"Pretty good so far," the trooper said.

Cody shook his head. "Why did the feds go after them the way they did? It isn't illegal to own firearms. This is Montana. Most of the folks I know have plenty of guns in their own houses. Hell, I've got a whole room full of 'em, and I know it isn't that unusual."

"Remember the time," Legerski said. "It was around Waco and Ruby Ridge. The feds were on a rampage. And even though the church had the right to store firearms, they knew they couldn't fight the government and a P.R. war at the same time. Plus, the church was trying to hold on to a bunch of members who felt cheated because the world didn't end like they were told it would."

"But the church sort of got screwed," Cody said.

Legerski said, "It depends on your point of view. The feds were pretty pleased they got the church to agree to give up all the weapons and no one got shot or killed. And when the apocalypse didn't show up when it was supposed to, a lot of the members lost faith and moved on. Stacy Smith was moved to an assisted living facility in Bozeman and she passed away quietly a few years ago. The news didn't even raise a ripple. But that church is still there and there are a couple hundred hard-core members."

"So . . ." Cody said, lighting another cigarette off the end of his old one.

"Those things will kill you," Legerski said.

"Yeah, yeah."

Legerski said, "Have you ever heard the name Bill Edwards? Aka William J. Edwards?"

"No."

"Not many have. But he's the new leader of the church. He's not like Stacy Smith. He keeps to himself and doesn't give speeches or circulate around Livingston and Bozeman making friends. I'd guess there are very few people around here who've ever heard his name. But he's a serious man, and his goal is to build the numbers of the church up again. He wants to make it bigger than it ever was, and he has a plan to do it."

Cody saw where Legerski was going.

"The rumor I've heard is that Edwards thinks the key to building the membership back up is young attractive girls. If he can persuade them to join, men will follow. It isn't exactly an original strategy—think ladies' night—but it works better than anything else in the world."

Cody sat back. "So you think it's possible the church nabbed the Sullivan girls when they came through here?"

"Keep your voice down," Legerski whispered, shooting a look toward the bartender. Then to Cody, "I can't prove it. But it makes me think. There have been a few teenage runaways—I can think of three, one in Livingston, one in Bozeman, one in Big Timber—in the last year who just vanished. Three is a lot in this area. People are starting to talk, is what I'm saying. And that's *all* I'm saying."

With that, Legerski pushed away from the table. "Got to get rid of some coffee," he said, and he turned for the men's room which was designated by the sign, COWPOKES.

Cody mulled it over while he checked his phone. There was a single text from Justin five minutes before that read, "Nothing." There were two more e-mails from Cassie with links to news stories about the church, and one about the funeral for Stacy Smith the previous year in Bozeman. Either she was thinking along the same lines as Legerski, or Legerski's initial e-mail had put her squarely on the path.

He wasn't good at texting, but he asked Cassie to check the FBI's ViCap (The Violent Criminal Apprehension Program) databases for *Missing Persons*, *Unidentified Persons*, and *Homicides and Sexual Assaults* of young women in southern Montana. He wanted to confirm Legerski's story about the three missing girls as well as to see what else was out there. He also asked her to check out one William J. Edwards.

She responded quickly, "Will do."

While he waited for Legerski to return, another man entered the First National Bar. He was large, lumbering, fleshy, with light wavy red hair sprinkled with silver and a flat Slavic face. He wore grease-stained jeans, a pilled thick chamois guide shirt, and lace-up boots with heels like truckers wore. He seemed to make a point to approach the bar the most circuitous route possible from where Cody sat.

The big man sat heavily on a stool at the bar with his back to Cody and without acknowledging him. He ordered from Jimmy with no pleasantries, simply, "Coors Light."

Cody looked him over. The man seemed determined not to look back at him, which to Cody seemed odd, given the empty bar and the late hour.

Legerski didn't acknowledge the big man either when he returned from the bathroom. Cody's antennae went up. In a small rural community, everybody knew everybody. He wondered why Legerski didn't say hello.

The trooper sat down heavily with a serious look on his face, as if he were thinking hard about something.

Cody made sure the big man wasn't looking at them in the mirror and nodded toward the newcomer and arched his eyebrows, as if to say, "Who is that guy?"

"Not now," Legerski mouthed. He seemed to Cody to be a little nervous, or a little scared.

Cody changed the subject and leaned forward.

"Let's go out there and look around for the car," he whispered.

"The church compound?" Legerski whispered back.

"We should do it now. Before they get a chance to hide the car or change the plates."

"*Now?* What about a warrant?"

"Don't you know a friendly judge?"

"I do. But we need probable cause. We don't have jack shit at this point."

"Then let's go anyway."

"They've got a gate across the entrance on the other side of the bridge. If it's locked, we have to ask them to come on their property. And it's always locked."

Cody sighed in frustration. "We don't need a warrant. We just drive up and ask them if we can look around. They're supposed to be good people. If they don't have anything to hide they should let us on the property."

"And if they don't?"

"Then we have probable cause, don't we?" Cody asked.

Legerski leaned back and looked at Cody blankly.

"Can't this wait until morning? We can see most of the compound from the highway. We could be there at dawn with field glasses and spotting scopes and see if we can locate the car. Then we'd have a reason to go get Judge Graff."

"Too much time," Cody said. "If they did what you suggest they did, that would give them time to hide the car and stash those girls. Every minute counts in something like this."

"Man, I don't know," Legerski whispered.

"Think about it," Cody said, leaning back himself. He thought if Legerski refused he'd go anyway. There was nothing illegal or unethical about asking for permission to look around the compound. If the church people said no, they said no. And he'd figure out a way to access it anyway.

Cody leaned forward again across the table, and Legerski reluctantly did the same.

"So who is the guy who just came in?"

The trooper lowered his voice so even Cody could barely hear him. "He's a long-haul trucker who lives with his mother in a shack six miles away from here in the foothills. His name is Ronald C. Pergram."

"Seems like an odd one," Cody said, stealing a side-long glance. Pergram didn't look over. Jimmy had delivered his beer and stood hovering over him. Cody got the feeling Jimmy was letting Pergram know that Cody and Legerski were talking about him in whispers.

"This Jimmy," Cody said, "is he a good guy?"

"The best," Legerski said. "I've known him for years."

"He seems to be pals with Pergram."

Legerski snorted. "I doubt that. He's just being Jimmy. Jimmy knows everybody in this valley."

There was a quick vibration in Cody's pocket.

"Excuse me," he said, and withdrew his phone. Legerski watched him suspiciously.

CHECKING VICAP, Cassie had written in a text. FOUND SOME MISSING FEMALES WITHIN A 100 MILE RADIUS. LAST SEEN AT TRUCK STOPS. WILL KEEP DIGGING.

"You say he's a long-haul trucker," Cody said, closing the phone.

"Who was that?" Legerski asked, nodding toward the closed phone in Cody's hand.

"My son Justin," Cody lied. "He still hasn't heard a word from the Sullivan girls."

Legerski shook his head.

"Tell me," Cody said, "have there been any other reports of missing women here on Highway 89?"

Legerski looked back, puzzled. "What are you thinking?"

"Just a wild hair," Cody said. "Something to look at if our first theory goes kablooey."

Legerski nodded, but seemed to withdraw a little. Cody got the impression Legerski didn't like the direction the conversation had taken, and found it telling. The trooper had a theory he wanted to sell to Cody, and Cody wasn't entirely buying it, which seemed to unsettle the man.

"So," Cody said, pushing away from the table, "let's go to church."

"Man . . ."

"You can come with me or stay or go home. Your choice. But since it's your stomping grounds, I thought you might want to come along."

Legerski sat at the table and finished the last of his coffee. Cody didn't linger, but stood and pulled on his jacket and turned for the door. He didn't hear the trooper follow.

When he stepped outside through the faux bat wing doors onto the old wooden portico, Cody noted that the condensation from his breath billowed around his head like a helmet. He paused for a moment to let his eyes adjust to the darkness. There were no lights in any direction, only the hard white stars that appeared like cream wash in the night sky. The moon reflected off the river in the distance and the windshield of his car. He zipped up his jacket against the cold.

Something had happened inside the bar but he couldn't figure out what it was. The way the three men— Legerski, Jimmy, the truck driver—interacted without words around him was unsettling, but he couldn't unpack it. Why did Legerski seem so different—jumpy, intense—when he returned from the toilet? Cody felt he'd missed something but he couldn't put his finger on it. He wished the alcohol in his system had dispersed but it was still there, dulling his instincts and fogging his brain. He thought about turning on his heel and going back inside to order a drink. He knew from long experience that sometimes the hair of the dog resharpened his wits, at least temporarily.

"No," he said aloud to himself. *You've got to ride this out.*

As he stepped down toward the hitching post and his truck he heard the door open behind him and the bat wing doors swing out. They moaned on rusted hinges.

He turned to find Legerski, fitting on his trooper hat.

"Changed your mind?" Cody said, smiling.

"Completely," Legerski said.

"You want to come with me, or do you want me to ride along with you? Or take two cars and really impress the hell out of them?"

"Let's take your pickup. In case this thing goes haywire, I'd rather not be in my cruiser. Let me get my camera and my sound equipment in case we have to document something."

Cody grinned and climbed in. He was glad Legerski was with him. He started the motor and waited for the trooper to retrieve the items from his trunk. He watched him root around, find what he was looking for, and walk around the back of his pickup carrying a satchel. His taillights turned Legerski pink in the rearview mirrors.

The trooper climbed in and shut the door.

"Do you know how to get there?"

"I've seen the place," Cody said. "It's hard to miss."

As Cody reached up for the shifter all of his senses suddenly came alive but things happened too quickly to process. Straight ahead, up the wooden porch steps and to the side of the door, two faces looked out from opposite sides of the neon Miller Lite beer sign in the window. At the same time, he heard the rustle of fabric from the satchel on Legerski's lap as well as the sharp intake of breath from the trooper.

Instinctively, Cody glanced over but all he could see was the gaping silver-rimmed muzzle of a snub-nosed large caliber revolver an inch from his eye. The cylinder revolved, filled with dull lead bullets, as the trooper pulled the trigger.

There was a tremendous explosion of light and thunder.

He could no longer see out of his right eye, but it was more than that. There was no pain, only tremendous silence.

Then he was floating, light as air, as if his lungs had filled with helium. He passed through the sheet metal roof of his pickup into the night, which was no longer cold. As he rose his eyesight was restored but he no longer had feeling in his limbs and his arms hung loose at his sides.

He looked down. He could see the top of his pickup from above, the bed of his truck which was empty except for a crumpled fast-food wrapper in the corner, then the rusted metal roof of the First National Bar. The windows of his pickup strobed three more times but there was no sound and he felt nothing.

Cody's life didn't pass before his eyes, but he clearly saw the photo of Justin in his football uniform and a vision of Jenny sleeping in bed from years before they separated the first time and he rose until he could see the river and the ribbon of highway through the valley and Jimmy and the truck driver emerge from the bar and stand on the porch and he knew what happened to those poor girls and he felt both cheated and angry at the same time and he wished he could do it all over again, everything.

Especially the last five minutes.

Then nothing. No sound, smell, or sight.

Peace.

26.

3:53 A.M., WEDNESDAY, NOVEMBER 21

Cassie Dewell sat at her kitchen table in worn sweats and slippers with her laptop open in front of her. Although she'd switched to decaffeinated coffee two hours after she'd returned home from Cody Hoyt's house, she was still wired. And unsettled. Her stomach growled and burbled and sounded loud in the sleeping house, and each time it happened she found herself placing her hand over her middle with the same reflexive instinct she'd once used when she was pregnant with Ben.

She'd tried to sleep but couldn't, and thought she'd work herself into exhaustion. Instead, though, she found her mind racing.

She considered eating something but nothing sounded good except cake. There was some in the refrigerator—German chocolate—left there by her passive-aggressive mother for the sole reason, Cassie thought, to keep her fat. So instead of eating it, she drank decaf and her stomach growled as if she'd swallowed a wolverine.

Cassie sat back and tapped out another e-mail on her phone and sent it to Cody. This one, from the *Bozeman Chronicle* the previous winter, was entitled WITH DEATH OF CHARISMATIC LEADER THE FUTURE OF DOOMSDAY CULT IN DOUBT. She found it of interest because, at the time, the reporter stated there was no clear plan of succession for the church and several factions were stepping forward to claim it. According to the article, the leadership of the Church of Glory and Transcendence would likely fall to Stacy Smith's son Wayne, but no one was sure he either wanted the role or was up for it. There was a brief mention of someone named William Edwards, who represented a competing effort. There was no other information about Edwards in the article, and Cassie failed to find any other published information about him in her searches. The only reference she found to him was on the Web site of the church itself, which referred to him as "Terrestrial Caretaker." Wayne Smith wasn't listed at all, which she took to mean that Stacy Smith's son had either not stepped forward or had been defeated for leadership. As far as Edwards went, there was no photo, no biography. She pointed out that fact in a note accompanying the link she sent to Cody's phone, and wrote, "He seems to be the guy you'll want to interview."

Not that Cody replied. In fact, he hadn't acknowledged even receiving any of the texts or e-mails she'd sent in the past hour. She speculated that he was out of cell phone range, busy with something, or simply unresponsive and rude. All three were distinct possibilities. She began to understand why Larry Olson, Cody's former partner, became so frustrated with him.

She wasn't supposed to access the ViCAP database from anywhere other than an official departmental computer in the sheriff's department, but she justified it to herself by noting the laptop actually belonged to Lewis and Clark County, so what did it matter? Cassie had no intention of claiming the overtime on her sheet because she wanted to avoid problems and questions from Sheriff Tubman. Questions like why she was assisting a suspended deputy in his investigation of two missing teenage girls in the middle of the night with no formal complaint or referral—and outside their jurisdiction.

She didn't know how she would answer that question if it came up, other than it seemed like the right thing to do despite policy and protocol. That she felt unclean and guilty for being responsible for the suspension itself. That she didn't want to be regarded by her colleagues around the office as the sheriff's *tool*.

Cassie sat back in her chair and knuckled at her eyes with both hands. Her spine cracked and her stomach burbled again. The house was cold for sleeping—her mother insisted on turning the temperature down to sixty-two at night to "save energy"—and Cassie's feet were cold. But she didn't want to risk turning the thermostat up. The rumble of the furnace and the whoosh of forced air might awake her mother, who would ask what she was doing and why she was doing it so late. Cassie didn't want to deal with the questions now. Although

Cassie was in her midthirties and had a son, her mother
had a way of phrasing things—with a certain tone—
that always made Cassie act guilty, like she was still
twelve and trying to get away with something.

Although she was grateful her mother lived with her
and watched over Ben and cared for him while she was
at work, the situation was difficult and becoming worse.
While Cassie had aged and changed, her mother hadn't.
The quirks and passions her mother displayed when
Cassie had lived at home seemed more pronounced,
more set, more rigid. Cassie looked on helplessly, for
example, when her mother patrolled the house turning
off lights and unplugging electronics that weren't being
used at the time. Cassie was afraid Ben would take to
heart her mother's leftist rants and genuine hatred of
business, all Republicans, the military, and the police.
The police! Didn't her mother know what she did every
day? Didn't she know or care that Ben's father had
been in the army?

She swallowed the last of her cup of decaf and
leaned forward to her laptop and keyed in the pass-
words for ViCAP—one for the department, one for her
personally—and followed the prompts and she was in.

It took five minutes to narrow down the search. There
were actually twelve missing women from southern
Montana, but only four in their teens at the time of
their disappearance. Of the four, one case had been
open for five years, so she discounted it with a pang of
guilt and the recognition that missing Jessica Lowry,
age seventeen, Bozeman, history of drug abuse and

emotional problems—would for now remain shoved aside and forgotten. She didn't even want to look beyond the area, or statewide. Even in a state with a low population like Montana, the sheer number of missing people was overwhelming and depressing. Instead, Cassie keyed on the three girls she presumed Cody had asked about, and read up on each of them. She opened a document window aside from the Web pages so she could cut and paste relevant information to share with Cody, provided there was anything of note.

Erin Hill, Livingston, eighteen, white, brown hair (although possibly colored red), green eyes, five foot two, 160 pounds, reported missing by stepmother in July two years prior. Disappeared after being arrested for possession of meth, presumed a runaway. Divorced parents, lived with mother. An unconfirmed sighting of her was reported by a convenience store cashier at a truck stop on I-90 west of Billings. The cashier reported that a girl matching Hill's description had used the ATM in the store and lingered for an hour inside, but the cashier didn't speak to her or see her depart the store. The internal ATM video malfunctioned during the transaction and didn't get a shot of the user, but the subject had used Hill's PIN number to withdraw the last $120 from her savings account in a Livingston bank.

Shanna Marone, Bozeman, seventeen, white, long dark hair, brown eyes, five foot six, 140 pounds, tattoo of red lips on neck and Harley-Davidson logo tattoo on mid-lower back, reported missing eighteen months before after not showing up for classes at the alternative high school. Mother distraught, father not in the picture. A passing motorist on State Highway 205 (between Belgrade and Manhatten) reported seeing a person hitchhiking who matched the description of the missing subject, including a yellow down coat she was known to wear. No other verified sightings had ever been confirmed.

Chelsey Lybeck, Big Timber, fifteen, white, short blond hair, blue eyes, four feet eleven, 110 pounds, was reported missing by the father, a ranch foreman on the Lazy Double-Ought Ranch . . .

But she was found, Cassie realized as she read on. Her body was discovered last summer on the bank of Sweet Grass Creek by fishermen. Cassie recalled reading something about it in the newspaper. The body was too decomposed to determine the cause of death, but the Sweet Grass County Sheriff's Department speculated she'd died of blunt force trauma followed by exposure. To date, there had been no arrests, although the ranch foreman father had been questioned twice and the file remained open.

Cassie didn't include Chelsey Lybeck on the document she was building, but concentrated on Erin Hill and Shanna Marone. Both runaways, apparently. Both last seen—possibly—at a truck stop along an interstate highway and on a state highway. Both never seen again, if the ViCAP records were correct.

She thought of the Sullivan girls. Similar age. On the highway. Missing. Cassie forced herself not to make a leap of speculation based on such a weak and isolated set of circumstances.

Then she saw the link on the bottom of the ViCAP Web page for HIGHWAY SERIAL KILLER INITIATIVE.

She hesitated, worried about spending too much time going down a wrong path when there were other things she could be doing.

But she floated the cursor down and clicked on it. As she read, Cassie felt the hairs rise on her forearms and on the back of her neck.

First, she scanned a map of the United States covered with red dots. The dots were placed along interstate and state highways, looking like a strings of red pearls from coast to coast. The highest concentration of dots were in the east, Midwest, and southeast. But there were plenty in Montana and throughout the rest of the country.

In 2004, an analyst from the Oklahoma Bureau of Investigation detected a crime pattern: the bodies of murdered women were being dumped along the Interstate 40 corridor in Oklahoma, Texas, Arkansas, and Mississippi . . . ViCAP analysts have created a national matrix of more than 500 murder victims from along or near highways, as well as a list of some 200 potential suspects, almost all long-haul truck drivers . . . The victims in these cases are primarily women who were living high-risk, transient lifestyles, often involving substance abuse and prostitution. They're frequently picked up at truck stops or service stations and sexually assaulted, murdered, and dumped along a highway . . . the mobile nature of the offenders, the unsafe lifestyles of the victims, the significant distances and multiple jurisdictions involved, and the scarcity of witnesses or forensic evidence can make these cases tough to solve . . .

She took a deep breath and scrolled down to a specific incident report.

A passerby found the severed head on Feb. 10, wrapped in two plastic bags and stuffed inside a backpack in Barstow, Calif. Authorities still haven't identified the victim or her killer, but the circumstances point in a particular direction.

The teenage girl likely had been killed days earlier, Barstow police say. Her head lay a few hundred yards from a truck stop just off Interstate 15, not far from I-40. To authorities, the proximity to the truck stop and the interstates suggests that the slaying might have been the work of a distinctive type of criminal: a serial killer operating along the nation's highways.

Cassie thought it remarkable and horrifying that there were so many missing women along the highways that a task force had been created in the first place. And her mouth went dry when she read that ViCAP and the task force had assisted local authorities to arrest no more than a dozen suspects—all long-haul truckers. There had been two convictions, but more than five hundred open cases were unsolved.

The fact there was an actual federal task force on highway serial killers disturbed her greatly. Cassie's father had been a long-haul truck driver. The story of how her parents met was a sweet one—how her mother had been hitchhiking, back in the days when people actually hitchhiked across the country, en route to a Grateful Dead concert in Big Sur—when the ex-Marine with a buzz cut named Bill Scribner picked her up in his Kenworth. The unlikely pair disagreed on everything except their attraction for each other.

Scribner was based in Wyoming and he drove his truck for eleven months and hunted elk the other, and he could quote Shakespeare and Paul Harvey without missing a beat. He wanted to marry but Cassie's mother refused to engage in the formality of a ceremony and a contract, so they had an understanding of sorts. He doted on Cassie during his rare overnight visits, and he'd taken her on several cross-country runs when she was ten and eleven. While he drove and the country went by, he told her that Americans had a restless gene and he must have been double-dosed with it. But he said he performed an important and honorable service, and he was proud of his profession. He told Cassie that professional long-haul truck drivers like himself were "Knights of the Road" and they had their own code of conduct and civility. She remembered him telling her he was "building America, one truckload at a time." She was proud of him also, and noted how other truckers looked up to him with respect and admiration when he strode into truck stops or met foremen to pick up or drop off a load. There was even a time when she thought she'd like to follow in his footsteps. She wanted to be a Knight of the Road, too.

But Bill was struck down with inoperable brain cancer that took him down so quickly he was dead by her thirteenth birthday.

Still, though, she thought of her father and those glorious trips through a warm sentimental haze. And she was disgusted there were a few drivers out there who had penetrated the knighthood in an evil way.

From the darkened doorway, Ben said, "Momma, what are you doing? What are you looking at?" and she was jolted back to the present. She reflexively reached up and closed the laptop screen.

"Ben . . ."

"I miss Dad," Ben said, and stepped into the light. He was five years old, wearing his flannel pajamas with the cowboy print. His feet were bare and looked cold. He was dark-headed and chubby, like his mother.

"Come here," she said, sliding back in her chair and opening her arms.

He shuffled forward, arms to his sides, and thumped his head into her breasts.

"I miss him," Ben said, his voice muffled by her clothing.

"I know you do, honey. So do I. But you need to get to bed and get some sleep."

"I'm hungry."

"Ah."

"Maybe if I got a snack."

"I'll get you a glass of milk."

"And maybe some cake . . ."

"No cake," she said, extricating herself. "Milk and off to bed."

As he settled into a chair she poured a glass of milk from the refrigerator after checking the expiration date. Her mother was loath to throw anything away until it was consumed. The milk was okay.

"What are you doing?" Ben asked when she sat back down.

"Working. Sometimes I have to work late."

He nodded, not very empathetic, and gulped the milk down and shivered.

"Don't drink so fast," she said.

He shrugged.

Before he could settle in, she guided him out of the kitchen and down the dark hall. As they passed the bedroom occupied by her mother, she heard, "Cassie? Is everything all right?"

"Yes, Mom."

"I heard talking."

"Ben."

"Is he sick again?"

"Just sleepwalking," she said. She wasn't sure why she fudged on the answer.

"I'm *not* sleepwalking," Ben whispered over his shoulder. Cassie shushed him.

"There's cake in the fridge," her mother called out.

"I told you," Ben said accusingly.

"Good *night*," Cassie sang through the door to her mother.

Her mother said something else she didn't hear, and

Cassie ushered Ben to bed and tucked him in. She straightened up his blankets and quilts against the cold and kissed him good night on the cheek.

"Night, Ben."

"Night, Mom. I love you."

"I love you, too."

A shaft of moonlight from the window illuminated the framed photos on Ben's dresser. Three photos of his father Jim Dewell, one in the dress uniform after basic, two in his desert fatigues. In the one Ben liked best, Jim leaned back against a wall of sandbags cradling a machine gun. He wore a pistol on his belt and a smirk on his face.

Ben didn't actually miss his father because he'd never met him. But he knew if he said it, Cassie would always react with sympathy. Cassie knew it, too. She sometimes wondered if she'd done the right thing, raised Ben the right way. But she was new at this, and didn't know better. She'd had no real road map from her own mother.

Ben was a boy through and through. He spent hours wordlessly disassembling his toys and putting them back together. He knew the makes and models of cars and trucks on the street, and he'd declared recently that as soon as he could he wanted to hunt deer and elk. There was a poster of Tim Tebow when he was the Bronco quarterback, on his wall despite her grandmother's disdain for the man and his overt Christianity. Ben's career path, he'd stated without doubt over breakfast cereal the week before, was to be an NFL quarterback, join the army, and drive tanks and later tractors.

He wouldn't get married and he'd eat elk meat for dinner. Cassie had stifled a smile when her mother reacted to the declaration with outright horror.

She closed his door and padded down the dark hallway, considered going to her own bedroom, and decided against it for now. She was still too wired. She thought of the missing Sullivan girls, Cody out there somewhere not responding, the way the sheriff had played her, and raising a boy in a home with a mother who worked too many hours and a grandmother who was crazy as a tick. She tried not to resent Jim for getting killed and abandoning her. It always bothered her that she'd never seen that gleeful smirk he showed in the photo in real life. Like he was really enjoying what he was doing and Afghanistan in general, and certainly much more than working back at the state highway shop to pay the mortgage with a fat wife and a crying baby at home.

He'd died in the Battle of Wanat in 2008 in Afghanistan. She was eight months pregnant at the time. The official letter from the Department of Defense said Jim Dewell had been killed when two hundred Taliban guerillas attacked the village in the province of Nuristan. Eight other Americans had been killed and twenty-seven wounded. An investigation launched by the government concluded that no negligence was involved and that "by their valor and their skill, they successfully defended their positions and defeated a determined, skillful, and adaptable enemy." Words from a different era, she thought when she read them, about a battle no one had heard of in a war no one cared about.

Except Ben, of course, who idolized his father with Cassie's encouragement. To Ben, his father was a hero and a god. No man—or Cassie—could compare with poor dead Jim. She was proud of her husband, that he'd given his life for the country. They knew she was pregnant when he shipped out. They'd married the week after she told him. And if he hadn't been killed, he was due back for the birth. She wondered if he thought of her in his last seconds. She wondered if he thought they'd had a happy marriage. And she wondered if she did. It seemed so long ago.

Then *bam!*—five years. Five years with Ben as the only man in her life. Five years where she didn't dare bring a man home who would pale in comparison with the mythic Jim Ben believed in. Not that there hadn't been a few opportunities. Unmarried—and a few married—men at both the academy and the sheriff's department had tried. A couple were even, maybe, okay. Not drug addicts or rednecks or total losers. Maybe there would be a right time, and a right man. When Ben could handle it, and maybe even encourage it. But Cassie couldn't imagine when that would be.

Cassie stopped and closed her eyes and tried to picture Jim in her mind. It frightened her she couldn't see his face anymore. And it bothered her that when she thought of him she recalled the photo on Ben's dresser instead.

She checked her cell phone on the table for messages. There were none. Then, keeping the laptop closed, she hesitated for a moment and called Jenny Hoyt's phone.

Cassie didn't want to get immersed again in the contents of her laptop, or speculate without evidence.

Jenny answered after one ring.

"I'm sorry to call you so late. Were you sleeping?"

"I wish I could. But it's okay. I was just sitting here waiting and when the phone rang I thought it might be Cody."

Cassie paused. "So he hasn't been in touch?"

"Not for a while. Two hours, to be exact. He texted Justin and asked if he'd heard anything from those girls, and he sent me a text saying he was meeting with a highway patrolman in Emigrant. I haven't heard anything since."

Cassie imagined Cody drinking, spewing his philosophy and buying rounds for the local alcoholics. Forgetting to check his phone or not caring enough to do so.

"My mind just keeps conjuring up things," Jenny said as much to herself as to Cassie, Cassie thought. "Like maybe he got into some kind of trouble. Or if he's on another goddamned toot. I want to think that isn't the case. I know there are dead spots down there without cell service. But . . ." she trailed off.

Cassie wasn't sure what to say. "I haven't heard from him, either."

"I'm his wife," Jenny said sharply. "He knows the rules. He's supposed to check in."

Silence.

Cassie tried to make her voice professional, to jolt Jenny out of her pique. "I'm working on the case with him. I was corresponding with him back and forth. He needs me to do background. When was the last time you called his phone?"

"Fifteen minutes ago," Jenny said, her voice cracking. "Even though he made me promise years ago not to call him when he was on an investigation. He was always afraid he'd forget to mute his phone and the ring would create a problem. But this is an emergency, so I called. But it rang a few times and went straight to his stupid message."

"I see," Cassie said.

"I'm getting scared. And Justin is"—she lowered her voice to a whisper—"wrung out. He's not sure to be mad at his father or worried about him. And this Ted Sullivan has called twice wanting to talk directly to Cody. He's getting hysterical, like he blames us for this. He acts like I'm keeping Cody from talking to him or something. I want to tell him to piss up a rope, but I understand how he feels. I can't even imagine what he's going through. Or the girls' mother."

"Let me know if Cody calls or texts," Cassie said.

After a beat, Jenny said, "I will."

"I'll do the same."

"Okay." Then, "Now I'm really getting worried."

Cassie didn't respond.

"If he's on a toot," Jenny said, "I'll personally kill him. I will, I swear."

Cassie nodded. She understood. "I'm getting off the phone in case he calls."

"Good idea. Me, too."

Cassie sat back down at the table and glanced at the clock. Too long, she thought. Even if Cody had lost

control of himself he would have at least lied to them
by now.

On impulse, Cassie keyed Cody's cell phone number
and pressed SEND. It rang twice and she was surprised
by the soft electronic click on the other end. Cody had
answered.

"Cody, Cassie Dewell. I haven't heard back from
you—"

The call terminated. She looked at her phone to verify what happened. Cody had answered, but immediately dropped the call. Or was the cell signal on the
other send so poor it couldn't maintain the connection?

She tried again. When it went directly to voice mail,
she repeated herself and said, "and neither has Jenny.
Obviously, we're getting concerned. Contact us as soon
as possible, even if you don't have anything to report. If
I don't hear from you in fifteen minutes, I'm going to
blow the cover off this. I assume you don't want that to
happen."

She hesitated, wondering if she should say more,
then killed the call.

Then she glanced at the digital clock on the stove
and noted the time.

27.

Ronald C. Pergram, the Lizard King, nosed the Case tractor onto the trailer for the second time that night. The cold night air within the cab smelled of diesel fumes and upturned soil. Hard white stars undulated through the spires of exhaust from the engine.

When the tracks and tires were firmly on the platform, he killed the engine and climbed out. His back ached and his neck was stiff from tension and concentrating on the work and he could barely turn it. Because of the harsh white light thrown by the headlamps of the tractor as he dug the second large hole in the floor of the mountain valley, his eyes weren't yet acclimated to the dark. His ears rang from the percussive rattle of the engine that was now ticking furiously as it cooled. So furiously, he almost didn't hear the burr of the cell phone in the dark behind him.

So instead of chaining the tractor to the trailer and

tightening the turnbuckles, he stepped off the platform onto the soft dirt and cocked his head toward the sound. He saw the phone light up in the gloom about twenty feet away at belt level. Then it rose and illuminated Legerski's wide face in the light. Pergram saw Legerski press the phone to his ear for a second or two, then lower it and kill the call.

He waited. Legerski just stood there in the dark, saying nothing. Then: "Shit."

"Who was that?"

"Some woman," Legerski said. "Trouble, maybe."

"Meaning what?"

The trooper held the phone out. "She might be the one who's been sending him stuff all night."

Pergram was confused for a moment, but the confusion was overtaken by sudden anger. "You kept that deputy's phone? Why didn't you throw it in the hole with the truck? What the hell are you thinking?"

Pergram's last glimpse of Cody Hoyt's pickup was as he pushed it into the huge hole with the blade on the front of the tractor. From the height of the cab, he could look down over the bed of the vehicle and see Hoyt's body doubled over on the passenger seat floorboard. The side and back windows of the vehicle were spattered from the inside with blood and hair and brain matter. Legerski had stood off to the side as if supervising the work, which the Lizard King resented the hell out of. As far as he was concerned, someone who'd never operated heavy equipment had no right waving his arms around or shouting, "Can't you make the hole deeper?" Nevertheless, he'd dug out a fifteen-foot-deep casket-shaped hole, pushed the truck into it, and carefully backfilled the excavation and run his treads over the top to tamp down the soil. When he was through it looked similar to the excavation he'd done earlier in the night and multiple times before: like a grave for a giant. When the hole was filled, he raked over the mound with the teeth of the backhoe to make it look more natural to the naked eye. After a winter of heavy snow and the spring runoff, they'd seed it with prairie grass seed pinched from the highway department shop that would sprout on the top and reclaim the bare ground. Within a year, it would be difficult to tell the topsoil had ever been disturbed. While he worked, he ignored Legerski in the dark but was aware the trooper was standing there, head down, looking at his phone.

But it turned out it wasn't his phone. It was Cody Hoyt's phone. And Legerski still had it.

"We might have a problem," Legerski said.

"Hell yes we do. I'm working my ass off to erase all the evidence and you're carrying around the phone of a cop you murdered. Why didn't you get rid of it? Throw it in there? Wasn't the hole big enough for you?"

"Shut the fuck up," Legerski said. His voice was flat.

Pergram shut his mouth.

"Do what you need to do to get that tractor secure," the trooper said. "We need to talk inside."

He gestured toward the cab of the one-ton truck they'd used to bring the tractor out. Pergram had driven, keeping tight to the bumper of Hoyt's pickup, which was driven by Legerski, now in civilian clothes. The trooper had left his uniform in his cruiser and hidden the cruiser behind the First National Bar.

As Pergram secured the chains from the trailer to the tractor and tightened the turnbuckles, he seethed with resentment. He didn't like the way Legerski had spoken to him, in that tone, the way he put him off and said he'd wait inside. The way he'd been talking to him all night, ordering him around, giving him commands since the shooting. And the whole time he was holding Hoyt's phone—a piece of equipment that could tie them directly to the dead cop.

The Lizard King didn't like to be told what to do. Still, though, he'd done what Legerski had ordered. They really hadn't talked since the shooting; it had all been one-way.

Pergram paused for a moment before climbing up into the cab of the one-ton. He hadn't quite processed what had happened or how they'd deal with it. The girls he'd brought in seemed like a vague and distant memory because so much had transpired since. He needed sleep, rest, food, and time to gather his thoughts. The handful of white crosses—known as "trucker speed"— he'd taken earlier would soon wear off. Then he needed the kind of release he dreamed about.

He climbed up into the cab and shut the door. Legerski sat there, staring out the dirty windshield.

"Start it up, will you? I'm freezing to death."

Pergram started the motor and goosed the heater fan.

"It'll take a few minutes."

"Yeah."

"You shot a fucking *cop*," Pergram said. "That isn't what I signed up for."

"And you buried him."

"But what now? We're fucked. You know what they do when you shoot one of their own, you of all people."

Legerski shrugged. "He used to be a cop. Not anymore. He was suspended. And he wasn't well liked. He had a reputation for going off the reservation."

"Still . . ."

"I know," Legerski said. "I can tell you're pissed at me. But what did you want me to do? Let him dig until he figured everything out? Is that what you would have done?"

Pergram shook his head, uncertain what the trooper was talking about.

"That's right," Legerski said. "The guy was a fucking bulldog. I tried to steer him toward the church but he wanted to start kicking doors down *tonight*. And he wanted me to go along with him. We wouldn't have had time for any kind of damage control before the shit hit the fan."

The trooper held out the phone he'd taken from Cody's body. "He's got someone working the back end, some broad. I think I know who it might be. She's been sending him texts and e-mails all night. That was her who called—someone named Cassie. Most of the stuff she sent is just things she pulled off the Internet and forwarded. But I saw where he asked her to pull the cases on those missing girls."

Pergram just stared. He didn't get what Legerski was saying.

"You're the one who pointed him toward the church," Pergram said. "He was going where you pointed him."

Legerski sighed impatiently and his eyes flashed in the moonlight. For the first time, Pergram wondered if the trooper would pull the gun he'd used on Hoyt and kill *him* now that the dead cop and his pickup were buried. After all, he could pin everything on the Lizard King. . . .

"Try to keep up with me here," Legerski said patiently. "I thought he'd work through the sheriff's department in Livingston or through the state. That means *me,* where I could direct traffic and make sure the investigation got stymied whenever it got too close. I had no idea he'd be crazy enough to show up tonight, or show up at all himself. Normal cops don't do things like that. He's not even in his county, so even if he wasn't suspended he'd need permission and cooperation down here. But by coming here himself . . . it screwed up everything. I had no choice."

"But did you have to kill him? I didn't like the asshole either, but—"

"He was starting to ask about you," Legerski said. "Tonight. We hadn't even gone out to the compound yet and he was already asking about *you.*"

Pergram felt his mouth go dry, and it wasn't just a symptom of the white crosses.

"He was going to put things together pretty fast," Legerski said. "When the church thing didn't go the way he wanted—and you know the situation there—he was going to shift his attention to you. With his helper up in Helena checking missing persons and with access to all the law enforcement databases, it would be a matter of time before he came after you."

Pergram said, "Which means you might be exposed."

"Which means I'd be exposed."

"For a minute there, I thought you were trying to help me," Pergram said. "I feel better now when I know you're only looking out for yourself."

Legerski snorted. "We've got this thing. But we aren't exactly blood brothers."

Pergram acknowledged the truth of that with a nod. He wished he wasn't so addled from exhaustion right now so he could think more clearly. He had the suspicion Legerski was setting something up but he couldn't figure out what it was.

Why wouldn't Legerski simply pull the untraceable throwdown piece he'd used on Hoyt and pop him? Then set up some kind of semiplausible narrative where the Lizard King went down for his acts?

Then it came to him. And he relaxed. He hoped his face didn't portray what he'd just realized—that Legerski could never harm Pergram as long as Pergram knew where evidence was that could incriminate him.

"So what do we do next?" Pergram asked, thinking of the steps he'd need to take to make sure the trooper didn't get ahead of him and figure out how to eliminate him from the picture.

"I know what we don't do. We don't spend any time

with those girls except to dump off some food and water."

"Fuck that," Pergram said. "I didn't deliver them so we could keep them holed up. I need what I need."

"You'll get it," Legerski said, his tone once again fused with the firm arrogance he'd used earlier. "But you'll have to wait until we're clear. Once we're clear, we do the whole thing just like we talked about. But not until I say we're clear. Got that?

"It'll get hot for a couple of days," Legerski said. "I've got to be nimble. This broad"—he shook the phone as if she were inside—"knows he met with me. I'll be the first stop when they look into it, so I've just got to cooperate and not throw off any suspicion. I can do that—I've done it all my life. And it won't take long before things go cold. They always do when there aren't any solid leads."

Pergram stared hard at the trooper. Not for the first time, he considered what his world would be like without him. He thought about the .380 in the pocket of his jumpsuit, and ran through a scenario where he drew it, worked the slide, and put a bullet into Legerski's face. He'd practiced the move enough so he knew he could do it quickly.

But then what? The next steps flummoxed him, although he savored the thought of having those girls to himself. At least until they came for him, the cops.

And he recalled why they'd gone into business together in the first place. Legerski needed a delivery mechanism for victims. And Pergram needed local protection.

"We still need each other," Legerski said, as if reading his mind.

"Yeah."

"So we stay away from them except to dump off the food. We do this together or not at all."

"Yeah, okay. But how long are we talking about? I've got another run in two days."

"That should be enough time," Legerski said.

"So what are you going to do?"

Legerski turned from him and fixed on something in the dark outside the windshield. "I'm going to work it from the inside," he said softly. "I'm going to stay on top of everything that's going on by making sure I'm in the middle of it. I'm going to take control, because that's what I do and that's what I'm good at. I can take this thing to dead-end after dead-end until there's no place else to go. The case will probably stay open for years, but there's no way they'll ever close it. I'll make sure it gets tied up into knots."

"You can do that?"

"Hell, yes. I've already gotten rid of the only real threat. If someone follows up they won't have that crazy look in their eyes. We're dealing with the typical nine-to-fivers here and they don't have anything to go on."

Pergram tried to think like a cop, now that he was more relaxed. "But instead of two missing girls we've now got a missing cop, too."

"Ex-cop," the trooper said. "And no one can ever determine where the girls went missing unless you fucked something up somewhere. They could have disappeared in Yellowstone, or Wyoming, or Idaho. No one knows where they ended up, right? You didn't fuck anything up?"

"I don't think so," he said, his mind spinning, recalling everything that had transpired.

"Then all they've got is a suspended alcoholic who drove down here in the middle of the night and never came back. No one saw him except you, me, and Jimmy. They sure as hell won't find his vehicle. How are they going to figure that one out? Especially if the lead investigator on the highway—me—gently steers them to where there's nothing to go on?"

Pergram nodded. He got it. Legerski was way out ahead of him already. So far ahead, Pergram thought, that he'd probably already figured out how to throw him under the bus. Except . . .

"What about Jimmy?"

"We can trust Jimmy."

"Can we?"

"Yeah," Legerski said softly, "I'll make sure Jimmy is no problem."

He said it in a way that gave Pergram confidence.

"What about the gimp?" he said. "She's probably running her mouth and scaring the shit out of those new girls. She'll have them wanting to die before we get to them."

Legerski nodded, agreeing. "You take care of her."

"When? Tonight?"

"How long do you want her to keep talking?"

Pergram saw the logic in it. "I'll never get to sleep," he said, moaning.

"Neither will I," the trooper said, gesturing to the phone.

"I need to get all the texts and e-mails off of it so I know what she knows and who I'm dealing with. Then I'll flush the SIM card and trash the phone. There won't be a trace of Cody Hoyt to be found. Believe me, I know how to do this."

The Lizard King nodded. Then, softening his voice, "We could go to the basement now and see how those girls are doing. Before the sun comes up and things start happening."

Legerski started to object, but caught himself. He seemed to be considering the idea. Pergram felt buoyed.

At that second, the phone in Legerski's hand lit up and a text message chimed. He looked at it and spat a curse, then turned it toward Pergram.

It read, CASSIE: I'M ON MY WAY.

28.

"Do you know what time it is? What day, even?" Gracie asked Danielle.

"I'm not sure," Danielle said in a soft, slurred voice.

"He took our phones."

"Yeah."

Danielle had awakened an hour before and had been sick to her stomach, like Gracie had been. Gracie had cradled her sister, supporting her, while she threw up in the far corner of the room. There was nothing to clean up the mess, though, and the stagnant air was sour.

There was no light and no seepage in the walls to indicate whether it was morning or night. Gracie had become used to the gloom. The single space heater hummed and glowed orange, creating long dark shadows. It didn't throw out enough light to illuminate the corners of the room but, like an open fire, it had become the center of their world and she found herself staring at it; thin red coils stretching from left to right, the warm air pushed out by a tiny humming fan. Gracie and Danielle sat cross-legged a few feet from the heater, which was positioned next to the ragged woman. She didn't give any indication that she planned to move from her spot. The concrete beneath them never really warmed up. They shared a thin blanket. Gracie found herself constantly shifting her position as her buttocks and legs got cold. The blanket was too short to double over so both of them could sit on it, and cold seeped through the fabric.

Danielle slumped forward with her arms wrapped around her knees and stared straight ahead. Her face was slack and her mouth was parted. When Gracie reached over and turned her sister's face toward her, Danielle's eyes looked frightening—as if there was nothing behind them. And her sister didn't resist Gracie's gesture, or blink.

"Danielle?"

No response.

"*Danielle.*"

Danielle leaned back and pulled away. Her sister had always been annoying, but in a superconfident, bubbly way. She'd never seen her like this, even in Yellowstone.

Gracie closed her eyes. The situation they were in seemed like a horrible dream. Her head was foggy and she didn't feel fully conscious. She wondered if she were in shock, and she preferred the sense of cushion of unreality to what it must really be like to be half-naked and imprisoned in a dark cold room with a frightening one-legged woman.

"I feel sick," Danielle said, wiping at her mouth with the back of her hand. "I feel like I could throw up again." She shot a glance over her shoulder toward the dark corner.

"Try to hold it," the woman said. "It reeks enough in here as it is."

The woman's voice was grating; scratchy and louder than necessary in the small room, as if she could only speak at one level: annoying. It was the kind of harsh voice that penetrated walls.

"Do *you* know what time it is?" Gracie asked her.

The woman snorted. "You lose track after a while when it's dark all the time. I don't have a fucking clue."

"I'm worried about my sister," Gracie confessed.

"She's sick because of the roofies," the woman said to Gracie. "They usually inject you with roofies. You'll both be feeling it for a while. My advice is to enjoy it while you can."

When the woman spoke, her face seemed to collapse in on itself because of her missing teeth.

Gracie nodded, remembering the driver leaning into the car with the needle. Feeling the sharp pain of the needle prick.

"You know," the woman said, "the date rape drug."

Gracie nodded, unsure. She feared with Danielle it was something much worse.

Gracie said, *"They?"*

"What?" the woman asked.

Danielle looked over, confused.

"You said *they*. We only saw one guy, the truck driver. Are you saying there's more than him?" The idea terrified her. Not just that there was more than one, but that what the woman suggested was that they were organized. That this wasn't a first-time thing. That Danielle and her and the woman weren't the first victims. This room, this terrible place, was a victim *factory*.

No, Gracie almost yelled out. She couldn't let it happen to her and her sister. She'd step up and figure out a way to fight back. First, though, she needed more information in order to help form a plan.

"What's your name?" Gracie asked the woman, taking her off guard.

"What's your'n?" the woman asked back, cocking her head suspiciously.

"I'm Gracie Sullivan. This is my sister, Danielle."

"She don't say much."

"That isn't normal, believe me."

"Danielle and Gracie," the woman repeated, trying the names out as if they were a foreign language. "I'm Krystyl. That's spelled K-R-Y-S-T-Y-L. It's the second *y* that fucks people up. Krystyl Meecham. I go by my given name, not the name of the asshole I used to be married to."

Gracie nodded. She'd never met a real person named Krystyl, and thought if she ever did she would probably look like the skeletal one-legged woman a few feet away. But she didn't say anything, and wanted to get the conversation back to where she'd left it.

"I'm from Salt Lake," Krystyl said. "Originally.

That's where my family is from. My dad used to say we're just a tribe of wild-ass redneck jack-Mormons who wouldn't come to no good. I guess you could look at me and say he was right."

"You said they," Gracie prompted.

"Yeah," Krystyl said, screwing up her face in obvious revulsion. "There's two of them most of the time, but sometimes there's three. All of 'em are repulsive fuckers."

Gracie felt a chill run up her back and it wasn't from the cold room.

"What . . . what do they do?" Gracie asked in a whisper.

She couldn't tell if Krystyl was smiling or grimacing when she said, "What don't they do? Whatever they can think of. Whatever they want to. You're just a piece of meat and they do whatever."

Krystyl sighed and readjusted herself and leaned forward. When she did her body blocked half of the grille panel of the space heater and Gracie felt the absence of heat immediately. "They ream you everywhere. They make you bleed and then they yell at you for bleeding. They put things into you they brought along with them. They'll laugh and make you feel like a piece of trash until you beg them to just kill you. And they got a camera. They play to the camera."

Gracie thought Krystyl sounded almost perversely pleased to tell them, and she was physically repelled. Krystyl seemed to have accepted her fate. Gracie couldn't conceive of giving in.

"I got to admit," Krystyl said, "I just shut myself off

now. I don't think about what they're doing to me and I try to think of something nice. I let my mind go far away. Dad used to take us fishing for catfish. I didn't like it much but that's what I think about while they're goin' at it. Another time and place."

"Jesus," Gracie gasped, tears welling in her eyes. She turned to Danielle, horrified. Her sister would likely get the worst of it. But Danielle didn't seem to understand the conversation.

"Danielle," Gracie said, "Please *talk* to me?"

Her sister didn't respond.

Krystyl said, "Maybe they'll be nicer to you girls. You're all young and tight and I guess they'd like that. Me, I'm a hag. I wasn't always this bad but they made me worse. When you get treated like an animal you turn into one, and I'm no better than a fucking animal to them. Or to me." Strangely, she cackled at that.

"How long have you been here?" Gracie asked.

"Fuck if I know," Krystyl said, "Couple weeks, I guess. Longer, maybe."

"Were there others?"

Krystyl cackled again. "Look at the walls, see the scratch marks? See the blood all over the walls and the floors? There have been plenty of others. I met one of 'em when I first got here. Her name was Bonnie. She was from Oregon somewhere, and she was a bitch on wheels. A real nutcase, but maybe she was because of what they done to her."

Krystyl shook her head and coughed. "I think she was sort of getting used to them, kind of looking forward to them coming to get her. She acted kind of possessive toward me, like I was the other woman or something. Like I was here to break them up. They put us together once and it was a disaster, so they got rid of her."

"What do you mean?" Gracie asked.

"One of 'em just took a gun and popped her in the back of the head. Right there in front of me. I ain't never seen something like that before.

"Now I've been thinking they're getting tired of me. They'd rather use me as a fuckin' punching bag than anything else anymore. But I figured they might keep me around until they could get some fresh meat. And it looks like they did."

Gracie found it hard to breathe, and she closed her eyes.

"The driver?" Gracie asked.

"Yeah, he's one of 'em. He likes to be called the Lizard King. I don't know his real name and I don't want to know. And don't ask me who the other two are, I don't know. All I know is one is big and fat and the other ain't. You better do whatever they say or they'll fuck you up."

"Where are we?" Gracie asked her. She knew the answer would include the word "fuck" since everything else did.

"Fuck if I know."

"Are we in Montana?"

"It don't matter, does it? We're in fucking hell. That could be Montana."

Gracie scooted herself toward Danielle on the blanket, as much to be closer to her sister as to feel more of the heat from the space heater Krystyl was blocking with her body.

"Where did they grab you?" Gracie asked. "The truck driver, I mean."

"Outside Gillette, Wyoming," Krystyl said. "I was workin' the truck stop servicing drivers . . ."

And she suddenly stopped speaking and sucked in her breath. Her cheeks went hollow and her eyes bulged.

"What?" Danielle said in sudden terror, but Gracie shushed her. She'd heard it, too. Or felt it. A footfall or thump of some kind outside the room that vibrated through the concrete.

The three of them sat frozen for a moment. A rectangular metal panel slid back on the door revealing a dim wedge of yellow light. Then a pair of eyes filled the wedge for a moment. The man was looking in at them. The slider slammed shut and they heard a jangle of keys outside the solid wood door.

Danielle grasped Gracie by her arm and they scooted back along the floor, legs pumping. They didn't stop until their backs were flat against the right corner of the room, the corner where Danielle hadn't gotten sick.

Gracie watched as if in a dream. She was almost beyond terror at this point. The more sounds there were—jangling keys, the thunk of a bolt being thrown back, the aggressive squeak of rusted hinges—the more her mind seemed to check out. It was as if she'd stepped aside into another room to watch herself, like she wasn't actually there.

The door swung open and someone filled it. Someone large and blocky, like the driver had been, but she was blinded by an intense flashlight beam in her eyes. Because there had been no real light in the room, the beam blinded her fully. She felt Danielle cower next to her, felt her sister pull up her legs and bury her head behind them, sitting in a tight fetal position.

Although she couldn't see past the light, the man said, "And how are my two sweethearts doing?"

Gracie couldn't speak and didn't want to.

"You'll get used to it," the man said. Then Gracie could hear him sniffing.

"If you're going to throw up, use that chemical toilet over against the wall. Don't foul your own nest. I'll bring you a mop and a bucket later to clean this place up."

Gracie had seen the white plastic box but didn't know what it was. The flashlight burned her face and she shut her eyes against it.

"Don't act so damned scared," the man said.

"Who are you?" Gracie asked.

"Your new best friend," he said, and prodded the flashlight beam toward Danielle. "What—don't she know how to talk?"

"She's scared. We're both scared."

Then, turning and whipping his flashlight away from them toward Krystyl, "What kind of shit has she been feeding you girls, anyway?"

Neither answered. Gracie heard the scuffle of heavy shoes on the concrete floor, the voice no longer directed at them. She opened her eyes to see the beam of light still on Krystyl, who refused to look at it. The powerful light made hollows out of her eyes as it hit the side of her face.

"What have you been telling them, anyway? You been lying to them? Filling them with your shit?"

"No." Krystyl's voice was resigned, as if the lie was perfunctory.

"Come with me, gimp."

Gracie couldn't tell if there was more than one man at the door. She didn't think so but there was no way of knowing it.

The man clicked off his flashlight and it was totally dark.

"I said"—and there was a heavy blow and a grunt of expelled air from Krystyl—"*come with me, gimp.*"

"I ain't movin'."

"The hell you ain't."

And with that Gracie heard two more solid blows, the slap of flesh, and a pathetic scream that faded into a low moan.

"Here," the man said to them, "Here's something to eat." She heard the sound of a paper bag hitting the floor and a second later something cold and cylindrical bumped against her foot. The sensation of it made her jump.

"Scc you girls later," the man said, and Gracie blinked and looked up.

Through and around green spangles in her eyes from being blinded, she saw Krystyl's body being dragged across the floor by her hair. The man was strong and pulled Krystyl through the door quickly. Then the door shut and the keys jangled and they were alone.

She looked down, still not quite there, and saw that the object that had rolled into her foot was a bottle of water. There were several other bottles on the floor as well, scattered when the bag broke open. It looked like convenience store food: packages of burritos and sandwiches and candy and nuts and a tin of Altoid mints.

Although it was impossible to determine if it came from outside the structure or simply from the other side of the door, she heard a scream, then a pop.

"Oh Jesus, we've got to get out of here," Gracie said with urgency.

Danielle didn't respond.

Gracie thought, *We will escape. We will survive.*

She would find a way. And it was up to her, and her alone.

29.

Cassie Dewell was wired and tired. She sat fuming in
the predawn in the county Ford Expedition last used by
Cody Hoyt to plant evidence at the Tokely crime scene.
It had been a bad morning so far and she couldn't
anticipate the day getting better. She'd parked in an
alcove of skeletal aspen trees on the shoulder of the
county road as the sky turned a rose color over the
western mountains. An icy breeze rattled the dried
leaves and sent them skittering down on the hood of
the Ford and the asphalt of the road. Through her windshield, she surveyed the vast immensity of Sheriff Tubman's frosted lawn and the magnificent home at the top
of the hill flanked by tall Austrian pines.

Wired and tired, she thought.

Inside, it was as if Cody were sitting next to her. It
smelled of stale cigarette smoke, fast food, and Cody's
lingering musky male odor. On the way there on the

winding mountain road, she'd spilled half the go cup of coffee from McDonald's on herself, and she'd cursed the girl who hadn't fitted the plastic lid on tightly before passing it through the drive-through window. The sting of the hot liquid on the skin of her inner thighs had ceased, but her slacks were stained and she sat in a soggy puddle. Cody was very particular about keeping the Ford neat and free of detritus that was a given in a vehicle used for long drives and stakeouts. He'd glare at her if she didn't properly dispose of a wrapper and he'd bark if she forgot to clear the cup holders of empty cans or bottles whenever they stopped to get out. They'd spent hours together inside the Ford and this was the first time she'd been alone in it or spilled anything inside. She didn't like it, either.

The empty Ford only reminded her she was on her own. Although she'd found the strength to raise a child and pursue her career without a husband around, this was something new. It was so much easier to second-guess Cody than it was to take the lead, and Cody was right: she *didn't* have the experience to confidently make the right moves. Lacking experience, she had to draw on a well of strength that, she hoped, wasn't running dry.

Steam from the spilled coffee fogged the inside of the windshield, and she reached forward and cleaned a loopy circle of it with the few dry McDonald's napkins she had left. Through the circle, she could see the long circular driveway that cut through the lawn to the Tubman house and exited fifty yards farther on the county road. The house was three stories and built of varnished logs. It had a steep roof, gables, and knotty pine columns out front hung with arts-and-crafts-style iron lanterns. On the side of the house was a trailer topped with four four-wheelers and another trailer with snow machines. A gigantic fifth-wheel recreational trailer nosed out from the trees from behind the structure.

The whole scene reminded her of a description she'd heard Cody Hoyt use more than once: "That's a pile of Montana money." Meaning the place was ostentatious in a laid-back, rural mountain way. But there was no doubt it cost a bundle.

She'd kept the Ford running to keep warm but placed it in park. Far up on the driveway, near the porch of the sheriff's home, was a small, orange, cylinder-shaped object. That morning's copy of the Helena *Independent*, delivered while it was still dark. She knew how important the newspaper was to Tubman, how he pored over every item and article that might mention the department, the county, his rivals, or him in particular. She assumed he'd come out soon to retrieve it.

When he did, he'd be in the open. And, she hoped, surprised by her presence and subsequent request.

A light came on in one of the upstairs windows. No one looked out. She waited, and another light lit the windows on the bottom floor on the right side of the house. She assumed it was the kitchen. Tubman was probably making coffee. Retrieving the paper would be next.

She reached up and grasped the shifter and engaged the transmission and rolled slowly forward. If this didn't go as she envisioned it, she thought, she might be doomed within the department and out on the street looking for work. Her stomach burbled and she set her mouth.

Wired and tired . . .

Earlier, Cassie was at home at the kitchen table in front of her laptop at four forty-five in the morning when her mother had flowed into the room. She'd spent the last three and a half hours digging deeply into Google and ViCAP and RIMN, both law-enforcement databases, finding what she could on the principals from the Church of Glory and Transcendence.

Cassie found it notable how information about the church, its membership, and its leadership had stopped abruptly following the death of founder and leader Stacy Smith three years before. Prior to her death, communication from the church was everywhere. Smith was quoted in local newspapers, national newsmagazines, and radio and television interviews. She seemed warm, kindly, and charismatic. Citizens in the area around the church seemed to tolerate and even like her and her membership in a "live-and-let-live" manner. But when Smith died, it was as if a clamp had been placed on the outflow of information. As if the new leadership wanted to operate in secrecy, or at least keep their heads down so they wouldn't be noticed. There was also a dearth of statements from ex-members as there had been before Smith's death.

She wondered if the membership, once burned, was quietly stocking up and rearming again for the apocalypse. Only this time, they wouldn't let their neighbors

in on the date? Arming up, Cassie knew, wasn't an unusual phenomenon at all in the state and throughout the
Rockies. With the poor economy and national financial
crisis, sales of guns and ammunition were at record
levels. She'd read departmental memos about it. More
and more people were dropping out, arming up, and
stockpiling food and gear.

Cassie speculated that the remaining membership
was literally bunkered in. All indications were that the
membership had foresworn interaction with the locals,
and they'd made a conscious decision not to engage in
any outreach. Since the membership had been built in
the first place through aggressive proselytizing, this
new tack seemed to go against the grain. How would the
church survive and pay the mortgage on the property,
Cassie wondered, if they didn't grow?

Maybe, she thought, they were adding to their ranks
by abducting young, lost people found along the nation's highways?

She felt sorry for the parents of the Sullivan girls
who were no doubt entertaining terrible scenarios of
their own. She tried to put herself in their place. What
if Ben was missing?

It was too horrible to contemplate.

She'd also delved deeply into the information provided
by the FBI's Highway Serial Killer Task Force. She'd
been reading about a trucker named Bruce Meersham
who'd been arrested and convicted of killing and dis-
membering a truck stop prostitute the previous year.
Meersham had been caught by happenstance by a high-

way patrol officer at Interstate 24 near Nashville. The trooper had been hidden in a speed trap and couldn't be seen from the highway, and the truck hadn't been speeding. But as a tractor trailer passed by, the highway patrolman observed a plastic bag thrown from the window that landed twenty yards away.

The trooper noted the license plate of the semi, then checked out the bag of refuse and found a pair of severed female hands. He called it in, and Meersham was arrested fifty miles away at a weigh station. Inside the cab of his Mack, law enforcement found three more tightly wrapped plastic bags of body parts all belonging to the same woman. Meersham was arrested and later convicted of murder, and he refused to cooperate further although it was highly suspected he'd been involved in multiple similar crimes across the country. He entered prison at age fifty-seven. Cassie shook her head. There was no way a man *started* doing that at age fifty-seven. She wondered how long he'd been at it, how many women he'd kidnapped, raped, mutilated, and scattered across the country over the years, and how many others like him were out there. She wasn't sure why she couldn't tear herself away from that line of inquiry in regard to the missing Sullivan girls. But the more she read, the more agitated and angry she became.

When this was over, she vowed, when the girls were located and Cody was found, she wanted to learn more about the phenomenon because it chilled her. She knew from the academy and her limited experience that when someone was missing or a body found, the investigation became intensely local. Who knew the victim? Who might want to harm the victim? Who might know the history of the victim and their interaction with others in the area? That's where they started. In fact, that's exactly the methodology Cody used to target B. G. Myers.

But if the killer wasn't local, if he was simply passing through the state and would be gone again in hours, how could law enforcement track him down? And if a serial killer was strategic and diabolical, what better profession to take up than becoming a long-haul trucker?

She shivered and felt the hairs on her arm rise.

And Cody hadn't checked in with her. She'd expected a reply of some sort to her text telling him she was on the way. Either warning her off or telling her where to meet him. But there had been nothing.

Her mother walked heavily across the linoleum in the kitchen in her bare feet, her robe billowing around her.

"Your constant clacking is keeping me awake and giving me a headache," her mother said dramatically. "I hope I haven't used up all the Tylenol."

"My *clacking*?"

"What you do on your computer," her mother said, mimicking Cassie by holding her hands up and waggling her fingers as if typing manically on a keyboard.

"I've tried to be as quiet as I could."

"Plus, I can hear you moan. And sometimes you snort."

Cassie sighed and sat back, her concentration broken. She stared at her mother. She was wearing the robe Cassie disliked, the one with the huge batik face of Che Guevara wearing his beret across the front. "I know," her mother said, gesturing at her robe. "I know you hate it."

"He was a totalitarian and a cold-blooded murderer."

"You have your opinion," her mother said, sniffing.

"It's not my opinion. He was a brute. Do some *research*, Mom. He's nobody to celebrate. Around Ben, especially."

"It's just a sentimental thing to me," her mother said. She'd once claimed she bought the robe from a vendor on the way to Woodstock in 1969. Around the time she'd changed her name from Margie to Isabel because Isabel sounded more exotic and revolutionary. Cassie knew Isabel's participation at Woodstock never happened, although she had no doubt her mother had come to believe it over the years. If all the people of her mother's generation who claimed to have been at Woodstock had actually been there, Cassie knew, the concert would have hosted millions more kids than were actually there. But there was no point in getting into that argument again.

Isabel looked down at her robe and said, "Besides, he's very handsome."

"For a killer."

"How did I raise a girl to be so judgmental?" her mother said, distracted by the difficulty of the child-proof cap on the bottle of Tylenol.

Cassie bit her lip. She wanted to say, *You never raised me at all. You dumped me with Grandma and*

Grandpa while you chased around the country for your causes. Sometimes I saw more of Bill than I saw of you. But it was a fight she couldn't have, because she needed her mother there for Ben. Isabel had spent the first half of her life neglecting her and the second half engaging in unspoken extortion.

"Let me open it," Cassie said, and her mother handed over the bottle.

Cassie unscrewed the cap and gave it back.

"What's so important that you need to keep me awake all night with your *clacking*?" her mother asked, shaking three tablets into the palm of her hand.

"I've got a pair of missing teenage girls and now a missing partner," Cassie said flatly.

Her mother paused and looked at her with discomfort. She was sixty-two years old, wide-faced and blousy, with once-red hair that was so infused with gray it looked pink. She didn't like uncomfortable subjects, like missing people.

"Here in town?" her mother asked.

"No. Somewhere out on the highway."

"Why is it your concern?"

"*I'm a cop.*"

"I know," her mother said, turning to fill a glass of water, "I just like to pretend you aren't."

"What would you rather have me do?" Cassie asked, feeling the heat rise in her neck. And immediately regretting she'd asked.

"I don't know," her mother said with a sigh, and Cassie was grateful she'd diffused the question. Anything to avoid an argument with her strong-willed daughter. After all, nasty little asides and innuendos worked better for her over the long run and always had.

"Mom," Cassie said, "I'll probably have to go out of town for the day."

Her mother swallowed the pills one by one before saying, "When will you get home?"

"I don't know for sure."

"I have my book club at six. You know that. We're doing a Wally Lamb book and you know I have some things to say."

"I know," Cassie said. "I don't ask you to do this very often. But I might not be able to get back by five."

"This is happening with more frequency," her mother said. The words weren't said in anger, but in a kind of martyred resignation.

"This is important, Mom. I really appreciate you being able to take care of Ben, and I know it's tough on you. But we're talking about the lives of two girls, and who knows what with my former partner."

Isabel screwed up her face at the mention of Cody Hoyt. They'd not hit it off when they met for the first time the previous summer. Cody and Cassie had been headed toward the Justice Center to clock out for the evening when they saw half a dozen people chanting on the courthouse steps. Cody pulled to the curb to ogle them, and Cassie pointed out her mother, who had brought Ben along to the Occupy Helena demonstration. When Isabel walked over with Ben in tow, Cody had sized her up from head to foot, from stocking cap to Keen sandals, with a sneer on his face. He waited until Ben was out of earshot and told Isabel, "Only lazy slackers on food stamps have the leisure time to chant slogans. The rest of us have to work."

Isabel said, "He's the awful misogynist redneck you work with?"

Cassie nodded, surprised by the half-smile pulling at her mouth. "He's not a misogynist, necessarily," she said. "He hates everyone equally."

"Well, if I were you—"

"You aren't," Cassie said, cutting Isabel off. She closed her laptop harder than necessary.

Cassie had dressed and driven her Honda to the Justice Center and exchanged her car for the Ford at the transportation desk. The officer behind the counter was surprised she was in so early and wanted to talk, but Cassie signed out the vehicle, took the keys, waved him off, and walked down the silent halls of the sheriff's department. She hoped she could find somebody interested in going with her to find Cody, even though the prospects were slim.

As she passed forensics, she saw a bar of light under the door and knocked. Alexa Manning, the young crime scene tech, let her in. They were both surprised to see each other. Alexa was tall and slim with bone-white skin and short-cropped black hair and small brown eyes. Cassie didn't know Alexa well, but the two had a bond because they were both single women in the department and had each heard grumbling and whispered asides about their unavailability because "one was fat and stuck up and the other one's a dyke."

Alexa was working late on the Tokely case, she said,

because her vacation started that day and she wanted to get as much work done as possible before she and her partner went to Moab for the holiday weekend. Cassie sighed, resigned to the fact that Alexa wouldn't be able to go with her either, and asked Alexa what she'd found out. Alexa beamed.

"We've got B. G. Myers at the scene," she said.

Cassie sighed. "I know about the wrappers you found in the trash can."

"We've got more."

"Really? What?" Cassie was genuinely surprised.

"On the south side of the house there was a set of tire tracks and boot prints frozen into the mud. Do you remember seeing them?"

"No."

"Cody pointed them out to us and we made plaster casts. And guess what? The tire treads match up with the tires on Myers's pickup. And the boot prints are the same size and sole as Myers's work boots."

Cassie took that in. "So that means . . ."

"We've got that guy dead to rights that he was absolutely there at Roger Tokely's house."

"So the wrappers and the stuff we found in the trash?"

"That's good, too, but we can't use them because Cody put them there. Luckily, they steered us in the right direction and we found more to corroborate the theory. The more evidence, the better, right? That's what you guys always tell us."

Cassie looked at the plaster casts on the workbench and the photos Alexa had taken of the tires and B. G.'s boots. They matched up.

"Good work," Cassie said.

"You don't sound that excited. Shouldn't you be more excited? I am. This is the first murder investigation I've been on and we cracked it, man."

"I am excited."

Alexa laughed uncomfortably, as if she couldn't figure out what she'd done wrong.

"Really," Cassie said. "This should do it. Thanks for working late to nail it down."

Alexa nodded, still perplexed.

"One question," Cassie said.

"Shoot."

"If you and Tex didn't have that receipt and the wrappers, would you ever have thought to go up to B. G.'s place and photograph his tires? Or his boots?"

Alexa looked at Cassie as if she were crazy.

"Of course not," Alexa said. "What—do you think we'd drive around the whole friggin' county trying to match up this plaster cast to a hundred thousand random tread patterns? Do you realize how many old trucks there are in Lewis and Clark County?"

Sheriff Tubman padded down his driveway in a blue bathrobe cinched tight and fat moccasin slippers. His hair was mussed and his ankles were skinny and mottled and so white they almost looked blue in the dawn. As he bent over to retrieve his newspaper he heard the sound of the motor and looked up, puzzled.

Cassie watched him closely as he registered who was in the county Ford. As she pulled up in front of him and stopped, he rose to full height and squinted at her through the windshield, holding the newspaper down at his side. His studied arrogance hadn't kicked in yet, which is what she counted on.

She shoved the big Ford into park and climbed out. The front bumper of the vehicle was just a few feet away from him. She got out and shut the door but kept the engine running. The purr of the motor was the only sound.

"Nice place," she said, walking up alongside the vehicle. She took a side step at the front and leaned back against the grille and crossed her arms under her breasts. It was a posture she'd seen Cody Hoyt assume many times; passive but judgmental at the same time. She'd been surprised how many times perps started yapping and volunteering information they never would otherwise because they assumed Cody had the goods on them.

"Why are you here so early, Officer Dewell?" Tubman asked. "I haven't even had my coffee yet. Did something happen during the night and you couldn't get ahold of me?"

"I never tried," Cassie said. A burst of dawn wind came up hard and cold and she saw leaves flee from trees in her peripheral vision.

"So what brings you up here to my home?" he asked, trying to smile. But it looked like a grimace.

"I've got a request."

He seemed to recover from the surprise for a moment and he stood tall and relaxed his shoulders. "What kind of request?" he asked, assuming command.

"No," she said, "It isn't a request. It's a demand."

He snorted, and looked over his shoulder at his house, as if expecting reinforcements.

She said, "You took advantage of me. You set me up to bring down my partner because you never liked him. I resent what you put me through and I don't like the results. You put a good man out on the street."

As if he couldn't help it, he lifted the small rolled-up newspaper, like there was something in it she must be angry about. She hadn't seen the paper that morning but realized there must be a story about Cody being fired. Tubman had likely called it in himself to make sure he was portrayed as a man who wouldn't tolerate dirty cops.

"Look," he said, "I haven't seen the story yet. I do know I praised your work to high heaven, the way you exposed a dishonest officer. You're probably going to come out of this as a big hero, so I don't know what your problem is."

"My problem," she said, "has nothing to do with your story. It's about two missing teenagers you've never heard of. Even though you screwed him, Cody drove down to Livingston last night to try and find them. He did it because he wanted to do the right thing."

"Livingston?" Tubman said, shaking his head and appealing to the shaft of sunlight that had flashed over the mountain and sequined the frost on his yard, "That's out of our jurisdiction. I don't know what the hell you're talking about, Dewell, and I think you need to consider what you're saying to me. And think about the fact that you're at my house in a county vehicle giving me a ration of shit for no reason I can think of."

She noticed that his face was flushed and if he had a chin it would be thrust at her. For a moment, she was taken aback. Then she remembered why she was there.

"Those girls I mentioned are missing," she said. "Teenagers from Colorado, aged sixteen and eighteen. They vanished last night off the highway between Yellowstone and Helena and they haven't been seen since. Cody's son knew them, so Cody drove down there to try and find them and as of a few hours ago he hasn't communicated back to me or to his family. We've got three missing people in Montana in the last thirteen hours. You know that every minute that goes by something bad could happen. I know how you feel about Cody, but this is bigger than that. I want the time to go down there myself and help him if I can to figure out what happened. And I want you to approve it."

Tubman again glanced over his shoulder at his home, as if to verify where he was. Then he turned his head and locked her eyes in.

"Cody Hoyt is drunk in some county jail or passed out on the side of some low-rent bar," he said. "This thing about missing girls is news to me and we'll deal with it through the proper channels if we're requested to even get involved. I've not heard a damned thing about it. So if you're asking to take leave right now, in the middle of a murder investigation and after I've praised you up one side and down the other to the media for your good work, you need to think long and hard about this."

He paused, and glared at her. "Because if you run away right now for your own stupid reasons, I can't defend you and I won't even try. You're needed here. We've got a murder investigation. You're the primary on it. And everybody's watching."

She said, "You're not hearing me. This isn't a debate. I'm taking the county vehicle down south and I'm going to find out what happened to Cody and those girls. Roger Tokely was murdered by B. G. Myers. We've got the proof. If you don't believe me, talk to Alexa Manning. Your renter, B. G., killed your other renter, Roger Tokely, over drugs."

At the word "renter," Tubman flinched. He simply stared at her with contempt she'd never seen from him.

"I know the deal," Cassie said. "Cody told me. I know what's going on with you and your payments. And when I look at this place," she said, gesturing toward the house and the recreational vehicles and the fifth-wheel trailer, "I know he was right. You let that feud go on in the Big Belts because you didn't want your rent checks to bounce. And you put me out front with the press because you'd get credit for bringing me into the department. And you sent me up there to shadow Cody to get rid of the one guy who could take you on. So don't patronize me now. I won't stand for it.

"I'm taking this Ford," she said, and patted the bumper of the vehicle without looking down, "and the authority of the department down to Park County. You need to notify the sheriff down there I'm coming, and request they cooperate with me as if this is the highest priority item on your list. And you're going to organize the whole department and impress upon them that they're to do everything they can to find these girls and Cody."

She stopped talking and was as appalled at her words as Tubman was. The seconds mounted up in silence except for the burbling of the exhaust pipe of the Ford.

Finally, he said, "You know that as of this moment everything has changed between us."

"I do."

"And you know if you go down there like you're talking about you're just going to find that miserable drunk in some bar or whorehouse?"

"Maybe."

Tubman broke his gaze and looked past her, as if there was something fascinating over her shoulder. She almost turned to look, but she didn't.

"Go," he said.

"Thank you, sir."

He glared at her. "Don't think this doesn't change everything, Dewell. You're on my list now, just like Cody Hoyt was. And you know what happened to him."

As he said it, he lifted his nonexistent chin.

"Try it," she said. "But remember you aren't the only person who can talk to the press."

He started to smile, but suddenly cut it off when he realized what she was saying.

"You made me the hero because I'm a fat single mother you hired personally to add diversity to the department," she said. "They ate it up. Now, if you try to destroy me, you're the one who loses. Think about it."

Tubman inadvertently dropped the newspaper near his slipper. He feinted to pick it back up, but rethought it and stood up to face her. But he looked whipped, she thought.

"I'll check in," she said. "But you need to call out the cavalry."

"Tomorrow's Thanksgiving," Tubman said. "A whole lot of folks are going out of town for four days."

"I know it. That's why we need to find them today."

He nodded, but didn't speak. No doubt, she thought, he was thinking of the next election. So far, he was unopposed except for the lunatic county coroner, Skeeter Kerley. But if one of his own ran, a female who looked and acted like a normal female, who would attract the housewives and liberals and voters who already didn't like him for one reason or other, a female who had been praised as a tough investigator by the sheriff himself . . .

"Keep me posted," Tubman said. "I'll do all I can to help find those girls."

"And Cody," she said.

"Yeah," he said sourly. "Him, too."

30.

Ronald Pergram drove his mother's white 1986 Buick Riviera past the unmanned National Park Service window at the north entrance to Yellowstone and goosed it on the straightaway before beginning the switchback climb to Mammoth Hot Springs. The car, like his mother, was repulsive. It was low-slung and underpowered and its 3,300 lbs of steel rocked atop a mushy suspension that gave him the feeling of driving a car with four flat tires. The top of the coupe was peeling tongue-like strips of faux leather and the paint job looked sandblasted. The windows were cloudy with grime. The backseat was filled with garbage bags and newspapers and he'd had to clear the front seat of empty Big Gulp containers just to squeeze inside. The trunk contained two dead bodies wrapped in plastic, one on top of the other.

Although there was a CCTV camera mounted on

the side of the entrance station, he knew there was no reason to worry about being identified. The NPS operated on banker's hours during the off-season, and they rarely had a ranger on duty to collect entrance fees before eight in the morning, much less someone viewing the monitor at park headquarters. As long as he entered the park before eight or after five, America's first national park belonged to the Lizard King.

He kept a wary eye out, though, in front and behind him. There was always the chance—although remote—that an overeager park ranger would pull him over for speeding or simply note his presence in the park if questioned later. But like the entrance booth personnel, traffic rangers seemed to vanish from existence once the hotels and visitor amenities inside the park closed for the season.

That was one of the reasons he liked to use his mother's old car. If the camera caught the license plate and some ranger had the gumption to check out the owner, Pergram couldn't imagine them going after a sixty-eight-year-old local widow who didn't look like she even had the money for a day pass. Plus, he simply liked the idea of driving that old bat's car with the bodies of two women in the trunk.

The body of the gimp was wrapped in plastic and wedged around the spare tire. It weighed next to nothing and wouldn't even provide ballast on icy roads.

He'd made this trek more times than he could recall.

Pergram deliberately drove right by the small battered sign on the side of the road that read POISON SPRING

TRAILHEAD. The sign was so low to the ground it was partially obscured by tall grass, and the area itself was dark with nearly constant shadows because of the tall and close walls of lodgepole pine on both sides of the road. There was no pullout at the trailhead to park but a quarter of a mile farther was a single concrete picnic table virtually hidden from passing cars. He slowed and turned into the campsite and drove as far into the small clearing as he could. Pergram turned off the motor and got out. He could hear the tinkle of a tiny creek through the trees in front of him, and there was a low rush of cold wind in the crowns of the lodgepole pines, enough to rock the trees back and forth slightly.

He stood still and listened. There was no road traffic. He wanted to make sure no one was coming and could catch a glimpse of what he was doing as they passed by.

When he was sure he was alone, Pergram unlocked the trunk and slung the body of the gimp over his shoulder and took it fifteen feet into the timber and let it drop with a thud.

The dead lot lizard underneath was stiff as a board. Out of curiosity, he'd unwrapped the plastic around her head to see what she looked like. Her face was wan and emaciated and frozen into a leering grimace. Her eyes were open but filmy, and they seemed to stare right into his heart. So he wiped that leer off her face with a jack handle, then wrapped the plastic back over what was left and put the body into the backseat. It was like carrying a bundle of branches, it was so stiff and bony.

Then he returned to the Riviera and inspected the plastic-lined interior of the trunk for spots of blood. It was clean. He stripped the plastic out and balled it tight and shoved it inside his coat. Then he closed the trunk lid and went back for the bodies.

Even though the gimp weighed no more than a hundred and ten pounds, he was sweating by the time he reached Poison Springs because he'd already carried the body of the lot lizard. As always, he eschewed the old trail to get there that began at the road and wound through the timber, instead cutting directly through the trees from the picnic table to approach it from the side.

Someday, he thought, he would surprise a bear. Or the bear would surprise him. And that would be that. The park service would have a hell of a time figuring it out, he thought.

He smelled it before he saw it. Poison Spring had a particular sulfur and steam odor that could tear his eyes if the wind was just right.

As always, he stopped and paused and got his breath back. He'd never seen hikers at Poison Spring, even during tourist season, but he couldn't let himself get complacent. But it was silent all around.

The spring looked deceptively enticing. The opening in the ground was twelve feet by twenty feet and it was filled with clear water that appeared sapphire blue and lapped gently at the crusty edge of the opening. Steam and fumes wafted from the surface and always reminded him of hot bathwater. When the light was right, as it was now, he could see deeply into the cavern. The sides were uneven and coral-like, with shelves of built-up mineral deposits jutting out here and there. On one of the shelves, through the steam and undulating water, he could clearly see a femur bone. That bone had been there on that ledge for two years. He wished there was a way to reach down and knock it off. Luckily, he thought, it looked enough like a bone from a deer or elk that anyone else glimpsing it wouldn't be alarmed.

It was called Poison Spring because it was. The pure water contained large amounts of natural sulfuric acid.

Pergram was no chemist. He didn't know how long it took for the sulfuric acid in Poison Spring to dissolve a human body, or two in this situation. He didn't know what was left after a month or two deep in the depths of the spring. All he knew was that it suited his needs and it had worked so far.

After he'd unwrapped the gimp's body and weighted it down with heavy rocks, he rolled it toward Poison Spring until it was balanced on the crust of the edge. This next part always scared him a little, because he had no idea how thick and strong the crust was and if it might break under his own weight and burn his own skin. Once he had the body poised near the opening, he found a stout pole in the timber and used it to lever the body in.

There was no splash and it sunk out of sight so quickly he didn't get a good last look. There was no foaming or agitation in the spring from the arrival of the new carcass. He went through the same procedure with the lot lizard.

He stood there, watching and listening, then balled the plastic he'd wrapped it in with the plastic from the trunk around another rock and tossed it in.

The entrance gate had a ranger in it as he drove out of the park, but he simply waved. The ranger, a decent-looking young woman with red hair, green eyes, and a pug nose and freckles, waved back. He felt a stir when he looked at her, and noted her for a future possibility. Seasonal rangers and temporary workers in the park often hitchhiked to and from work along the highway. He'd not yet given any of them a ride. But it was something to consider . . .

Pergram slowed down as he approached Emigrant en route to his house. There were two vehicles parked in front of the First National—Legerski's cruiser and a black Ford Expedition with Lewis and Clark County plates. The realization hit him that at that moment, inside the building, Legerski was having breakfast with the cop who'd texted: I'M ON MY WAY.

He was momentarily torn. Should he stop and go inside and see what they were talking about? Sit at the bar and order some eggs and bacon and eavesdrop on the conversation as he had the night before?

He didn't trust Legerski not to give him up. The man was a sociopath and would do anything to save himself. Sure, he'd said he'd take care of everything. But what if the lady cop was smart? What if she saw through Legerski's lies?

If that happened, Pergram had no doubt the trooper

would turn on him. Jimmy was harder to figure out, but because he was friends with Legerski—Legerski had brought him in—he guessed the bartender would sell him out as well.

Pergram cursed and drove on. It was his fault he'd let them in. He regretted it, although at the time it seemed his only choice.

As he drove on, he recalled how the scheme had taken shape, when it had changed from his own personal secret world into something he was forced to share.

Two and a half years earlier, he'd been returning to Livingston from delivering a load in the Pacific Northwest. It was dusk and less than ten miles out of town when he saw the light bar of wigwag lights in his side mirrors. He checked his speed—he was two miles under the limit—and wondered why the trooper was behind him. Why the cop wanted to pull him over in the first place. Pergram felt absolute terror for the first time in years, and thought his life would be over.

He'd eased his Freightliner to the side—it was before he bought his Peterbilt—and waited. The trooper probably wanted to check his papers, he thought. Sometimes they did that; random harassment checks of truckers to make sure they'd done the proper paperwork at the last weigh station. Later, he recalled that he should have noted that the trooper didn't sit in his cruiser and run his plates before exiting his car. That should have been a clue. But at the time, all he could think of was that he was caught. And what he might have to do to get out of it.

The lot lizard was bound and gagged in the bunk of his sleeper, just a few feet away from him. She was still under the influence of the roofies he'd injected into her, but her breathing was ragged. He'd planned to take her to that shack by the river where he always took them. Then, when he was done, to Poison Springs.

He had no excuse if the trooper saw or heard her. And no explanation.

Pergram watched as the Montana State Highway Patrolman walked up alongside his trailer. The man moved slowly and deliberately, his right hand resting on the butt of his sidearm. Pergram reached down and opened the console between the seats and touched the butt of his .357 Magnum revolver. He knew that he might have to kill a cop, right there on the side of Interstate 90. Cars and trucks sizzled by in the eastbound lane. A couple of the drivers slowed to rubberneck before continuing.

The trooper approached the driver's side door and knocked on it. Pergram took a deep breath, tried to act inconvenienced, and opened his door.

Legerski's face stared up at him, probing with his hard cop eyes.

"Something wrong?" Pergram asked. "I know I wasn't speeding. Do I have a light out or something?"

"Operator's license, registration, and bill of lading, sir," Legerski said with false courtesy.

Pergram wanted it over as fast as he could so he didn't argue. He handed the documents down and sighed. "Everything's there," he said.

"Are you deadheading it back?" the trooper asked, checking the papers.

"This time. I always try to bring back a load but the dispatcher was an idiot and didn't hook me up. So yeah, I'm deadheading it back."

The trooper nodded, then handed the papers back. For a brief moment, Pergram thought he was in the clear.

Then Legerski said, "You've been around here for a long time but you spend most of the time on the road. So tell me, do you have a girl in there now with you?"

Pergram was too shocked to answer. His right hand twitched on his lap. Eighteen inches to the right was the butt of the Ruger .357. It was double-action, he wouldn't even need to cock it, just aim and pull the trigger.

Pergram tried to swallow but couldn't. "What?" he asked, and his voice cracked.

"I asked you if you had a girl in there."

Pergram couldn't speak.

"Are you all right?" Legerski asked. "You act like something's wrong."

"I'm coming down with something," Pergram said in a croak. "Something I ate, I guess."

"That damned trucker food," Legerski said, shaking his head.

"What was it you asked me about a girl?" Pergram said. "I don't know what you're talking about." Lame.

Legerski tipped his trooper hat back on his head. His hand was still on his pistol but he hadn't pulled it. His voice became conversational.

"I picked your mom up a week back for missing a headlight," Legerski said. "She cussed me out but good. She said she was a good driver, just like her son, the long-haul trucker. She said you live with her when you aren't on a run, and since I'd just spent a week looking for a missing girl on that stretch of highway I gave it some thought. I asked around a little, because we really kind of live in the same neighborhood. I pulled your log and determined that there were more than a few missing prostitutes and runaways in this part of the state in the last couple years. And each time there was an incident report *you* were on the road on your way back here. I think that's more than a coincidence."

Pergram simply stared back. To this day, he wondered what it was that stopped him from killing Legerski right there. Was it something in the trooper's eyes, or the tone of his voice? Or simply because the thing was playing all wrong?

Then Legerski said, "I think you might be a man after my own heart, is what I'm saying."

It took a moment to understand.

"I bought some property down south of here. You know the old Schweitzer place?"

Pergram found himself nodding. He was familiar with it because it was less than four miles from his mother's house. Eighty or ninety acres in a steep mountain valley surrounded by walls of mountains on each side. There was a beat-up old house with the windows smashed out on it, but that wasn't what was unique about the property. Schweitzer, it was said, was a crazy old coot. He'd built a bunker somewhere on his land. A concrete underground bunker that would withstand a nuclear or chemical war. But he'd died before he ever had to use it. The property had been on the market for years because it was remote, without good water, and didn't have enough grass for a profitable herd of cows.

"I know it," Pergram said.

"How about you meet me out there? When I get off duty, say six thirty tonight?"

"I can do that."

"Bring your friend."

That's how it started.

He parked the Buick on the side of the house and got out. The wind had picked up and was shaking the Russian olive bushes, vibrating them with angry urgency.

Pergram rubbed his face with his hands before entering the house. The white crosses had worn off and he was dead tired and hungry. But he was also excited. Seeing those two girls in their underwear when he grabbed the gimp, knowing they were there, stirred him. The gimp had done nothing for him. There was some relief, sure, but it was temporary. It was like eating a dish of dry dog food when steaks were a few feet away behind a closed door.

As silently as he could, he entered the house. He couldn't see or hear her. He hoped she'd gone back to bed and was still sleeping. But as he navigated through the passageway toward the kitchen he smelled coffee and there she was, at the table where she'd been the night before, glaring at him.

"I seen you out there," she said. "You took my car again without asking."

He flushed.

"Where do you go when you take my car? Why don't you take your own truck and use your own gas? I'm on a fixed income. I can't afford to keep putting gas in that car when I'm not even using it."

"I'll fill it up later today," he said, shinnying around her and kicking a stack of newspapers aside so he could open the door of the ancient pantry.

"When you going back out on the road?"

He ignored her. The pantry was crammed full with canned goods. Some of the labels were so old they were yellow and peeling off the tin.

"What are you looking for, Ronald?"

"Something to eat that isn't shitty or expired."

"There's nothing wrong with those cans," she said, disgusted with him.

He reached in and pulled out a Campbell's soup can of split pea soup and shook it at her. "This has been in here as long as I can remember. I remember looking at this when I was ten years old and wondering what kind of people wanted to eat it. And here it is today."

She scowled and looked away.

He fixed his eyes on the back of her head. Her hair was white and wispy. He could see her scalp through it. For a second, he considered how hard he'd have to hit her with the can to break her skull.

"I can cook you something," she said. "There's some Dinty Moore stew in the refrigerator."

"I told you I *hate* that."

He snatched a fairly contemporary can of pork and beans from the pantry, slammed the door, and left her there.

He closed and locked the door of his room and stood there for a few minutes to make sure she wasn't on the other side. Sometimes she did that, he knew. Just stood there on the other side of the door to listen to what he was doing. He should have brained her with the can of soup, he thought.

Pergram opened the beans with his Swiss army knife and wolfed it down. He put the empty can in the garbage. He hated clutter, unlike her.

He lay on his bed in the dark and closed his eyes but visions of those two girls started showing up on the inside of his eyelids. The way they cowered in the corner, those firm long legs on the nice-looking one.

He opened his eyes because he knew what he had to do next or he'd never get any sleep.

His collection of videotapes was hidden beneath the floor under his bed. Dozens of tapes and DVDs he'd made of his conquests. Along with the girls, Legerski was in many of them. Jimmy was in a few. He'd made a set for the trooper, in fact, but refused to hand over the originals when Legerski asked for them.

The tape collection was now what kept him alive, he thought. Legerski wouldn't dare turn on him if there was a risk the tapes and disks could be found that would implicate him. Pergram had insinuated more than once there was.

"You're fucking lying," Legerski had said, "there is

no way I can be identified." But there was a hint of panic in his voice.

"Maybe, maybe not," Pergram had said back.

The tapes were Pergram's life insurance policy.

On his hands and knees, he reached under his bed until his fingers closed around a ring bolt. He opened the lid and set it to the side, then reached into the hole.

Under the floorboards were two green army surplus ammunition cans fitted with tight swing-back covers that kept the contents safe and dry and could be opened by prying up on a side panel. The stencils on the sides revealed them to have once stored .50 caliber machine gun rounds. He didn't disturb the can he thought of as his "Oh Shit" box. It contained carefully thought-out and collected items he'd need if his world went completely upside down and he had to run for it.

The other box was the collection of tapes and DVDs that was the history and culmination of his secret world; old VHS tapes and newer digital DVDs. He brought it out and opened it and fished through the collection, trying to find one that matched his mood. He selected one from three years before, the time he'd defied Legerski and dragged two girls into the room for himself. He didn't want to see Legerski, to be reminded of him right now.

Legerski had retaliated for him breaking their agreement that they both be present with the girls at the bunker. He'd disguised himself and made his own tape and did depraved things to the two lot lizards there at the time and killed them both afterwards. Then he left the tape to be discovered and viewed by Pergram, who would instantly understand the message sent. Without telling Legerski, Pergram had made an additional copy.

Later, over breakfast at the First National Bar, Legerski looked up and said, "This is what happens when you fuck with me, Ronald. Now you've got to go get another one."

He did. And he never defied Legerski since. He'd viewed the disk only once, and now he set it aside and chose another.

Pergram sat on his bed and inserted the disk into his laptop computer and put on his headphones. It started with him looking into the camera, grinning. The two girls were in the background, bound and gagged.

Again, he wondered what Legerski and the lady cop from Helena were talking about.

And how long he had.

31.

Cassie Dewell's egg-white and mushroom omelette arrived at the center table in the First National Bar of Montana, delivered by the cook-slash-owner named Jimmy. Jimmy placed a set of silverware wrapped tight in a paper napkin by her plate and said, "You said without the bacon or sausage that comes with it, right? I hope you like it. I don't make too many of those around here."

"Thank you," she said. She could feel Jimmy's eyes on her as well as the eyes of Montana State Highway Patrol officer Rick Legerski, who sat across from her. She knew they were poking fun at her a little, checking her out. She was used to it.

Legerski had ordered "the Rancher": three eggs over easy, chicken-fried steak with gravy, hash-brown potatoes, and toast.

"You know what a Montana vegetarian is?" Jimmy asked, hovering just behind her. By the way he asked it she knew it was a well-worn joke and often told.

"What?" she asked, looking over her shoulder.

"Someone who only eats meat once a day," Jimmy said, and grinned. His top teeth were long and yellow like horse teeth and he was missing most of his bottom teeth.

She smiled politely and said, "I'm from Montana."

"You're from Helena," Jimmy said, "that ain't Montana."

"Jimmy," Legerski said, cutting in, "I could use some more coffee."

Jimmy looked at Legerski and Cassie could see something exchanged between them, but she couldn't discern what it was.

"Coming up," Jimmy said, and turned on his heel.

"Thank you," Cassie said to the trooper in a low mumble.

"He doesn't have very impressive people skills for a bar owner, does he?" Legerski said after Jimmy was out of earshot, "But he makes a hell of a breakfast. And he's kind of famous for his big cinnamon rolls."

She tried her omelette. It was passable, but she envied Legerski, who dug into his massive plate of food. She was always embarrassed to eat in front of men she didn't know because it called attention to her weight. So she ordered food she wasn't crazy about. Even if they didn't say anything—and they rarely did—she knew what they were thinking.

* * *

She'd found the place easily enough. It was the only bar and grill in Emigrant, after all, and trooper Legerski's cruiser was parked in front. She'd called him en route since he was the last person she was aware of to see Cody Hoyt, and he suggested they meet there. He said he didn't work out of an office—most highway patrolmen didn't and took their patrol cars home every night—and the small conference room at the Department of Transportation shop outside Livingston was being used that morning. Since she hadn't had anything to eat since lunch yesterday, she realized she was starved and agreed to meet him at the First National.

After ordering, they'd sniffed around at each other at first, talking about the weather and state politics until their food arrived. She didn't know what she thought of him yet. He was polite enough, more formal than she was used to, and had stood up when she came in. His big mustache hid his mouth and he had the dead-eyed cop look down cold. His hands were huge and reminded her of bear paws when he grasped them together on the table. Legerski seemed serious, if somehow forced, as if he were playacting at being vigilant and extremely sincere. He had a gruff low voice and a drawn-out, western way of speaking. Legerski chose his words carefully and seemed to want to use as few of them as possible. He didn't wear a wedding ring.

She'd said, "I understand you were married to the sister of our dispatcher, Edna."

He'd nodded, and said, "Love is grand, but divorce is a hundred grand."

It was the kind of thing men said to each other and generally didn't say to women, she thought. But she gave him the benefit of the doubt and hoped he thought of her as serious, as well as a colleague. Since he was a state trooper and she was an investigator for an out-of-county sheriff's department, the hierarchy was clear. But he didn't act superior.

"Thanks for meeting me this morning," she said.

"You bet," he said, between mouthfuls of food. "But it's kind of a busy time."

She looked around: there was no one else in the place except Jimmy.

"Not here," he said, reading her movement. "But it's the day before the holiday. Hell of a lot of traffic on the roads, and we're expected to be out there in the middle of it."

She nodded. For the second time that morning, she'd been reminded it was Thanksgiving tomorrow. Thanksgiving, and her halfhearted intention of planning a dinner and cooking a turkey at home for Ben and her mother had been set aside.

"When do you go on shift?" she asked.

"Couple of hours."

"So we have a little time."

He shrugged his shoulders, as if to say, "A little but not much."

"You know why I'm here," she said, recapping the night before. She left out the extraneous information about Cody's suspension, her role in it, their meeting at the bar, and started with Justin Hoyt's announcement that the Sullivan girls were missing. She said her last communication with Cody had been at two forty-seven that morning.

Legerski sopped up the last of the gravy with a piece of toast. He seemed to be listening patiently, but he asked no questions.

"So last night you met with Cody Hoyt?" she asked.

He pushed his plate aside, sat back, and raised his eyebrows. "You get right to it," he said.

"I don't think I have much time," she said. "If those girls are lost or have been abducted, well, you know. Every minute is important."

"I think I know that," the trooper said softly with a dollop of defensiveness. "I've been in law enforcement for over twenty years."

"I'm sorry," she said. "I'm tired this morning."

"And a little tightly wrapped," he said, but finished it with a smile.

Then, "You're wondering if I was the last person to see him."

She nodded her head.

"That I can't tell you for sure. I don't know who he ran into after he left here. But yeah, I met him last night. Right here, in fact. We'd been in touch for a few hours and he swept the highway from Livingston south and I covered Yellowstone north to here. Neither one of us found that Ford Focus."

She thought he answered her question but without an ounce of elaboration. Obviously, he'd testified many times in court and had learned to keep things short and to the point.

She listed to the side and reached down to her hand-bag near the chair. "Do you mind if I take some notes?"

Legerski said, "Is this an official interview?" He seemed put out by the prospect.

"Nothing like that. I'm just trying to establish a time line for my own benefit."

She opened her notebook to the page she'd begun back at her house. Times were noted from when Justin Hoyt entered the bar to when Cody left Helena. Since there had been no contact or incidents from that point on, the time line ended at Cody's last text.

"It takes two and a half hours to drive from Helena to here," she said. "So what time did you meet with him?"

Legerski looked toward the ceiling for a second, and said, "He got here at two thirty. Yeah, that's right. That's a half hour after Jimmy usually closes, so I'm sure of the time."

She scribbled it down.

"So you asked Jimmy to stay open late?"

"Yes. He owes me a few favors."

"How long did you and Cody talk?"

He hesitated, again being very deliberate. Then he turned in his chair. "Jimmy, do you remember what time it was when that Hoyt fellow left here?"

Jimmy looked up sharply, and she found his reaction surprising. He seemed alarmed.

"What, like twenty minutes?" Legerski asked Jimmy.

"Something like that," Jimmy said after a beat.

Cassie wrote down that Cody left the bar at approximately two fifty.

"That's not very long," she said.

Legerski shrugged again. "There wasn't that much to discuss. I told him I hadn't found the car or the girls, and he told me the same thing. I knew there was a state-wide and regional alert out by then, so we weren't the only ones looking."

She gestured toward Jimmy with a nod of her head toward the owner. "I'm surprised he can't remember how long you two were here. It seems to me that if he was waiting to close he might pay more attention to the exact time than usual."

"That's Jimmy," Legerski said, as if it explained everything.

"Did you discuss any other possibilities of what might have happened to them during your twenty-minute talk?"

"Like what?"

She looked up and met his eyes, trying to figure out if he was playing games with her. He held her gaze.

"Like maybe people at the Church of Glory and Transcendence might have something to do with the disappearance?"

"Yeah," Legerski said quickly, and leaned forward on the table and clasped his big hands together and lowered his voice. "I threw that one out there. The reason being we've had a few missing girls in a hundred-mile radius over the past few years and those folks out there on that compound keep to themselves. I probably shouldn't have said anything to him because I've got no evidence at all to back this up, just like I shouldn't be repeating it to you. But yeah, I speculated some—" he cut himself off in midsentence.

"What were you going to say?"

"Nothing. I've said too much already, probably."

For reasons she couldn't quite explain, she didn't tell Legerski she'd spent hours researching the church and had speculated the same thing.

"Are you the one he was texting?" Legerski asked.

It took her by surprise and she didn't respond.

"When he was sitting here last night, every time I turned my back he'd be tapping away on his phone," he said. "Was that you?"

"Yes," she said. "He's my partner. But if he was texting anyone else? I don't know that."

Legerski opened a packet of white sugar from a bowl on the table and poured it out on the surface. Then he took his big forefinger and drew a line through the spill, severing it in half. She determined there was no point to his actions, other than impatience with her and her questions.

"Deputy," he said, almost sadly, "I don't know you at all but I'm getting tired of you because you're asking a lot of pointed questions and you aren't being up-front with me. I don't really have time for this."

"What do you mean?" she asked, and felt her face flush.

"He wasn't your partner anymore. He was suspended yesterday. He told me himself he was on his own, investigating as a private citizen. Even though that was the case, I not only met with him on my own time but I cased the highway looking for those girls. And this morning when you called, I dragged my sorry ass out of bed after not enough sleep to meet with you before I went on shift. And the whole time you've been here you've been interrogating me like I'm a suspect or something. I don't know how you do things in the state capital, but that's not how we do things around here."

With that, he sat back, dug a wad of bills out of his front uniform pants pocket, and tossed them on the table between them.

"I've got to get to work," he said.

She was stunned, and felt both guilty and incompetent. Everything he said, she thought, was true.

As he started to push away from the table, she reached out and touched his hand. He glared at her, but didn't push back further.

"Look," she said, "I'm sorry. I'm new at this and I feel like the world is crashing down on me. I'm under pressure and I'm probably in over my head. I came on too strong. I don't mean to offend you, I really don't."

"Am I a suspect?" he asked indignantly.

"Of course not," she said. "I don't know anyone around here and you do. There are two missing girls and a missing cop. I really need your help if you'll give it to me."

He didn't respond, but she thought she saw something soften in his eyes.

"So as far as you know," she said, "after Cody left here last night he was going to drive to the compound?"

Legerski nodded. "That's what he said, anyway. I can't vouch for where he actually went."

She thought that through for a few seconds, but before she could ask he said, "He wanted me to go with him because I've got a live badge and he didn't. But I told him I wouldn't go down there without probable cause. So as far as I know, he went there alone."

"It doesn't surprise me he'd go there without a search warrant," she said with a weak smile.

"We discussed that. He said he'd go to the gate and ask for entry. If they didn't give it, he somehow thought that might convince a judge to write up a warrant."

That sounded right to her.

"Do you know a friendly judge?" she asked.

"You mean now?"

"Yes."

He seemed slightly flustered. "Well, yeah, there's Judge Graff in Livingston. I've worked with him a lot over the years and he's a good guy."

"It seems to me," she said, "if you go to him and tell him about the missing girls and the fact that Cody vanished last night after he said he'd go there, we've got probable cause to search the compound."

The trooper looked pained. "There's no telling if Judge Graff is around or if I'd find him. Hell, he might have left the state already for the holidays."

"But you'll try?" she asked.

It took him a moment to agree. "Yeah, I can stop by the courthouse on my way through town. But, lady, I've got to get to work."

"Thank you," she said. "And one more thing."

"What?" he asked, looking away.

"If you can see the judge and get the process going,

please brief the Park County sheriff about what's going on. I'll call my boss and remind him that he agreed to ask the local sheriff for cooperation. Maybe we can get four or five deputies down here to help with the search."

Legerski seemed reluctant. She noticed his neck seemed flushed where it wasn't earlier, even when he was angry and ready to leave.

"If we do what we can to apply pressure around here and let everyone know we're serious, someone might tell us something we don't know," she said. "Will you do it?"

Legerski showed his teeth—not really a smile, but a facsimile of a smile, she thought—and said, "Yeah. I'll do it. But I can't guarantee anything."

"I realize that," she said. "We don't have much to go on. But we also don't have time to waste."

He took a deep breath and held it in and stared hard at something over her head. She got the feeling she should be bracing herself for some kind of "experienced cop tells the newbie how it really is" speech. She was right.

"Deputy," he said.

"My title is Investigator," she said sharply.

"Okay, Investigator," he said with a tiny smirk, "I'll break it to you. These girls have supposedly been missing for less than fourteen hours, right?"

She nodded.

"Officially, this isn't even a missing persons case yet. And your friend Cody—who knows? You haven't talked to him in seven hours, that's all. From what I know about him, he's probably curled up with a bottle in his pickup somewhere sleeping it off.

"What I'm saying is that what's urgent to you right now won't seem urgent to anybody else until more time has passed or until we get some kind of new information. You seem to think that everyone in Park County should drop everything they're doing and rush here and start kicking down doors. But how do we even know the two things are connected? We don't even know *that*."

Legerski stood and clamped his trooper hat on his head. To Cassie, he said, "Not enough time has passed for the kind of reaction you want, is what I'm saying."

To Jimmy, who was hovering behind the bar looking ashen, Legerski said, "Money's on the table."

Jimmy nodded.

She wondered again what the relationship was between them because it seemed both intimate and disquieting.

As the trooper went out the door, she felt immense relief. Something was happening. She'd set things in motion, and that's all she could hope for at this point. Cody called it "flooding the zone."

She snatched up the wad of cash Legerski had tossed on the table and matched it with bills from her purse. Clutching the bills, she followed the trooper out the door and caught him before he slid into his cruiser. When he looked up and saw her pursuing she thought she caught a quick reaction of startling contempt. But it was gone as quickly as it had been there and she hoped she was mistaken.

"Here," she said, handing him the cash. "The least I can do is buy you breakfast."

He shook his head and made no move to retrieve it. "Not necessary," he said.

"I know it's not necessary, but let me do it. I'm grateful."

"You're pushy," he said, then caught himself. It was as if it had slipped out.

"A little," she agreed. "Hey, I've got one more question."

He didn't turn toward her, but looked straight out the windshield. But he didn't slide his window up.

"Cody asked me last night to check on those missing girls you mentioned. I did some research and didn't find anything to work with, but I was reading up on the FBI Highway Serial Killer task force. It got me to thinking."

"Thinking what?" the trooper asked with a flat voice.

"That if we don't find anything on that church compound, we might want to do some interviews around here of long-haul truckers. You probably know them if they exist. What do you think?"

"I think I'm going to be late for my shift."

"You've got my cell number, right? You'll call when you know about the warrant and the assistance?"

"Got it," he said. He seemed to be in a hurry to get away from her.

"Thank you again," she said.

He nodded, backed out, and paused at the asphalt of the highway before turning left toward Livingston.

Cassie was buoyed with herself and watched him

go. Before he wheeled out onto the pavement their eyes met in his rearview mirror and he mouthed something that she couldn't hear but that pierced her like a knife in the heart.

Stupid cunt.

She tried to hold herself together and not react, and she turned sharply on her heel and walked away. Of course, she'd heard the word before. Of course, she'd been called it, especially from criminals she and Cody had apprehended. By the time she reached the end of the small gravel parking lot she was breathing again and she lifted her head.

It was cooling down outside. The wall of mountains on the other side of the valley had simply disappeared as if they were never there. In their place were roiling white clouds and spoors of snow falling toward the river. She hugged herself rather than go back to the Expedition for her coat, and walked aimlessly around the side of the First National toward the back. Her stomach hurt from tension, lack of sleep, the egg-white omelet, and what Legerski had called her. She doubted he knew she could see his mouth in the mirror. Maybe, she thought, he simply didn't like the idea of a woman in charge of the investigation. Or maybe she had come on too strong, too pointed, too suspicious.

But a man didn't use a word like that except to demean. And he no doubt meant what he said. It hurt.

As she meandered behind the bar she dug out her cell phone and called Sheriff Tubman.

Tubman was cool and dry, and grunted in affirmation

as she updated him. He said he'd already contacted Sheriff Bryan Pedersen of Park County and Pedersen agreed to try and spare a couple of uniformed officers to drive down into Paradise Valley to help serve the warrant at the compound, "If there is one," Tubman cautioned.

"Is that the best he can do?" Cassie asked sharply.

"It's his county," Tubman answered wearily. "He's got spare guys going off shift early this afternoon for the holidays. He's got to keep his essential personnel close in case they need to respond to something."

"Christ," Cassie said, "what could be more important than two missing girls and a missing cop?"

"Ex-cop," Tubman said acidly. "And we don't know where the girls went missing, Cassie. If we knew it was Park County it would be higher priority with him, but it's all speculation at this point. We don't know where the hell they were last seen."

After she terminated the call, she called Jenny Hoyt. Jenny was weary and seemed resigned to very bad news. No, she'd not heard a word from Cody, and Justin had heard nothing from the Sullivan girls. No, Cody wasn't sleeping it off in any town or county jails anywhere in southwestern Montana. No, the Sullivan parents hadn't received a call or text from their daughters, either. Ted Sullivan, Jenny said, was flying to Helena that morning and had asked her about the investigation thus far.

"Don't send him down here," Cassie said. "He'd only get in the way."

"I'll do what I can," Jenny said. "He sounds frantic on the phone. I'm not sure I can keep him here."

"I'll call you as soon as the warrant arrives," Cassie said, leaning against a battered open Dumpster behind the bar, "and I'll keep you posted after we go to the compound."

"Thank you." After a beat, Jenny said, "So are you thinking he might have gone there last night and someone did something to him? Maybe those church people?"

"I don't know."

"I remember reading about them a few years ago," Jenny said, "They seem like a strange bunch of people. But why would they hurt a cop? That doesn't make sense."

"No, it doesn't," Cassie said.

She closed the phone and dropped it in her bag. A light wave of pinprick snow washed through the air. The storm was sudden but didn't seem long-lasting, she thought. All she needed was to get socked in before the nascent investigation even got going, she thought with gloom.

Whether it was the name Legerski mouthed about her or the questions he'd raised at the table, the simple weight of doubt seemed suddenly very heavy. All along, she'd assumed the disappearance of the Sullivan girls and Cody's disappearance were of course related. But what if they weren't? What if the girls had taken a wrong turn and hooked up with some boys their age, and Cody had simply kept driving? There *hadn't* been enough time yet to conclude they were officially missing.

What if an all-out effort by Legerski and the Park County sheriff's department turned out to confirm only that Investigator Cassie Dewell had overreacted for no good reason? She could guess what her colleagues would say about her, and knew what Sheriff Tubman would instigate.

She felt very alone. So alone, she wished Cody were there with her.

There was nothing to do but wait until she heard from Legerski about the warrant. She hoped it wouldn't take long.

If nothing else, she thought, she could use the interim time getting a better feel for the highway and the valley. Figure out where the compound was and look it over from a distance. Drive the road south toward Yellowstone to see if she could find anything about the Sullivan girls or Cody the trooper had missed.

As she turned away from the blowing snow she found herself facing the open trash container. Cody always had a thing about garbage cans, she knew. He explained it by saying that when people threw things in the garbage it was almost like ridding the items from their lives. Out of sight, out of mind, he'd said. More than half the valuable evidence he'd retrieved in felony crimes came from rooting through garbage cans, he said.

So she raised up on her toes and looked in. It was obvious Jimmy didn't have his trash hauled away very frequently. Hundreds of empty bottles, food containers, and open packages were inside almost to the top. She thought that the entire social history of the bar for the past month could be determined by the layers inside; what customers drank, what they ate, what they'd tracked in.

On the very top was a fairly clean empty box that had probably held the cinnamon rolls that were on the breakfast menu, she thought. She smiled, remembering what Legerski had said about Jimmy's famous rolls. But obviously, Jimmy didn't bake them: they were delivered.

She reached in and opened the box. The bottom was scored with caramel-colored swirls from where the rolls had been, but that wasn't what caught her attention. Because in the corner of the box was a small heap of ashes and cigarette butts. Jimmy had obviously used the empty box as a dustpan when he cleaned up that morning. She recognized the Marlboro Red butts as the kind Cody left everywhere.

Cassie removed the box and carefully poured the contents into a clean paper bag she found next to it.

She looked inside and counted: eight. Eight cigarettes. She could have them tested for DNA but she had no doubt who'd smoked them. Even Cody wasn't capable of smoking eight in twenty minutes. Which meant he'd been there much longer than twenty minutes the night before.

She wondered why Legerski had lied to her. And why Jimmy had gone along with it.

She decided to question Jimmy herself to find out,

but as she walked around from the back of the building she heard a motor start up and a hiss of thrown gravel.

Jimmy's old Jeep Wagoneer was sizzling down the highway to the north. He'd hastily hung up a SORRY FOLKS, WE'RE CLOSED sign in the front window.

32.

Ronald Pergram was awakened by the burr of his cell phone on his pillow. He grunted and reached to turn it off, assuming it was the dispatcher calling to tell him about his next load, but the number displayed on the screen jolted him awake. It was a temporary number of a prepaid cell phone Legerski used only for emergencies.

As Pergram rolled to his side in bed the laptop that had been perched on his white belly slid off onto the mattress. He'd fallen asleep watching the DVD he'd selected, even before he got satisfaction from it. He was still bone tired and he'd not come close to having enough sleep.

"Yeah."

"Meet me at the place," Legerski said. He sounded agitated. Pergram could hear road sounds in the background. Legerski was calling from a moving vehicle.

"Now?"

"Fuck yes, *now*," Legerski said. "We've got problems."

Pergram closed his eyes. Pure red anger gathered in his chest and pushed up his throat. But he was wide-awake.

"Isn't that your department?" Pergram said. "I do the hunting and run the heavy equipment, and you solve the problems. That was the deal."

"Jesus, this isn't the time. Just get your ass to the place as soon as you can. I called Jimmy and he's on his way."

Pergram's heart leapt. "Are you talking about a session?"

"Don't be a moron. We don't have time for that until we're in the clear. I'm talking about a stupid cunt cop snooping around. She doesn't have a clue what she's doing but she's got me worried."

His hopes dashed, Pergram slid his feet out of bed and placed them on the cold floor.

"Okay, I've got to get dressed."

"Bring the tapes," Legerski said. "All of them."

Pergram glanced down at the collection in the ammo box near the side of the bed.

"The DVDs too?"

"Of course the DVDs, too. You know what I meant."

"Fifteen minutes," Pergram said, killing the call.

Yeah, Pergram thought, *I know* exactly *what you mean.*

* * *

Before leaving his room, Pergram checked the loads in the magazine of his Taurus .380 ACP and shoved it into his waistband at the small of his back. A blunt two-shot Bond Arms .45 Derringer went into the front right pocket of his Carhartt parka. His sheathed bone-handled skinning knife fitted nicely into the shaft of his right work boot, and a razor-sharp throwing knife went into the left.

He got back down on his knees and retrieved the "Oh Shit" box and bolted the floorboard hatch.

Locking his room behind him, he carried an ammo can in each hand and went as quietly as he could through the tunnel of refuse toward the front door. Although he couldn't hear her, he felt her presence and turned his head sharply. She glared at him from an ancient over-stuffed chair in an alcove of boxes and translucent containers packed with items that still had the price tags fixed to them. Her wide feet were up on a stool made of milk crates and the fat from her sides pooled over the armrests. She'd been just sitting here, in the shadows, waiting.

"Where you going?"

"Out."

"What you got there in your hands?"

The ammo cans. He didn't look down at either when she asked, but the handles felt like they were burning his flesh.

"Might go to the range," he said.

"Go ahead and lie to me," she said. "You're up to no good. I can see it on your face. I've always been able to tell when you're out causing trouble."

The rage hadn't receded far, and it climbed into the base of his throat again. Three steps and he'd be on her. Three steps swinging two heavy steel containers. He wondered how long it would take them to find her in all the garbage.

"Not like JoBeth," she said. "JoBeth never caused no trouble. She was the opposite of you. I still don't know how the two of you grew up in the same house. It just don't seem possible."

He said, "I'm taking your car again."

Her mouth dropped open. The reaction was worth it, he thought.

"What if I need to use it?"

"It'll wait."

"I'm going to have to hide the keys from you, Ronald. I swear, I'll hide the keys."

"I've got a spare set," he said, turning for the front door.

The last thing he heard was, "Put some damned gas in it this time!"

There was a winter storm blowing in from the north and Pergram drove into the teeth of it. The sky was dark and close, the bumpers of the individual clouds tainted slightly green, the clouds themselves blocking out the omnipresent mountains. Thin smokelike waves of snow twisted across the highway, rolling like sidewinder snakes he'd seen firsthand in Texas. The heater in the Riviera wasn't working worth a damn and the air the vents expelled smelled like radiator fluid. The ammo box filled with tapes and DVDs was on the passenger seat next to him.

She always brought up JoBeth, he thought. She used JoBeth like a blunt object to beat him with. Thin, lovely, athletic JoBeth, his little sister. Two-sport all-state athlete, honor roll, Future Farmers of America award winner. Somewhere in all that shit back home were her clippings from the Livingston *Enterprise*, each one of them painstakingly scissored out an eighth inch from the text and pressed into a three-binder scrapbook that used to sit prominently on the front coffee table when it could still be found. JoBeth's official U.S. Marines induction photo was on the wall, her clear blue eyes gazing out with a sense of purpose as straight as her jawline. When the word had come that the Humvee she was riding in in Iraq was destroyed by an IED, Pergram had mixed emotions. His mother didn't. She went off the deep end and found some kind of solace in "collecting." Collecting, Pergram thought, and acting the martyr. Her perfect child had been taken away, leaving her with . . . *him*.

Not for long, he thought.

Out of habit, Pergram checked traffic ahead and behind him on the highway—there was none—before slowing and taking an unmarked two-track that wound through high sagebrush toward the mountains. Tiny pellets of snow rattled across the hood of the car and against his driver's side window. Twisted fingers of forsaken lone sage scraped the undercarriage of the Riviera as he drove.

The old road took him through a narrow stand of old mountain ash trees and down a switchback slope. He crossed an ancient bridge constructed of railroad ties that sagged over a creek. Every time he drove the tractor over it he expected it to cave in, but it never did.

The trees cleared and he topped a rise and the old Schweitzer place was laid out in front of him. It wasn't really a ranch because it had too few acres—maybe a thousand acres—to feed enough cows to make a go of it, he'd heard. But when crazy old man Schweitzer bought it in the early 1950s, ranching wasn't his main priority. His thought then was to find a location that would withstand a nuclear war with the Soviet Union or Red China. That's why he chose acreage with high mountains on all four sides, far away from any population center that might be a target. That's why he built the bunker beneath his house with three-foot reinforced concrete walls and ceiling. It wouldn't withstand a direct hit, but humans inside could conceivably live through just about anything else. The air-filtration system was on its last legs but it still worked. They'd know when it failed when they found asphyxiated dead bodies inside. So far, though . . .

Just get your ass to the place as soon as you can. . . . Don't be a moron. . . . Bring the tapes.

Pergram reran those words through his mind over and over again. Each time he did he got angrier. He wondered what that woman cop had said to Legerski to cause his reaction.

He remembered a time a few years before when his

secret world was his and his alone. Before Legerski bullied his way into it. Before Jimmy joined them. Things weren't perfect back then because he was always afraid he'd get caught. But he learned as he went along, got better and more cautious all the time. He'd never been arrested or even questioned. The only person who seemed to suspect him—and blab about it—sat in a ratty old easy chair with her fat feet up back at home. She didn't know the extent of his secret life and would be shocked to find out. She just knew he was inherently rotten and she didn't mind sharing that opinion with anyone who asked. Rick Legerski had asked, apparently.

Things were so much better before, he now realized. At least no one ever called him while he was sleeping and told him to get his ass anywhere. Or called him a moron.

No one, Pergram thought, had the right of status to say that. No one had the right to treat him like a simpleton, an idiot, a mouth-breather who would do what he was told and not question the reason why. Not unless they'd been through what he'd been through and done what he'd done on the highways. *He* was the one who had started this, he thought. *He* was the one who made it happen. *He* was the one who delivered the goods to people who not only didn't appreciate it but started to think they were better and smarter than he was.

Pergram knew there were others out there on the highway, but it wasn't like they were in some kind of club or association. They didn't have a Web site where they could share videos or stories or tips. He wasn't sure he'd even like meeting another one.

Once, at a bank of urinals in a truck stop out of Valentine, Nebraska, he'd stood next to another trucker who seemed to emanate a certain aura of familiarity. The other driver was pudgy and dark and had dead, ravenlike eyes. As he zipped up, Pergram looked over to find the man staring at him in an unexplainable knowing way. Pergram nodded and the man smiled slightly, then turned away and zipped up himself. They'd exchanged something, a common thread, but didn't mouth a word to each other. Pergram just *knew*. He'd waited outside in the hall for the driver to come out. He wanted to ask him about methodology, tactics, disposal. But in the end, he chickened out. He was on the road south toward North Platte before the other driver came out of the truck stop and mounted up.

There was a small white house on the valley floor. Next to it was Legerski's cruiser and Jimmy's Jeep Wagoneer.

He parked next to Jimmy's Jeep and climbed out of the Buick with the ammo cans from the seat. But instead of walking toward the sagging front door of the house he went to the side where there was a thick concrete abutment emerging from the ground.

He leaned over and grasped the steel handle of the door and pulled. It was unlocked.

As he went down the wide stairs, his rage suddenly morphed into absolute calm and he became the Lizard King without even willing it to happen.

33.

Danielle sat with her back against the wall near the space heater, hugging her bare knees close. Her eyes were wide open but she was in a world of her own. Gracie observed her closely but Danielle didn't seem to know it or care. Danielle was silently chanting something, her lips moving in a kind of rhythm.

Gracie tried to figure out what her sister was chanting while she sipped on one of the bottles of water the man had tossed in earlier. Neither had eaten anything that was in the bag except for sharing a package of beef jerky.

Gracie said, "Danielle?"

Danielle didn't look up, didn't stop her mantra.

"Danielle, goddamn you!" Gracie shouted.

Her sister stopped murmuring and slowly looked over. Gracie had never cursed at her sister before that way, and it seemed to have penetrated.

"What?"

"What are you saying to yourself?"

Danielle's voice was soft and hoarse. "I'll never fall in love again. I'll never trust a boy. I'll never fall in love again. I'll never trust a boy."

"Got it," Gracie said, alarmed. Then, "What does that have to do with anything?"

Danielle gestured to their surroundings, as if it answered the question.

"That's not the problem," Gracie said. "The problem is you won't take any real responsibility, that's what. We aren't here because you care so much, Danielle. You blame this whole thing on the fact that you were trying to get to Justin and convince him to come back."

"That's what happened."

"No, it wasn't," Gracie said. "We aren't here in this place because you wanted Justin and you trusted him."

"Please don't blame me," Danielle said softly. "I can't take it if you blame me."

"I'm not *blaming you*," Gracie said, wrapping the thin blanket over her shoulders. "But you're not getting it. How about 'I'll never lie to my parents.' Or, 'I'll always get my car checked out at the mechanic shop so it won't die in the middle of nowhere.' That's what I mean."

The vacant look returned to Danielle's face.

Gracie said, "Or maybe, 'I won't put my little sister in danger ever again by being stupid.'"

"We're going to die here," Danielle said softly.

Gracie had no response. The situation they were in was too immense and horrible to think through. Twice in the last twenty minutes they thought they heard sounds from beyond the heavy door. Each time, they stopped talking and stared at it, terrified of it opening. Each time, nothing happened.

"It's not like we have any weapons or what we could use as weapons," Gracie said, looking around. The only objects in the room were the cheap space heater and the plastic chemical toilet Danielle refused to use. She wondered how long her sister could hold out before she slipped into madness. Danielle seemed perilously close to just . . . *going away.* Gracie thought that if she could somehow engage her sister, create a task—something to keep Danielle in the present—they might have a chance.

"We can fight them," Gracie said.

Danielle arched an eyebrow of doubt.

"We can kick him in the balls and scratch his eyes out. We bash him on the head with the space heater. We can surprise him."

Danielle shrugged.

Gracie held up a corner of the thin blanket. "We do have this."

Danielle said, "A blanket?"

"It's really dark in here, especially if you're coming in from outside. It has to be hard to see at first. Maybe if we were ready for him when he comes back we could hide in the dark and throw the blanket over his head the second he comes in."

Danielle simply looked at her.

Gracie continued, "We knock him down and kick him in the face and balls, then we run out the door. We don't stay around because he could kill us. We just run. We're not like Krystyl—we have two good legs."

Danielle narrowed her eyes and seemed to think about it. Gracie thought, *I'm getting through.*

"If we're quick," Gracie said, warming to the idea. "I throw the blanket over his head and you shove him down as hard as you can because you're stronger. Then we kick the shit out of him and run. That's how it would have to work, I think."

"Where do we run?"

Gracie shrugged. "We just run and don't stop. I think we could outlast him if he chased us."

"What if he manages to grab one of us?"

"The other one keeps running until they can find somebody and call the police. That's all I can think of. If we stop to help each other, he might get both of us."

Danielle nodded. Gracie couldn't tell if Danielle was still with her or was simply reacting to react. She feared she'd lost her sister again.

Gracie sat in silence, fuming and fighting tears, then suddenly bolted up and grabbed the tin of Altoid mints. She picked it up, squinted at it, saw how it fit in her palm. The brushed metal on the bottom of the tin reflected the orange bars of the space heater.

"We'll use this," she said.

Danielle looked up again. "Mints?"

"No—the tin. Look at it," she said, holding it up. "It's the size and shape of a cell phone. It fits in my hand like a phone."

Gracie turned it upside down and mimicked tapping

out a text on the surface of the tin with her thumbs. "See . . ."

Daniella shook her head, puzzled. She was not getting it.

"It looks like a cell phone from a distance if it's partially covered by my fingers. What if that driver looks in here and sees you sitting there acting like you're sending a text? Maybe he'll panic and think somehow he missed one of our phones when he threw us in here? He'll think he didn't miss anything but he may not be absolutely sure. He'll panic and come rushing in. I'll be on the other side of that door," she said, gesturing. "That's when I throw the blanket over his head and we kick him and bash him with the space heater and run."

Gracie paused, her eyes wide and expectant.

But Danielle shook her head. "That won't work."

"Why not?"

"He'll know it's not a phone."

Gracie stamped her foot. "How will he know that if you really act like you're texting? If you *sell* it."

Before Danielle could object again, Gracie blew up and threw the tin of mints at her sister as hard as she could. The tin smacked the wall with an explosion of little round white candies.

Gracie screamed, "Listen to me! We've got to *do* something. We've got to *try*. Look at this room. Those men are going to rape us and kill us no matter what. They can't let us go. Don't you want to try and get out of here?"

Danielle looked away but after a beat, she said, "Yes."

"Then work with me here."

"You didn't have to throw that at me."

"I'll knock some sense into you if I have to," Gracie said, feeling their roles reverse from big and little sister. "Now take that tin and pretend you're texting."

Danielle slowly found the tin, shut it with a snap, and listlessly bounced her thumbs off the metal.

"Sell it to me."

Danielle texted furiously.

"That's better."

As she watched, Danielle slowed her movements until they stopped and the tin slipped to the hard concrete floor.

"Danielle?" Gracie yelled, but it was like screaming at an empty shell. She'd lost her again, and maybe forever.

Gracie began to weep.

After a WHILE, Gracie said, "Maybe we should pray."

They were seated together again side by side. If nothing else, Gracie wanted to offer some comfort to her sister. And she needed some herself.

Danielle didn't respond.

"To God," Gracie said. She reached over and grasped her sister's hand. It was clammy and barely responded to her touch.

"Please God," Gracie said, "help us out of here. We know we haven't paid much attention to you but we're asking you now to help us."

When she looked over, Danielle had tears in her eyes that glistened in the orange glow of the heater.

"Maybe we could pray for Mom and Dad?" Gracie said. "Can you imagine how they must be just freaking out?"

Gracie grasped both of her sister's hands in hers.

"Look at me, Danielle."

After a long moment, Danielle's eyes met hers. Gracie leaned close enough that their faces were inches apart. She didn't know how to pray formally. She didn't know the words and the religious phrases she could think of seemed stuffy and false.

"Please, God," she whispered, "if you're up there please help us find a way out of here. And please help my sister."

Gracie steeled herself. If she made the choice to believe she couldn't back out of it later. She wasn't sure how that would change her life or improve their situation, if at all, but she thought she was willing to do it. She needed something to believe in, something greater than herself to help her through this. God had always been out there in her peripheral vision, she thought, but she'd refused to turn her head and look at Him directly. Now was the time if there ever was a time. She liked the idea of handing herself over to a greater power.

But she wondered how many girls in the same room had prayed to be let out? All of them, she guessed. And did it work for any of them?

While Gracie and Danielle touched hands, there was a slight vibration in the floor. Their eyes met. It was the third time there had been some kind of movement from the other side of the door. This time, though, it was followed by a distant and faint deep male voice. Gracie couldn't make out any individual words, but she got the feeling more than one man was speaking.

"They're outside," Danielle whispered. She was terrified.

Instinctively, Gracie and Danielle scrambled across the cold cement floor to the far corner. Gracie noticed that Danielle had left the tin on the floor when she pushed back.

When Gracie looked over at her sister she saw the glimmer of lucidity was gone again. Danielle had slipped back into darkness with her eyes wide open.

34.

Ronald Pergram paused on the bottom of the dark stairwell before opening the door. He stepped back to give himself some room, then practiced reaching back through his open coat for the .380 from his waistband and brandishing it. He was quick. He made sure there was a cartridge in the chamber so he wouldn't have to rack the slide. He thumbed the safety off and fitted it back into his jeans. Then he reached down into his coat pocket and repositioned the .45 Derringer so it pointed forward. He cocked the hammer and left it there. He knew he could reach down and fire it through the fabric of his coat, if necessary. As long as he was close, the firepower was tremendous.

Then he opened the heavy door and stepped inside the room without a word. He took a step to his right with his back against the wall and his right hand in his pocket, gripping the Derringer. His senses were tingling almost as if he'd summoned more white crosses into his system. The door wheezed shut behind him.

Jimmy and Legerski were already there. They didn't leap up to confront him and didn't seem surprised by his sudden entrance. Legerski sat in a plastic lawn chair, leaning back so the front two legs were suspended a few inches above the concrete floor. He was in full uniform and his arms were crossed over his big belly. Although he was mostly still, his jaw worked furiously on a piece of chewing gum. He eyed Pergram with calculation. Pergram noted Legerski's holstered service weapon on his belt, safety strap buttoned. Because of the trooper's crossed arms and relaxed posture, drawing the weapon would be a production.

Jimmy paced. He had a jerky, disconnected way of moving, especially when he was nervous or excited. He kept bringing the palms of his hands together in front of his chest, then dropping them to his sides as he walked. His head bobbed to an interior monologue Pergram had no interest in hearing. Although he might have a weapon hidden somewhere in his clothing, he appeared to be unarmed. Jimmy liked to dress old-fashioned western, in tight jeans and form-fitting faux-pearl snap-button shirts, so it would be difficult to conceal a pistol unless he had one in the shaft of his cowboy boots. He wouldn't be able to draw fast, either. But Pergram wasn't concerned with Jimmy.

Really, this was between him and Legerski, Pergram thought. Jimmy was a sideshow and always had been.

Pergram raised the ammo box so Legerski could see it.

"Are they all in there?" Legerski asked. This was the big question.

Pergram said, "Mostly."

"I need them all. I need to be positive I can't be identified in any of them. I've been so careful. . . ."

"Not careful enough maybe," Pergram said. "But you just keep believing that."

The chewing stopped. Pergram could see Legerski's face harden into a mask.

"What are you guys talking about?" Jimmy asked, obviously aware of the tension between them.

Schweitzer had built the underground concrete bunker in the shape and dimensions of an unbalanced barbell. The room they were in was by far the largest, and it had once been crammed with stacks of metal shelving containing crates of freeze-dried food, water barrels, weapons, and survival gear necessary to live for years after the nuclear apocalypse. The shelving had been cleared out but some of the original items remained. An old gasoline-powered generator also remained, but they'd never started it. The power for the bunker and the air-filtration system came from outside, from the power grid. Switching over from outside power to the inside in an emergency was a matter of flipping a switch and firing up the generator.

Schweitzer was a prepper—preparing for the end— long before the description was common. In those days,

Pergram knew, the threat was perceived to be external. These days, with preppers, the threat was thought to come from within. Those church idiots, he thought, were ahead of their time.

To the right was the makeshift studio. That's where the bed was located. What made it different from a normal basement bedroom, aside from the lighting and camera tripod, were the ringbolts in the concrete walls, the wooden box of sex toys and leather restraints, and the curled-up garden hose just out of camera view that was used to wash off the walls and floor after they'd used it. Under the bed was a large grated drain. The fitted sheet over the mattress was heavy duty plastic, so blood wouldn't soak through.

There was a dark hallway leading off the studio area that led to another room. That room was unfinished and had never been used by Schweitzer. It's where they kept the girls Pergram brought back, on the other side of a heavy steel door with a single one-inch-by-three-inch viewing slot closed by a steel slider.

"Mostly," Legerski echoed, shaking his head and glaring at Pergram. Pergram shrugged.

"What are you talking about?" Jimmy asked again.

"Shut up, Jimmy," Legerski said sharply. Jimmy shut up. For a moment he stopped pacing and nodding. He seemed to finally sense a confrontation brewing in his feral way, Pergram thought.

"What do you mean when you say *mostly*?" Legerski asked.

"I think you know," Pergram said. "Why should I cash in my insurance policy just now?"

"You aren't fucking thinking clear," Legerski said. "You're leaving loose ends around. You're leaving *evidence.*"

"They aren't loose. They just aren't with me here."

Again, Jimmy said, "What are you two talking about?" His voice went up an octave as he asked.

They ignored him.

Pergram said, "Maybe you shouldn't have killed that Hoyt guy. You acted alone in that. Maybe you should have thought about what that could bring down on our heads."

Legerski flushed. He was angry, but he didn't want to show it. He said, "If I didn't we'd already be fucked. It was something that had to happen, given the circumstances. I already explained this to you. And if you really think about it, you'll see I made the right decision at the right time."

Pergram hesitated, then said, "Maybe. But you also said you could handle whatever came afterwards."

Legerski held out his hands, palms up. "This lady cop from Helena. I could never have predicted her showing up this morning. I figured if anything they might send a cruiser down from Livingston to check out the roads and check in with me. I know all those guys up there and I get along with all of them. No way did I think someone from Helena would just show up like that. She could really screw everything up."

"I thought you said you could handle it."

"This is different," he said, looking down at his boots. Pergram felt his stomach roil.

"What's so special about her?"

"Nothing," Legerski said. "She's got no real experience. I checked on her and she's new to the department. She's a diversity hire and shouldn't even be there. Her husband was in the military and got whacked in Afghanistan, so she's a single mother, and if she was smart she'd just ride things out and do her time and build her pension."

"So what's the problem?" Pergram asked, starting to get annoyed with Legerski. "You're supposed to sweet-talk people like that."

"Normally, I could," Legerski said. "But she's taking everything personally. She knew this Cody Hoyt—he was her partner. She wants to find out what happened to him and she thinks it's connected to those girls back there." When he said it he jerked his head toward the dark hallway. "She's getting the Park County Sheriff's office involved and she asked me to go to Judge Graff and get a warrant to search the compound."

Pergram was confused. "Isn't that what you wanted? For them to suspect the church?"

"Yeah," he said without conviction. "I wanted them to go out there and hit a dead end. You know, cast some suspicion on the members and interview a few of them even. Then the investigation would just sort of fade away because she wouldn't find anything to implicate them. But she's not your average cop. Like I said, she's taking this personally and asking a lot of questions I never thought would come up.

"Look," Legerski said, "I know cops. I am one. I know the difference between mailing it in and getting in your hours and really going after something. I mean, she's down here on her own time. I can't see her just filing a report and going away. She talked to me like I was a suspect. She fucking *interrogated* me. But she just kept hammering away with *one more thing, one more thing*. Then she asked me if I knew any long-haul truckers who lived around here."

Legerski let that sink in.

"Ask Jimmy if you don't believe me."

Pergram looked to Jimmy. Jimmy said, "Yeah, it was at my place an hour ago. She's a bitch. She's got no sense of humor. One of those types, you know?"

Pergram felt a stab of red rage rush up his throat. "You didn't . . ."

"No, I didn't tell her anything she could go on," Legerski said, waving Pergram's question away with a big paw. "Like I said, she got me to agree to see the judge this morning and get the warrant. I don't have a choice. It was that or come off like I was impeding her investigation. So that's where I'm headed as soon as we're done."

"What did you tell her?" Pergram asked.

"Nothing. But she's not going to let go of it once she clears the folks on the compound. If she starts to ask around it's no secret you and me know each other. Locals will tell her that. I can't deny it if she asks." Legerski leaned forward and the two front legs of his chair lowered to the concrete.

"So what if you know me?" Pergram said.

Legerski flushed. "It's the same thing Hoyt asked, is what I'm saying. You're a kind of logical conclusion given the circumstances. I can see it plain as day. They've got a bead on you even though they don't know who you are. It's just a matter of time before she puts two and two together."

"What?"

"You're a type, Ronald," Legerski said. "You fit the profile. I always knew it."

Pergram felt suddenly angry. "What *profile?*"

The way he said it made Jimmy's eyes go big. He stared at Pergram gap-mouthed, as if this was all new to him.

"Jesus," Legerski said, glancing again at his boots, "I'd hoped it wouldn't come to this. But it's the same way I found you in the first place. I looked back at the cold case files and found that friend of your sister's. What was her name, Melody? Yeah, Melody Anderson. Seventeen, high school athlete in Livingston. Tall, a little crazy. She vanished, as you know."

Pergram stepped back involuntarily. He had no inclination Legerski knew about Melody. His first. And his first mistake, in a way. He'd learned things since, he wanted to shout. No more locals. Obviously, they'd look close when it came to locals. So to ensure a steady supply and avoid area gossip and suspicion, he'd learned to cast his net much wider. And concentrate on targets with no support system, no anxious friends, family, or relatives. So that when they were gone no one would really miss them. It took a while to get it figured out, but he'd mastered the system. But Melody, the first, would always sit back there calling at him. Like she was now. Since then, he'd always been so careful. . . .

"You're a fucking poster child for the profile," Legerski said. "Think about it. Late forties. Single. Gone for long periods of time. A determined cop could start to match up known disappearances with your long-haul trucking logs if they did the research. Hell, I did it. They'd start to see a pattern of missing women that corresponded with your routes. So when Hoyt asked I looked into his eyes and I saw he was one of those rare bulldogs. He was going to grab this thing with his teeth and run this out. What I did to him saved your miserable life, Pergram."

With that, Legerski grabbed the cheap plastic arm-rests of his chair and pushed himself up until he was standing. His right hand hovered over his weapon.

"And for saving your life, you give me this shit," Legerski said to him.

Pergram looked around the room, trying not to meet Legerski's or Jimmy's eyes. He had to think for himself and not be influenced by them.

He said to Legerski, "You're making this out like you were saving me. But you were really saving your-self because you didn't know where the videos were hidden, or how many copies I made."

The trooper's mask cracked. Pergram knew he hit home. The illusion was shattered. Until Legerski had all of the videos in his possession, he wouldn't be in complete control of Pergram, and they both knew it.

Pergram said, "You did what you did to save your hide. You never gave a shit about me. I'm the one who made all this possible. I never needed you, or this bunker, or anything else. I started this and you and Jimmy weaseled your way in. So don't get high and mighty and say you killed a cop to save me.

"You don't care about me," Pergram said.

Legerski filled his huge chest with a deep intake of air, as if it was a response. His eyes and face betrayed his defiance and acceptance, Pergram thought.

No words were spoken for a minute. Pergram and Legerski glared at each other. Pergram thought about dropping his right hand into his pocket and grasping the .45 and pulling the trigger.

Jimmy suddenly said, "I want to see them girls. I want to do them now."

Legerski said, "You're out of your fucking mind, Jimmy. This is not the time."

Jimmy rolled his eyes theatrically and put his hands on his hips. "You two have seen them. I haven't even seen them yet."

"Later," Legerski said.

"Bull-*shee-it*," Jimmy moaned. Making the word stretch over three syllables. "We got girls back there I've never even seen. Young meat, from what you told me. But you two assholes are standing around struttin' like peacocks. I say we go back there and see what the Lizard King brung us."

"I said," Legerski whispered, "not now, Jimmy. You know the rules. We all participate or none of us do."

"We're all here," Jimmy said, sweeping his hands toward Legerski and then Pergram. "I been up all night with your bullshit. Now it's time to meet the new chickens."

Pergram stared hard at Legerski. The only reason Jimmy was involved was because the trooper had brought him in. Pergram never wanted additional participants. It made things too complicated.

"Fuck you two," Jimmy said, turning on his heel toward the dark hallway. "I'm gonna go get them and bring them out here and we're gonna have a good time. Why the hell else would I even agree to come here?"

"Jimmy," Legerski cautioned.

"From what you said, we might all get busted," Jimmy said over his shoulder, "so I want what I want in the meantime. Ya'll can come along with me or stay around here arguing about who done what first."

Pergram hated the fact that things were chaotic. The idea of Jimmy getting to those girls first was an unspeakable affront.

"This was my thing a long time before you two came into it," he said. "You two shouldn't even be here."

Legerski ignored him, and filed in behind Jimmy as he went down the hallway.

Pergram closed his eyes for a moment and despised Legerski for being involved. And despised Jimmy for what he was doing. Then he followed them both down the hallway.

Why not? he asked himself. He thought of those long bare legs on the dark-haired one. Those spindly freckled legs on the other. Still, though, the timing and desire needed to be right. . . .

Jimmy got to the door first. Legerski was behind him and to his right. Despite the poor illumination, Pergram thought he saw Legerski reach down on his right side and unsnap his sidearm.

Then Jimmy whooped and reached for the door.

35.

Gracie felt more than heard footfalls coming toward the door. The talking, the low rumbling, had stopped.

"Oh, Jesus, they're coming," Gracie whispered to Danielle.

On the other side of the door, a man yelled out with a high-pitched cry. Like he was cheering something.

She felt her sister's hand squeeze hard.

The vertical viewing slot in the door was thrown back, and a pair of eyes filled it for a moment before it was closed again.

There was the sharp report of a bolt being thrown, metal on metal. Then the door opened inward and there was a flood of light silhouetting two figures. Not two, she thought. *Three* of them. One after the other. Their bodies melded together into a single wide mass but three heads stuck out at the top. The first one wore a cowboy hat with the side brims bent up sharply. The middle one wore a peaked cap of some kind.

The last man to enter was hatless but the blocky shape of his head was familiar. He was the trucker who'd brought them here and the man who'd pulled Krystyl out of the room by her hair. Gracie saw the glint of a badge on the second man, and for a brief electric moment her heart soared. *The police had come to rescue them.* Then she realized the man with the badge was in the middle of the three, not in back where he should be. He wasn't prodding the men into the room—he was one of them.

A voice she'd not heard before, high and twangy, said, "Hello, girls." Then: "Gimme that flashlight."

A few seconds later Gracie was blinded by a beam. He'd shined it directly into her eyes. She raised her hands up and covered her face. Even through her closed eyelids she knew the bright light was still on her.

"That skinny little one looks like a damned boy," the first one with the flashlight said. He was describing *her*. The beam left Gracie and swept to the left.

"Now, that's what I'm talkin' about," the man said, his voice rising again until he sounded giddy. "That's what I'm *talkin'* about. Ha!"

The light, of course, was on Danielle.

"I was getting bored with them whores," the man said. "You done good this time, Ronald. You keep this up and we won't have to call you the Lizard King no more."

Now that the light was off her, Gracie spread her

fingers so she could see between them. The tall skinny one had come further into the room and now stood above them about fifteen feet away. She didn't have the nerve to look up toward the flashlight or his face. In the reflected light she could see his scuffed pointy-toed cowboy boots, tight jeans, and an oval bronze belt buckle. The two men behind him, the trucker and the one with the badge, were still in shadow.

"Woo-eee," the skinny old man said, dragging the word out.

She raised her eyes. The man with the badge behind the cowboy bent over, stood back up, and extended his hand toward the cowboy's neck and she saw the outline of a gun in it.

The *bang* was concussive in the closed room and the skinny man dropped straight down. She heard the thud of his knees on the concrete and he was directly in front of her. The flashlight rolled away from him toward her, strobing across the side wall.

She got a glimpse of his face in the flashing light: long and horselike, sallow cheeks, unshaven skin sequined with silver whiskers like some kind of backwoods hillbilly type from the movies. His mouth was open slightly to reveal long yellow teeth and his eyes looked right at her but there didn't seem to be anything intelligent behind them. He looked surprised.

The big man in the uniform stood behind him and pressed the muzzle of the gun to the back of the cowboy's head and there was another explosion. The cowboy stiffened and fell over face-first.

Something hot and viscous landed on her bare leg but she didn't look down to see what it was. She could smell gunpowder, blood, and burned hair.

"Dumb son of a bitch," the man with the gun said. And to them, he said, "Sorry you had to see that, girlies."

Gracie asked, "Are you here to help us?"

"Hardly," the man with the badge said. Then, to the man behind him, "Ronald, help me drag this dumb son of a bitch into the corner for now."

36.

Ronald Pergram watched it happen; Jimmy striding into the room blathering and whooping, asking for Legerski's flashlight and reaching back for it, clicking it on and shining it on the girls in the corner, the beam playing on them like an evil eye. Then down and to the right, in the corner of his eye, he saw the trooper squat down surprisingly quick for a man of his bulk and tug up on his pant leg to reveal the butt of a revolver jutting out from an ankle holster, pulling it, and with one motion raising it up so the muzzle was four inches behind Jimmy's ear. Jimmy never sensed it coming or looked around.

When the man went down, he watched Legerski fire the kill shot into the back of Jimmy's stupid head.

Pergram didn't make a move to stop the sequence. He just watched. There was no fear whatsoever that Legerski would turn on him.

Because he was the Lizard King, he had insurance, and right now he was bulletproof. Legerski turned and brandished the gun.

"The throwdown I used earlier," he said, meaning it was the same untraceable weapon he'd used on Hoyt.

The trooper said, "Don't worry. I'll get rid of it soon enough."

Jimmy's body was light. Pergram grabbed a leg and dragged it toward the wall. He could feel Jimmy's muscles twitch and quiver beneath the denim. Jimmy's broken head left a wide spoor of black blood behind him like a wake behind a boat.

They got the body into the corner and Legerski kicked the stray flung-out limbs into some kind of order.

"Get the flashlight and help me."

Dutifully, but resenting the hell out of following any man's orders, Pergram closed his hand around the barrel of the flashlight on the floor. It was sticky from rolling through the blood. He carried it over to where Legerski was bent over Jimmy's body. The trooper was looting his pockets of change; a folding knife; his wallet; and a wad of credit cards, receipts, and notes to himself Jimmy kept bound with a rubber band in his shirt pocket. Legerski unbuckled Jimmy's belt and pulled it free through the loops.

"So they don't have something to use as a weapon or to hang themselves."

Then he took Jimmy's cowboy boots off and tossed them through the open door into the hallway.

The act made Pergram remember the door was still

open and it seemed to do the same to Legerski, because
the trooper pivoted on his boots and pointed his finger
toward the girls in the corner.

"Don't neither of you even think of running through
that door. There's no place to go and we'll stop you before you even get there. You seen what happened here,
what I'm capable of. You have *no* idea what my partner
is capable of. So just sit there quiet until we leave."

Pergram turned and hit them with the flashlight.
They hadn't moved, but he saw something flash in the
younger girl's eyes. She'd been thinking about it, thinking about trying to dash by them toward the door. He
smiled but he knew she couldn't see him do it.

The girl with the dark hair said, "You're going to
leave him in here?"

"For a while," Legerski said. "Until we figure out
what to do with him."

Pergram watched as Legerski looked around, saw
the old blanket on the floor, and snatched it up to cover
most of Jimmy's body. "There," the trooper said, "now
we don't have to look at him."

Pergram didn't want to talk, even though Jimmy, the
stupid old coot, had actually said his name. So had
Legerski. Even so, he doubted the girls would remember it, given what happened. They'd heard his voice before, but why push it now?

The older one buried her face into her hands and
Pergram heard a sob. He looked at the younger one.
She looked back, grim, her face a mask of defiance.

He thought, *She'll be fun to break.* All that misplaced
attitude based on nothing he could see. She was just

another one of those overachiever types like his dead sister JoBeth. She didn't know how the world worked. How could she, when she'd spent her life being coddled, being told how smart and special she was? At least the older was crying. Maybe, on a gut level, she understood. If not, she'd find out soon enough, he thought.

Even though it was the wrong time, the absolute wrong time, he felt his insides stir and his blood rise.

"You ready to go?" Legerski asked him.

Pergram nodded reluctantly. First things first.

As Legerski jammed Jimmy's possessions into a plastic bag in the other other room, he said, "We'll be better off without him."

"Yeah. I never wanted him involved in the first place."

The trooper looked up. "I know that. I wish I wouldn't have brought him in. But you know what happened. He started asking me questions about our comings and goings. I knew he was a deviant, but I didn't know he'd be reckless."

"I did."

It had been an unbelievably stupid move on Legerski's part. Six months before, Jimmy had asked why it was the trooper kept ordering food to go in quantity when there was only one of him still left in his house. Asking him things like, "You got a dolly you ain't telling me about?" Things like that. One night when the trooper was drunk and off duty, Jimmy showed him his porn collection, which was extensive and revealed his rough inclinations. Legerski noticed a few items that could only be trophies—locks of hair, panties, a pair of glasses. One thing led to another, and the next time Pergram and Legerski went to the bunker for a session Legerski had brought Jimmy along.

Pergram thought letting Legerski in had been his first mistake, although he didn't feel like he had a choice at the time. Letting Jimmy in compounded the problem.

"It is what it is," Legerski said, knotting the plastic garbage sack. "No one around here will be very shocked that Jimmy just closed up and hit the road. He's done it for months at a time before."

Pergram nodded, but a bad thought was forming.

"You mean you don't have a real cover story for Jimmy going away?"

"Not really."

"You're just winging it? I thought you were supposed to be the great planner?"

"We didn't have no choice. Jimmy was going to go in there and get them girls before we could get to them first. That was never the deal. He got greedy and stupid. Plus, we don't have the time for that now. We've got to take care of our situation first and get the heat off."

Pergram nodded for the sake of nodding.

"Look," Legerski said, "I've got to get to Livingston and see that judge. That cunt cop is probably wondering where the hell I am now. I've got to get up there and cover my ass."

"And leave mine hanging," Pergram said.

"No, it's not like that."

"The hell it isn't."

"Ronald," the trooper said, "you've got to step up now. I've been doing all the dirty work. It's time you stepped up."

Pergram leaned back and looked at Legerski through slitted eyes, waiting. The bad thought was turning into a freight train headed right at him.

"That Helena cop knows me," Legerski said. "She don't know you. You can get close enough to her to hit with a roofie. You can either take her to your secret spot in the park or bring her back here, I don't care. But we've got to get her off the street before she stirs things up around here and asks too many questions and starts putting things together."

Pergram said, "You saying you want me to kill the lady cop?"

"That's what I'm saying."

"Won't that bring down seven kinds of hell on us?"

Legerski stepped back from the table. "It could," he said, "but not if we do it quick and thorough. The Park County sheriff's deputies aren't due for hours. She's completely on her own. If we take her out now, it'll be a mystery but no one will know jack shit unless we screw it up.

"In fact," Legerski said, warming to it, "I can steer things a different direction. I can say I saw the two of them—Hoyt and Dewell—getting intimate in a car on the side of the road. Who's to say they didn't just run off together? The disgraced cop and his lover and partner? It sounds like something Cody Hoyt would do. It's just crazy enough people will believe it."

Then he grinned, and said, "I'll work on the story. I've got between now and seeing the judge to work on it. I can plant the seeds with the Park County guys I know. There might be some holes but for now I'm liking it."

Pergram didn't say he did, didn't say he didn't. All he knew was that everything he'd built over the years was piled up between the tracks and that freight train was coming. All he'd accomplished was coming apart and spinning wildly out of control and the person running the show was standing right in front of him with a trash bag of a dead man's remains in his hand.

Legerski grasped the handle of the ammo box Pergram had delivered with one hand and held the plastic bag with the other. For a moment, Pergram refused to let go and the two men stared in each other's eyes. Then Pergram released his grip and let Legerski take it.

"You know I've got more copies," Pergram whispered.

"I'll need them, too."

"Not until I decide to give them to you."

"You might get us arrested if you keep them."

"Yeah," Pergram said, "but if that happens it'll be the both of us. We'll go down together."

Legerski gave Pergram his best cop dead-eye, but Pergram didn't crack. He'd been on the receiving end of cops and their looks for years.

Pergram gave it a beat, didn't want to ruin Legerski's

good time. He changed the subject and said, "What does this cop look like and what is she driving?"

The trooper described the Ford Expedition and the Lewis & Clark County plates. He said, "Midthirties, heavy-set, medium-length brown hair, brown eyes, wearing a dark pantsuit and a white blouse."

And added, "She has a pretty face."

37.

Cassie sat in the parked and idling Ford Expedition on the shoulder of the highway and thought about Thanksgiving, churches, and God.

The compound for the Church of Glory and Transcendence was across the river on the other side of Yankee Jim Canyon. She'd seen it years before as she passed by but she'd never studied the layout or paid much attention to it overall. Now, she looked at it through field glasses, building to building, hoping to find something that would lead to solving the disappearance of the Sullivan girls and Cody Hoyt. She saw no fresh tire tracks on the moist dirt road leading to the compound or on the roads within it, and she saw no red Ford, no sign of Cody's pickup.

The morning sun, fused through winter storm clouds, came soft and late to the valley. Colors, shadows, and contours appeared flat. There were so many days of sunshine in Montana that a day without it always felt odd to her, and it somehow dampened her earlier enthusiasm that she was doing the right thing and that the investigation was going somewhere.

A hundred yards up the road was a closed gate. The road beyond the gate wound down her side of the river to a two-lane bridge over the river to the compound. It looked to be the only way in and out, although she couldn't tell if there were roads into the mountains from behind the buildings, and guessed there must be.

The compound was laid out on a huge bench of land directly across from her. Sharp-walled foothills rose in back and to the sides, and it looked as if the mountains were cradling the compound in the palms of their open hands. There was a kind of military precision to the layout. To the left, there were four or five long neat rows of small white single-family houses, all with green roofs. In the middle of the assemblage was a massive chapel marked by a pointed steeple. The four rows of stained-glass windows indicated there were at least four floors within it, or at least the front half. The chapel was also painted white. A two-level clapboard building served as the school, she guessed, based on the playground equipment in a fenced area adjacent to it. To the right were large anonymous buildings, garages and equipment sheds and storage facilities, she guessed. That would be the place to look for the missing vehicles, she thought. The rest of the bench to the right was a plowed field that was fuzzy green with early shoots of winter wheat.

What was remarkable about the compound, she

thought, was the utter lack of human activity. Sure, there were wisps of woodsmoke from the chimneys of the houses and curlicues of steam from the roof pipe of one of the outbuildings, but there were no people about. She wondered if they were all underground, and the thought unnerved her.

She tried to imagine the network and scope of the underground complex that supposedly existed underneath the buildings. Except for odd concrete abutments that appeared for no rhyme or reason in the gravel yards in front of the homes and within the outbuildings, there was no reason to suspect it was there.

During one of the long spells when her mother was gone, Cassie had been shuttled to her uncle Frank's place on a small, windswept cattle ranch outside Miles City, Montana, on the eastern plains. Uncle Frank and Aunt Helen had four boys, two older than her and two younger, none of whom still remained in the county. Until Uncle Frank lost the ranch and moved to town, she was one of the boys when it came to ranch work. Although her uncle wanted to spoil his only girl, she'd have none of it. Part of the reason was to avoid teasing from her cousins, the other part was her desire to fit in. She built fence, delivered calves, and pulled the flatbed behind the truck or tractor; loading hay bales in the summer and feeding the hay to the cattle in the winter.

Every Sunday they'd go to church in Miles City, the First Congregational Church. Her cousins hated it, but she secretly loved the opportunity to dress up once a week, be a girl, drive to town with brothers who smelled clean and looked nice. She never understood why they went to the Congregational Church, and never understood the difference between Congregationalists and Lutherans or Baptists or Presbyterians. She knew Catholics thought themselves special and she always envied them for it because they seemed to know something she didn't. There were a few Mormons in town and they had the most modern church, with a basketball court inside, and she envied that, too.

She decided she was a Christian back then, and she figured she still was. When she glassed the compound she wondered about the members who were so devout they'd uprooted and moved there years ago so they could be with like-minded believers. She envied them like she'd envied the Catholics and Mormons because they seemed to believe in something. She didn't think they were stupid, or ignorant. In fact, maybe they were smarter than her in a spiritual way. At least they believed in *something* that could help guide them through their lives.

She didn't hear the bell but it must have rung for recess, because suddenly the yard near the school was filled with children. They filled the swing sets and lined up for the slide. Boys squared off for a football game. Children who didn't get to the equipment or the organized games stood in knots in the corners of the yard talking among themselves. Three adults bundled in parkas supervised by walking around.

She zoomed in. The children varied in ages from probably five to gawky teenagers. They looked healthy and well dressed in conservative but not tremendously dated clothing. She noted the rosy cheeks of some of the girls in the cold morning, and the clouds of condensation that floated above their heads like thought bubbles.

Cassie moved the binoculars and focused on a group of five or six small children in the corner of the yard. They were apart from the older kids and kept to themselves in the natural tribal order of children on a playground. Their coats seemed too large and bulky for their size—probably hand-me-downs—and their little legs stuck out the bottom like twigs. They weren't much older than Ben, she thought. Two of the boys could *be* Ben. The thought made her heart swell and she fought off a sudden and unexpected urge to cry.

Cassie sighed and wiped at her eyes with the back of her hand and lowered the binoculars to her lap. She was not getting any kind of suspicious feeling from what she saw that the church members across the canyon were malevolent, that they'd be involved in the disappearance of teenage girls or Cody. It was silly to think that, she knew. Evil people often didn't look evil from the outside. That was one of the revelations of police work for her; that the man out mowing his lawn could be as awful as the crackheads who lived in the rental cabins above Lincoln. She knew God-squad types could be capable of great crimes. But she just wasn't getting the vibe, despite what Trooper Legerski had said.

She wished she could ask Cody for his thoughts on

the situation. He put more stock in intuition than most cops she'd met. Once, he'd said, "When something feels hinky, better go with it." But nothing she saw or felt in the compound seemed hinky.

Cassie considered driving up to the gate and asking them to open it. That had been her original intention. But when she thought more about it, she decided she couldn't risk it even if it was what Cody likely would have done—and possibly did. If they didn't let her in and she had to wait for the warrant to arrive, that might give them hours to hide and dispose of evidence if there was any. And if they let her in and her intuition about them was wrong—there she was. They could disappear her the same way they'd disappeared the Sullivan girls and Cody.

So she'd wait until the Park County deputies arrived with the warrant, and, if necessary, they'd use it for access. She had plenty of time to kill and wonder if what she was doing made any rational sense.

She checked her wristwatch. An hour and a half toward lunchtime, an hour for lunch, then maybe three or four more working hours left in the day before everyone took off for the Thanksgiving holiday. It took forty-five minutes from Livingston to get where she was, so that cut down the available time for the Park County deputies to help her even further. She cursed the timing of it all. Why couldn't this have happened on a Monday, instead?

The Sullivan girls had been missing for barely thirteen hours, and Cody eight. If they were being held alive in the compound or elsewhere, what were the chances they'd still be alive after the four-day weekend? After ninety-six hours of captivity? She'd seen the crime statistics for kidnapping at the academy. The odds were slim to none.

Then she thought again about Ben. He deserved a Thanksgiving dinner. He deserved some kind of normalcy and tradition, the things she never had growing up with her mother. She'd get back to Helena, she decided, as soon as she could. The Albertsons stayed open late and if they didn't have turkeys left she'd buy a ham. If necessary, she'd cook all night.

The thought of being at home with Ben while the Sullivan girls and Cody were still missing brought a nauseating wave of guilt. But what could she do if they found nothing to go on?

Cassie tried to jump-start the process. She called the Park County Sheriff's Department on her cell phone and asked for Sheriff Bryan Pedersen directly. The receptionist placed her on hold, and enough time went by that Cassie imagined a conversation between the sheriff and the receptionist to concoct the best cover story they could come up with to refuse the call.

Finally, "This is Sheriff Pedersen." His voice was dry and high, not pretentious.

"This is Investigator Cassandra Dewell of Lewis and Clark County," she said.

"Right, Deputy Dewell. Whenever I hear your name I think of Deputy Dawg, the cartoon character." There was a beat. "I hope you aren't offended."

"No, it isn't the first time I heard it."

"Sorry, then." He chuckled. "So what can I do you for?"

"Has Sheriff Tubman contacted you this morning? He said he would."

"Oh, yeah," Pedersen said, "it slipped my mind. We've got everybody out on assignment right now but I might be able to spare a couple of guys after lunch."

"After lunch?"

"Yeah, I got Gadbury and Simmons I can send down there. They're two of my best investigators." Meaning plainclothes detectives, similar to Cassie and Cody.

"What about some uniforms?" she asked.

"Not likely. We're running a skeleton crew as it is because of the holiday coming. I've got to have a couple guys here on call and I've got to man my jail. I can't pull anybody to drive down there today."

She closed her eyes and breathed deeply to remain calm. Legerski's words came back to her, that just because she was having a crisis didn't mean anybody else was.

"Sheriff, we've got three missing people. Trooper Rick Legerski is on his way up there to get a search warrant from the judge, and I really need some manpower from your department to help serve it."

"This is for the church compound?" Pedersen said, an unmistakable note of reluctance in his voice.

"Yes."

"Yeah, I guess I know about this," Pedersen said.

She waited for more, but more didn't come.

"Sheriff, is there a problem?"

A long sigh. "No, I told Tubman I'd help you out. I owe him a couple. But you have to understand something, Deputy Dewell. This whole thing sounds flimsy to me. You're asking us to go down there and turn a church group upside down the day before Thanksgiving based on what you suspect? How do you suppose that's going to play with them or with the residents in the valley? It seems damned heavy-handed, if you ask me."

I didn't, she wanted to say. Instead, she said, "Look at it this way. The quicker we clear them the quicker we can look other directions. I'm sure they'll appreciate that."

"You think?" he said, dubious. Then, "You're determined to do this today?"

"Yes."

"Less than twenty-four hours after these girls were reported missing . . . *somewhere?*"

"Yes."

"Are you sure it can't wait a little while? Say after the holiday weekend? We'll have more guys available then and we might have more to go on. We don't even know if those girls disappeared in the canyon for sure, do we?"

"No. But Investigator Cody Hoyt told me personally he was coming here last night to investigate. That's the last we heard of him."

Groaning, Pedersen said, "I know Cody. He's an obstinate son of a gun. I guess I shouldn't be surprised he thinks it's just fine to cross the county line and start an investigation out of his jurisdiction without bothering to inform or involve the local authorities."

"He's on his own," she said, knowing she sounded defensive.

"He always is, and that's the problem with guys like that."

She said, "We can debate Cody's methods or we can try to save some lives, Sheriff."

Pedersen sighed again.

"I heard you were kind of tough to deal with."

"Who told you that?" She suspected either Tubman or Legerski. Either way, as much as she wanted to deny the feeling, it cut into her. Then she thought: not Tubman. Even sheriff to sheriff, he wouldn't cast aspersions on his own high-profile diversity program hire.

"So Trooper Legerski has been in contact with you this morning?"

"Just a few minutes ago, as a matter of fact. He wanted to know if the judge was in chambers or off for Thanksgiving."

So she knew. Legerski.

She said, "Is the judge in?"

"Until noon. After that, he's on the road."

"Good. We should be able to get the warrant."

"I suppose, Investigator Dewell. But he might have some of the same questions I do. He may wonder why we can't wait."

She closed her eyes, fighting real anger. She said, "If it turns out those girls and my partner were hurt down here and we could have prevented it, maybe then you'll be able to explain to everyone why it was best to wait over a four-day weekend to save them."

"Calm down, little lady—"

"I'm not anyone's little lady, Sheriff."

"And no wonder. But never mind. I'll send Gadbury and Simmons like I said. And if I can rustle anyone else up, I'll send them, too. I'll ask them to give you a call when they get close so you can arrange a place to meet."

She said, "At the locked gate that leads to the compound. Tell them to meet me there."

"All *right*."

He said it as if he couldn't wait to get off the phone.

Fuming, she noticed as the Expedition idled there was only a quarter of a tank of gas left, and she decided to run the ten miles farther to Gardiner to fill up. As she pulled back onto the highway toward Gardiner, she replayed the conversation with Sheriff Pedersen in her head, and got even angrier. *Little lady?* Legerski had poisoned the well. Why?

She thought again about the number of cigarette butts she'd found in the Dumpster. She thought about the furtive way he'd acted when they met that morning. She speculated what the trooper had told the sheriff in their conversation about her other than she was "tough to deal with." She thought about what he'd mouthed when he left.

Cassie opened her phone again and speed-dialed Edna's cell phone back in Helena. She didn't want to talk to the chief dispatcher over the radio where anyone listening could hear.

After recapping what had happened and where she was, Cassie asked, "Didn't you say your sister still lives in Gardiner?"

"Yes, hon. Sally. She owns the little quilt shop there. Yellowstone Quilt Shop."

Cassie nodded. "I have a little time. I might just drop by and see her."

"I'll call her and tell her you're coming. I'll bet she'll do a twenty percent discount for you if I ask."

"Edna," Cassie said sharply, "please don't call her. I'll just drop by. I want to ask her a couple of questions about her ex-husband Rick Legerski. I'd rather she didn't know that before I got there."

Edna paused and said, "She's a private person. But if she trusts you she has plenty to tell. Okay, I won't call her."

"Thanks, Edna."

38.

The snow squall had stopped for the time being but the storm clouds to the north looked to be gathering, bunching, closing their fists to deliver a much harder blow later in the day. Pergram bounced the old Buick down the rutted private road toward his home, a sense of black calm in his head and heart.

Although he did poorly in school and barely graduated, he'd always had an innate ability to plan and figure, to think several steps ahead. If he was ever called to write his formulas down on paper he couldn't do it. But he had learned over the years from trucking that he could outthink and outmaneuver his fellow drivers and keep himself ahead of the game. He was *superior* to them. That's why he kept his load just under the 80,000 pounds gross vehicle weight by not filling both 125-gallon tanks all the way and adding the extra weight of fuel. When he ran he never used cruise control but used his

gears to avoid unnecessary stress on the motor, and he
kept it below the speed limit, between sixty-two and
sixty-four miles an hour, optimal speed for fuel savings. He knew his truck would get 6.2 miles per gallon
in the summer and 5.5 in the winter and he planned
accordingly; putting on more fuel in low-tax or rebate
states like Illinois and driving across high-tax hard-ass
Minnesota without stopping at all. He ate and slept in
his cab and didn't waste money at truck stops unless he
could help it. He perfected the art of shifting his load
slightly from the front of the trailer to the rear and vice
versa by applying pneumatic air to different parts of
the trailer as he drove over scales.

All those strategies gained him time, saved him
money, and ended up on his bottom line every month.
Over the years, he'd earned tens of thousands by not
being stupid, not being brash, just trucking along thinking a hundred miles in front of him while the scenery
rolled by.

He did that now, as he drove to his house. He could
see a hundred miles ahead of him and he knew what he
needed to do.

The "Oh Shit" box sat on the passenger seat next to
him.

The flimsy old curtain in the living room opened a few
inches as he noted the scarred foot of a cane holding
the fabric back. That's how she looked outside these
days without actually standing up. She leaned forward
in her chair and parted the curtains with her cane. He
pretended not to notice her.

Pergram didn't go straight into the house. Instead, he carried the "Oh Shit" box to his Peterbilt, hoisted himself up, and climbed inside. The box went between the seats. Then he shut the door and leaned on the coil and started up the Cat 15 motor. It was cold at first and he sat quietly and feathered the fuel until the racketing of the diesel motor smoothed into a familiar hum. He checked the stacks and observed them until the exhaust turned from oily black to chalky to clear.

He checked his gauges, fuel level, air pressure, temperature, fluid levels. Everything was beautiful. It felt good to be back inside his cab. It felt *right*, a warrior mounting his warhorse, he thought. His foray onto solid ground this time had been a disaster.

He left the truck idling and swung out of the cab and clambered down the steps to the dirt. He knew she hated it when he left his truck running outside so close to the house.

Pergram went in through the front door and shinnied his way through the tunnel toward his bedroom door. As he passed her she was still in her chair where she'd been when he left. She shook her cane at him and her mouth moved and sounds came out. He didn't even look over.

He unlocked his bedroom door and strode inside. Within a minute, he'd packed his laptop, video camera, digital cameras, and VHS to DVD converter into a hard-sided case. Standing on top of his bed, he reached up through the cheap paneling squares and grasped a grocery bag containing copies of all the original discs and tapes he'd delivered to Legerski. The bag had so many video sessions preserved he could barely fit it into the case. But he managed, and he clicked the hasps shut.

The door remained open as he left the room. No need to lock it, he thought.

The droning, cackling sound he heard as an irritating soundtrack came into focus because he let it. He paused a few feet short of the alcove of stacked treasures where she still sat.

"Ronald! You know how I feel about that truck running right outside my window. I can't hear myself think it's so loud. It's like somebody is shaking me. I can feel the whole house shake. I can smell the fumes and they make me sick. What have I asked you about leaving that truck running?"

He didn't respond. Just stood there.

"Ronald, I know you're there. I know you can hear me, you rude son of a buck. I know you're right there."

He nodded to himself as if answering.

"Did you fill my car up with gas like you promised? If we're going to have a nice Thanksgiving I need to go into town and stock up. I don't want to run out of gas, Ronald."

Then, "Are you going on another run? Is that why you started that truck? Does that mean you won't even be here to share Thanksgiving with your old ma? Is that what you're trying to tell me?"

Pergram reached out with his free hand and placed it on a column of newspapers, magazines, and folded empty brown grocery sacks that rose from floor to ceiling. He put some weight into it, and it leaned a little. Dust motes floated down from the top level into the shaft of light from the front-room window. He leaned the stack toward the open aisle that led to her chair in the alcove of debris.

"Ronald, what are you doing? You be careful there."

"What did I say about all this shit?" he said finally.

"I'll clean it out. I told you I'd get rid of it."

He sighed.

"What about Thanksgiving, Ronald?"

"I guess you'll be able to spend it with JoBeth."

She paused.

"*What did you say?*"

"I said I guess you'll be able to spend this Thanksgiving with JoBeth, Ma."

"You're talking nonsense."

"Tell her I never could stand her."

She gasped, speechless for once.

"Tell her I couldn't stand her friends, neither."

"Ronald, don't say that. Don't say it."

He put more weight behind his hand against the stack. A few of the newspapers from the top fell off into the aisle.

"This place is a fire hazard," he said. "*How many times have I told you that?*" Mimicking her tone and cadence.

"Ronald, be careful. That ain't funny."

"It's kind of funny," he said as an aside. Then, "You told that highway trooper you thought there was something wrong with me. That I was up to something."

"What highway trooper?"

"The one who pulled you over a few years ago. Legerski."

"I don't even remember, I really don't."

"That being the case," he said, "I wonder how many other folks you talked to about me you can't remember, either? Just because what you say doesn't mean nothing to me, that doesn't mean other people might not listen to you. Ever think about that?"

He shoved hard and the column collapsed, sealing the aisle.

"Ronald!"

All he could see of her back there among the garbage was the top of her silver head. It rocked back and forth as she yelled.

"Ronald, I told you that would happen. Now you've got to help dig me out of here. Some of them things fell on my legs."

He stepped back and reached into his breast pocket with his free hand and withdrew a book of matches that read JUBITZ TRUCK STOP/PORTLAND OREGON. That was one of the good ones, he thought. No lot lizards there.

He opened the cover, fingered back a match, and rubbed it across the strike strip. The smell of sulfur was sharp and a curl of smoke hung in the stagnant air.

"What are you doing, Ronald?" she asked, finally scared.

He tipped the book so the flame spread to all the matches. It flared and he nearly dropped it because the heat singed the tips of his fingers. Then he flicked it toward the fallen stack.

"Ronald . . ."

He backed out the door and could already feel the heat on his face.

He checked his side mirrors as he ran through the low gears and the Peterbilt pulled away. The mirrors were filled with flame and roiling black curls of smoke coming out through the windows and doors of the old house. It wouldn't be long, he thought, before the Buick went up with it and rendered any hair or fiber evidence to ash. Already, the dense Russian olive bushes on the side of the house were crackling with flame.

Pergram slowed as he approached the junction to the highway, checking both lanes. He took the turn wide as he had hundreds of times, careful not to let the end of his trailer clip a delineator post, and pointed the snub nose of the Peterbilt south toward Gardiner.

Looking for that fat lady cop from Helena.

39.

The Yellowstone Quilt Shop was a former residence on Scott Street, the main road through town. It stood between a white-water raft outfitter company closed for the winter and a pawn shop with a sign that read GUNS! It was a neat Victorian, narrow with a steep roof of wooden shingles and a covered wooden porch on the front. A hanging sign made of quilt squares hung in the window and indicated it was open.

Cassie parked the Expedition along Scott Street in front of the shop and climbed out and brushed crumbs from her lap and the front of her coat. She'd filled the tank and eaten a half-dozen miniature chocolate donuts at a convenience store near the bridge that crossed the Yellowstone River. The clerk behind the counter, a bald man with a full beard who wore suspenders, said he'd never heard of the quilt shop. A woman customer behind her chewed the man out for being oblivious and gave Cassie directions.

She could hear the roar of the river behind the row of shops. It was far below them in the canyon, but the sound of rushing water carried.

White lace curtains on the inside gave it a homey, quaint feel, Cassie thought. It stood out from the elk antler look of the rest of the town. The shop, like all the buildings on the block, was close to the street. Only a narrow strip of brown grass behind the white picket fence separated if from the sidewalk.

A small bell rang as she pushed through the door. The shop was small and filled with fabrics on tables and displayed on the walls. A slim dark-haired woman looked up and smiled shyly from behind a sewing machine at an antique desk at the front. The machine she was working with went silent.

"Good thing you made it," the woman said. "I was planning to close at noon today for the holiday. But not to worry. You can browse as long as you like. The fabric on the tables is marked twenty percent off, and I'm running a nice special on fat quarters."

Cassie was embarrassed not to know what a fat quarter was and didn't ask. She always felt guilty about knowing so little about quilting and other sewing crafts. Instead, she squared her shoulders and said, "Are you the owner?"

"Yes."

Sally Legerski looked gentle and almost elegant, Cassie thought. She had high cheekbones, a wide mouth, and large blue eyes and she was slim and petite. Cassie could see very little of Edna in her facial features or build. Although she guessed Sally to be in her late forties, it wasn't hard to imagine that she'd been quite a beauty in her teens and twenties. Quite the contrast with Edna.

Cassie dug into her purse and withdrew her wallet badge and let it flop open.

"Mrs. Legerski, I'm Investigator Cassandra Dewell from the Lewis and Clark County Sheriff's Department. I'm in the area investigating the disappearance of two teenage girls last night and I hope you can answer a couple of questions."

"Oh, dear." Cassie could tell it was an expression of concern for the girls, not alarm that Sally was being questioned. Cassie had deliberately not mentioned Cody. For some reason, she didn't think that would help her.

"Two girls from Colorado on their way to Helena were last heard from after they passed through town. Since then, we've not been able to locate them or their vehicle. It's been over eighteen hours."

"I see," Sally said, obviously puzzled where the line of inquiry would go from there. After a beat, she asked, "Are you wondering if I saw them?"

Cassie raised her eyebrows. "Did you?"

"I don't think so," Sally said. "It's possible, though. There is quite a lot of traffic that passes down that street out there right outside my window. You know, people going to and from the park. Right now it's very quiet, but in the summer it gets kind of ridiculous. It gets noisy and I tend to just tune it out. What time did you say they came through town?"

Cassie checked her notes. "After nine."

"P.M.?"

"Yes."

"Then I'm sure I didn't see them. I was home by then. I live up on the hill where I can't see the road. I hope someone saw them, though, and you're able to find them. This whole town is dead by that time in the winter. I get so worried about young girls driving alone on the highway. Are you asking me because they were quilters or something?"

Cassie felt a flush of embarrassment in her cheeks.

"Not that I know of."

Sally Legerski nodded, and said, "Well, *okay,*" as a polite way of saying, *Then why are you here?*

Cassie took a deep breath and chanced a concerned smile. She said, "I should probably just come clean with you."

Sally cocked her head slightly to the side, puzzled.

"I want to ask you some questions about your ex-husband, Trooper Rick Legerski."

At the sound of his name, Sally's eyes and expression iced up. It was a visceral reaction, Cassie thought. Sally pushed back from the table and folded her arms over her breasts.

"What about him?"

"Mind if I sit down?" Cassie asked, gesturing to a folding chair on the side of the table.

Sally nodded her okay.

Cassie sat down so the two were much closer, so it

would seem more like a conversation than an interrogation.

"I met with him this morning about the missing girls since he's the only patrolman on this stretch of highway," Cassie said. "I guess we didn't hit it off very well. I came away with the feeling he was holding something back on me. I got the feeling there were things going on behind the scenes he didn't want to tell me about. I'm new to this job and I'm a stranger down here in Park County. So I was wondering . . ." she faltered. What is it exactly she wanted to know? Did she want an ex-wife to dish dirt on her ex-husband? What was the point of that? To get revenge on the man who called her a horrible name?

"Let me guess where you met," Sally said, "The First National Bar in Emigrant, right?"

Cassie nodded.

"And was the owner there? A tall creepy guy who kind of hovered around the whole time saying inappropriate things?"

"Jimmy."

"Yes, Jimmy," she said, and her top lip curled slightly as she said the name. "If I ever see Jimmy again for the rest of my life it'll be too soon."

"I didn't like him, either," Cassie said.

"He's bad news. I always hated going in there, even with Rick. Those two . . ." She didn't finish, but looked up suddenly at Cassie. She seemed startled at her own vehemence. "I'm sorry," she said. "You're dredging up some bad memories for me."

"That's not my intention," Cassie said. Although it was.

"What do you want to know about Rick?"

"I'm not sure," Cassie said. "I guess I want to know what kind of man he is."

A shadow passed over Sally's face and it turned into a mask.

She said, "I've closed that chapter in my life and I really don't want to open it up again. I've moved on, and I'm not the kind of woman who gossips about her ex-husband. I've got no respect for women who trash their ex-husbands as if they didn't bear any responsibility for choosing them in the first place. I hope that's not what you expected of me."

"I'm not meaning to pry." Cassie took a breath, unsure how to proceed.

"It sounded like you were."

"No. Let's keep this entirely professional and not personal. You were with him as he advanced in rank and moved around the state. So he must be a good highway patrolman?"

She spoke as if reciting. "Rick was a great law enforcement officer. He worked hard, put in more than his share of hours, and he didn't cut many corners. He likes to throw his weight around a little—make sure everyone knows who's boss—but that isn't unusual with some state troopers. He maintained that it was part of his job. After all, those men are usually out there on the highway all alone. They don't have partners and in a state like Montana, backup could be twenty minutes away. Asserting authority defuses situations that might become volatile.

"Believe me," she continued, "moving around the State of Montana with him through the years, I met a lot of highway patrolmen. I guess what I'm telling you without saying it very well is his job comes first."

Cassie nodded for her to go on.

She didn't. "Are we done here?"

"Yes. Unless there's something you want to tell me."

"I really don't. It's personal."

Cassie was ashamed of herself. She didn't know what direction to go. In her mind was a furious tangle of different threads and none of them came together in any logical way. There was Cody's disappearance, the presence of the church compound, the cigarette butts, the rebuffs by both Legerski and the Park County sheriff, the missing girls out there . . .

Sally said, "No one can ever really understand what goes on in the marriage of other people without being there. It's the most complicated thing in the world. I've completely stopped trying, you know? There was this wonderful couple who lived right behind me. Married forty-three years. Every time I saw them they doted on each other. The man, Walt, called her 'honeybunch' instead of Wilma, her name. I really envied them. Then one day, he says he's going out for groceries and he never comes back. She won't talk about what happened, and I have *no* idea."

Cassie shook her head.

"You always hear the arguments are about money or sex, and that's probably true. But sometimes it's just about a bad vibe. Sometimes you can look across the table at someone you've been with for years and realize to your horror you know *nothing* about them. That they are living another life right in front of your eyes. That you have absolutely *no idea* what he's doing out there away from home and he won't even offer a fake explanation why sometimes he'll roll in looking flushed and used up."

Cassie felt her scalp twitch.

Sally said after a beat and without prompting, "I'll tell you one thing: he keeps some *strange* company for a cop."

"You mean Jimmy?"

"Him, too," Sally said.

Before Cassie could ask, the silence of the shop was filled with the clatter of a diesel engine outside on the street.

"This is what I meant earlier," Sally said, raising her voice to a near shout to be heard, "it's a great location to catch the tourist traffic but a lousy one when you're trying to concentrate or carry on a conversation. Especially when it's those big trucks."

Cassie followed the shop owner's line of sight and turned in her chair. A massive black truck with a long silver trailer was right outside on the other side of the Expedition. It was stopped in the street. She leaned down and tried to see the driver through the lace curtains but the cab was too high from her angle. The truck had stopped in the street near Cassie's Expedition. She waited for the truck to move on so they could resume their conversation.

Cassie stood up and walked around the fabric tables to the window and pushed aside the lace and looked outside. A stout, heavyset man in jeans and an oversized tan coat pulled himself up into the cab of the truck and shut the door. She couldn't see his face or even a quarter profile—only a band of light-colored hair beneath the band of a greasy cap. Why had he stopped and gotten out of his truck?

With a hiss of air, the truck lurched and rolled away.

"What was that guy up to?" Cassie asked.

"I don't know," Sally said from behind the table. "I can't see."

The clatter of the truck subsided as it vanished from sight down the street. It made a wide turn on the end of the block and Cassie strained to see the license plate but all she could discern was it was commercial and from Montana.

She said, "I'll be right back," and went out the front door. The bell rang as she stepped out onto the wooden porch. Although she could no longer see it, she could track the black truck by its sound. It had turned and turned again, and was coursing up the next street over, laboring back the direction it had come.

As she walked out to the Ford, she unbuttoned her coat and reached back and rested her hand on the butt of her Glock.

She peered into the vehicle through the passenger side window and could see something on the driver's seat. She hadn't locked her door and someone—no doubt the truck driver—had opened it and placed it inside.

Cassie walked around the car and looked in. On top of the seat was a misshapen white square package. She pulled on her left glove and opened the door to retrieve it.

Three square white envelopes bound by a rubber band. She recognized them as the kind that covered CD or DVD disks. And on the white smooth surface of the outside envelope was spidery writing: *There at the Schweitzer place.*

40.

Cassie returned to the quilt shop with her briefcase and the package just as Sally Legerski rotated the hanging sign in the window from OPEN to CLOSED. She paused on the porch but Sally waved to her through the window to come in.

"That's for my customers," Sally said as Cassie closed the door behind her. "What happened out there?"

"That truck driver left me something."

"You're kidding," Sally said. "Do you know him?"

Cassie stopped. She hadn't even considered it. "No. But it's just weird because I've been thinking a lot about long-haul truck drivers lately."

Sally nodded, understandably unsure what she meant.

"He left this," Cassie said, gesturing with the envelopes.

"Oh, my."

"Can I use the table here to check them out?"

"Sure, let me clean it off."

"Don't worry about it," Cassie said, dragging the folding chair over to a table covered with folded yards of fabric. She opened her briefcase and withdrew the county laptop and opened it on top of the fabric. Sally hovered behind her, and Cassie turned her head and said, "You might not want to see this."

"What is it?"

"I'm not sure, but I've got a very bad feeling about it."

Sally returned to her chair behind the counter. From where she sat, Cassie didn't think Sally could view the screen.

As Sally started ringing out the register for the day, Cassie slid the first disk from the envelope and fed it into her DVD drive. There was no label or marking on the disk, and she thought it might contain fingerprints. She decided to save the other two for the evidence techs if necessary and not handle them further. She found her headphones in the briefcase and plugged them in. If there was sound accompanying the video, she didn't want Sally to hear it.

Without preamble, the video launched. A man's face masked in a balaclava filled the screen. She could see his eyes but they were so close to the lens they were blurry and unrecognizable. He wasn't looking into the lens. Instead, he seemed to be fiddling with the camera itself. There were thumping and static noises. Then he stepped back and turned with his back to the camera and came into focus. Cassie unconsciously placed both of her hands on the sides of her face.

He looked large and blocky, wearing a black long-sleeved sweater and black sweatpants and lace-up boots. A huge belly extended out over the waistband of the pants. Large white hands extended from the cuffs of his sweater. She looked for a distinguishing mark or wedding ring but saw neither. Still, she was struck by the size of his hands. He had Legerski's frame, she thought, but so did a lot of men.

The masked man turned slightly, stepped aside, and swept his arm to present a stark bedroom of some kind. He said, "And here we are once again. This ought to be a good one because it stars . . . *me!*" His voice was electronically altered and sounded disembodied, inhuman.

Cassie noted the camera was at shoulder height, likely on a shelf or tripod. It wasn't high-quality video or audio and the lighting was bright but garish.

"Wait just a second until I bring out the talent," he said, and went off-screen. The camera didn't move with him.

After a minute of nothing but still life, the man re-appeared holding what looked like a leash. No, Cassie saw, not a leash. A chain. It snaked out of his hand and extended behind him. Then he gave it a sharp yank.

A skinny naked woman was pulled into the shot and she sat down on the bed and glanced at the camera. The chain was attached around her ankle. She looked terrified. Cassie stared back at those haunted eyes. The man in black took his end of the chain and snapped it to get her attention, then fastened it to a ringbolt on the wall next to the bed. She could see the chain was long enough to allow movement around the bed but no further.

As he did, Cassie tried to see the girl better. Her face seemed familiar, Cassie thought. Then it came to her: she was one of the missing three local girls she'd researched the night before. She couldn't remember which one, couldn't attach the name, but she knew she'd be able to connect them when she had her files in front of her.

For the next few minutes, time stood still and Cassie was transported into a real-life version of hell. Even as she watched it, she knew she'd never be able to scrub the images from her mind for the rest of her life. She had to remind herself to breathe.

The man seemed jaunty and cruel at the same time. When he glanced back at the camera—there was a second of wide-spaced deep eyes—there was no doubt he seemed to be enjoying himself.

It came in horrible flashes, and Cassie found herself fast-forwarding, getting the gist but not dwelling a second longer than necessary on the actual details.

The man shoved his crotch into the girl's face and grabbed at his zipper with one hand and her hair in the other . . .

Fast-forward-fast-forward-fast-forward

The camera never moved or zoomed in, to Cassie's relief, and she assumed there was no one else in the room even though the monster liked to address the lens himself as if hosting a show.

At one point, after he'd turned the girl over facedown on the bad and waddled up behind her, he addressed the camera with a flushed red face and jabbed his finger at it and said, "Don't fuck with me again, Lizard King!"

Lizard King? she wondered.

Fast-forward-fast-forward-fast-forward

The poor girl, Cassie thought, feeling her own eyes fill with tears as the girl cried and begged for him to stop. He backhanded her hard enough that she fell off the bed. As he bent down to pull her back up, Cassie noticed a large discolored mark of some kind on the skin of the small of his back. Like a stain or a botched tattoo. As if he realized the same thing himself, he self-consciously reached back and tugged down the hem of his sweater, hiding it again.

Fast-forward-fast-forward-fast-forward

Staggering and spent, the man lurched to his feet and stood there, the girl curled up on top of the bed. He breathed hard, glowered at the camera. Then he lurched toward the screen and went out of view.

The girl lay on the bed in a fetal position, hugging her knees, her back facing the screen. Cassie could see her bent spine, her shoulders heaving from crying. On the small of her back was a tattoo and Cassie recognized it as the Harley-Davidson logo. She remembered one of the missing girls had the tattoo . . .

Then he returned, holding a long bladed knife that looked like a bayonet. He lurched across the screen toward the girl in the bed, and stopped to look back over his shoulder and smile.

Fast-forward-fast-forward-fast-forward

Blood, everywhere. . . .

* * *

Cassie felt as disgusted and abused and as horrified as the murdered missing girl as she removed the headphones, closed her eyes, and croaked, "Holy Mother of God."

"What?" Sally said, alarmed. "You look like you've seen the devil himself."

"I have," Cassie said and wiped furiously at her face as if it would remove the images. It didn't.

"Something's bleeding," Sally said.

"What?"

It took a moment for Cassie to realize Sally wasn't referring to the girl in the video, but to her own hand. She'd balled her fist so tightly when she watched that she'd cut into the palm of her hand with her fingernails. She had smears of blood on her face.

"Here," Sally said, approaching with a Kleenex.

Cassie slammed the laptop closed, even though the video was over, so Sally couldn't see it.

"What?" Sally asked again, as Cassie clutched the Kleenex with her right hand and opened the laptop and restarted the disk and then froze it during the opening minute. She froze the image of the spare bedroom itself before the girl was brought in.

"I need your help," Cassie said. "I want you to look at something."

Sally looked scared.

"Don't worry," Cassie said. "I've paused it. I just want you to identify a location for me if you can. You've lived around here for a while and you may recognize it as local."

Sally Legerski took a deep breath and came around

the table. She leaned down so closely Cassie could smell her scent.

"Do you know this room?" Cassie asked. She watched Sally's face and saw a twitch of recognition in it.

"What happens in that room?"

"Never mind that. Do you recognize it?"

"Possibly."

Cassie felt an electric charge fire through her. She tried to remain calm.

"Where is it?"

"I said *possibly*."

"Is it connected to your ex-husband?"

"I just don't know without seeing more."

"That's not going to happen," Cassie said firmly.

Sally sighed. "Rick bought this place, this old abandoned ranch, not long after we moved down here. I thought it was idiotic at the time and I still do. He made noises about fixing it up for our retirement home, but the house was a wreck and the well hardly worked."

"This bedroom is in the old house?"

"No," she said, "the man Rick bought it from built this underground shelter. I don't know how much it must have cost, but he claimed it would withstand a nuclear war. It's right outside the house, the entrance, I mean. This looks like the bedroom that was down there. I never spent more than ten minutes in that shelter because it creeped me out and I was mad at Rick for blowing our savings on it, but this sure looks like the bedroom but I can't swear to it."

Sally pointed toward the screen. "I recognize the concrete walls but those ring things are new . . ." her voice trailed off when she seemed to realize what she was saying. "What happened in it?"

Cassie ignored the question and said, "Is it known as the Schweitzer place?"

Sally said, "How did you know?"

"I think it's where the girls are," she said.

It wasn't "There at the Schweitzer place" as written in the ungrammatical scrawl. It was: "*They're* at the Schweitzer place."

Sally reached out for the side of the table so her knees wouldn't buckle beneath her.

Cassie walked toward the back of the shop, through a packed storeroom, and through a storm door into a tiny backyard. She needed air, and she needed a few minutes. There was a chain link fence along the end of the yard. Just a few feet beyond the fence was the rim of the canyon where the Yellowstone River roared far below.

She gripped the top rail of the fence with both hands and closed her eyes. When she did she could see the terrified face of the girl on the video looking back, then the set of his shoulders when he approached her with the bayonet. She'd read enough and learned enough at the academy to know most serial killers kept trophies of some kind to remind them of their victims. Photos and videos weren't unusual. But she'd never actually looked at them, and she wished she could somehow unwatch what she'd seen. She wondered how many victims were on the second and third disks.

Then she raised her head and opened her eyes. She

was suddenly furiously angry, and she cursed herself for taking the time to gather her thoughts, to regroup. It was time the Sullivan girls—and possibly Cody—couldn't afford to have wasted because of her indecision.

She glanced at her watch. Enough time had lapsed. She felt a pang of guilt regarding the dirty trick she'd played on Sally, leaving her in there with the laptop. But she had no doubt Cody would approve.

Cassie turned on her heel and marched back into the shop. Sally Legerski sat again behind the counter but didn't look over as Cassie sat back down at her computer. Sally looked shell-shocked. The paused image on the screen included the man and the girl. It was just after he'd yanked her back onto the bed.

"You watched some of it," Cassie said.

"I had to." Then, "It's him. It's Rick."

Cassie felt a surge of excitement. "How can you be sure? We never see his face."

Sally wouldn't meet Cassie's eyes. "That birthmark on the small of his back. You can see it when his shirt pulls up. I recognize that birthmark. It's purple and it covers most of his back. He was always self-conscious about it because it's sort of in the shape of a skull. He used to call it his death's-head, and it does kind of look like that."

"You're sure?"

Sally looked over with fury in her eyes. "It's *him*."

At least, Cassie thought, looking at where the video was stopped, Sally hadn't advanced it to the end.

"What's your Wi-Fi password?"

Sally didn't respond. She seemed to be in a rage.

"Sally, what's your password?" Cassie asked sharply.

After Sally told her, Cassie went to work. Sally talked in a wooden voice, as much to herself as to Cassie.

"He is a very controlling man."

Cassie acknowledged her with a "Um-hmmm."

"For the first few years, I didn't mind it that he wanted to know everything I did during the day and who I might have talked with. I found it kind of endearing that he was so jealous. But it wasn't just jealousy—it was possessiveness. Like he didn't trust me at all and he was suspicious of everything I did or said. He'd go over the phone bills and ask about strange numbers, or check the computer to see what Web sites I looked at. And he'd get *angry* if I didn't agree with him on something, even if it was trivial. After a while, I felt suffocated and I couldn't stand it."

Cassie could guess the next part, and it came.

"But I never thought he was capable of something like *this*."

After the last five minutes of the video file was copied to her hard drive, compressed and sent, Cassie opened her cell phone and redialed the most recent number called. Again, she got the receptionist at the Park County Sheriff's Department.

"This is Lewis and Clark Investigator Cassandra Dewell. I need to talk to Sheriff Pedersen right now. It's an emergency."

"He might have left for the day, ma'am."

"Then patch me through to his cell or his house. *Right now!*"

The receptionist paused as if to argue but thought better of it.

After a minute, Pedersen came on the line. It didn't sound like he was using his cell. "Yes, Deputy Dewell?"

She ignored the irritation in his tone. "Where are you?"

"Here, at the office. But I was planning on packing it in early this afternoon, why?"

"Is Trooper Legerski still there?"

"I'm not sure. He might have left after he talked to the judge."

"Please look," she said.

"Can you tell me what this is about?" he asked, still annoyed.

"Legerski's a rapist and a murderer. He's probably got the Sullivan girls imprisoned right now on some land he owns and I don't know if they're dead or alive."

The silence was infuriating. Cassie said, "Sheriff, find Legerski and lock him up before he knows what's going on. He's a fucking monster, and if you check your e-mail you'll see proof. But detain him first, and *then* watch it if you can."

"Hold on," Pedersen said, and she could hear the receiver clunk down on his desk. In the background, she heard Pedersen ask, "Is Rick still here?"

There was an exchange of voices she couldn't make out, then Pedersen was back on the phone.

"He was in the squad room bullshitting with a couple of deputies but I guess he left. If you hadn't heard, the judge turned down your request for a warrant."

"Doesn't matter," she said. "Go find Legerski and take his firearms away and put him in your jail. I'm not kidding, and if you don't do it right now everybody in Montana will want to know why when this thing breaks."

"Look," Pedersen said, "I know Rick pretty well. What you say comes across as kind of crazy. I can't just arrest him based on your accusation and with no evidence."

"I told you," she said, her voice rising until it was a shout, "*The evidence is in your goddamn e-mail inbox*. You'll see proof of your buddy raping a girl who's chained to a wall and then gutting her like a deer. It's the worst thing I've ever seen, and the man who did it was in your office. Get him secured away and then cancel all the holiday vacations and get every officer you've got on their way to the old Schweitzer place off U.S. Highway 89."

She paused and looked at her screen. "The coordinates for your GPS units are Latitude 45-10′06′ North, Longitude 110-51′45′ West. Got that?"

Silence. Then Pedersen moaned, "Jesus. Oh, my God . . ."

Cassie said, "You're looking at the video file I sent."

"Oh, man." Then: "*Oh, my God*. Where did you get this?"

"Somebody left it for me."

"I can't see his face. How do you know it's him?"

"He's got a birthmark on his back. There's a point in the video where you can see it."

"But—"

"His ex-wife is sitting right in front of me and she made a positive identification. She says it's him."

"Are you sure this thing isn't faked?"

"It doesn't look faked to me. Does it look faked to you?"

"Repeat the coordinates," Pedersen said, suddenly all business.

She did.

Then, "Sheriff, don't put the call out over the radio to apprehend Legerski. If you do he'll hear it and run for cover. It would be better if you sent some guys to find him and pull him over."

"I agree."

"I'll meet you at the Schweitzer place," she said. To herself, she whispered, "Hold on, girls. Hold on, Cody."

41.

Gracie and Danielle stood huddled together along the side wall of the room under a metal air grate. It was the one place in the room they'd found where the odor from the dead body in the corner and blood on the floor was the least likely to make them gag.

Gracie's bare feet were cold from the concrete and the cold seemed to be seeping up through her bones. She held Danielle tighter, hoping to transfer her sister's body warmth, but didn't know what to do to warm her feet. Sometimes when she exhaled, her breath came trembling out.

She thought about snatching the blanket back from where it was draped over the dead body, but she couldn't yet make herself do it.

Danielle stood wordlessly chanting her mantra and rocking.

"The next time someone is at that door, do the cell phone trick, okay?" Gracie said to her sister.

Danielle hadn't spoken or looked up in an hour. It was the longest she'd ever gone without talking, Gracie thought.

"Danielle, pretend Justin is on the other side of the door."

Danielle rocked. Gracie hoped there was some way to reach her.

"What do you say? Will you do it this time?"

There was a remote vibration in the floor and despite her freezing feet, Gracie could feel it. Danielle could, too, because her head jerked up and she stared at the door in wide-eyed terror.

Gracie whispered, "They're back. Start texting and sell it."

Danielle gathered up the tin and sat with her back to the wall, the Altoid box poised in front of her, her thumbs at the ready. Gracie was thrilled.

She rose, yanked the blanket from the dead body, and stood poised next to the door.

Gracie heard more distant and muffled sounds, but no conversations like before. Gracie was sure they were out there, but what were they doing?

After a series of heavy footfalls the sliding metal plate on the door slid back. Gracie stared in terror at the pair of shadowed, piglike eyes as they moved around the room until they settled on her sister.

"There you are," the man said. She recognized the voice as belonging to the man with the badge, the man with the gun who'd shot the tall man in the corner.

"How're you girls doing?"

Gracie looked over at her sister. Danielle had lowered the tin between her knees out of view. She wasn't going to go through with it, and Gracie sighed and let the blanket slide to the cement floor.

"I see one of you," the man said to Danielle. "Where is the other? Where's your sister?"

Gracie froze. The man couldn't see her because she was out of the sight line of the sliding panel.

Instinctively, Danielle's eyes moved to her.

Gracie felt as if she'd been stabbed in the back by her sister.

"Come out where I can see you," the man said.

Gracie stepped into the center of the room.

"Hiding, huh?" the man said. "You're not the first to ever try that trick."

Gracie looked down at her bare feet. She was afraid if she looked at Danielle she'd dive at her and try to tear her sister's hair out.

"I shouldn't really be here," the man said, as much to himself as to Gracie, it seemed. "But I wanted to see how you're doing."

She nodded.

"Has my other friend been here since we left?"

"No," Gracie said, looking up.

"You're not lying to me, are you?"

"No."

She could see him nodding through the slot in a satisfied way. He said, "I believe you since you're standing."

"I'll be back in a few minutes," the man said. "But you two need to keep something in mind. Your role here is to satisfy *me*. As long as you can do that, I'll keep you around. I won't let that trucker hurt you, and believe me—he will. He likes the sound of bones snapping. You saw what happened to Krystyl and the cook there. Think about them, and then think about *me*. Think of ways to make me happy. If you do that, girls, I can protect you from the trucker and we can discuss your future later. Got that?"

Neither said a word.

"Good," the man said, and slammed the slider shut.

"If he doesn't kill you, I will," Gracie growled at her sister.

Danielle shrugged, tears in her eyes.

At the same time, Cassie Dewell kept one eye on the road and the other on her GPS unit as she coursed up Highway 89 north from Gardiner. If she'd programmed the coordinates correctly, the screen said she'd be at the old Schweitzer place in six minutes.

Six minutes.

Back at the quilt shop, she'd debated with herself whether to wait on the highway for the contingent from the sheriff's department in Livingston to storm the Schweitzer place en masse or to find it herself. Finally, she thought: What would Cody do?

She smiled grimly at the thought: WWCD.

Then she said good-bye to Sally Legerski, who was

still in shock behind her silent sewing machine, and went out to the Ford. She made a vow to go back when it was over and offer what comfort she could. There were so many victims of crime, she thought. So many friends, relatives, and family members on the periphery of evil.

As she sped along the highway she noticed a black spoor of smoke to her right, toward the mountains. A big fire of some kind several miles from the highway. It seemed odd in the late fall/early winter when there was no wildfire danger. The low pressure of the storm front kept the smoke from rising straight up and flattened it on the top so it looked like a T. Because her driver's side window was open, she caught a hint of the stench. It smelled like burning plastic and rotten garbage.

Her mind raced, fueled by adrenaline, lack of sleep, and horror. She imagined how horrible it would be to be a prisoner in the shelter without an inkling of who out there might be trying to find her, if anyone was. Every minute would be its own nightmare. The only positive aspect she could think of was how unlikely it was Legerski could have molested the Sullivan girls in such a short time since their abduction. She had to remind herself it had been less than twenty-four hours, and for much of the time Legerski had been entertaining Cody Hoyt and her. Inadvertently, that might have spared the Sullivan girls the fate of the girl on the DVD. But she couldn't be sure, of course, and if he was given more time she had no doubt what their fate would be. One of the jarring impressions she had taken away from viewing the DVD was that he was well practiced.

She'd told Sheriff Pedersen she'd meet him at the Schweitzer place, but she didn't say *at the same time he arrived.* She wanted to get there first, find and free Cody and the girls, and wait for the cavalry to arrive. She wanted to see Cody, put an end to the investigation, be the hero, and get home for Thanksgiving. It was something she could tell Ben about some day; how his mother was a hero like his father had been.

The GPS indicated she should turn off the highway within 0.5 miles, so she slowed down. The road displayed on the screen was nothing special; an ungraded private two-track with no official name. She looked ahead and saw that it wound up through the sagebrush and up and over a rise to what looked like a valley on the other side. As she turned she noticed a series of fresh tire tracks in the mud of the road, more activity than she thought there should be for such a forlorn location, and her heart began to whump.

And it was as if Cody was back in the Expedition with her, chain-smoking and doing one of his cynical monologues about human nature and the corrupt judicial system. She could hear him laying out the pros and cons, the very real scenario where everything they tried to do right turned out for shit.

What would happen if the evidence itself, the DVDs, turned out to be tainted somehow? What if the man who'd given them to her had stolen them? Would they hold up in court? What if Legerski claimed they were fraudulent, that some video sharpie with digital equipment had the know-how and technology to make it appear that he was raping and killing women? Isn't that what they did in Hollywood—created realistic images of beings and people via computer? CGI—computer-generated imaging. What if they couldn't find corroborating evidence to back up the images, or if the evidence they found was thrown out due to some technicality like an illegal search and seizure? After all, Cassie had made the decision to proceed with speed and force instead of careful deliberation. She hadn't even tried to obtain a search warrant for the Schweitzer place or the shelter. . . .

There was still the truck driver who had blown the case open by leaving the disks. She didn't know why he'd done it, whether he was somehow involved or whether he was a Good Samaritan who wanted to steer her in the right direction but leave himself out of it. Either way, the speed in which he'd driven away and his method of passing the damning evidence indicated he wanted to get out of town fast. She'd not called him in or put out an APB on his all-black truck, not wanting to risk Legerski hearing about the incident over his radio and panicking. She wanted Trooper Legerski to be caught before he knew he was a suspect.

Finding the driver and his truck shouldn't be difficult, she thought. Although she didn't know all the particulars of long-haul trucking, she did know the drivers were heavily regulated and their identities available through a national database. It wouldn't take long for investigators to name him and pull his license plate number and put out the word to highway law enforcement. Plus, he had U.S. Department of Transportation numbers stenciled on the door of his truck for identification. There was no way, she thought, for a trucker to stay unidentified for very long, once the word was out to highway patrolmen, federal and state DOT officials, weigh station attendants, and truck stop cashiers. It should be a matter of hours or days before he was apprehended and brought back. She looked forward to questioning him. And maybe thanking him for being a knight of the road.

When she topped the rise and drove down into the steep mountain valley she made a decision. She thought again: WWCD.

Maybe it was seeing Legerski's highway patrol cruiser parked beside the run-down old house in the valley below. Maybe it was the two rectangles of fresh upturned soil out in the hay meadow, and the outline of a half-dozen similar disturbances that were visible because the light snow from that morning clung to the natural grass around the rectangles and exposed them to her naked eye. She didn't understand the reason for the plots, but they were certainly discordant and suspicious to the landscape.

She parked next to the highway patrol cruiser and got out. A slight icy breeze rustled her hair and she pushed a strand of it out of her eyes. It was obvious there was no one in the old house because the windows were broken out and the front door hung open like a gaping mouth.

Cassie reached back through her coat for her weapon. It was a .40 Glock 27 with nine rounds in the magazine and one in the chamber. She'd never fired it in the line of duty, and had rarely pulled it out of its holster except at the qualifying range. It was a compact weapon that fit her hand and had plenty of firepower. She'd always wondered if she'd be capable of killing another human being, but what she'd seen on the DVD changed all that.

She followed several sets of tracks to the concrete abutment on the side of the house. It reminded her of a storm cellar entrance but the construction was thick and solid and it looked impregnable. It had been there long enough that blue-green veins of lichen climbed the sides. There was a set of closed wooden doors at the mouth of the passageway that swung out. She noted the rusty hasps on the edge of the doors but saw no lock on them.

She took a deep breath and squared her shoulders, then bent over and opened the doors one at a time, revealing a steep set of concrete steps that led to a closed steel door on the bottom of the landing. She started to climb down, hesitated, and then retreated back up to the opening.

Instead of descending into the shelter, she leaned into the stairwell and shouted, "Trooper Legerski! It's Cassie Dewell. Are you down there? I saw your car outside."

Silence for a moment, then she heard what sounded like a thump behind the closed door.

"Trooper Legerski, are you down there?"

She tried to keep her voice from trembling or sounding shrill. She wanted it to come across as normal as possible and as clueless as he thought she must be.

She was ready to throw herself to the side if he came out blasting. Instead, she heard a bolt thrown and saw the door crack open a few inches but she couldn't yet see him.

"Mr. Legerski, are you down there?"

"What do you want?" He sounded gruff, but somehow false, like he was attempting to sound understandably annoyed. "What are you doing here?"

"Your ex-wife told me you owned this place; that's how I found you."

"Sally? Jesus Christ." But there was a hint of relief in his voice.

"Did you get the warrant from the judge? I've been waiting for you to call and let me know."

She heard him sigh. "Didn't you hear? He wouldn't issue one. He said there wasn't enough probable cause, just like I told you would happen."

"Damn," she said, and stomped her foot. "No, I didn't know that. Hey, can I come down there and talk with you? We need to go to Plan B." She thought she sounded sincere.

"Jesus Christ, lady," he said. After a beat, he said, "Stay there, I'm coming up."

"What kind of place is this, anyway?" she asked the empty stairwell. She heard him curse and say something under his breath, then open the door. He was in uniform, although he looked as if he were buttoning up the top of his shirt. That did it. Why else would he be partially unclothed in a place like that?

At that moment, she was sure he had the girls down

there and he didn't want her any closer to them than she already was.

He filled the narrow staircase as he climbed. He stepped heavily, lurching from side to side as if each step was a chore. His wide shoulders nearly brushed both walls as he came up.

She waited until he emerged from the shadow and she could see his face in a band of sunlight. He was six steps from the top when she set her feet in a shooting stance and raised the Glock with both hands.

He looked up and saw the gun and his horrible fleshy face went slack. Then his eyes widened and he opened his mouth to speak but she didn't let him and she didn't stop pulling the trigger until the slide of the gun locked back, the magazine empty. Legerski tumbled backward in slow motion, arms and legs flopping lifelessly, a sack of meat kicked down the stairs, blood spatter everywhere.

Cassie ejected the magazine and slammed another one home and followed her gun down the stairs, using the handrail when the steps became slippery with blood.

She stepped over the massive twisted body, turned, and shoved it on its side with her boot. It was heavy, and his uniform front was black with blood. He had holes in his cheek, neck, and hands.

She bent down and grabbed a handful of his uniform tunic where it was tucked into the back of his belt and pulled hard until it came free. His skin was pasty white but there it was: an oblong purple birthmark on the small of his back nearly eight inches high. There were two flesh-colored spots within the mark that looked vaguely like eye sockets. It *did* remind her of a death's-head . . .

Cassie drew a glove from her coat pocket and pulled it on her right hand. She found his service weapon and removed it from its holster. There was another gun in an ankle holster, a snub-nosed revolver with the serial number filed off. A throw-down. Cody always packed a throwdown or two, but she didn't need one. She put the revolver back in the holster and tugged the pant leg hem down to hide it so it would be discovered later.

She stood and stepped back, breathing hard. She looked down into his open eyes but there was nothing there. He didn't look so tough now, she thought.

Then she aimed Legerski's service weapon up the stairwell and fired two shots through the opening into the sky, and tossed the gun up the stairs.

She said, "Poor guy—killed by a stupid cunt."

When the sliding steel window plate opened, Gracie looked up. Instead of the leering piglike eyes of the man who'd been there earlier and said he was coming back, she saw two blue eyes belonging to a woman barely tall enough to look in. Her heart swelled with hope.

Of course they'd heard the shots, one after another, in rapid succession like so many firecrackers.

Pop-pop-pop-pop-pop-pop-pop-pop-pop-pop. Then, two more.

"Gracie and Danielle Sullivan?" the woman asked.

"Yes," Danielle replied softly.

"God, yes!" Gracie squealed, both at the voice outside and Danielle's reaction to it.

"I'm Investigator Cassie Dewell of the Lewis and Clark Sheriff's Department. Trooper Legerski is dead. Are you all right?"

"Yes," Gracie said.

"Did he hurt you?" Dewell asked.

Danielle said, tossing the tin aside, "He took our clothes and our phones and put us in this room . . ."

"But did he *hurt* you?"

"No," Gracie said, understanding the meaning if Danielle didn't. "Not yet," she added.

"Thank God," Dewell said with genuine emotion. "Is Cody in there with you?"

Gracie and Danielle exchanged puzzled glances and looked back.

"Is that the name of the dead guy in here?" Danielle asked.

The only Cody Gracie knew was Justin's dad.

"Let me get this door open," the woman said, dropping her eyes from the slot.

The door opened and she swung it out. She was short and solid with an open face and large eyes. There was a gun in her hand. Gracie ran to her and Cassie wrapped her arms around her in a firm hug. "It'll be okay," Cassie said into her hair, "it'll be okay now."

Gracie didn't want to let go but Cassie gently pried her arms away. Gracie watched as Cassie approached the body in the corner and produced a small flashlight. She twisted it on, revealing the man's face. There was a gaping red hole from an exit wound where the man's right eye should have been. Gracie looked away and Danielle closed her eyes. Cassie stood and said, "Jimmy."

"We never heard his name," Gracie said.

"Maybe that means Cody is still alive," Cassie said. "Do you girls know of anyone else who might be down here?"

Gracie shook her head, and said, "There was a girl named Krystyl. I think he killed her."

"But no Cody Hoyt?" Cassie asked.

"Justin's dad?"

"Yes."

"Why would he be here?" Danielle asked.

Cassie shot Danielle a look that was a little accusatory. "He was looking for *you*."

"No," Gracie said, "we never saw or heard about Mr. Hoyt."

Cassie nodded, then smiled. "Let's get you two out of here and get you some clothes."

"Thank you," Gracie said.

Cassie nodded.

As they reached the top of the stairwell with blankets from the shelter draped over Gracie and Danielle, Cassie looked up to see a stream of law enforcement vehicles, lights flashing, pour down the road toward them.

Thursday,
November 22

*The act is unjustifiable that either begs for a blessing,
or, having succeeded, gives no thanksgiving.*
—Francis Quarles

42.

By the time Cassie topped the sagebrush hill to return to the Schweitzer place it was almost unrecognizable. In the small valley below, backhoes, earthmovers, tractors, dump trucks, and law enforcement vehicles were all over the meadow. She could see huge mounds of black soil next to excavated holes, muddy and dented vehicles parked in a loose row, and county workers walking from hole to hole with shovels. A large forensics tent had been put up over the concrete abutment that led to the underground shelter, obscuring it from view. There were at least two dozen local, county, and state cruisers as well as unmarked cars and SUVs parked around the old ranch home.

A uniformed Park County deputy sheriff held out his hand, palm up, to stop her before she descended into the mountain valley. He walked from his cruiser to Cassie's Ford Expedition and crossed across the front and indicated she should roll down her window by twirling his finger. She did. He was painfully young, red-haired, and lean. His uniform looked too big for him, she thought.

She reached in her purse for her badge and wallet before remembering she no longer had them.

He said, "Crime scene. There's no unauthorized entry—" then he stopped.

She looked up from her purse to find him staring at her, his young face a picture of awe.

"You're her, aren't you?"

"I'm Investigator Dewell."

"You're the one," he said, and stepped closer and removed his hat.

She couldn't help herself from flushing. She looked away.

"It's an honor to meet you," the man said. "What you did was unbelievable."

"Can I get through?" she asked, embarrassed. She wished he hadn't used the word *unbelievable,* although it was meant as a compliment.

"Absolutely," he said, stepping aside.

Sheriff Bryan Pedersen looked grim as she entered the tent, and he glanced up at her with haunted eyes. One by one the twenty or so people inside the huge tent stopped what they were doing and stared until she felt like her face would melt away.

Finally, after an uncomfortable ten seconds, someone applauded. It was Alexa Manning, the evidence tech from Lewis and Clark County. Others joined in.

Cassie blinked away tears and was both angry and surprised at her reaction. She mouthed, "Thank you," and made her way toward Pedersen.

As she passed Alexa, Cassie said, "I thought you were on vacation."

She shrugged, "I was halfway to the airport when they called me back on duty. And I'm not the only one."

Cassie nodded, now seeing that the people inside the tent were a mixture from Lewis and Clark County, Park County, the state patrol, and a few she'd never seen before. Several of the men wore heavy gray shirts with PARK COUNTY MAINTENANCE embroidered over their breast pockets.

Sheriff Pedersen held a clipboard with one hand and a portable radio with the other. He nodded at Cassie as she approached, then gestured with his chin for her to follow him outside. As she did, she noticed a tech behind a plastic evidence table dutifully logging her ten ejected .40 casings with evidence tags.

When they were outside, he said, "Walk with me."

Bryan Pedersen was tall with broad shoulders, long legs, and had pinched brown eyes and a drooping gunfighter's mustache. She thought he might be handsome in a different set of circumstances, and she instinctively looked down at his big hands and saw the wedding band.

"Inquest go okay?" he asked.

She nodded. For most of the previous evening and all morning, Cassie had given statement after statement to state Division of Criminal Investigation officers who were called in whenever there was an officer-involved shooting. They'd impounded her gun and badge and she'd given her statement a half-dozen times and answered the same questions over and over.

I didn't wait for the sheriff's team to arrive because I was convinced the Sullivan girls were there and were in imminent danger . . .

He was coming up the stairwell and I saw him pull out his weapon and fire twice, so I started firing back in self-defense . . .

I didn't count as I pulled the trigger. I didn't realize I'd emptied the magazine until after . . .

Never once did she regret killing the monster Legerski. Her only concern during the inquest was getting tripped up over the details of the shooting and somehow incriminating herself. She'd learned from the best, though, and never wavered.

Then, as if he'd just thought of it, Pederson said, "I was hoping you could clear something up for me regarding the shooting of Legerski."

She felt her legs get weak but she said, "What's that?"

"The Sullivan girls said they heard a series of rapid shots then two more afterward. Does that make any sense to you?"

Cassie shook her head. The state inquest team had asked the same question.

"It was just the opposite," Cassie said. "Legerski fired first, and I returned fire. It's understandable they got the order wrong, given the circumstances and the stress they were under. The girls must have been confused by the sequence."

Pederson held his gaze for a moment, seeing if she would waver. She didn't.

"Good enough for me," he said. She wasn't sure she'd convinced him, but she was sure by his manner that it no longer mattered.

"We took a look at those DVDs," he said.

She didn't comment.

"Worse thing I've ever seen," he said. "There are four different women—girls—altogether. They all end the same way. There's no way somebody faked all that to frame Legerski. No way in hell. It's him. Luckily, we've identified two of the victims so far and we're putting their images out nationwide. We'll figure out who the other two are."

Pedersen shook his head slowly. "I've never seen anything like it before and I hope I never do again," he said.

"Four," she said. "Any possibility he killed more?"

"I'd bet a million dollars there were a hell of a lot more than four victims," Pedersen said. "Maybe he didn't record them all or maybe we just haven't found the other disks yet. But when you look at that horror chamber he's got down there, and the scratch marks on the walls of that room—there were more than four."

She nodded, and felt a chill worm up her spine as she recalled the room. "I know," she said. "I was in there. So did you dig up the bodies?"

"No," he said, "And that's the thing. We haven't even found the four. We don't know where he buried them, or burned their remains, or what. I've made a request

to the feds for body-sniffing dogs and imaging technology so we can go over this little ranch inch by inch. I'm
scared as hell to find out how many there are.

"I wonder how high the count will be," Pedersen
said. "Think about it. This is a damned human slaughter-
house. Two of those girls on the CDs aren't local, so
who knows where they came from or how many there
will turn out to be? We're going over that bunker with a
fine-tooth comb finding hair and fiber evidence, blood,
DNA . . . we'll get an idea," he said.

"We know that he didn't bury them with the cars
we've recovered out there," he said, gesturing toward
the roaring backhoes and heavy equipment working in
the meadow.

She said, "You've found entire buried *cars?*"

"We've dug up eight vehicles so far. A couple look
like they've been buried for three or four years. He
didn't even bother to take the plates off, so we'll figure
out who owned them soon enough. But the scale of it
just blows me away, Deputy Dew"—he corrected himself in midword and finished with—"Investigator."

"Eight buried cars?" she said, now knowing exactly
what had been beneath those churned-up rectangles
she'd seen the day before.

"The thing that just pisses me off is he used county
backhoes, right from our shop," Pedersen said. "It looks
like he checked them out under a fake name and drove
them out here. Our own equipment! Legerski was running this thing right under our noses using our own
resources."

All Cassie could think about was if she'd waited, if she hadn't killed Legerski, the trooper might confess his crimes and identify the victims.

Cassie said, "How long do you think he's been doing it?"

Pedersen shrugged. "Years, I'd guess. But he wasn't alone."

"You mean there were more involved than Legerski and Jimmy? Is that what you're saying?"

Pedersen looked hard at her. "You mean you don't know? The Sullivan girls said there were at least three of them."

Cassie shook her head. "I haven't talked to the girls since we were separated on the top of the stairs yesterday. All I've done is interview after interview."

"Oh. Well, yes, they say there were three."

"Who is number three?"

"They say he was a truck driver. He was the one who pulled them out of their car."

The news pummeled her. "I can't help but assume the truck driver is the same one who gave me the evidence."

"That's what we're thinking. And we've got a suspect."

"Who?"

"A local named Ronald Pergram. He's a weirdo, all right. He's got a place near here but it burned down yesterday. That's what led us to think it might be him. His body might be inside, but we don't know yet. His truck wasn't there, but we don't know if it might be garaged somewhere or getting tuned up, or what. Just in case he's running, though, we've got an APB out on his truck but no hits yet. We'll find him, though, one way or the other."

"I hope so."

"It's not like you can just hide an 80,000-pound truck."

Something dark passed over Pedersen's face. He said, "You need to see something. That's why I brought you out here."

"See what?" she asked, her insides still knotted.

He gestured with his chin toward one of the huge fresh mounds of dirt in the pasture.

She knew before she saw the entirety of the pickup partially hidden by the excavated dirt. Cody Hoyt's battered old Dodge, listing to the side due to a flattened tire. The bed was filled with loose dirt and the windows were broken out. The top of the cab was dented in, probably by the ton of dirt dropped on it to fill the hole.

Pedersen put his hand on her shoulder. "We dug up a fresh excavation and he was inside," he said. "The only body we've found. It looks like Legerski or somebody shot him at close range. Powder burns on his face, that I could see for sure."

Cassie closed her eyes and felt her knees get weak again. She was grateful when Pedersen stepped over and put an arm around her shoulders and pulled her into him.

"I notified Sheriff Tubman, who called his ex-wife," he said. "I'm damn sorry. It's hell to lose a partner."

"I can't believe it," she said. "I can't believe he killed him."

"He would have done the same to you if you'd let him. But you got the guy who pulled the trigger," Pedersen said. "There's that."

As he walked her back to the tent she saw Sheriff Tubman's SUV swing into the makeshift parking lot. He was out of uniform but wearing his Stetson with the factory curl, and appeared to be doing his best to look grave. But by his bearing and step, she could tell he was practically ecstatic.

"I'll leave you two," Pedersen said, releasing her. "I've got to get back to the tent."

She wished he would have kept hugging her, and felt instantly resentful toward Tubman for breaking it up. There was nothing romantic about Pedersen's intention, but the man was solid and reassuring and those were two things she could never say of Tubman.

"There she is," Tubman said as he walked up. "There's my girl."

"I'm not your girl."

"You know what I mean," he said, brushing her comment aside. "I'm just proud of you. You're a hero."

She grunted.

"You wouldn't believe the calls I'm getting—from all over the country. The networks want to interview us, and they're sending camera crews—it's mind-boggling.

This is the biggest thing to happen in this part of the state in years, and *you're* the one who got the bad guy. I'm just . . . so proud."

Cassie glared at him with contempt. She knew she'd probably guaranteed his reelection. He could continue to preen and collect rent money from drug dealers for another term.

"What?" he asked, genuinely surprised she didn't share his triumph.

"They found Cody's body," she said. "Did you forget?"

"Of course not. I'm sorry. I conveyed my sympathy to Jenny and his son Jarrod."

"Justin," she corrected.

"Justin, right."

"How'd she take it?"

He feigned gravity. "Hard. But it's not like she didn't expect something like this, given who he was."

Cassie stepped back from him and said, "I know what Cody would say to you right now if he was here."

Tubman arched his eyebrows as if to ask what.

"He'd say, 'I shot a highway patrolman yesterday and got away with it. Now I'll try for a sheriff.'"

Tubman looked stricken. "That's not funny," he said.

"It wasn't intended to be," she said. "If they hadn't taken my weapon from me this morning for the inquiry, I'd blow your head off."

He tried to grin but couldn't. He said, "You can't talk to me like that."

"I just did."

He looked out toward the meadow. "Dewell, I'll pretend this conversation never took place. I'll chalk it up to stress, and postcombat fatigue, so to speak. I want you to take a few days off after this. I'll make sure you get paid for them. I'll ask the therapist to get in touch with you and set up some grief counseling. Now I think I'll turn around and get back to my Thanksgiving dinner with my family."

"You do that," she said.

"You're taking this all wrong," he said. "Instead of letting me praise you for solving a tremendous crime that makes all of us proud, you're taking out your bitter feelings on me personally. I've put up for years with one Cody Hoyt," he said. "I don't need another one."

"Get in your car or I'll *borrow* a weapon," she said.

Tubman walked back to his SUV shaking his head. She got a small amount of satisfaction from that.

Before going back into the tent, Cassie called her mother.

"Oh, we're doing just fine," her mother said. She sounded winded but exuberant. "The turkey is just about done and I'm finishing up mashed potatoes and green beans. Ben and a couple of guests are watching football."

Cassie said, "A couple of *guests*?"

"Oh, yes, didn't I tell you? I invited a couple of friends. They didn't have any place to go and it's Thanksgiving, after all."

"You invited some of your Occupy Helena derelicts to my home?"

"As I said, dear Cassie, they had no place to go. Isn't that what Thanksgiving should be about?"

"Let me talk to Ben," Cassie said.

She told her son she'd be home as soon as she could.

After terminating the call with her mother, Cassie called Jenny Hoyt's home. It was tough to press SEND.

Justin answered.

"Justin, this is Cassie Dewell. I want to tell you how sorry I am."

He obviously didn't know what to say for a moment, and she felt for him.

She said, "Just always remember that he died in the line of duty. He died trying to save the lives of two innocent girls, and if he hadn't come down here they'd be hurt or worse by now. We probably wouldn't have ever found them."

"Yeah," Justin said. "But it's tough, you know? It's really hard."

"Of course."

"I'm glad you shot the guy. I wish I could have been there to see it."

"No, you don't," she said.

She could hear voices in the background. One sounded familiar.

"Are Gracie and Danielle there with you?"

"Yeah. Their dad, too. He flew in from Omaha. Their mom is coming up later today."

"Are they doing okay?"

"I guess. Do you want to talk to them?"

"Let me talk to Gracie, if she's willing."

When Gracie came on the line, Cassie identified herself and asked, "How are you doing?"

"Fine, I guess. I want to thank you again for—"

"Never mind that," Cassie said. "I just want to tell you I admire you. You're tough. I can't believe you held it together the way you did for someone your age."

Cassie hoped Gracie was smiling and blushing. Gracie said softly, "Thank you."

"How is your sister?"

There was a pause. "There are some counselors here. Danielle's going to need some help. But she seems to be okay, I think. At least she seems to be in the same room with us, which is good. She'll be all right. I'm fine."

"I hope that when this is all over we can get together just to talk. You seem like a girl after my own heart. I've got a young son but no daughters. If I had a daughter, I'd want her to be like you."

There was silence for a moment, then Gracie asked, "Have you found that truck driver yet?"

"No, but we will."

"You need to *find* him," she said, her voice cracking.

The Pergram home was still smoldering when they arrived. Cassie recalled seeing the smoke in the distance the day before but she'd attached no significance to it, and apparently no one had called the county fire department.

"There's nothing left," she said as Pedersen drove in close. "And like I told you, his truck is gone."

"Looks like the son of a bitch covered his tracks," Pedersen said, shaking his head. "I wish those DCI guys would have let us know the girls claimed they were abducted by a truck driver. I guess they thought we knew that already."

The home had burned hot and completely to the ground. The air stunk of burned plastic and burned fuel. An older model car was close enough to the flames that it had burned as well, and blackened skeletons of Russian olive bushes littered the perimeter of the scene.

"I think his mother lived at home," Pedersen said. "I hope to hell she wasn't inside."

They exchanged glances.

"We'll find him," the sheriff said, reassuring her. "You can't hide for very long in an all-black eighteen-wheeler, for Christ's sake. We know his license plate number, and his DOT registration, and the description of his truck. The word is out everywhere. Every trooper in the west is looking for him. We'll get the son of a bitch."

Cassie nodded dumbly, but it all came crashing in on her. She'd let him escape by not calling it in when she found the package in her car. She knew it, Pedersen knew it, Ronald Pergram knew it.

"He set up Legerski," she said, "and he used me to pull the trigger."

"Don't beat yourself up. You did the right thing. You couldn't have known," Pedersen said.

"He thinks ahead," she said, gesturing toward the

smoldering ruins. "He plans things out. He probably
has a plan of some kind to get away with this."

She closed her eyes. "Instead of killing the monster
I killed the monster's sidekick. The monster is still out
there."

And Gracie's voice echoed: *You need to* find *him.*

Friday, December 7

There's a killer on the road
His brain is squirming like a toad
—Jim Morrison, "The Hitchhiker"

Afterward

Two weeks after Ronald Pergram became Dale Everett Spradley of Oakes, North Dakota, he stood alone under a television monitor at a Love's truck stop outside Tulsa to check the load board. He'd unloaded thirteen pallets of Washington State frozen salmon at a grocery warehouse at midnight, which left ten skids in his trailer to deliver to Little Rock in the morning. He was looking for a partial load he could pick up in the area to maximize his trip to Arkansas and he found it: ten skids of frozen farm-raised catfish in Inola, Oklahoma, needed to be trucked to Hot Springs, Arkansas. The foray would take him a couple of hours out of his way, but as usual he was ahead of schedule.

He jotted down the telephone number for the dispatch broker, checked his wristwatch, and made the call. It was a nice $4,500 deal and he took it. No reason to run his new truck LTL (less than a load) when he could pick up a partial en route. It was free money.

The truck stop was empty and quiet except for two drivers huddled together drinking coffee in the twenty-four hour diner. He nodded at them as he passed and they nodded back. No recognition at all. He smiled to himself. The storm had passed.

He was ready to go hunting again. He *needed* to go hunting again.

The first twenty-four hours after he drove out of Gardiner were the most stressful, even though he'd swapped out his Montana license plates for Oregon plates he'd stolen the year before and stored in his "Oh Shit" box for just such an emergency. It wasn't difficult to black out the DOT numbers on his driver's side door with black Krylon spray paint and replace them with stick-on numbers that looked good enough even though they couldn't be traced to anyone. He'd driven straight south without stopping, using his piss-jar to urinate, and taking back roads through tiny sleeping towns to avoid interstate highways and weigh scales. He'd dyed his hair jet-black in the sink of a remote rest stop, and added a big drooping false mustache that matched his new color. He'd wear it until his own grew out. He'd added thick horned-rim glasses with clear lenses and except for the intensity of his eyes he barely recognized himself in the mirror.

Because his trailer was empty he didn't have to re-fuel until he entered New Mexico, where he bought diesel for cash on an Indian reservation notoriously lax for keeping a sales log. He spotted three troopers en route to Brownsville, Texas, but they didn't look back.

He'd seen his own face on a television tuned to Fox News behind the counter as he paid for fuel. They'd used the one from his driver's license, and he looked ruddy, washed-out, and jowly. The attendant didn't look over his shoulder at the screen, and Pergram didn't look up.

At an infamous used truck outlet in Brownsville next to the Mexico border, he took a loss on his truck and trailer and traded up for a two-year-old bright yellow Peterbilt Model 389 with a Cummins ISX15 engine, an eighteen-speed Eaton-Fuller transmission, a Unibilt Ultracab with a seventy-seven-inch bed, a microwave and refrigerator, blackout curtains, and 190,000 miles on the gauge. The cost with trade-in was $105,000. He added a $70,000 reefer trailer and got the salesman to agree to lose the paperwork in exchange for an all-cash payment that took most of the stash in his "Oh Shit" box. He knew his old truck would be resold south of the border within a few days. Down there, they didn't care about DOT numbers or plates that didn't jibe.

While they got his new rig ready, Pergram walked to an Internet café he'd found several years ago. The owner of the place specialized in documents, and sold most of them to coyotes or illegals coming across. But for his last $25,000 in cash, the man produced a new commercial driver's license (CDL) in the name of Dale E. Spradley as well as a social security card, medical examiner's report, and a clean CSA scoresheet that showed Spradley was a damned good driver who kept his nose clean and played by the rules. Pergram/Spradley used one of the rental computers to purchase load insurance online, and he was back in business.

A week prior, he'd scored his first big load as an independent owner-operator. He picked up twenty-four pallets of frozen salmon in Washington to deliver among four warehouses coast-to-coast. As he dropped each partial load he used the load boards at truck stops to arrange smaller loads and keep his trailer full and making money.

Because he was working for himself, he wouldn't ever again have to worry about satellite tracking, or overbearing dispatchers, or Qualcomm units that noted his every move. He'd negotiate his own deals from his prepaid and untraceable cell phone and keep his truck on the road, always moving forward. He'd eat on the road, sleep in his truck, keep his logs clean, and stop at every weigh station to rebuild his track record. It wouldn't take long.

He thought about what had happened back in Montana but he didn't dwell on it. He admitted his mistakes—involving others, primarily—and learned from them. Never again would he have a fixed address, a home base, an obsessive mother with a big mouth. There was no need.

Although he was Dale Spradley of North Dakota, he would never have to actually set foot in Oakes.

In a spiral notebook he kept in his console he'd sketched out the reason why he'd never have to rely on

a home or somewhere like the Schweitzer place ever
again. That's because he'd carefully designed where
he'd weld a false wall inside the nose end of his trailer,
cutting the overall load capacity from fifty-three feet to
forty-eight feet. Forty-eight feet was a standard load
length, and he doubted anyone would ever notice the
missing five feet of length inside with a naked eye. Behind that false wall would be an eight-foot-by-five-foot
compartment. Big enough for a cot fastened to the floor,
sturdy enough for ringbolts in the walls, wired for
video and audio, and soundproofed from the outside.
He would be able to carry his Schweitzer place with
him.

He felt unleashed.

Like a shark, he'd always keep moving. No one
could ever pin him down again. He'd pick up a load on
one coast and deliver it to a warehouse on the other and
never return to a house or a town. The scenery would
roll by day after day and he'd keep his eyes out for opportunities.

On the way to Inola on old Route 66 for the skids of
frozen catfish, dawn broke over the horizon. It was clear
and cold and there were commas of snow on the Oklahoma prairie. He had to tap his brakes to prevent running into an older model Honda weaving unsteadily on
the two-lane highway. As he swung around it, he could
look down and see inside.

A disheveled brown-haired teenaged girl in sloppy
lounge pajamas, her hair askew, was squinting hard
over the wheel and barely keeping her car on the road.

Hungover, he thought, and driving home in the morning after a long hard night of beer and sex and privilege.

She looked up at him, obviously annoyed that he was staying right with her.

The Lizard King had returned.

Acknowledgments

The author would like to thank Butch and Dana Preston of Montana, two wonderful long-haul truck drivers, for offering technical assistance and answering all my questions during that cold January ride on I-90 from Billings to Chicago.

I'm also grateful to my first readers: Laurie Box, Molly Donnell, Becky Reif, and Roxanne Box. Special thanks to Ann Rittenberg—who was right as always.

Thanks also to Don Hajicek, Jennifer Fonnesbeck, and the terrific St. Martin's Minotaur team: Sally Richardson, Andy Martin, Hector DeJean, Matt Baldacci, Matthew Shear, and my peerless editor Jennifer Enderlin.